MY SALTY MARY

Books by the Lady Janies
My Lady Jane
My Plain Jane
My Calamity Jane

My Contrary Mary
My Imaginary Mary
My Salty Mary

MY

CYNTHIA HAND

SALTY

BRODI ASHTON

MARY

JODI MEADOWS

An Imprint of HarperCollinsPublishers

HarperTeen is an imprint of HarperCollins Publishers.

Library of Congress Control Number: 2023944810
ISBN 978-0-06-293010-1

Typography by Jenna Stempel-Lobell
24 25 26 27 28 LBC 7 6 5 4 3

First Edition

For people who love pirates.
And for people who love mermaids.
But mostly, for people who love books.

She laughed and danced with
the thought of death in her heart.
— Hans Christian Andersen, *The Little Mermaid*

MY SALTY MARY

Author Note

Ahoy there, reader!

Before we get started, we think it's important to remind you that sometimes (okay, all the time), we're taking real history and softening some of the sharper edges in order to tell a funny, lighthearted story. This book is no exception.

Pirates of the historical variety were not very nice people, what with the actual murder and pillaging and real-live keelhauling they did on a regular basis.

Also, this period of history sucked for Black and Indigenous peoples, who were being kidnapped, colonized, and enslaved.

In the interests of telling an enjoyable story, we've softened—but not erased—these aspects. Our Caribbean is a different version of the Caribbean you'd find if you had a time machine: less murdery and racist.

Therefore, we encourage you to take the story of *My Salty Mary* with a grain of salt.

Prologue

You definitely know this story. A mermaid saves a handsome prince from drowning and, in the process, falls madly in love with him. An evil sea witch magics her into becoming human—all for the low, low price of one beautiful singing voice—and it seems (for a minute there) like the mermaid is going to get her much-deserved happily ever after. But then the prince decides he's madly in love with another girl.

As for what happens next? Well, there are a few versions. In one, the mermaid battles the sea witch, triumphs, and marries the handsome prince—the story is sweet and satisfying (with maybe a few catchy musical numbers) and everything turns out just how it should. But in the older, *original* version of the story (the one that probably shouldn't be told to children), our heroine loses everything. The prince marries the other girl. The little mermaid dies of a broken heart and turns into sea foam.

That's right: she dies.

But there's another version. A better one. Ours.

Yes, our story is about the little mermaid. But it's also about treasure. And true love. And pirates.

A little history on pirates. Piracy has pretty much always been a thing since boats were invented, but 1719, when our story takes place, was part of what's known as the "Golden Age of Piracy." It had all started with a war: England versus Spain, with a little France thrown in. Spain was winning, so the queen of England gave a bunch of guys with ships permission to attack Spanish ships and steal the gold and supplies the Spanish were stealing from the Indigenous peoples of the Americas. These crown-approved guys with ships—aka privateers—thought of themselves as the Robin Hoods of the sea (if Robin Hood had kept all the money for himself). It was a pretty sweet gig if you liked to sail and didn't mind risking your life.

Then—as all good things must come to an end—England and Spain made peace with each other.

Overnight, the permission to plunder those shiny Spanish ships was revoked. And, overnight, a bunch of guys with a very specific set of skills no longer had jobs.

So, what's a bunch of out-of-work privateers to do?

Piracy.

But they decided to be civilized about it. They founded a

brotherhood in which they supported and treated one another as equals. They set up a code of honor—specific rules for how they would operate—as they continued to relieve the Spanish of their (stolen) gold. (They also took it upon themselves to liberate the gold of the English and French.) And if they happened to come across a ship that was stealing people from, let's say Africa, the pirates might take the ship, welcome the formerly enslaved men as new recruits, and make a stop at a nearby island to let off everyone who didn't want to be a pirate.

This didn't go over well with those who were trying to build an economy on human trafficking, so the rulers of Europe collectively decided that seriously, piracy should stop being a thing. England hired a ruthless captain named Jonathan Barnet to hunt down all the most infamous pirates. To set an example, you see.

You may have heard of some of these pirates, like Captain Blackbeard, the most notorious swashbuckler to sail the seven seas. (Our version of Blackbeard is actually a combination of Blackbeard, Black Sam Bellamy, and a few other pirate-y guys who had "black" in their names.) Then there are some buccaneers you probably haven't heard of, like Mary Read and Anne Bonny, the most notorious *women* pirates in the Caribbean. Being a lady pirate wasn't half-bad. On a pirate ship, you didn't have to wear a corset. Your worth wasn't decided by who you married or how many babies you birthed. You could be free.

But it wasn't all sunshine and rainbows, of course. A woman on a ship was considered bad luck, so you had to dress as a man if you didn't want to get thrown overboard. It was difficult to find good shampoo. And oh yeah, you occasionally got chased by Jonathan Barnet. And if he caught you, well, that was it. You died.

That's what the historians say happened to Mary Read: she was captured, tried, and found guilty of piracy, but died in jail before she could hang.

But—bah!—what do historians know?

They certainly don't know that Mary Read and the little mermaid were the very same person. A girl who loved books so much she gave herself the last name Read. A girl who learned the hard way that romance isn't a fairy tale. A girl who's going to start out our story feeling pretty darn salty about love.

But don't worry. She'll come around.

HOW IT STARTED

Our Version

"I'm getting married!" the prince said again.

Mary sank down onto the edge of her bed, stunned. When he'd said it the first time she'd assumed he meant they—he and she—were getting married, and she'd been confused because she was pretty sure that the proposal was supposed to come *before* the wedding. But then he kept talking—about something called a dowry, which was apparently a negotiation with the bride's family—and Mary slowly came to understand he wasn't talking about her. Which meant that Charles—aka the prince, aka the *love of her life*—was getting married.

To someone else.

"You'll be there, of course," Charles went on. "Even if Lavinia didn't want to invite you, I insisted."

Mary stared at him.

"Oh, right." Charles gave a sheepish smile. "I should have mentioned: I'm marrying Lavinia. Oh, and the wedding is tomorrow," he added.

Mary's mouth dropped open.

"I know, I know," said Charles. "I should have told you earlier." He took in her expression and gave a pitying laugh. "You're shocked, of course. This must be most unexpected news."

Or it was the sort of blindsiding news that could kill a person. Thankfully, she didn't turn into sea foam.

Yet.

Where Mary came from, it was a well-known fact that getting one's heart broken was fatal. And where she came from, that was what happened when a person died: they burst into a mass of fluffy white sea foam and floated away on the next tide. Yes, it sounds drastic, but where Mary came from, people lived for three hundred years. Why, Mary had a grandmother who was two hundred and ninety-two years old. But Mary herself was only sixteen. The last thing she wanted was to die of a broken heart.

She pressed her hand to her chest and found the organ in question still stubbornly beating. It hurt, yes—there was an unpleasant squeezing sensation—but it hadn't killed her.

Yet.

"You're disappointed." Charles gave a dramatic pout. "Please try to understand. I'm so fond of you, truly."

She gasped. He was fond of her! She knew it!

Charles pressed on. "But you've seen Lavinia. She's undeniably beautiful. And you're so tall—you're nearly taller than I am—and you're—" He grimaced, as though struggling with how to explain it. Finally, he held his hands person-width apart, palms facing each other, and made a straight line down.

Like a box. Like the shape of her.

Her heart gave a painful twist. She wasn't beautiful, she knew, not by human standards. Not like Lavinia, whose perfectly symmetrical face actually *was* in the dictionary next to the word *beautiful*. (Mary had been there the day the dictionary people came to take Lavinia's sketch.) But so what?

She *loved him*.

The first time she'd laid eyes on Charles, on the fine ship where he'd been celebrating his birthday, she'd known that they were meant to be together. She'd seen fireworks that night—literal fireworks, exploding in the sky over their heads—and what she'd felt for Charles was like the fireworks, so bright and loud in her heart.

She loved him. Like Juliet loved Romeo in her favorite story.

He *had* to love her back.

"You understand, don't you?" He cleared his throat uncomfortably. "The truth of the matter is, I'm a prince. You know how everyone here calls me 'the prince of Charles Town.' And as a prince, I must marry a . . . princess, of sorts. It's a rule—well, an unspoken rule, but a rule nonetheless. And Lavinia's a princess."

Mary opened her mouth to tell him that *she* was a princess. A real one. Unlike Lavinia, Mary was the daughter of an actual king. She had a crown and everything. But the words didn't come, not because she couldn't speak—she could; she'd spent months learning how to speak English—but because even now, at this crucial moment, she couldn't tell him the truth about who she really was. He wouldn't believe her. And she was always tongue-tied around Charles, like she was so dazzled by him that it was as if he reached into her throat and stole her voice away.

Mary hurried to the trunk at the foot of her bed and rifled through her belongings.

Charles watched her warily as she found what she wanted. "What's this?"

Proof, she wanted to say. But instead she just held up the crown.

It was crafted from a single piece of coral, which shifted from orange to pink depending on the light, and gave off a kind of ethereal glow. Pearls, white and black and every shade in between, had been set in intricate designs along the front. The crown had belonged to Mary's mother, passed down upon her death. It was the only thing Mary had taken with her when she'd come Above.

It proved, beyond a doubt, that she was a princess.

Gently, Charles took the crown and inspected it. "This is beautiful," he breathed.

A lump formed in Mary's throat. She nodded. "I—"

"It's perfect," Charles said, still gazing at the crown. "This will look exquisite on Lavinia tomorrow. She's been desperate to find a tiara to match her veil." He began to prattle on about the details of the wedding. "It's to be held aboard my father's finest ship: the *Fancy*. Won't that be nice? I know how you love the water. Come, you must help me with the preparations. There's much to do before tomorrow."

The stabbing pain returned to Mary's chest. *This is it*, she thought. *Sea foam*. But she remained very much alive, red-faced and speechless, when Charles smiled his heart-melting-est smile and held out his hand to her.

"Please, my little foundling?" he pleaded.

She took his hand. She'd taught herself how to speak English, but she'd never learned how to say no to him.

His little foundling, Mary fumed the next day as she stood aboard the *Fancy* and watched Charles say his wedding vows. He never called her by her name, she realized suddenly. Not the name she'd been given at birth nor the human name she'd chosen. She'd picked *Mary* because she'd often seen it in books, and it was a name humans seemed to revere. She loved that name—it just fit her somehow.

But Charles always called her his little foundling.

Little. What a joke.

"I do," Charles was saying now.

Mary's jaw clenched. How could he do this to her? She'd given up everything for him.

"I do," Lavinia cooed back to Charles.

That codfish.

The priest announced that Charles could kiss the bride.

Mary glared down at the deck. Humiliation burned through her. She was sure everyone was looking at her, laughing at her, because everyone had known she and Charles were together. But now he'd cast her off. *How did this happen?* she asked herself. She loved Charles. And he loved her.

Didn't he?

Wait, *didn't he?*

She was beginning to have her doubts.

Everyone clapped, and Mary looked up to find Charles and Lavinia facing the crowd, smiling bashfully, holding hands.

It was done. He was married.

Her heart gave a great squeeze. She pressed her palm against it as she blinked back tears and somehow didn't become sea foam right there in front of everyone.

What a scene that would cause. The onlookers would be shocked. There'd be screaming, perhaps even some fainting. The wedding would be spoiled.

It was a petty but comforting thought.

That night, after the food and cake, the dancing and toasting, after the newlyweds retired to their room belowdecks and everything had gone quiet, Mary stole a bottle of rum and sat on the bow of the ship. She liked rum, she discovered as she watched the moon gleam on the black, rolling ocean. The liquid burned its way down her throat, warming her stomach. It reminded her that she wasn't foam.

Yet.

Just then, a head breached the surface of the water, followed by a set of pale arms, a torso, and a long, shining green fish tail. Effortlessly, the creature climbed up the ship and hoisted itself to sit on the rail.

It was a mermaid, obviously.

It also happened to be Mary's sister, Big Deal, who—when she'd been giving everyone secret human names—Mary had dubbed Karen.

Mary rushed to the rail to help her onto the deck. *"How did you find me?"* she cried in Merish.

(A note, dear reader, about Merish: when Merfolk speak to one another, they're directing their thoughts-as-words like a type of targeted telepathy. The range of Merish is similar to that of out-loud speech—one can whisper or yell or anything in between. To us humans, however, Merish would sound totally silent, as we don't have the part of the brain that can detect it. So Mary's cry wasn't really a cry, but you get the idea.)

"Oh, you know. Magic." Karen fixed her gaze on Mary's feet. *"Seriously? All that fuss over those things? And what are those nubby stumps on the ends?"*

Mary resisted the urge to tuck her feet under her, out of sight. They were blistered and red. The fancy wedding shoes she'd borrowed had made her feel like she was stepping on knives whenever she walked. She'd tossed the heels overboard right after the wedding. *"There's more to being human than just feet,"* she said stiffly.

Karen scoffed. *"So you're happy? Is being human everything you thought it would be?"*

There was a knowing glint in her eyes. Somehow—Mary didn't know how, but somehow—her sister knew about her predicament.

"Does everyone know?" she asked. Everyone, meaning the other Mers.

Karen nodded grimly. *"So it didn't work out with the human. Gee, who could have predicted that?"*

"I'm fine," Mary insisted, her face burning. *"It's true that I didn't marry the prince, but I'll figure out something else. I can take care of myself."*

This wasn't true, and Karen could tell. (It is supremely difficult to lie while using telepathy.) Mary didn't honestly know how she could live in the human world without Charles. She had no way to provide for herself.

"I'm fine," she lied again.

"You're remarkably calm, considering," Karen said. *"I mean, you have, what, half an hour left to live? It's nearly dawn."*

"Um," Mary said. *"What do you mean?"*

Karen put a hand to her scaly hip. *"Everyone knows the rules: 'The day after your one true love has wed another, when morning breaks, so shall your heart.' And then . . ."* She pursed her lips and blew a frothy raspberry.

Sea foam.

Right.

"Oh." That seemed awfully specific to Mary's particular situation. Had the Sea Witch (aka Aunt Witch, to Mary, since the Sea

Witch was her father's sister and therefore her aunt) said anything about that? Mary hadn't been paying the best of attention that night; she'd been in such a hurry to be reunited with her darling prince. What a fool she was!

An improbable laugh escaped her, along with a rum-tasting burp, which just made her laugh and sob harder.

Great Waters, she'd given up everything for Charles. And now . . . And now . . .

The sky was lightening on the horizon. It was almost morning.

"We can fix it," Karen said. *"Aunt Witch sent me to give you this."* She began digging through her bag.

Hopefully she'd brought Mary a potion that would magically solve all her problems.

Instead, Karen pulled out a long, sharp knife.

Mary reared back. *"Aunt Witch wants me dead? But aren't I about to die anyway?"*

Karen snorted. *"No, stupid. It's a magic knife. Obviously. I traded my hair to Aunt Witch to get it for you."*

Mary gasped, just now noticing how her sister's hair was cropped up to her ears. What an enormous sacrifice! A mermaid's hair was considered her pride and joy; it had magical powers, in fact, like the ability to stay shiny and untangled while submerged in saltwater twenty-four hours a day.

Karen gave the knife to Mary. *"Aunt Witch says to plunge this into the heart of the human who hurt you. Let his blood spill over your weird, disgusting legs, and they will become a proper tail again. Then you'll come home and we'll all pretend this humiliating incident never happened."*

"Stab him?" Mary's mouth dropped open. *"I can't do that!"*

Karen rolled her eyes. *"You can if you want to live to see tomorrow."*

There was a sudden phlegmy cough from somewhere down the ship. Karen dropped into the water with hardly a splash.

"You'd better do it quick," she called up when she surfaced again. *"I'd estimate that you have about ten minutes. Maybe fifteen."*

Mary shivered. *"I don't know if I can."*

"Don't be a baby," Karen snapped. *"Just do it. And don't forget to bring Mother's crown back with you. One day, when I'm the Sea Queen, I'll need that crown for my coronation. You can't just take things that belong to both of us."*

Mary's mouth opened and closed. *"All right. I— All right."*

Then Karen was gone, back down to their watery home, aka Underwhere (yep, you heard that right: Underwhere, as in W-H-E-R-E), aka the Kingdom of the Sea.

Five minutes later, Mary was standing at the foot of Charles's bed, glaring down at him and Lavinia. They were spooning.

Mary's palms were sweating. The knife felt slippery in her grip.

She really, really didn't want to die in five minutes.

But could she actually do it?

Just then, Charles turned over onto his back, perfectly positioning himself to be stabbed in the heart.

Mary lifted the knife, trembling. Her thoughts were muddled— thanks largely to the rum. She tried to work up the rage she'd felt earlier.

She loved him. But he didn't love her—and never had. It was so obvious now.

Her fist tightened around the knife handle.

Charles gave a sudden snort. His chest, with its very stabbable heart, rose and fell as he began to snore like a chain saw (although chain saws hadn't been invented yet).

The trembling in her hand grew worse.

If she did this, she could go home. She could live the rest of her three hundred years trying to forget him. But no one else would forget it. She'd always be the littlest princess. The silly one, who tried to be special and ended up getting dumped. She'd never live it down.

She couldn't go back.

But the alternative was not living at all.

And time was running short.

It was now or never.

It's him or me, she thought. *I have to do it. I must.*

No.

She couldn't.

She lowered the knife to her side. In the mirror over the armoire, she caught sight of herself, a wild and desperate girl, her blue eyes red-rimmed and sorrowful. The fancy updo she'd fixed herself for the wedding had half fallen down now, framing her face in lank strands. Her gown didn't suit her, either. It was a pale blue satin number that was too tight in the shoulders, and too loose in the hips and chest. It would have been beautiful on someone with Lavinia-like curves, a *proper* woman, the kind Charles would have wanted to marry.

Suddenly Mary couldn't stand to be wearing the dress for a moment longer. She tore at the laces.

The dress didn't budge.

She tried to wriggle out of it.

It stuck fast.

Then she remembered she had a knife in her hand. She hacked her way out of the dress and hurled it onto the foot of Charles's enormous bed, where he and Lavinia still slept obliviously.

Calmer now, Mary stole a shirt and breeches from the armoire and put them on. Then, because she'd said she would, she glanced around the cabin for the crown. Not on Lavinia's head, not on the chest of drawers, and not on the heap of clothing.

Oh well. Mary couldn't spend any more time looking for it, since she had a, uh, deadline.

She returned to the bow of the ship and used the magic knife to saw off her hair, as a show of solidarity with Karen. She hoped her family would understand. She hoped her father would stop being mad at her and maybe feel a teensy bit sorry for her instead. (But he'd probably stay mad. The last time she'd seen her father, they'd been screaming at each other—silently, that is—and she'd said she hated him.)

She couldn't go back.

Before she could change her mind, Mary flung the knife into the sea.

It was dawn. The sky was washed with shades of pinks and

peaches. The sun breached the horizon in an orange flare. Mary closed her eyes, savoring the feel of the wind tugging at her, the salty sea air, the warmth of morning on her face. . . .

The pain hit her again, this time in her stomach. (Reader, this could have been the rum.) She squeezed her eyes shut, waiting to become foam.

It didn't happen.

Perhaps it was going to take a moment?

But the ship was beginning to wake. Mary couldn't stay here and burst into foam in front of everyone. That now seemed down-right undignified. So she did the only thing she could think to do: she ran to the starboard side and hurled herself, unceremoniously, over the rail.

She expected to explode into foam the instant she struck the water, but no. The only thing that happened was that she bounced painfully against the hull a few times. Then the ship kept sailing away, and Mary discovered something significant:

She couldn't swim.

She was momentarily drowning until she figured out how to doggy paddle. But even then, she quickly tired. *I could really use some help*, she thought, and thankfully, just then, a helpful sea turtle came along and let her rest upon its shell.

An hour passed. Two. And still she had not turned into sea foam.

"All right. What am I to do now?" she asked the sea turtle.

The turtle didn't answer. It did, however, abruptly decide that it had somewhere better to be, and Mary was back to treading water.

She wondered if Charles had found her dress yet. She imagined him standing on the deck, clutching the blue satin to his chest, gazing out at the water with deep sorrow. He would regret everything. He'd weep for her. Wouldn't he?

No, she thought bitterly. *Probably not.*

She was so tired of treading water. How easy it had been to navigate the world as a mermaid, slipping through the depths with a flick of her strong tail. Karen was right. These weird damn legs weren't getting it done. She couldn't go on.

So it's to be sea foam after all, she thought as she slipped under the waves. Broken heart no longer required.

"Man overboard!" someone yelled.

Mary startled, her head breaching the surface. Had Charles come back for her?

A hulking shadow fell over her: a ship. There was a splash—someone jumping into the water—and then strong hands around her middle. They hauled her into a net, which hoisted her up and onto the deck, where she was dumped out, coughing and sputtering.

Another shadow fell over her.

Mary brushed water out of her eyes and squinted up to see, not Charles, but a man dressed all in black. He wore a faded black shirt with a black leather vest atop it, a very shiny and fancy pistol tucked into his belt alongside a wicked-looking cutlass. He had a short scruffy beard and wore the top part of his hair tied back, revealing several piercings along the outer edges of his ears, the rest of his hair loose about his shoulders. His skin was weathered and tanned (because sunscreen hadn't been invented yet), and his eyes seemed permanently squinted. Mary noticed that his knuckles were scabbed over, as if the man had recently been in a fistfight. He grinned down at her, a glint of gold in his teeth.

"What a strange catch we have today," he said in the lowest, raspiest voice she'd ever heard. "What say you?"

Mary gaped up at him, speechless.

The man who'd jumped in after her—*not* the one with the deep voice, we should clarify—turned out to be a young man about her age with brown skin and dark eyes. He smiled kindly. "Can you stand?"

With his help, Mary rose unsteadily to her feet. Her head was woozy. Her stomach hurt. She was really starting to regret that rum.

"Here, have some rum," said the man in black, thrusting a bottle under her nose.

Mary took a swig. Then she ran to the side of the ship and spilled her guts over the rail.

"Ha! A lightweight," scoffed the man as Mary stumbled back, wiping her mouth on her sleeve. "Where did you come from, boy?"

Boy?

It hit her instantly, that now-familiar rub of not being slim enough or curvy enough to be considered a real woman. Yes, she was wearing men's clothes, and she'd cut her hair, but even so, if she'd ever been *girl enough* there would have been no question.

But just as she was about to blurt out that she was a girl—a *woman*, thank you very much—she noticed that there were an awful lot of men on this ship. Only men. She didn't see a single woman, in fact. So given the circumstances, perhaps it was in her best interest to be viewed as a boy. "I came from a—a ship. I fell off."

"Well, that makes it simple enough!"

Did it? She glanced around again. All the men were grinning like they knew something she didn't. She noticed then that the men weren't all what humans referred to as "white," like the sailors from the *Fancy* had been. Many of them had brown skin—like the young man who'd saved her—and black skin. The range of skin tones was more like Mary was used to in Underwhere. And some of these men had eye patches. One had a peg leg. And another had a parrot perched on his shoulder. "Is this a merchant vessel of some kind?"

The man in black laughed huskily, which the rest of the men copied. "This is a pirate ship, lad! I am Captain Vane. And you, my young friend, have the good fortune of being the newest member of our crew."

Mary straightened, her heart (which was obviously functioning just fine, in spite of everything) picking up its pace.

Pirates.

In her time as a human, Mary had come to understand two things about pirates: they were scary and bad. Scary as in the mere *mention* of pirates made grown men shiver. And bad as in they were criminals, although she wasn't sure what kind of crime they were involved in. As Mary had been rather focused on Charles, any other details about pirates had escaped her.

"It's not so terrible," the kind young man whispered. "You'll see. You can start as a cabin boy and work your way up the ranks. Maybe you'll even like it. We go where we please and take what we want. It's not a bad life."

"It's better than being sea foam, I suppose," Mary said.

"Aye, it is that," he said with a good-natured laugh. "I'm Tobias, by the way. Tobias Teach. I'm glad to meet you." He stuck out a hand.

Mary shook it. "I'm Mar— Mark." That was a boy's name, right? And there should be a surname. One that wasn't *Foundling*.

She wasn't sure how surnames worked, exactly. During her time in Charles Town, she'd met a Mr. Baker (he'd cut Charles's hair) and a Mr. King (he'd looked after Charles's horses). Charles's last name was Worthington. That codfish! She was doing entirely too much thinking about Charles. She was going to stop thinking about him. She was never going to think about him again. Starting . . . now.

What had they been talking about? Oh yes. A surname.

Perhaps she could simply name herself after something she liked.

"Reading," she blurted out. When she'd lived in Underwhere, she and her best friend had sometimes found human books amid the wreckage of ships. They'd spent hours poring over them together, reading and discussing the stories. "Mark, uh, Read," she amended quickly. "That's my name."

Captain Vane snapped his fingers at a bespectacled man standing nearby. "You, Quint. Get this down."

"How do you spell it?" The man whipped out a small ledger and a quill. "M-A-R-K . . ."

"R-E-A-D," Mary said slowly, and Quint wrote it down.

"Glad to make your acquaintance, Mr. Read," growled Captain Vane, clapping her on the shoulder so hard her teeth clattered together. "Welcome aboard the *Ranger*."

Then he waved all the men back to work.

Tobias gestured for her to follow him away from the captain and the multitude of rowdy men. "You're not from around here, are you?" he asked when they were out of earshot of the others.

Mary actually *was* from around here, as they were surrounded by ocean. But of course she couldn't say so. "I came from . . . Charles Town." Her jaw tightened.

The *prince* of Charles Town. What a joke.

She hoped Charles got sunburned on his honeymoon.

She was going to stop thinking about Charles. Starting . . . now.

"Ah, Charles Town," said Tobias. "I've never been there myself, as I quite enjoy my freedom, but we sail up that way sometimes. If you wish to return, I can help you, miss."

She almost didn't catch it; he said the word *miss* so softly.

He knew.

"My name is really Mary," she confessed, lowering her voice to match his.

He shook his head. "You should stick with Mark. At least until we can get you back to Charles Town."

"No! I won't go back there!" she declared.

Wow, she'd almost yelled. She'd used her voice. It felt rather good.

Tobias gave her a crooked smile. "All right. No one will make you."

"What I mean is, I'd rather be a pirate," she said. After all, being a little mermaid hadn't worked out, and being a little foundling had worked out even worse. She'd do better as a pirate, she thought, even if she'd have to pretend to be a boy. She'd go where she wanted. Take what she pleased. It sounded like a fine life, indeed.

So Mary decided right then and there that she was going to be more than just a competent pirate. She was going to be a *great* pirate, whatever that entailed. She'd be the strongest. The richest. The most fearsome. The scariest and baddest of them all.

I'll be the best pirate who ever sailed, she promised herself fiercely, staring out at the rolling blue of the ocean, which already seemed different, like an opportunity there for the taking, brimming with treasure and fun.

And she promised herself something else, too: she would never give anyone the power to make her feel so small as Charles had—she was going to stop thinking about him now, seriously. She would never fall in love. Ever, ever again.

HOW IT'S GOING

One Year Later...

Mary

ONE

A sharp whistle pierced the air. "Sails!" cried the lookout from the crow's nest. "Sails, to the port side!"

Mary took the stairs to the quarterdeck two at a time. She turned toward her left and lifted a spyglass to her eye. Sure enough, against the bright horizon was a three-masted ship with red crosses on its sails. A Spanish galleon. Down from Port Royal, probably. Ripe for the taking.

The entire crew buzzed with excitement.

"She's riding low," said Quint at Mary's side. "She's sure to be hauling a heavy cargo."

Mary peered across the water until the ship's name came into focus: *El Chango*. Translated from Spanish, it meant: *The Monkey*.

"She's carrying rum, do you think?" guessed Diesel, the ship's gunner. "Molasses? Tobacco?"

"Could be anything," said Quint, rubbing his hands together. "I hope it's Spanish gold."

Mary lowered the spyglass. "Whatever it is, it's about to be ours." Then she noted the conspicuous absence of their fearless leader. "Where's the captain?"

"Haven't seen him all day," said Diesel with a shrug.

Nor had she, but she wasn't about to let this prize get away. "I'll find Vane," she told Quint. "Keep on them, DuPaul," she ordered the helmsman.

"Aye, Mr. Read." The man nudged the wheel.

She turned to the assembled crew. "Are you up for a little hunting?"

"Aye!" called the crew in unison.

A thrill shot through her, adrenaline flooding her veins. Her heart was already drumming sweetly, her breath quickening, even her skin atingle with the anticipation of the chase.

It turns out, dear reader, that Mary had broken her promise.

She'd fallen in love again, almost immediately.

With being a pirate.

She hurried to the captain's cabin and put her fist to the door.

Tobias opened it. "Ah, Mr. Read." He stepped aside to let her in, revealing Captain Vane sitting on the edge of the four-poster bed in the back, a bottle of rum dangling from his fingers.

"What's all the noise about?" Vane peered up through blood-shot eyes. "What all-important news do you bear, Mr. Read, that you would interrupt my heartsore seclusion?"

Mary exchanged glances with Tobias. He gave the smallest of eye rolls, which Mary interpreted easily enough: Captain Vane was (still) feeling wounded over Bess, the pretty lady who'd broken things off with him during their last visit to Nassau, and he was (still/again) attempting to drown his sorrows in rum. Which Mary knew from experience wouldn't work.

She cleared her throat. "A ship, sir. A fat Spanish galleon. Shall we pursue?"

Vane heaved a sigh. "I pursued Bess, you know. Really gave it me best effort. Flowers. Fancy dresses. Jewels. And she just took me heart and—" He opened his hand, palm up, and pantomimed crushing.

This was exactly why Mary had sworn off love. The *Ranger* was one of the most profitable ships in the business, and Vane one of the most feared and well-respected of pirate captains, and yet here he was, brought low by an ill-fated romance. She fought the urge to grab Vane by the shirt collar and tell him to pull himself together. "Yes, so tragic," she said instead. "But about this ship. We've got the wind on her, sir, but who knows for how long."

Vane took a deep swig from his bottle, groaned, then finally nodded. "Fine." He got to his feet, staggered, clutched at his head, and fell back again. "You handle it, Mr. Read. I'll come out for the fighting."

A second glance with Tobias. This was the third time this week the captain had been too heartsore/drunk to do his job.

Tobias's look said, *Save me from this nightmare.*

Mary's responding look said, *Sorry. Sucks to be you.* Then, out loud to Vane, she said, "Very good, sir." With another nod at Tobias, Mary jogged back to the main deck. "He'll come for the fighting," she reported to Quint.

Quint's expression went carefully blank. "Again? That's the third time this week."

Mary shrugged, then cupped her hands around her mouth as she called out, "Make ready! We're going after her! Raise the canvas!"

The crew cheered again and hurried to their stations. Mary returned to the helm.

And just like that, the chase was on.

Wind caught the sails and the ship surged forward, quickly closing the distance between itself and the *Chango*. By now the other crew would have noticed they were being pursued. They, too, had fully unfurled their sails and were moving away as fast as they could, but their ship was large, heavily laden, and couldn't possibly outrun their attackers. The men on the *Chango* would know that. The fear would be building. The gravity of their situation would be sinking in.

Mary smiled. This next part was delicate.

"Fifty more yards, and we're in range," yelled Diesel.

She nodded. She waited until they were quite close—almost on top of the other ship—and then rolled up her sleeves. It was time. "Hoist the black!" she yelled, and soon, Vane's personal pirate flag—three red symbols on a black field: a dagger, a skull's profile, and an oddly shaped heart—was flapping in the wind. Mary had always thought the flag looked silly (the heart, she thought, was a bit much) but it got the job done.

Immediately, the *Chango*'s crew began to panic.

"¡Piratas!" The shouts could be heard across the water. They were speaking in Spanish, but everyone basically knew what they were saying: Pirates! (The tone of "Let's get out of here!" is universal, dear reader, as is "We're all going to die!")

Mary knew the captain of the *Chango* must be giving up now on the idea of getting away.

"There she goes!" bellowed Quint, and, as expected, the merchant vessel slowed and began to turn. Fifteen cannons slid from the gunports, compared to the mere six the *Ranger* boasted. But Mary wasn't worried. Much.

At her command, the *Ranger*, too, came about. "Fire a warning!" she shouted.

A great *BOOM* rocked the ship. A cannonball flew across the water, just missing the galleon's bowsprit.

Now she was giving the captain of the *Chango* a choice: surrender, or fight.

Plenty of captains surrendered. That gave them a chance of survival, after all. Their crew might be spared. Sometimes, even the captains were spared and left to sail away, their holds empty of everything valuable. But they got to live . . . as long as they found somewhere to make port before they died of hunger or thirst.

Mary preferred the ones who chose to fight. She liked the challenge, the thrill of battle. The danger. She lived for it, actually.

"Come on," she whispered, peering through the spyglass. At the helm of the other ship, the captain, a tall white man with a powdered wig and fancy coat, was looking back at her through his own spyglass.

She gave a playful wave.

The man dropped his spyglass, sending it spinning across the deck as he shouted orders. He raised his arm as though to make a chopping motion.

"Guns!" Mary grinned. "On my mark!"

At the rails of the *Ranger*, the men who were crouched there cocked their various muskets.

"Fire!" Mary shouted.

The men stood and fired. A flurry of iron musket balls screamed across the water. Some hit the *Chango*'s crew above decks, but most were aimed toward the gunports. The idea was to take out the men on the gun deck so they couldn't fire on the *Ranger*. But muskets weren't terribly accurate, so most of the bullets just bounced harmlessly off the galleon's sturdy hull.

And then the *Chango* fired back. With cannons.

(Reader, this is one of the more unbelievable parts of the age of sail. When two ships got into a fight, they really did come parallel to each other, giving the enemy the biggest target possible. The goal was to hit the other ship with more cannonballs than they could hit you with. But put too many cannonballs in another ship and you'd sink it, which was undesirable when you were a pirate and you wanted to loot the other ship before all that treasure sank to the bottom of the ocean. Hence the *Ranger* firing at the cannon people. And why the *Chango* had no problem opening with cannon fire—they would have liked nothing more than to sink the *Ranger* and sail away safely.)

The cannonballs from the *Chango* slammed into the side of the *Ranger*, sending splinters of wood flying everywhere. Thankfully, nothing tore through—yet. She was a good and sturdy ship.

"Fire!" Mary shouted again. More muskets. A few faces from the opposite gun deck vanished, but were quickly replaced. They weren't leaving Mary much of a choice. "Cannons, Mr. Diesel!" she cried. "Fire! Fire at will!"

The fuses were lit. Within seconds, nine-pound iron balls hurtled across the water, some striking their marks, some falling short. Both ships rocked on the water, waves cresting the side of the decks.

After a bit of back-and-forth with this, Mary's men (ahem, Captain Vane's men) managed to slow the barrage of cannon fire from the other ship.

Now it was time for the fun part.

"Board!" she yelled. Pirates echoed the order along the ship until, on the gunner's count, half a dozen men threw grappling hooks at the *Chango*, grabbing the side of the ship so they could maneuver themselves closer.

"Heave ho!" they cried, pulling the lines. "Heave! Ho!"

Slowly—so slowly—the ships came together until their hulls nearly touched.

At once, men high in the rigging swung out toward the other ship. Of course, that meant the *Chango*'s musket men started firing on the *Ranger*'s men. But Mary's musket men (er, Captain Vane's musket men) fired back. For several minutes there was utter chaos—until Mr. Quint gave a sharp whistle, signaling for the rest of the men to come aboard.

"On the rails! Come with me, lads!" Mary said, throwing her body over the top of the rail and onto the nets they'd thrown below. "Let's show them what we're made of."

Tobias landed beside her. "I *know* you weren't trying to leave me behind, Read."

Mary pulled herself onto the deck of the *Chango* and drew her cutlass. "Well, I wasn't about to go back into Vane's cabin and risk getting trapped there."

A huge orange-bearded man ran at them, bellowing, but they easily slipped out of his way and pushed him over the side.

"That's fair." Tobias blocked as another man lunged at them, his sword swinging. "If I didn't have to be there, I wouldn't. I'd rather swab the deck than listen to his moaning about."

Mary thumped the newest opponent on the head and tossed him overboard, too, to join his friend. "What do you say we play cards after our shifts? That'll give you some time away from Vane. And I wouldn't mind winning some money off the other officers. They're sure to be feeling rich and foolish after this raid."

"Aye," Tobias said, fighting another man from the *Chango*. "That'd be good."

Mary swung her sword at a different sailor, their blades meeting with a bone-jarring clang. The other man was stronger, but she was faster, lighter on her feet. She spun and dodged and ducked, then kicked him over the side to join the others. Then she turned to meet her next foe.

"I was thinking"—Tobias ducked a blow—"that we should get a better table for the shack."

"What's wrong with the one we have?" Mary knocked her opponent to the deck; he didn't get up.

"It's got three peg legs and the top gives you a splinter every time you touch it."

"Oh yeah." Now that he mentioned it, she hated that table.

"I'd like something better for drawing."

Mary grinned. Maps—that's what Tobias loved to draw. He was good at it, too, which was part of why he was the ship's navigator. "Fine," Mary said, pulling on a rope; the boom swung around and smacked several of the *Chango*'s sailors. "We'll get you a new table. An extravagant one with four original legs and a smooth top."

Tobias laughed as they came back-to-back to fight off the next guy, and the next.

Sometimes it was hard to believe this was her life. Every day since she'd jumped off the *Fancy* with no plan except sea foam, she'd discovered a new kind of strength in herself, and a new sense of purpose. At first, that purpose had been simply to take Captain

Vane's messages to and fro, as she'd been a mere cabin boy. Then her purpose had been to mind the rigging and learn how to go aloft, trim the sails, and not get splattered across the deck for poor Nine Toes to clean up. And now she bested men and captured ships, alongside her best mate, Tobias.

They made a fine pair, she thought. She felt comfortable with him in a way she hadn't felt with anyone in a long time. But Tobias didn't know about the mermaid thing. Or the princess thing. She didn't know how she would even begin to bring that up.

The fighting was over quickly, after that. Her men were fierce and seasoned pirates, and the young sailors of the *Chango* were no match for them.

"Mr. Read," Tobias said quietly. "Your hair."

Mary felt around the back of her head, where, indeed, her hair had come loose from its tie. Well, she couldn't threaten the *Chango*'s sailors like this. "Check on the cargo, Mr. Teach," she said to Tobias. "I'll join you in a minute. Also," she added more quietly, "thanks for the warning."

"Glad to be of service." He grinned, tipped his hat, and turned to see about the cargo. Mary's gaze may have lingered on his backside a bit too long, but then she spun and strode quickly into the captain's cabin where she could fix her hair situation.

The room looked empty. But if Mary's experience told her anything, it was that on a pirate ship, looks can be deceiving.

"Come out from there!" Mary barked. "I'm going to count to five. One, two—"

"Don't kill me!" A man slid out from under the bed.

"Get out!" Mary ordered.

The man didn't have to be told twice.

When the door slammed shut after him, Mary took a moment to root around the chest of drawers and wardrobe until she discovered a brilliant yellow ribbon. She stuffed her hat into her pocket and, finger combing her hair, moved to stand in front of the mirror.

At the sight of herself in the tarnishing silver, she went still. In the year since joining the crew of the *Ranger*, she'd grown tanned and strong. Her face (which, according to *some people*, had suffered from RBF, aka Resting Bossy Face) looked *right* under the cap she always wore, with a strong jaw and high cheekbones.

This was the life she wanted, one of high seas and adventure. And if the price for having this life was needing to keep her hair tied back every day, bind her chest, schedule bathroom breaks for when she could be alone, pretend to shave, deepen her voice, and act like she thought the men were actually funny—well, then so be it.

The door flew open just as she finished pulling her cap back down.

"You'd better come," Tobias said urgently. "There's a problem with the cargo."

"What problem?" Mary frowned.

"It's bananas," Tobias said.

"Bananas? How so?" Mary followed him out of the captain's cabin.

"As in, the cargo of the ship consists entirely of bananas." He gestured to a huge stack of the bright yellow fruit on the deck.

"No," Mary said in dismay.

Tobias then took her down to the cargo hold, where there were boxes and crates stacked everywhere—all full of bananas.

"No," Mary groaned.

Tobias led her to the next room. More bananas. Bananas from floor to ceiling.

"Has Captain Vane seen this?" Mary asked.

"Nope." Tobias popped the *p* on the word. "Which is a good thing, because the only items of value on this entire ship that aren't bananas are a bottle of banana rum and . . . this." He held out a worn-looking book. Mary snatched it and flipped through it.

Banana recipes. Every single page held banana recipes.

"Ugh! This is a nightmare." She shoved the book back at Tobias.

They returned to the main deck, where the crew of the *Ranger* was in an uproar, apparently having discovered the banana situation.

Mary climbed to the quarterdeck to address them.

"WHERE'S OUR TREASURE?" bellowed the pirates, seemingly in one voice.

Mary held up her hand, nodding, and the men quieted down to listen.

"We all know that treasure's a relative term," she yelled. "We're pirates, aren't we, lads? Which means we make the best of what we find. When life gives you bananas, you make . . ."

"You make what?" asked one of the surlier men.

Tobias flipped through the banana cookbook. "You make banana cream pie?" he offered.

"You make banana cream pie!" Mary agreed.

"I do like banana cream pie," mused the man, apparently mollified.

"So let's gather up the fruit and get back to our own ship," said Mary, and the pirates set to work.

"Thank you," she said to Tobias as she stepped down from the quarterdeck. "Now, we must see to the *Chango*'s crew."

They were all bound and lined up on the deck, awaiting their fates.

The *Chango*'s captain was tied to the mainmast, looking miserable in his powdered wig. Mary was glad Captain Vane hadn't showed yet. He would likely want the other captain dead as an example to those who would cross him. (He wasn't one of the most feared pirates for nothing.)

She drew her cutlass again and stepped toward the line of men. "So you've been captured by pirates. Now what?" She looked down the line. All the men looked nervous. And rightfully so.

"Are you . . . Captain Vane?" asked one of the men, literally shaking in his boots.

"My name's Mark Read," she answered. "I'm the quartermaster of the *Ranger*. Captain Vane is currently occupied with far more important things than you lot, so I'll be the one taking care of you today. Know that you'll come to no more harm, so long as no one decides to be foolish. I'm what you'd call a gentle pirate—I've no heart to injure you, but that doesn't mean I won't disembowel you if provoked. Now, I'm sure you already know your options, but for any of you who might be new to this business: you can either join the crew of the *Ranger* and live—or you can walk the plank and brave the drink. There is no third option."

How easy she found it to talk now. Even if she had to slightly alter her voice so they'd believe her a man. The words just flowed.

One of the *Chango*'s crew raised his hand.

Mary used her cutlass to point at him. "Yes? You in the back?"

He lowered his hand. "Can we have a few minutes to think about it?"

Mary considered. "I'd like to give you the time. Honestly, I would. But this is one of those decisions you're going to have to make right now. Either line up there, over by the plank"—she pointed—"or be ready to sign on as a pirate. I recommend the pirate life. If you find it disagrees with you, you can always walk the plank some other time."

"Aye, that's a good point," said the man. "I'll be a pirate."

"Me too," said another.

"But if you're a pirate, you'll be marked for death anyway," the captain of the *Chango* burst out suddenly.

"Wait, how's that?" said the man who'd just decided to be a pirate.

"Haven't you heard of the great pirate hunter, Jonathan Barnet?" the captain asked dramatically. "He roams the sea, looking for pirates, and when he finds them, he always bests them. If you become a pirate, he'll hunt every last one of you down, and you'll die on the end of his sword, or he'll take you back to hang for your crimes."

"Could somebody get this guy a gag?" Mary asked.

"Better to jump ship now than meet your demise at the end of a rope!" the captain cried. "Beware! Bewaaaaaaaaaare!" Then Quint stuffed a rag into his mouth.

The men of the *Chango* looked a lot less certain than they had moments before.

"Oh, please," Mary laughed. "It's a simple choice here, lads. Live as a pirate. Or worry about some Barnet boogeyman and take your chances with very real sharks."

Every single man on the *Chango* chose piracy (spoiler alert: no one ever chose the plank), which meant they formed a new line where they'd march up to Mary and Tobias, who would record their names and jobs, and swear to work hard and serve faithfully on the *Ranger*. There had only been one casualty from her crew (poor Judd was dead). Her ship was largely undamaged, except for a cannonball hole here and there. And they'd gained thirty-six men, among them a new cooper, which was great because they'd really been scraping the bottom of the barrel when they'd hired the old one. In spite of the unfortunate situation with the bananas, Mary felt the day had been a success.

"Stop everything!" Captain Vane's raspy voice came from the rail where he was crossing over onto the *Chango*. "I see a woman! There's a *woman* on my ship!"

Mary's heart jumped into her throat. Tobias took a step toward her, panic written on his face.

She'd known this time would come, hadn't she? Something would give her away, some stray lock of hair, a loose piece of clothing. She had to do something. Now.

Wait, Tobias mouthed. His gaze cut to Captain Vane.

And just like that, Mary became aware that *everyone* was looking at Captain Vane, who was pointing. *Not* at Mary.

Everyone swiveled to look at a young Black sailor from the *Chango,* her hair tightly braided and shoved down the back of her shirt. She was small but strong-looking, with cords of muscles running up her forearms.

"Aye," she admitted. "I am a woman. What's it to you?"

There was a single collective gasp from both crews. Someone dropped a banana.

Mary's panic for herself sank into dread. This was going to get bad. She just knew it.

"A woman," Diesel muttered. "Haven't seen one of those in . . . a while."

"Ye think she knows the rules?" Mr. Swift (the *Ranger*'s musician) asked.

"She must, or she wouldn't have been hiding, you dolt."

"When you say rules," the woman asked almost primly, "are you referring to guidelines?"

"There are rules on my ship." Vane snapped his fingers at Tobias. "Mr. Teach, the rules, if you please."

"Yes, Captain." Tobias drew a small leather book titled *Captain*

Vane's Definitive Guide to Piracy and Mayhem from his inner pocket.

"Read the rule about women," Vane commanded.

"Yes, Captain." Tobias scanned through the book. "Let's see. Every man has a vote, every man gets his fair share of the booty, lights out at eight o'clock, keep your piece, pistols, and cutlass clean and fit for service, ah yes. Here it is: *no woman is to be allowed among us.*"

"That rule makes no sense," said the woman. "I'm as good a sailor as any man here. I dare you to prove otherwise."

It was a sound argument, one that Mary would have made herself if she had ever been found out. She was a good pirate—a great one, even. But she also knew that Vane would not be won over by reason.

He drew his cutlass. "Women at sea are bad luck. Very bad luck, I say! I knew the moment I came aboard that there was something off here." He kicked at the pile of bananas. "No treasure—bah! I want her off this ship immediately."

There was only the rolling blue ocean on every side of them.

"Mr. Read," Vane directed. "Fetch the plank."

"It's already fetched," Mary said hoarsely. She'd had it set up during her "join us or die" speech earlier.

The woman's eyes widened slightly. Then her expression went carefully blank.

"Not so bold now, are you, honey?" Vane sneered. "Go on, then. Walk the plank."

"No," the woman said.

Vane nodded to Nine Toes and Squinty. "Help her, lads."

Each of the pirates took one of the woman's arms and began to drag her toward the plank.

Mary had to do something. She had to stop this.

"Wait!" She stepped forward. "We can't go throwing people off the ship. That's murder. It's immoral."

Vane sighed. "Mr. Read, we've had this discussion before. We're pirates. We have no moral code but the one we make for ourselves. We force people to walk the plank all the time. They need to fear us."

But at the plank, Nine Toes and Squinty had stopped, waiting for their captain and quartermaster to finish arguing.

"Wait," Mary said again. "Doesn't she look familiar to you?"

Tobias shifted his weight. "She looks familiar to me. What's your name, miss?" he asked the woman.

"Effie." She lifted her chin. "Effie Ham."

A groan spread across the deck of the ship and Captain Vane said, "Effie Ham as in *John Ham's* sister?"

"That's right. John's my big brother." She wrested her arms free and crossed them over her chest, staring coldly at Vane. "I was making my way to Nassau to meet him. Won't he be angry when he finds out *you* fed me to the sharks?"

"Captain," Mary said, keeping her voice low. "You can't throw John Ham's sister off the ship. It'd be like a declaration of war."

Vane scoffed. "John Ham doesn't scare me. He has one little ship—a pink, no less."

"But he's a fierce one, Captain. He's been known to take down ships twice his size," said Quint.

"And he's also known to hold a grudge," Effie said.

"I think we can risk the bad luck just this once," Mary said. "We're handling the banana situation just fine."

The captain seemed to be thinking for a few moments as he looked back and forth between Tobias, Mary, and Effie Ham. Then he heaved a sigh. "Fine. This once. But never again." He turned and picked up the bottle of banana rum and marched off the *Chango* and back to the *Ranger* without another word.

Effie strode over to Mary and Tobias. "Thank you," she said. "You stuck your necks out for me. I'll be sure my brother knows who spoke up and who kept silent."

Mary wasn't so sure that sticking up for Effie had been a *good* idea. The look the captain had given her sent shivers down her spine. But keeping Effie out of the drink had been the moral choice—one she wouldn't take back.

"Don't worry about him," Tobias said as they watched Vane disappear into his cabin. "He'll forget all about this by the time we reach Nassau. He might not even remember Effie Ham at all."

Mary wasn't so sure about that.

TWO

Tobias

Reader, Captain Vane definitely remembered Effie Ham. He'd been lying flat on his back in bed for hours, drunkenly ranting about the various deficiencies of women as a whole. "They're the worst!" he was saying now. "And you know who else is the worst?"

"Is it Bess?" Tobias asked glumly.

"She just doesn't understand me," Vane blathered. "I tried to explain that being a pirate is who I am, but she just looked me dead in the face and said, 'You're going to die if you don't retire,' and I honestly couldn't believe how mean that was."

"That's terrible," Tobias said, because it was somehow his job to comfort this man.

Technically, Tobias's job was to be the ship's navigator. He was good at it. His crewmates liked to call him "the Artist," as if his reading maps and understanding ocean currents were a mystical art, rather than a science. Tobias didn't mind the nickname. He liked maps; the way they transformed the chaos of the unknown world into the order of the known. If you could read maps, then you always knew where you were—and where you were going.

But the maps on this ship were kept in the captain's cabin.

Which meant that now Tobias was, unfortunately, playing babysitter/therapist for the mopiest captain to ever sail the seven seas.

"Pirates don't retire," Vane ranted on. "She can't just tell me to choose between her and my ship. I should be able to have it all!"

"Of course you should," Tobias agreed.

"I mean, have I ever asked her to give up being a madam? No!"

"Land ho!" came the call from outside.

"Oh thank God," said Tobias.

"Oh no," Vane rasped. "Are we there already?"

Tobias lurched to his feet. "Perhaps he was mistaken. I'll check." He stepped out onto the main deck and looked to the horizon, where the lookout was pointing from the crow's nest. Sure enough, Tobias saw a dark smudge there, where the sea met the sky, and within a few minutes, that smudge became the familiar shape of the island of New Providence.

He smiled, relieved. Finally, they were coming home.

Tobias returned to the cabin and began rolling up and putting away his maps and charts.

"So we're there?" Vane surmised.

"Aye, Captain."

Vane took a long swig of banana rum and wiped his mouth with his sleeve. He grimaced. "I don't know how I'm going to face her."

"Didn't she say she never wanted to see you again?" Tobias reminded him.

"Yes, but perhaps she'll have seen reason, since I've been at sea risking my life and well-being *for her*, you know? Bringing back this bounty, for her!" Vane went to gesture at all the treasure he'd gathered, but then realized it was (this time, anyway) only a humongous pile of bananas. He shook his head sadly. "I know I'm getting up there in age, but I can't retire, Toby. What would I do without this?"

Tobias fought the urge to say what he really thought. First of all, he knew Bess, and she was a good woman, and she was also a pretty good madam (not that Tobias knew such things firsthand, but that was her general reputation), and she didn't need Vane's stinking bananas. She'd been good for Vane when they were together. She'd tempered him somehow.

Secondly, Vane *was* getting old, about thirty-six now, Tobias reckoned, and he couldn't name a single pirate over the age of forty.

Thirdly, there was plenty a man could do, in Tobias's opinion, if he couldn't be a pirate. Tobias knew what *he* would do. He thought about it all the time. He'd love to retire from piracy, but he was only nineteen, and certain things were expected of him.

"Bring her in easy, DuPaul, and try not to scrape anyone like last time!" came Mary's voice just above them, barking orders from the quarterdeck.

Vane gazed down into his lap, momentarily ashamed that Mary was doing his job. Then he straightened up. "Mr. Read's too soft. He should not have contradicted me on the *Chango*. And over a woman! He made us look weak."

"Oh, I don't think—"

"He doesn't want to keelhaul people. He stands up for women, but you know, I don't think I've ever seen him with a lass. Doesn't he like women?"

"Uh." Tobias thought fast. "Sure, I've seen Mark with women. So many women. He leaves a trail of broken hearts in his wake, one after another. Yep. That man's a serial heartbreaker. Nassau is just full of women he's courted and cut ties with. If they don't speak of it, it's because they can't bear to."

Vane narrowed his eyes. "Is that so?"

"Yes," Tobias said urgently. "It *is* so. But Mark doesn't kiss and tell. He's very private."

"If you say so." Vane took another swig of rum.

Whew. That had been awfully close.

"I'll be staying on the ship," Vane announced. He took another drink. "I can't risk seeing Bess."

"Yes, Captain." Tobias thought this was probably wise.

"Oh, and see to the blasted meeting," Vane mumbled just as Tobias was about to flee the room.

Tobias paused. "Meeting, sir?"

Vane gestured to the bedside table, upon which was a rolled-up piece of parchment. Tobias unrolled it and read the fancy pirate script. (Reader, it was cursive.)

Calling all ye Prestigious Pirate Captains, it read. *A meeting of the most Serious Nature, to discuss the Future of Piracy. The Scurvy Dog, on the seventeenth of the Month, seven o'clock. Be there or be Keelhauled. Warmest regards, The Pirate King.*

Tobias glanced up. "The future of piracy?"

"Back in the day, being a pirate meant something," Vane said mournfully. "Gold ran like water. Rum flowed like, um, water. People respected us. Feared us. And now they see us as a nuisance or a joke. Indeed, it wouldn't surprise me, lad, if someday soon there are no true pirates in the world, just pretenders who like to dress up in 'comely pirate costumes' once a year and prance about seeking booty." He sighed. "Maybe I *should* retire."

Tobias nodded. "But you won't be attending this meeting?"

"Get Mr. Read to do it. And you'll be going, too, so I'll be well represented."

"I'll be going?" Tobias asked, alarmed. "Why would I be going?"

"Read the postscript."

Tobias glanced at the parchment. Sure enough, at the bottom was scrawled an extra message: *Toby, ye come, too.*

Of course. Tobias sighed. "Yes, I'll go, then. To see what he wants."

When he came out onto the deck again, the ship was already docked in its usual place in the harbor. The old fort on the hill loomed over the jumble of ramshackle buildings and palm trees that made up the town. Tobias could already hear the rowdy noise of it—raucous singing, dogs barking, and the occasional sound of a woman laughing. The air had a distinct fishy, rummy, man-sweaty smell. Tobias breathed it in deep, simultaneously repulsed and comforted by the stink. It wasn't a grand place, to be sure, but it was Nassau—aka Pirate Paradise, aka the Swashbuckling Capital of the World. Aka the only real home Tobias had ever known.

He hurried to the officers' quarters. Mary was already there, digging through a trunk. Tobias's heart gave a lurch at the sight of her. Unfortunately, at the same time, the ship also gave a lurch, and Tobias tripped and fell—as though he hadn't spent practically his whole life aboard one ship or another.

"Toby!" Mary hurried over, having no problems whatsoever with the motion of the *Ranger*. "You hurt?"

"Only my pride," Tobias admitted. "Hopefully no one else saw that."

Mary reached a hand down and—when Tobias took it—helped him to his feet. In those few seconds of contact between them, Tobias felt the familiar spark flare inside him. He liked Mary. *Liked* liked, if you know what we mean. And how could he not? Mary was amazing: strong and fast, clever and loyal.

But *liking* her was as far as anything could go. The risk of her being found out was too great.

"Gah." Mary snatched her hand back and wiped her palm on her trousers. "You're all sweaty."

And then there was that. She didn't *like* him the same way he liked her. Every time he thought he felt a connection, every time he found himself gazing into those sea-blue eyes a little too long, she pulled back, pulled away, and he remembered where he was.

If their relationship were a map, the little Tobias figure on the page would be squarely in the place Mary kept her friends.

Which was fine, he told himself. Totally fine.

"Ready to go?" Mary asked as Tobias threw his belongings into his bag.

"Aye." Tobias slung his bag over his shoulder, and within minutes, they were down the gangplank and heading into Nassau.

The town wasn't much to look at, just the several simple shacks and salt-sprayed storefronts where charlatans sold seashells by the seashore. (Your narrators offer our sincerest apologies to our audiobook narrator.) They were in one of the dodgier parts of a town that was entirely dodgy. It was actually pretty dangerous to walk the streets here. But this was one area where Tobias wasn't afraid. Pirates generally didn't mess with him, given that his father was the most infamous pirate in history.

Which reminded him— "There's a meeting tonight," he said to Mary as they began their long stroll toward home, handing her the roll of parchment he'd taken from the captain. "Vane says you're to go in his stead."

"No," Mary groaned. She read the paper. Scoffed. "The future of piracy?"

"I know," he said.

"And he wants to see you," she added, pointing to the post-script.

"Apparently." Tobias sighed.

"He probably just wishes to know if you're well." She gave him a sympathetic smile as they turned a corner. "You're his son, after all."

"Yes, it's not like he doesn't have scores more of us," Tobias replied dryly. It was true, his father had many sons—something like fifty-two, that Tobias knew of, and yet Tobias managed to be both the most disappointing and the most trusted of his pa's spawn.

"You're coming back aboard the *Revenge!*" the old man had declared the last time they'd spoken. "You've had your adventures on your own, but enough is enough. You belong at my side, not hunched over a bunch of maps taking orders from a lesser captain. Come with me, and we can rule this ocean as father and son! And when I'm gone from this world, you'll be the Pirate King, and your name—my name—will inspire terror!"

Tobias wasn't especially interested in inspiring terror. He *really* wasn't interested in being the Pirate King. He'd said so, and then his father had boxed his ears like he was still a lad.

"You're mad!" Tobias had yelled then, pushing him away. "Leave me alone! I like being on the *Ranger*. IT'S MY LIFE, blast it all! Not yours!"

It was so cringeworthy, when he thought back on it. Not that it wasn't true. He'd spent years on the *Revenge* in his father's shadow, and he'd never truly felt at home there. The *Ranger*, in spite of Vane's flaws, was better. Because there Tobias could be his own man. And because of Mary. But what he'd said about his father being mad (aka crazy)—well, that had been cruel. Everyone knew that the infamous captain had been slowly losing his mind for years, a side effect of the "French disease" (or what the French liked to call the "English disease"), aka syphilis. But Tobias should never have said it. He'd been feeling bad about it ever since. Perhaps, at this meeting he was going to, he'd be able to apologize.

He just had to figure out a way to do it that didn't make him look weak.

"All will be well," said Mary, although how could she possibly know that?

He tried to laugh off his own anxiety. "I might duck out along with everyone else at the end of the meeting and avoid the whole postscript part of the note. He can't get angry at that. I'll show up. That is all he required."

Her lips pursed; she disapproved of this plan. "You should talk to him, Toby. Clear the air. Trust me, I know what it's like to deal with a father who can't hope to understand you."

This was the first time she'd ever spoken of her family to him. "Oh?" he said, struggling to keep his tone casual. "Was your father also a terrifying, powerful, and overbearing narcissist?"

"Something like that," she said mysteriously.

He wanted to ask more questions, but more than that, he wanted her to tell him on her own. She could trust him with her secrets. He'd keep her heart safe. She needed to see that for herself, though, so he wouldn't push.

Mary jogged ahead to the small shack where they lived when they were ashore. "We're here!" She unlocked the door and stepped inside, then crossed to the window and drew back the curtains. A beam of light shot through, hit their rickety old table, and the table fell over. "Home sweet home," she said.

Tobias glanced at Mary.

She sighed and nodded. *Yes*, her look said, *a new table. Soon.*

For now, Tobias jammed a peg leg back on the table and coughed at the dust floating in the air. It'd been weeks since they'd been here. But as shacks in Nassau went, this one was tidier than most. Two small cots were set along opposite walls at the far end of the room, each neatly made up with a woolen blanket and a single feather pillow. A trunk lay at the foot of each bed.

"I want to change clothes before the meeting," Mary said. She gave her armpits a sniff. "And get a quick wash. I smell like a bilge rat."

Tobias snorted. "It's not that bad. But I agree. Fresh clothes wouldn't hurt either of us."

He set about drawing the curtain around the small wash area—which held a tub, basin, and chamber pot—while Mary grabbed their bucket and went to get some water.

Initially, Tobias had been worried about living with a girl, but that was mostly because he hadn't known many before. It turned out that Mary was content to live just like he did, needing only four walls, a roof, and a private space to do her private business.

So he'd hung a curtain on rollers, allowing them to section off a space for general hygiene. And when she'd explained that she needed certain . . . accommodations once a month, he'd been able to procure rags that could be boiled clean after use. Finally, he'd taken charge of cutting her hair when they were home, because hers was unusually shiny, and it grew so fast it was sure to give her away if they didn't manage it.

It was easy here, at home where it was just the two of them. On the ship, Tobias had to make sure the head was empty before Mary went in, stall anyone who wanted to relieve themselves until Mary was finished, and run other kinds of interference—especially when the need for clean rags came up while they were out at sea. And if Mary was any crankier those weeks, no one on the *Ranger* noticed. As far as Tobias could tell, it just made Mary even more of a pirate.

The door opened and closed as Mary returned with a bucket of water. "I'll only be a moment," she said. "Then you can have a turn."

"Take your time." While Mary disappeared behind the curtain, Tobias slung his bag onto his bed and unpacked his clothes, his journal, and a modest roll of maps he'd been working on. The clothes went into the trunk, the maps were tacked onto the wall over his head, and the journal went under his pillow.

Then he turned his attention to the small bookcase in the corner, crammed from top to bottom with books. He had a new book they'd taken off a ship a while back, by a fellow named Daniel

Defoe. *Robinson Crusoe*, it was called, about a man trapped on a deserted island. Tobias couldn't wait to dig into it.

That had been one of the first things that he and Mary had found in common. They loved books. They'd spent many a night in this shack (or on the ship) curled up in their separate corners, reading. Sometimes they even read a book out loud, together, passing it back and forth between them.

"It's all yours," Mary said, appearing from behind the curtain. Her face and hands were freshly scrubbed, her clothes clean, and her hair combed and tied back.

Before he crossed the line from looking to staring, Tobias grabbed his change of clothes and went to take care of his business.

"We should get going," Mary said when he emerged. "The day is fading fast, and the Scurvy Dog will be crowded later. I want to get a good seat."

For what was sure to be the circus, she meant, of his father's meeting.

"If we must." Tobias would like nothing better than to stay here in the shack tonight, cook a little dinner, and, yes, read his new book.

"I think we must," Mary said.

"Fine. But I can't promise to enjoy it," he acquiesced, and was rewarded with the faintest of her smiles.

THREE

Jack⁵

We'd now like to turn your attention, dear reader, to the other side of Nassau, where a man by the name of Jack was strolling down the street, talking to himself.

"I'm getting married," he said. He tried to picture it: standing up before his friends and family, saying the sacred vows of matrimony to his beloved. But Jack didn't have much in the way of friends yet, and his family situation was . . . complicated, and he had never actually been to a wedding before, so he was fuzzy on what the vows would be. So the best he could do was imagine himself all dressed up and looking handsome, standing in front of a crowd. That much, at least, was easy to picture.

Bonn would be there too, of course, standing with him, holding his hand. He was having trouble picturing her in a wedding dress, but he could imagine her staring up rapturously into his eyes, smiling that wicked smile of hers.

"I do," she would say in her husky Irish brogue.

He'd say it, too, softly, meaningfully, from the depths of his very soul. "I do."

Then he was pretty sure they would kiss, a special, magic type of kiss that would seal the deal.

And then they'd be married.

Just like Romeo and Juliet in Jack's favorite story, theirs would be a love for the ages.

Now all he had to do was to get her to say yes when he asked her tonight.

Which he was fairly certain she would.

She obviously loved him. She hadn't said as much, not in so many words, but he could tell. And he loved her. That was all that was required.

"Darling," he said now as a way of last-minute practicing. "I know we haven't been together for very long, but I adore everything about you. Please consent to becoming my wife."

"ARRR!" An old peg-legged pirate passed Jack in the street and bellowed out the greeting.

"ARRR YERSELF!" Jack hollered back, the proper response. He put a hand on the dagger he kept in his belt, just in case violence was going to be required, but the grizzled old fellow just step-clonked along his merry way.

Now, where was he? Oh yes. The "consent to become my

wife" bit. Perhaps there was a better way to say it. "Please do me the great honor of joining me in official matrimony," he tried out.

Hmm. Not quite. Maybe his entire approach was too formal. Bonn was not the most formal of persons, even though she'd been educated well enough, back in Ireland. She was the child of a well-to-do lawyer and the family maid, a scandal from the moment she emerged into the world. Her father had eventually brought her over to America, where he had attempted to set her up as a fine lady and parade her around in high society. But it was not to be, obviously. Bonn liked to tell the tale of one fateful day, when she'd been stuck reading some tedious book of etiquette, near bored to tears, and finally could bear it no more. She'd flung the book into the bushes and run away—stowed away, actually—on the next ship headed out of port, which happened to be going to Nassau. And that's where Jack had first come across her, a happy three and a half months ago.

She was exciting.

She was everything.

"Marry me, Bonn," he said then.

But it shouldn't be *that* simple, should it? This was going to be classified as one of the most important moments of their lives. It should be memorable. It should be great. It should be EPIC.

This was turning out to be a lot of pressure.

He took a deep breath and tried again. "Say you'll marry me, Bonn, my darling, my only, my one. You are my sun, my moon, my starlit sky. Without you, I dwell in darkness."

That was pretty good. But how did Bonn feel about romantic

metaphors? He didn't want her to laugh at him.

"AHOY THERE, MATEY!" Another pirate approached, swerving in a way that suggested he'd had too much rum. (Reader, let's assume that everyone in Nassau had had too much rum.)

Jack, his hand once again moving to his dagger, stuck out his chin in acknowledgment. "AHOY!"

The man belched deeply.

"ARRR!" replied Jack.

The man, satisfied by their interaction, stumbled on down the street.

Jack relaxed. But then he tensed up again, because he realized he'd arrived at his destination.

Now, there was some debate on the island of New Providence about what was the best restaurant in Nassau. (Yelp hadn't been invented yet, nor had the concept of starred reviews.) The problem with classifying such a place was that there were, technically, *no* restaurants in Nassau, only pubs, dance halls, and brothels that occasionally served food. It was confusing when you were hungry and just wanted something good to eat, and even more confusing was the fact that every establishment in town basically sounded the same: a pirate adjective followed by a pirate noun. Pirate adjectives, Jack had noticed, could be separated into four basic categories: health related (like *lousy*, *festering*, *mangy*, or *rotten*), manners related (such as *churlish*, *artless*, or *lumpish*), adjectives impugning a person's moral character (*low-down*, *spineless*, *lily-livered*, *dastardly*), and arbitrary undignified things (think *quivering*, *slithering*, or *squelching*). Pirate nouns were a bit simpler, as these were always animals: cur, dog, jellyfish, bilge rat, snake, pelican, and so forth. Jack had recently seen an advertisement for a new place called the Shrieking Sea Cucumber, and while that was an alarming thought (sea cucumbers, in Jack's experience, were typically the silent type), it totally tracked with Nassau's general vibe.

The nicest building in Nassau (i.e., the one that was the most structurally sound and well furnished) was a place called GIRLS GIRLS GIRLS. (We know, that doesn't have a pirate adjective or noun, but just go with it—it's the exception that proves the rule.) This had been at the top of the list Jack had considered for Romantic Locations to Propose to the Love of Your Life, because it was one of the only places in town with good lighting and relatively clean floors. But it was also a dance hall (*cough* brothel *cough*) and Jack had wanted somewhere more, er, private.

Next he'd deliberated on the place with the best rum in Nassau—because Bonn loved a good rum—but that had already been booked for some big pirate event.

So he'd picked the Poxy Parrot, a small pub in an out-of-the-way corner of town that reportedly made a damned good corned beef on Thursdays. He'd talked to the owner yesterday about reserving a table in a quiet corner, maybe lighting a few candles, you know? Then he'd asked Bonn to meet him there tonight with no other explanation, because a little bit of mystery is a good thing in any relationship. And now he was there, standing outside the door, trying to work up the nerve to go inside.

Jack was normally an optimistic person. A glass half-full, float where the tide takes you kind of guy. So while he was nervous now, feeling that this was about to be one of the Most Significant Moments in his life, after a moment he shrugged, thought to himself, *Well, here I go; I'm sure it will all turn out well*, and walked into the Poxy Parrot.

Bonn was already there. She liked to be early to appointments, which seemed to Jack a bit out of character for someone with such an obvious disregard for the rules of polite society, but she always said something about birds and worms that he'd never understood. It was easy to spot her, given that she was currently standing on top of the bar, a tankard of rum already in hand, belting out a rousing rendition of "YO, HO, HO (AND A BOTTLE OF RUM)" (one of the two pirate-themed songs that were on a constant loop pretty much everywhere in Nassau) at the top of her lungs.

Jack took a moment to admire her.

His true love.

Even in the overall dimness of the pub, Bonn was so beautiful it took his breath away. She wore a plain white linen shirt with a jaunty green vest over it that matched the spring-leaf color of her eyes, and an unremarkable brown skirt that she'd hitched up in the front, revealing tall leather boots to her knee. It was quite warm there in the Poxy Parrot, and she'd rolled her shirt to the elbows and unbuttoned the collar. A comelier figure he'd never beheld. But it was Bonn's hair that most caught his eye. He'd never encountered a person with such red hair before he'd met her. It was like a living flame, her hair, a mass of copper curls that tumbled all about her freckled heart-shaped face. He loved to tangle his fingers in that hair, to pull a curl and watch it spring back into form.

So here they were. He loved Bonn and her wild red hair. She loved him and his undeniable good looks and easy charm. They made a good match. He would ask her to marry him.

And she would say yes.

It really was that simple.

He located the table he'd reserved. (There was a piece of parchment set up in the middle of a table in the corner that read, Don't Ye Sit Here Unless Yer Jack Rackham, accompanied by a big red X over the figure of a person sitting, for those who couldn't read.) A single stubbed candle on the table cast just the right romantic glow. The owner had even put a bedraggled yellow flower in a mug in the center.

Excellent. Jack cleared his throat.

This was it.

"Marry me, darling?" he said quickly—one final bit of rehearsal.

"Well, maybe I'd consider it, if you asked me real nice," said the barmaid, who'd been scrubbing down the next table over. As he turned to her, surprised, she looked him slowly up and down, then gave him a crooked-but-sultry smile. "I definitely would."

Yes, yes. He was considered attractive by most everybody. Jack knew this.

"Alas, I wasn't speaking to you, although I'm sure you're delightful," he clarified. Then he stepped away from the table, cupped his hands around his mouth, and yelled, "Bonn! Hey, Bonn! Darling, over here!"

Bonn didn't pay him any heed, partly because Jack couldn't be heard over the singing, and partly because by this time Bonn had leapt from the bar and was now enthusiastically punching some unsuspecting pirate in the face.

Jack beamed. So gloriously scrappy, his Bonn.

"BONN!" Jack bellowed, and then he pushed his way through the raucous fray until he reached his love, who he managed to wrest off the back of the bewildered pirate. This almost earned Jack a punch to the face himself, as she took a defensive swing at him. He stepped back just in time. "BONN, IT'S ME!" he cried.

Her bright green eyes lit up. "JACK! GAWL, AND I ALMOST CLOCKED YOU THERE, RIGHT IN THE KISSER."

Or at least that's what he thought she said. It was hard to know for sure, what with the general din of the place and Bonn's accent. He loved the way she talked, an intriguing mix of highborn lady and gutter rat.

He took her by the elbow and steered her to their table, pulling out a chair for her to sit.

But she didn't sit. Instead, she read the sign on the table, and then cocked her head at him quizzically. "What are ye doing? And why, for that matter, did you wish to meet me here? It's a wee bit out of the way, isn't it?"

He cleared his throat for dramatic effect. "It's a special place for a special night."

She raised an eyebrow at him. "Special? How so?"

"Because . . ." He swallowed, his heart banging hard against his ribs. "Because I had something special I wanted to ask you."

He'd been planning to wait until after dinner to pop the question. But everything was feeling vastly more imperative now, with the barmaid still leering at them, and his heart beating fast, and his nerves jangling so that his hands were trembling. Best to get it over with as soon as possible.

He dropped to one knee.

"Oh dear God," Bonn breathed. "What are you up to, Jack?"

"You'll see in a minute," he said. "Just stand still and let me do this."

A hush fell over the pub as people noticed him kneeling there. So now it was more than simply the barmaid gawking at them. Now there were about forty pirates in various stages of drunkenness gazing in their direction, all beginning to point and stare.

"Woo-hoo!" one of them whooped. "Go get her, lad!"

"Good luck!" said another. "Yer going to need it with that one!"

"ARGH!" said a third, which Jack understood, in this instance, to be a form of encouragement.

Jack took Bonn's small rough hand in his suddenly-very-clammy one. "I haven't had time to woo you in the way you deserve," he said softly, "with fine food and flowers and starlit walks along the sand, but I've known you were the one for me, Anne Bonny, from that first night when I came upon you beating the tar out of those two rogues who'd tried to rob that old blind woman. You're the person I want to be with, always. Will you . . . will you have me?"

"Of course I'll have you," she laughed, but her voice was a bit strained, like she was nervous, too. "Now get up."

"Wait, I need to give you this." He reached into his pants pocket, drew his fist out, and held it up, uncurling his fingers so she could see what he offered.

A ring. A beautiful golden ring with a large dark emerald in the center, framed by a group of small diamonds. He didn't know her ring size (because ring sizes hadn't been invented yet) but he hoped it would fit her.

"Gawl," she breathed. "Oh, Jack. Where did you get this?"

"I, uh . . . found it." He thought it best not to tell Bonn where he acquired things. It would naturally lead to questions he didn't know how to answer.

"Right," she said with a little smirk. "You *found* it."

She thought he was a thief. He had never tried to correct that assumption, and he wasn't about to start now.

"Do you like it?" he asked.

"I . . ." She seemed uncharacteristically at a loss for words. "I love it. It's beautiful."

"So you'll marry me?" he said.

Her mouth opened and then closed again.

"I swear I'll make you happy, Bonn. You're my sun, my moon, my starlit sky—"

"I know, I know," she murmured. "But, you see . . ."

Oh bollocks. There was something wrong. Some minor impediment to their bliss.

"I haven't told you everything," she said.

"Oh, that's all right," he said with a nervous laugh. "I haven't told you everything, either." In fact, he'd told Bonn nothing of his past outside of the barest of details. He'd considered telling her loads of times, but at first he didn't know how to do it in such a way that she could ever believe him, and then, after they'd been together for a while, it felt weird to bring it up. He'd never even told her how old he was—she thought he was older, twenty at least. But none of that mattered to Jack. "Nothing you could tell me would change how I feel," he insisted.

"I feel the same," she said. "I . . ."

"See? I'm sure it's fine," he said.

She shook her head. "I'm sorry. But I cannot marry you, Jack."

The men around them made an audible AWWWW sound, not like *AW, that's adorable*, but *AW, how very disappointing we find this*.

"But . . . why?" Jack asked hoarsely.

"I am already married," she blurted out.

The crowd of pirates made an *OOF* sound.

"I did not see that coming," said one.

"Nor I," said another. "I thought she'd just say no because she's the kind of lass who don't want to be tied down."

"I really thought she'd say yes," another said. "Because he's so pretty."

Jack said nothing. He was frozen in place on the floor in front of her. Very slowly, he closed his fingers around the emerald ring.

Bonn caught his aghast expression, and it was like something broke loose inside her and all the words just started to pour out. "Gawl, I wish I weren't—I kind of married this fellow by accident. I didn't know the rules, you see. When I first arrived here, in Nassau, I mean, I didn't know anything about anything. I didn't have a place to stay. I hadn't any money besides some jewelry I'd been wearing when I ran off. I was so hungry and tired and lost, and there was this man who took me in. He let me stay in his room, called me his roommate and everything. He even found me a job, he did, as a dishwasher at this little pub he went to, and . . . he was kind to me. Some days kinder than others. But I was grateful for the place to stay, and a job that wasn't wenching. But then one day he told me that I was his wife."

"He told you?" This was like a bad dream.

She nodded, tucking a fiery curl behind her ear as she gazed down guiltily into her lap. "He said that I was his common law wife. Because we'd lived together a certain length of time. Of course I told him off, told him I was nobody's wife, but he took me to the law house and showed me the record where it'd been recorded. I was his wife. There was nothing to be done for it."

"He tricked you," Jack said.

"He did. I tried to murder him in his sleep for weeks after. If he could make me a wife, I could make myself a widow, I figured. But he was too wily."

"So you unmarry him." Jack's knee was starting to hurt, so

he staggered up from the floor.

"Tried that," she said. "A divorce can only be granted with the husband's permission."

Jack started for the door. "Be right back, my love," he said.

"Where are you going?"

"To get his permission," he said.

It was not difficult to track down James Bonny—that is, after Jack had the presence of mind to double back and ask Bonn to tell him her husband's name.

James Bonny. It baffled Jack that she would have taken the last name of this man who'd hoodwinked her so badly.

"I liked the name Bonny," she'd admitted. "My name was Anne Brennan before. But Anne Brennan was a bastard, a girl of no importance in this world. And when my father brought me to Charles Town, he introduced me as his daughter, Anne Cormac, but I never fit into that name, either. But Anne Bonny—now that had a ring. And if I went by that, my father wouldn't be able to find me."

"It is a good name," Jack had agreed, and then gone to hunt down the scoundrel James Bonny who'd given it to her. Who some other pirates told him could be reliably found in a brothel called the Dastardly Cur. Which felt like a fitting name.

James Bonny, for his part, did not seem surprised to encounter Jack.

"She's a terror, ain't she?" James said conspiratorially when Jack approached him. He took a huge swig of rum, grimaced, burped. "Like a beautiful storm. But she's also like ringworm—she gets under your skin and you can't ever be free of her."

"You're going to be free of her," Jack said. "Tonight. Now, if possible."

Bonny laughed. "Am I? Says who?"

"She does not wish to be married to you," Jack pointed out.

"She's a girl," James slurred. "So it's not exactly her choice, is it?"

"You're going to grant her a divorce," Jack said steadily, working himself up for violence. Jack abhorred violence. He preferred conversation if at all possible, so he was preparing to use every advantage and connection he had to talk the increasingly loathsome Mr. Bonny into capitulating to his request. If that didn't work: intimidation. And if that didn't work, well, he did happen to know a lot of pirates, and pirates generally didn't have a problem with murder.

"I might consider it," Bonny said.

"You might?"

"For the right bride price."

Jack blinked at him. "I'm afraid I'm not familiar with that term."

"Listen here," Bonny said with a smirk. "Anne is my property, seeing as she's my wife. I can do what I want with her. But I might be willing to sell. If the price was right. And sure, you and Anne could try to murder me to get your way—Lord knows she did try often enough, but I'm a tough bugger to kill, and besides, all these people here have been listening to this here conversation, so it'd be suspicious if I was to show up dead now. And it would be a shame to see a pretty, long neck like Annie's stretched out by a hangman's noose."

Jack felt his stomach drop most unpleasantly. He didn't have much in the way of currency. At most, he had about a hundred and fifty pieces of eight saved up. That and an emerald ring. He swallowed hard. "How much?"

"She's a fine woman, my wife," said Bonny, then looked him right in the eye as he said this next bit. "A thousand would do. One thousand pieces of eight."

"So what happened?" Bonn demanded to know the moment Jack stepped through the door of the room they shared in the Jumping Jellyfish, aka Nassau's best boardinghouse.

"Uh . . ." He scratched the back of his neck. "We had a conversation."

Her green eyes narrowed to slits. "And?"

"I think I made it worse," he mumbled.

"Didn't I tell you that's what would happen?"

Yes. She'd said it a few times as he'd marched determinedly out to find James Bonny. She'd said, "Don't go, Jack. You're only going to make it worse."

"You did tell me," he mumbled.

"How much worse are we talking?" she asked.

He told her.

"A thousand pieces of eight! Gawl! He told me a hundred, and I thought *that* was going to be impossible."

"He told you a hundred?" Jack sighed and scrubbed his hand down the front of his face. "Darling, that might have been good information for me to have *before* I entered into negotiations, don't you think?"

(A note, dear reader, on "pieces of eight." In the time our story takes place, the most common coin used was the Spanish silver dollar. The value of a coin was decided by its actual weight in gold or silver, and it didn't really matter what the coin looked like. Merchants preferred Spanish coins because they had a distinct pattern on the edge, which kept cheaters from shaving bits of the coins off. And, to make change, it was just fine to cut the coin into pieces. So a piece of eight was one of eight pieces that had been cut out of the Spanish silver dollar, a tiny silver sliver of pie. A single piece of eight was worth about the equivalent of $12.50 in US dollars today. In other words, James Bonny had just raised Anne's bride price from the equivalent of $1,250 to $12,500. So yeah, Jack had made things a lot worse.)

She crossed her arms over her chest. "You didn't ask me. You just rushed off half-cocked before I could tell you any more."

He nodded. "That's true, my love. I behaved rashly. I apologize. But not to worry about the money. I'll get that thousand pieces of eight for you, no problem."

"You'll get it," she said doubtfully. "How?"

"The way I come up with all our money." He'd never managed

to get his hands on anything worth much more than a hundred pieces of eight, but he was sure he'd figure something out.

But Bonn had now apparently decided not to accept that answer. "And *how do you* come up with our money, exactly?" she asked.

"It's better if you don't know," he said.

And that was true. It was better.

For him.

She scowled. "Well. I have a different plan."

"Does that plan involve murder?"

She grinned for a moment, as if the idea was tempting, but then shook her head. "It involves us becoming pirates."

Oh. That again.

"Forgive me, darling," Jack said tentatively. "But haven't we tried that and failed numerous times?"

Her lips pursed. "I said I'll be a pirate someday, and I will. Give me piracy or give me death!"

He was always a bit alarmed when she talked this way. Death was bad, of course, but being a pirate wasn't that much better, as he understood it. It was hard and cold and sometimes hungry work, and it was also dangerous, in that it often ended in being run through by a cutlass, or being hanged by the various pirate-hating authorities, or, if you were really lucky, drowning in a shipwreck. So really one was likely to have both piracy and death.

But Anne—his little fiery Bonn—scoffed at such dangers. "I've tried the life of frills and frocks already," she'd told him the first time he'd expressed his various concerns. "Gawl, I was my father's porcelain doll for years. I'm ill-suited for such things. I'd rather die on the water, cutlass in my hand, stained with the blood of my enemies!"

She was passionate. She had goals. Jack admired that about her.

"Here's my plan," Bonn said. "Everybody in town's talking about how there's this big meeting of all the pirate captains, tonight, at this place called the Scurvy Dog. So we go there. We wait until the captains are assembled. Then I—dressed as a saucy lad—will pretend some slight and challenge Captain Blackbeard's quartermaster—a big, hulking fellow by the name of Caesar who Blackbeard trusts more than any other—to a duel, right then and there. And then I shall best Caesar, but not maim or kill him, of course, as that would truly offend the captain, and I'll demand that, in exchange for Caesar's life, I be given a spot aboard the *Queen Anne's Revenge*, a proper part of Blackbeard's crew."

"And me," Jack added. "I'll come on the crew as well."

"Right. You. Yes," Bonn said quickly. "Anyway, how could Blackbeard refuse if he sees my quality as a fighter?"

"Indeed," Jack said supportively. "You're a marvelous fighter. Best I've seen."

"And I'm a smart sailor. I could prove it to him if he liked."

"You do tie a mean knot," Jack said.

"And then, once he's said he'll have me—er, us—I will reveal myself to be a woman," she added. "I'll tell him that it's women who are the future of piracy! And because he's the Pirate King—if he allows women to become pirates, then all the captains might."

Jack nodded nervously. "That sounds reasonable. Where he leads, the others will follow."

"And if there's any argument," Bonn pressed on, "you'll stand by me and fight by my side."

"If you think that's best." Even though Jack was not the greatest fighter. He was absolute garbage with a sword, he'd discovered early on. Although he supposed he did all right with blunter objects. Like a frying pan. Still, he could not really picture himself prevailing over a pub full of angry pirates brandishing a frying pan. "But darling," he said delicately. "While I do love your plan, and I will happily go along with it—whatever you need—do you think the violence bit is absolutely necessary?"

She stared up at him blankly.

"Can't we just ask Captain Blackbeard if we can become pirates on his crew? Surely he's a reasonable fellow, a smart man, to have risen so high on the pirate career ladder. Can't we make him come around to our way of thinking with persuasive words instead of cutlasses?"

Bonn laughed. "Ah, my dear lamb," she said, patting Jack's cheek affectionately if not a bit too hard. "Violence is the language of piracy. We've got to speak their language, see? But don't worry, love. All will go according to plan. By this time tomorrow we'll be part of Blackbeard's crew. A true pirate, that's what I'll be, and I mean to chase every adventure on the seas. I'll plunder a hundred ships—nay, a thousand—steal my weight in gold, lounge naked in a bathtub filled with shining pieces of eight. Pay James back with interest and a kick in the ass. Yo ho, yo ho, a pirate's life for me!"

"Yo ho," Jack agreed, and she kissed him, and it was the good kind of kiss, the kind that always made him feel like he was floating, and after that he would have agreed to anything she asked of him.

And so it was that about thirty minutes later, Jack Rackham and a saucy freckled lad sauntered into the Scurvy Dog.

"Blast," Bonn muttered under her breath as they took in the crowded pub, which was near bursting with various pirate captains. "We're too late to get a good table. Do you see Captain Blackbeard?"

"What does he look like?"

Bonn gave him a look.

"Right," he said. "Black beard. Got it." He glanced around. "A good many of these blokes have a black beard."

"His is huge and bushy, and he sometimes puts fireworks into it, to terrify his prey before he boards a ship," Bonn said.

Jack wasn't sure how that would work without burning one's face off in the process, but he didn't raise the question. "No one with fireworks in their beards, no."

"He's not here," Bonn said grumpily.

"At least we haven't missed him."

"That's true," she conceded. "Let's find a place to sit. Ooh, there's a little table in the back corner! You go claim our spot, and I'll get us some rum. I hear this place has the best rum in all of Nassau."

She started in the direction of the bar, where there was a huge line of thirsty pirates already waiting.

Jack moved toward the table in the corner. He was feeling a bit jumpy. Bonn's plan, he thought, had some flaws. Like, how was she going to fight a man she'd described as "big and hulking" and win without injuring him? And would this Blackbeard fellow really accept the fact that she was a woman and still allow her on his ship? And how exactly did Jack fit into all of this? And he didn't have a frying pan or a sword, just this puny dagger that wasn't even sharp.

"I'm sure it will all be fine," he told himself reassuringly.

"YOU!" Right then, at a nearby table, a man jumped to his feet so quickly that his chair clattered to the floor.

Jack looked around. "Me? Excuse me? Have I offended you, good sir?"

The man stared at Jack with wide blue eyes, and then began to stomp toward him. "SON OF A WITCH!" he yelled.

Mary →
FOUR

Jack.

It was Jack.

He was taller than she remembered, slender of build, his face smooth shaven. His eyes were the color of the deep ocean, the exact same shade as Mary's, and his dark hair, which had always floated about his face, was long and loose but for a few small braids here and there. He'd tied an orange sash about the top of his head and lightly lined his eyes with kohl. And—for some odd reason—he'd decided to wear three belts at once, even though he only needed to hold up one pair of trousers.

But otherwise he was completely unchanged.

Except for the fact that he had *legs.* That was pretty different.

His mouth dropped open as she strode up to him.

"Littlest?" he breathed.

"Son of a Witch," she said again.

Because that was his Mer name. Jack's mother was literally the Sea Witch, aka the villain in every little mermaid story ever told. (Up to now, that is.) Aunt Witch did have a wicked sense of humor and her magic was quite powerful, but she'd never, to Mary's knowledge anyway, done anything verifiably evil. In fact, when Mary had been so desperate to be with Charles (bleh, Charles!) that she would have done anything, sacrificed everything, only Aunt Witch and Jack had truly been willing to help her.

The last time Mary and Jack had been together was when she'd chugged down his mother's potion to make her human, and then realized too late that humans couldn't breathe under the water and that she was far, far below the surface. (Oops.) Jack had been the one to get her Above in time. He'd gotten her safely to land. And then she'd never seen him again.

"What are you doing here?" she asked hoarsely.

He shook his head incredulously. "I could ask you the same question!"

They stood in silence for a long moment, their mouths opening and closing like two addled codfish, and then all at once, they threw their arms around each other and held tight.

"I can't believe it," Jack gasped against Mary's shoulder. "All this time, you were here, right above everyone's noses. Hey, you got an earring! Your father would be so mad!"

Mary pulled back abruptly. "Did my father send you?" The

thought unsettled her. Even though her father been right about everything. About Charles, anyway. (She hadn't thought about Charles in a long time. She *had* to stop thinking about him. And she was going to do it starting . . . now.)

"No, no, your father thinks you're foam," Jack said. "There was a funeral and everything," he added pointedly. "We *all* mourned for you."

Mary bit her lip. "Oh. I'm— I'm sorry. I should have . . . I just couldn't . . ."

Jack drew back from her. "You couldn't face your family and the way everyone would look at you like you were just a silly little minnow who'd only been saved from a broken heart because you were a princess. I understand," he said. Because of course he did. They'd been the best of friends back in Underwhere, which meant he knew all about her complicated feelings about their family. Not to mention, he'd been the only Mer who was as fascinated by humans as she was. They'd entertained themselves for hours talking about what it must be like to live in the world Above. To walk on legs. To run. To feel air and sun on your face and not just murky water. To use your mouth to talk and sing and laugh and burp and kiss. It had all sounded so wonderful, even if it had just been pretend.

But then it had been real. For Mary, anyway.

She'd left Jack behind.

"I'm sorry," she said again. She couldn't imagine how she'd have felt if their positions had been reversed. "It's so good to see you, Jack, truly," she said. "I forgot how much I—"

Missed you, she'd been about to say. But that sounded like she hadn't missed him. She *had*. She'd simply . . . put it aside so she didn't have to feel it. Just like she'd put the rest of her old life aside.

Jack shrugged. "I won't say I forgive you for swimming off and forgetting all about me the moment you spotted a pretty human. But I am glad to find you all in one piece."

"Please don't tell anyone, though," Mary said urgently. The last thing she needed was for her father to find her. "Promise me."

"I promise!" he said quickly. "No one will hear it from me. But how did you manage to survive a broken heart?"

"It's a long story," she said. "And what about you? How are you even up here? Another potion of your mother's?"

"No, I'm—" Then, all at once, he was speaking in her head—in Merish. *"I don't need a potion. All that's required to be human is for me to dry myself."*

"Dry yourself," she repeated, momentarily distracted by how strange and wonderful it was to speak her first language again, to have words jump so neatly between two people. *"Um, what?"*

He grinned. *"It turns out, I'm half human."*

Her mouth dropped open again. (It was doing that a lot today.)

He laughed. *"I know, right? I'm still shocked myself, and I found out six months ago. I'd just come back from the market, and I was a little upset because someone—okay, I won't lie, it was Karen; she really had it out for me right after you left—called me a landlubber again, and then out of the deep blue sea my mother gave me a handful of potions, said that I didn't belong in Underwhere anymore, and told me a wonderful little story about how she once saved a human man from drowning—sound familiar?—and then she brought said man to a nearby deserted island, where the two of them passed a lovely few weeks together."*

Interesting. Perhaps the fact that Aunt Witch had (apparently) fallen for a human was the reason why she'd been so quick to help Mary. But Mary had never heard of such a thing before. She'd always assumed she'd been the only one. The fact that the Sea Witch had not only fallen for a human but spent *a few weeks* with him was sort of blowing Mary's mind.

"No one noticed she was missing?" Mary asked.

Jack shrugged. *"Those were freer times back then, I guess. And during those days with him they sometimes, you know, seahorsed around, and then nine months later, I was born."*

"I didn't know that was even possible," Mary said.

"Well, apparently it is, because here I am. I can be in either form. When I'm wet, I have a tail. And when I'm fully dry . . ."

"You have legs!"

"I have legs. Tell me these aren't the best-looking legs you've ever seen in your life." He stretched a leg out for her to examine his calf muscle. *"I find that I have a fine ass as well, and changes to some other body parts that my mother really should have warned me about."*

"Oh, Jack," Mary said. *"It's like you always wanted."*

"We both got what we wanted," he pointed out.

Well, sort of. Mary wasn't exactly where she'd thought she'd be the last time she'd seen Jack, but this life suited her, she found. She had a job. She had a community. She had—

"Is everything quite well here?" Tobias said, coming up beside Mary.

Oh, ship. Mary had been so caught up speaking with Jack in Merish that she'd forgotten that—to anyone else—it would look like they'd spent the last five minutes silently staring into each other's eyes.

"Um, yes, everything's fine," Mary said. "I just need to speak with this man." There was still so much she wanted to know. "How long until the meeting?" she asked Tobias.

He checked his pocket watch. "Uh, ten minutes, assuming he's on time."

"That's long enough. Guard our table." With no other explanation (because she couldn't currently think of an explanation) Mary grabbed Jack's arm and dragged him bodily to the storage room. She shut the door behind them, and when her eyes adjusted—it was quite dark in there, with only a few splinters of light making it through a scattering of bullet holes in the door—she found that the room was filled with stacked casks of rum.

"Now we can talk," she said. "But we have to make it fast."

"All right, so tell me everything," he said. "How long have you been in Nassau?"

"A year!" she said cheerily. "I got picked up by a pirate ship, and I've been working my way up the ranks since then. I'm the quartermaster on the *Ranger* now."

"How wonderful! Bonn will be most jealous when she meets you."

"Bonn?"

Jack smiled brightly. "My true love. She's just out there, you know."

Mary frowned. "Out there? This isn't really the best place for a woman."

"You don't say." Jack scoffed good-naturedly, roughing up her hair like when they were minnows. "Bonn has a brilliant plan to become a lady pirate. That's why we're here."

Oh, this was going to be difficult to explain to Jack. Things were different in Underwhere. Gender roles weren't so sharply divided. "You see, up here, in this place, women—"

"Aren't allowed to be pirates," Jack finished for her. "Yes, I know. The no-women-pirates rule makes no sense, if you ask me. But as I said, she has a plan." He paused. "I'm a bit nervous about it, truth be told, but she's the love of my life, so what choice do I have? I have to go along with it."

Mary felt her teeth come together at the words *love of my life.* If her experience in the human world had taught her anything, it was that love—romantic love, anyway—was dangerous. She only hoped that, when Jack learned this, it wouldn't actually break his heart.

"Can't she just disguise herself?" Mary asked after a moment.

"Oh, she's tried," Jack said. "But her bosoms cannot be contained. She's always found out eventually."

Well, that was the extent of Mary's advice.

"But perhaps our luck is changing now," Jack said. "Can you help us get on a ship? I've been doing my best to keep us in room and board, but we've recently hit a snag where we're going to need more in the way of capital."

"Uh," said Mary, "like how much?"

"Oh, not so much. Just a thousand pieces of eight."

"A thousand pieces of eight!"

Jack waved his hand, like this wasn't any big deal. "I only need about eight hundred and fifty more. And I'll get it eventually, I'm sure, but I can't come up with that kind of money as quickly as I'd like."

"So you're . . . not a pirate?" Mary asked. "You look like a pirate."

"Indeed? Thank you, thank you very much," he said, his chest puffing out a bit. "But no, unfortunately, I'm not a pirate yet. I acquire items using another method and sell them to buyers willing to pay."

"What other method?" Mary prompted.

"Shipwrecks," he admitted. "You'd be surprised by the number of ships at the bottom of the harbor. All around the island."

Ah. So he turned into a Mer, swam down, and salvaged shipwrecks. That was clever.

"That seems risky," she said.

"No riskier than, say, you *pretending to be a boy on a pirate ship,*" he shot back.

Ouch. But that was fair. "Speaking of all that," she said, "I go by Mark here. Not Mary. No one knows that I'm a woman except Tobias—"

A faint creaking from somewhere deeper in the storeroom stopped them. There was a light scraping, accompanied by a wheezing cough.

Mary and Jack froze, staring at each other in silent panic.

"Do you think," Mary asked in Merish, *"there's someone in here with us?"*

"Possibly?" Jack tilted his head, listening.

But the sound didn't come again. In fact, Mary reasoned, it could have come from the other room. There was so much going on.

Even so, she peered through the gloom. Her night vision had always been quite good compared to anyone else's—probably because of growing up Mer—but the storeroom was almost completely dark. She saw only the vague outlines of casks and an old blanket someone had tossed in there.

Perhaps she'd imagined the noise had come from inside the storeroom.

Mary crossed her arms. "Anyway. Why, pray tell, are you in need of a thousand pieces of eight?"

"So I can get married," Jack said. "It's complicated, but that's the gist of it."

"Be careful with that," Mary said. "Don't . . . don't let your heart get broken."

"We'll be fine," Jack said. "She's the one I'm meant to be with, I'm sure of it. But speaking of true love, what does that mean, I wonder, that your heart didn't break? Perhaps that prince fellow wasn't your true love after all? Or are you fully hu—"

"No, my heart obviously didn't break," Mary interrupted. "And to be clear, Charles was not a real prince, that was all a long time ago, and I don't even think about him anymore."

She tried so hard not to think about Charles. It was getting easier with time. But sometimes the hurt and humiliation of it all washed over her anew, and she felt like she was right back there, watching him declare his love to someone else.

Jack snorted. "If you say so. But I get it. I've been in love a few times since I came Above."

"Since six months ago?"

"I can't help it!" Jack said helplessly. "I simply adore all the different people I come across. Tall ones. Short ones. Buxom ones. Muscly ones. I love them all, and they love me."

"Ah, what a hard life you lead," Mary said wryly.

Just then, the door was flung open, and a small figure stood framed by the brighter light in the main room. Her shadow stretched across the floor and over the casks. Her eyes were narrowed. Her fists were curled.

"What is going on in here?" she asked hotly.

"My love!" Jack cried. "We were just discussing you."

Bonn—because this could only be Bonn—reached in and grabbed Jack by the arm and yanked him back into the main room. On his way, Jack grabbed Mary's arm, dragging her along with him.

The storeroom door slammed shut behind them. But we're

going to stay here in the storeroom for a few minutes more, dear reader, because there *had* been someone in the room with Mary and Jack—a man, slumped behind the barrels—and once they were gone, this man opened his eyes.

It was Captain Vane, who was feeling pretty enlightened about many things he had not previously known, particularly that his own quartermaster was secretly a woman—and that somewhere out there, just in the other room, was yet another woman with designs on becoming a pirate.

"Good Lord," he breathed into the darkness of the storeroom. "They're everywhere!"

(Now wait just a minute, you might be saying to yourself, dear reader, and we wouldn't blame you. How is Captain Vane here? The last we saw him he was passed out in the captain's cabin of the *Ranger*, and he said—he said!—that he was going to stay aboard the ship and not go to the pirate meeting, because he didn't want to run into Bess, aka his ex–lady love. And yes. That's true. But then, after drinking some more, he decided that he really must see his Bess—he couldn't bear not to see her, in fact, so while Mary and Tobias were making their way to their little shack and preparing for the meeting, Captain Vane had cleaned himself up a bit and stumbled through the town to the brothel that Bess managed. But there he'd been turned away. He hadn't even been given the chance to speak to her. After that, Vane thought he could use a drink, and he decided also that he wanted to be present for this all-important meeting of the pirate captains after all. He was the captain of the

Ranger. Not Mr. Read. So Vane had stumbled his way to the Scurvy Dog. But when he got there, the meeting hadn't started yet, so he'd had a few more drinks. Then he thought a nap sounded nice, so he'd found himself a cozy place in the storeroom to catch a few z's, and he'd been sleeping there soundly until he'd been awakened by the arrival of Mary and Jack.

So now he was very much awake, and his thoughts were whirling for more reasons than simply the excess rum. His quartermaster—Mark Read!—was a woman! A traitor! She'd basically been making a fool of him this whole time! Like Bess! Like all women! GAR!

But we've had quite enough of Vane's misogyny for now, so we're going to return the story to Mary and Jack.)

Back in the main room of the pub, Mary found herself face-to-freckled-face with a very irate Irishwoman, who looked like she was an eyelash away from clocking Mary right in the kisser. (That is indeed what Bonn was considering. We're kind of amazed she hadn't done it already.)

And that, dear reader, is the moment when the soon-to-be-infamous Mary Read met the already-a-little-infamous Anne Bonny.

"And who's this now?" Bonn wanted to know, looking Mary up and down. "He's a bonny chap, sure enough." But the way she said the word *chap* held a certain sharpness that made Mary's breath catch.

Jack attempted an introduction. "Um, Mark, allow me to

introduce the love of my life, my bonny lass, the glorious Anne Bonny."

Mary might not have noticed at first glance, because the girl was wearing baggy clothes that obscured her figure, a large somewhat misshapen wool cap, and dirt on her face, but Mary had the impression that under all of that, Bonn was the sort of beauty who could make Lavinia jealous. Where Mary could be described as a box (by some people), Anne Bonny was an hourglass—and a fierce one at that.

"Mark who, exactly, if that is your real name?" Anne pressed, staring at where Jack had ruffled Mary's hair earlier. "And just what were you doing in the closet with my—my Jack?"

"Oh, darling," Jack said sweetly. "Are you jealous? How touching."

"Yes, what were you two doing in the closet?"

Mary closed her eyes. She'd know Tobias's voice anywhere. And when she opened her eyes he was standing in front of her, his expression a mix of concern and hurt—oh bollocks, she'd hurt him. It'd been rude and thoughtless for her to just grab Jack and run off like that, with no explanation. She was a fool.

"The meeting's about to start," he pointed out before she could voice her apology. "Would you and your friends like to sit?"

"Yes," she said. "Let's all sit down."

They retreated to their table.

Anne was still staring at Mary dubiously.

"I'm Mark Read," Mary said quickly. Then, because it seemed

like a good way to restore the peace, she added, "I'm the quartermaster of the *Ranger*."

Anne's eyes widened. "Are you now?" She glanced back and forth between Mary and Jack. "Well, that is an interesting development."

"Mark here is my cousin," Jack explained, "who I thought dead, but only now discovered alive and well."

"Your cousin, you say?"

"Your cousin!" Tobias said, his frown disappearing. Suddenly, his voice held an eager, curious note. "What a fortuitous meeting!" He held out his hand. "I'm pleased to make your acquaintance, sir. I'm Tobias."

Jack took the offered hand gently and held it in his own. "Jack Rackham, at your service."

He'd chosen Jack when they were kids, at the same time as Mary had chosen Mary. He'd liked this one story they'd read about a boy and a beanstalk. It was hard to say where he'd gotten Rackham, though.

"However," Jack went on, still holding on to Tobias's hand, "I prefer for people to call me Calico Jack." With his free hand, he gestured down at his shirt, which was, sure enough, made of blue calico. "I find calico to be a much better fabric for life here—it's light and breathable and comes in so many fashionable designs. I don't know why other people feel they have to go with heavy velvets and wools or those rough and boring linens." He motioned to Mary's shirt and shook his head disappointedly. "I think the calico thing is going to catch on eventually. So call me Calico Jack."

"O-kay," Mary said, prying Jack's hand off Tobias's. "Calico Jack is fine, I guess."

Anne took the opportunity to grab Jack's hand, now that it was free. "So, uh, *Mark*," she said.

Oh crap. She definitely knew. "Yes?"

"Is Tobias your . . . paramour?" Anne asked.

"No!" Mary and Tobias said at the same time.

"We're not like that," Tobias insisted. "We're friends."

"He's my best mate," Mary agreed.

Tobias turned to her. "I am?"

The way he said it—that soft tone, the tilt of his smile, the faint surprise—made Mary's heart flutter a little more urgently. She shoved the feeling aside. "Of course," she said as lightly as she could manage, "and I hope you'd count me as your best mate as well. Considering I saved your life at least twice today."

"I do!" he said. "And I saved your life *three* times, I should point out."

"My life was not in danger from that banana peel," Mary insisted.

"Banana peel?" Jack arched an eyebrow at her. "Is that what they're calling it now?"

Her face flamed. "No! We're friends! That's all, I swear."

"Right." Anne turned her attention to Tobias. "So are you a pirate as well?"

He sighed. "Yes. Although some days I question the decision."

"Well, it's not like you really had a choice," Mary said. She clapped Tobias on the back as he scowled. "Toby's father is none other than Captain Blackbeard himself."

"Gawl!" Anne gazed at Tobias with newfound respect in her eyes. "*Yer* the son of Blackbeard! Only the most famous pirate in the blooming world! The Pirate King!"

"Pirates don't have kings," insisted Tobias, and Mary knew this was a seamount (aka an underwater hill) he would die on. "We don't need a monarchy. It's ridiculous to call him the Pirate King."

Jack cocked his head to the side. "If your father's the Pirate King, does that make you the Pirate Prince?" he asked.

"No," protested Tobias. "Absolutely not."

"Although some people do call him that," added Mary. "And some people call him . . ."

"Don't do it," warned Tobias.

"Baaaaabybeard." Mary brought her hand up to pat Tobias's basically-smooth-except-for-peach-fuzz-and-a-few-errant-whiskers cheek.

"Stop," Tobias said with a groan. "You delight in torturing me."

"I do," she admitted, her hand still on his face.

"You do?" Jack asked, looking back and forth between them.

"Aye, I see the delight," Anne said. "Maybe *they* should go into the closet together."

Mary quickly dropped her hand.

"Speaking of fathers," Jack said, clearing his throat, "do either of you know Ted?"

"Who?" Mary and Tobias asked at the same time.

"Ted," he said again. "It turns out that Ted is my long-lost father. All my mother was able to tell me was that his name was Ted, he has dark hair, and that he's a sailor of some sort. But there are a lot more people named Ted here than I expected. So far I've encountered a Ted Danson, a Teddy Roosevelt, and a Ted Bundy, but none of those fellows were a good match for my father."

"I'm sorry," Mary said, "I don't know anyone by the name of Ted. What about you?" She looked at Tobias.

"Sorry," Tobias said. "I know a couple of guys named Bill and Ted, but neither of them is a sailor."

"Oh well," Jack said. "I had to ask."

"When is this blooming meeting going to start?" Anne asked, drumming her fingers on the table. She glanced around. "There's Captain Crunch, and Captain Hornigold, and Captain Obvious. Ooh, and over there's Captain Ahab. And behind him, Captain Morgan."

Wow. The woman really knew her pirate captains.

"And is that Captain Vane?" Anne added. "Ach, but he looks like he's been hitting the bottle hard."

Mary and Tobias swiveled around to look. And yes, sure enough, there was Captain Vane. His hat was on backward and he was sloshing rum onto the floor, but it was him.

"What's he doing here?" Mary hissed. "I thought you said he was staying on the ship."

"He was!" Tobias insisted. "I don't know. I guess he changed his mind."

Mary sighed. If she'd come to learn anything about Vane since she'd been aboard the *Ranger*, it was that he was unpredictable.

Just then, as if to prove her point, Vane spotted her.

"Why is he smiling that creepy smile?" Tobias asked out of the side of his mouth.

"No idea," she said out of the side of hers, but Vane's gaze was making the back of her neck prickle.

Then the captain turned away and yelled for more rum.

"Does this mean we can go?" Tobias said hopefully.

"Not a chance."

"You know who's not here, though? Captain Blackbeard." Anne looked at Tobias like it was his fault somehow. "Where's your pa? Isn't he the one calling this meeting?"

"He's often late," Tobias sighed. "He likes to make an entrance."

As if on cue, Mary became aware of a noise growing in the street, raised voices and bells ringing.

Anne jumped to her feet and started to roll up her sleeves. "This is it," she said. "Wish me luck."

"Uh, darling," Jack said. "Perhaps, since there's been this new development, we can try an alternate plan."

She scowled. "You mean like a plan B?"

"What's plan A?" Mary wanted to know.

"Uh, Bonn here is going to challenge Blackbeard's quarter-master, Caesar, to a duel, beat him—without harming him, of course—and then ask Blackbeard to make her a member of his crew, after which, she will reveal the truth about her, uh, sex."

"Her what now?" Tobias asked.

"Aw, Jack, don't go blabbing," Anne said.

"Oh, dear God." Mary had never heard a worse plan in her life.

"I've never heard a worse plan in my life," Tobias said. He looked really and truly alarmed.

"What, you think I can't handle it?" Anne cocked her head at Tobias. "Do you want to go, Babybeard?"

"Don't call me that," Tobias said. "And no. But you shouldn't fight Caesar. He's a good man. It would make him feel bad to have to kill you."

"I guess we'll find out," said Anne.

Just then the noise from outside spilled inside as the door of the Scurvy Dog burst open and a flood of pirates entered, filling the room, all speaking and shouting at once.

All four of them—Mary, Tobias, Anne, and Jack—tensed. Especially, Mary noted, Tobias.

But none of these men was Blackbeard. Or Caesar. Or anyone else from the *Queen Anne's Revenge*.

"What's going on?" asked Mary, but her voice was drowned by the hubbub.

Something, she thought with a sinking feeling. *Something was wrong.*

She climbed up to stand on the table, put a hand to her mouth, and gave a sharp whistle. The men in the bar quieted and turned to look at her.

"What has happened?" she asked.

"It's Captain Blackbeard!" cried a big ruffian near the front of the crowd.

"Yes, and what about him?"

"Jonathan Barnet got him. That pirate-hunting bilge rat! He killed Blackbeard." There were actual tears in the man's eyes. "He's gone to the great beyond."

"Blast!" burst out Anne. "Of all the rotten luck!"

There was a clatter next to Mary—the sound of Tobias dropping into his chair. His face had gone ashen. He looked like someone had punched him in the gut. "Toby," Mary said.

Tobias's mouth opened like he might say something. But nothing came out.

"The Pirate King is dead!" someone cried. Then all the assembled men in the room slowly turned and bowed to Tobias. "Long live the Pirate King!"

FIVE

Tobias

The funeral of Blackbeard was held on the docks the very next day at noon—any earlier would have been *too* early for pirates. All of Nassau was in attendance, crammed shoulder to shoulder on the half-rotted wood. They were wearing black, and each mourner carried a bottle of rum.

Tobias had been hoping to show up at the last minute and slip into the crowd unnoticed, but upon his arrival, the assembled pirates had immediately broken into song.

"God save our Pirate King! Long live our fearless King! God save the King!"

And by "king," they still—weirdly, ludicrously, most stupidly—meant Tobias. On account of his being Blackbeard's *favorite* son.

It was like his pa was getting the last word from beyond the grave. But Tobias had no intention of letting a crown anywhere near his head.

"Send him victorious," belted out the pirates, "wicked and glorious, long to reign over us, God save the King!"

This was his worst nightmare.

He felt a squeeze on his shoulder and opened his eyes. Mary. She gave him a sad, sympathetic smile.

"I hope wearing black at funerals doesn't catch on," she said, fanning herself.

(Reader, we had questions about this, too. Here's what we found out. While wearing black at a funeral is a tradition that goes back to the time of the ancient Romans, when funeral-goers would swap out their everyday white togas for black ones, in this particular time—the 1700s—it was not a normal thing. It wouldn't become standard until the 1860s—a good 130ish years from now—when Queen Victoria wore all black to mourn the death of her husband, Prince Albert. Because she was such a trendsetter, that Queen Victoria.)

"Yes, why black?" complained Jack from Mary's other side.

And yes, Jack was there, too.

When Tobias and Mary had arrived and the terrible singing had begun, Jack and Anne had (of course) spotted them and waved them over. Tobias hadn't wanted to socialize, but the couple would provide a decent buffer from the rest of the funeral, so he'd agreed.

Jack was wearing a black calico shirt with a very subtle white floral print (where he could have gotten this fabric is a mystery that we narrators have not yet solved) and tight-fitting black striped pants. Black sash. Black boots. Black tricorn hat with a white feather in it. He didn't dress like any man Tobias had ever met, but it suited him, somehow. As Tobias watched, Jack sniffed at his own armpit and grimaced. "Why on the good dry earth would anyone pick black to wear at an outdoor event?"

"To match the beard, I guess," Anne Bonny said. "I rather like wearing black."

"And you look ravishing in it, darling." Jack leaned over and kissed her enthusiastically, then abruptly pulled away. "Sorry, sorry," he said to Mary. "Is kissing inappropriate for a funeral? This is the first official one I've ever been to."

Who is *this guy?* Tobias thought.

Mary had been acting strangely from the moment she'd first seen Jack at the Scurvy Dog last night. They'd been having a normal conversation, talking about Alexander Pope's new translation of *The Iliad*, which they had both recently read, and then she'd suddenly gone still. Her face had drained of color. And she'd jumped out of her chair and yelled, "SON OF A WITCH."

Which was, to Tobias's mind, completely out of character for her.

Maybe, he'd thought at first, this was the guy who'd hurt her. The one she didn't talk about. The one he saw her thinking about occasionally, a mix of fury and humiliation passing through her azure eyes. The reason she refused to ever go to Charles Town. Maybe she was about to stick her dagger in that man's gut and be rid of him for good. As the bloke undoubtedly deserved.

But then there'd been the hugging and the super-intense staring into each other's eyes, and then she'd dragged Jack into the storage room, emerging all rumpled and flushed, and Tobias had been totally bewildered.

Bewildered and (let's just admit it) jealous.

Wildly jealous.

Unreasonably jealous, considering that Tobias knew perfectly well that Mary saw him only as a friend.

Then she'd introduced Jack as her cousin, and Tobias had felt, well, relieved.

But there was something odd between them, a way that Mary looked at Jack that reminded Tobias of how she sometimes looked at *him*. Jack had been her best friend, she'd said. And then Tobias had been her best friend. And now Jack was in her life again.

And Tobias was back to jealous.

But then Blackbeard was dead—he was gone, and his entire crew was gone, which meant that Tobias had also lost Caesar and an entire group of decent, brave men he'd basically grown up with—and Tobias was feeling way too many things to focus on jealousy: confusion. Relief. Grief. Anger. More confusion. Yearning. An awful numbness every time he thought of his pa. And, to top it off, something very close to outright panic whenever the pirates sang that damn "long live the king" song.

Stop singing that! he wanted to scream. *Pirates don't need a king!*

Mary squeezed his shoulder again. It helped. But it was not enough.

"Mr. Teach, you'll need to come with us," said Bess, aka Captain Vane's ex-sweetheart, aka the madam of the Saucy Siren. (According to our research, Bess had been tasked with organizing the event, which we think was smart. If Bess could manage a whole brothel, why not a funeral?)

"Oh dear God, why?" Tobias asked. Would they make him stand up and be anointed the Pirate King right here in front of everybody?

He wouldn't do it! He'd refuse to be anybody's Pirate King.

"To stand with the family," Bess said gently.

Oh. Well, that was only slightly better.

"It's all right, Toby," Mary murmured. "We'll be right here."

"Yes, cheering you on from a distance," added Jack. "We'll be sending you our very best in the way of moral support, won't we, Bonn?"

"Sure, we will," Anne agreed.

Tobias looked at Mary as if to say, *Who is this guy?*

And she smiled again, reassuringly, like, *It's fine. You should go.*

So Tobias hurried after Bess, who led him to the end of the docks to join his fifty-two brothers and Blackbeard's various widows.

"Watch your step." Bess pointed downward, where a long match cord snaked across the dock and vanished behind other people's legs and feet.

Then he realized there were about a dozen match cords.

"Uh, what's going on?" he asked.

"You'll see!" she said cheerily. Ominously. Then she moved on to speak to another son.

"Oh, Toby, my dear," one of the widows said tearfully. "Your father always spoke so highly of you."

He sighed. He didn't know this woman. And she obviously didn't know him.

The widows were interesting, though. Blackbeard had fourteen wives, and a multitude of lovers. They were a diverse group, women with a range of skin tones from deep black to pale white, but here, on the docks, they all wore long black dresses, veils, and gloves, and they were weeping copiously, wailing loudly, and wringing their hands, like there was some kind of competition between them over who could act the saddest.

And of course they were all expecting Tobias to be sad. Which he was. He thought he was. He was just feeling too many other things to be able to tell for sure.

He dropped his gaze to his boots, just waiting for the funeral to begin—so that it could end.

You're mad! Leave me alone!

He could still see the pain in Blackbeard's eyes when he'd said that. The disappointment reflected there. The betrayal. And now he would never get to make things right. He wondered, as he had so many times since last night, what Blackbeard had wanted to talk to him about when he'd written the postscript: *Toby, ye come, too.*

But now he would never know.

The bell tolled noon then.

A large, official-looking man (dressed in black, of course, but with a white collar) came forward to the front of the crowd. He wasn't a priest, Tobias knew. He was an actor, hired to play a priest. Because Nassau, not having much use for priests, didn't have any. But they had a surprising number of excellent actors. This particular fellow was called Herbert the Strong, because his name was Herbert and he was, well, strong.

"Dearly beloved, we've come together today," Herbert the Strong said in a grand, booming voice, "to remember the life and legacy of Captain Teach, also known as Blackbeard, also known as the King of Pirates. Let us have a moment of silence." The mourners all went quiet—as quiet as hundreds of people could be, anyway—and bowed their heads.

For about two and a half seconds, Tobias just listened to the rush of water against the piles. Then he was caught in a flash of memory that struck him like lightning on the water: himself as a boy of seven, peering through a doorway to see Blackbeard at a roaring fire, combing his copious beard. A white man but his father, the nurse had told him. (His mother had been a Black woman who had gone to the angels when Tobias was born.) And now Tobias was old enough that this man—his father, at last—wished to see him.

"Come in, lad," Blackbeard called, waving him forward into the welcoming heat of the room. "Come here, son. You're to be my new cabin boy. That means you'll go with me on a big grand ship. How does that sound?"

And to Tobias back then it had sounded so good. To have

a father. To be with him. He promised himself right then that he would be the best son Blackbeard could have asked for.

Tobias clenched his fists, bringing himself back to the present with the pressure of his fingernails digging into his palms. He'd been having flashes like this all day, memories that would strike him, randomly, vividly, about his father.

Herbert the Strong cleared his throat, breaking the moment of silence. "Whew! Glad that's over with! Let's talk about how great Blackbeard was. And by great I mean that he was the baddest, scariest, most talented scallywag to ever sail the seven seas!"

Blackbeard's other sons cheered. The widows wept harder.

"For one thing"—Herbert held up a finger—"Blackbeard could drink any man under the table. The Pirate King could certainly hold his rum."

Tobias remembered, in another flash, sitting at the table in the captain's cabin of the *Queen Anne's Revenge*, Blackbeard thrusting a brown bottle under his nose. "You're nearly a man now, my boy," he pronounced. "Time to get some hair on your chest." Tobias was nine then, and not sure he wanted to be a man just yet. But when he gazed back at Caesar, hesitant, the older man gave him a faint, encouraging nod, so Tobias sipped the rum and then coughed and gasped, making Blackbeard boom with laughter.

Tobias shivered when he thought of that laugh—it had been a fixture of his life as reliable as the rising and setting of the sun. It could be cruel sometimes—a hard bark that never failed to make Tobias's heart beat faster. It could be maniacal—the smell of sulfur and burning as Blackbeard lit the fireworks in his beard and turned his sparking face to his enemies. It could be kind.

He tuned in to the funeral again. Herbert was now in the middle of describing Blackbeard's capturing of a hundred different ships, his battles against the British (or Spanish or Dutch or French) military, all his bold and courageous exploits, which Tobias knew would not have been possible without Caesar and the rest of the crew. It didn't feel fair, that it was only Blackbeard being honored here, when so many other lives had been lost. *They always want to talk about the king*, Tobias thought a bit bitterly. *They never want to talk about the soldiers.*

"He was a great lover, a courageous fighter, and a shrewd leader," Herbert continued. "He was, to put it frankly, a pirate's pirate. Some say he was the richest pirate who ever sailed. Some say"—Herbert paused for dramatic effect—"he amassed the greatest *treasure* the world has ever seen."

Oh yes. The treasure. Tobias had almost forgotten about that.

"But I guess now we'll never know," Herbert said mournfully. "Seeing as he left no map to any treasure, and told no one of its whereabouts."

Tobias couldn't help it—he immediately pictured himself at age twelve following Blackbeard into a dark vault, lit only by the hot torch Blackbeard held out ahead of them.

"Look here, son," Blackbeard said reverently. "This is my legacy—everything I've worked for."

He'd stepped out from behind his pa and gazed around in

wonder. The walls of this room were covered in rich tapestries, all woven in different styles and featuring different figures. It was clear they had all come from the ships of very wealthy and important men around the world. There was a pianoforte, a golden chandelier, and even a desk with a massive ledger lying open.

But that wasn't what Blackbeard had wanted Tobias to see.

No, it was the huge chests of weathered wood and banded iron, stuffed so full the hinges looked ready to break.

"Go on," Blackbeard said. "Open one."

Tobias hesitated, certain the latches must be booby-trapped somehow and that he was about to humiliate himself in front of his pa. But the eager look in Blackbeard's eyes wasn't the booby-trap-related eagerness—Tobias was intimately familiar with that particular expression—so he reached out for the nearest chest and touched the clasp.

The lid popped open and gold came spilling out. Coins, trinkets, and even a few teeth.

Tobias was dazzled and delighted. "There's so much treasure, Pa! Are they all this full?"

"Open another and find out."

The next chest held silver—so many Spanish silver dollars that Tobias thought there had to be more than a thousand pieces of eight in here. Another chest held jewels: loose gemstones, necklaces, and dozens of rings (a few still on fingers).

"Caesar tells me you have a head for numbers," Blackbeard said gruffly. "Is that true?"

"Yes, sir." Tobias stood up a bit taller.

"Good, good. Toby, you're my cleverest son. The one I trust. You're the only one who could understand the value of all this. You're the son I choose to have by my side. This treasure—my legacy—will be yours and yours alone."

His eyes were suddenly hot. A headache throbbed at his temples.

"Unfortunately," Herbert was saying, "as dear Blackbeard and his crew could not be recovered, today's burial will be of the symbolic sort." He swept around to direct everyone's attention to a ship sitting in the middle of the harbor, a single-masted sloop with its sails furled. A small rowboat was rowing away from it as fast as possible.

That was when Tobias noticed the hissing.

He looked down just in time to see a flame racing along the match cord, winding its way between feet and along the dock until it reached . . .

A cannon, aimed out at the harbor.

An immense *BOOM* rocked the docks, and a moment later, the cannonball struck the sloop broadside, leaving a gaping hole in the hull.

The crowd roared with appreciation.

Then Tobias caught flames traveling the other match cords.

BOOM. Another hole in the sloop.

BOOM.

One by one, the cannons blasted holes in the ship. Out in

the harbor, timbers groaned and cracked until the entire vessel finally gave out and the poor sloop vanished beneath the waves. An enormous cheer filled the docks. Then, almost in one motion, the mourners lifted their bottles of rum.

"To Blackbeard!" Herbert the Strong called.

"To Blackbeard!" they answered, and drank.

Tobias lifted the bottle to his lips. He'd never really come to like the taste of rum. Or the burning. But he drank one small swig for his pa.

After the drinking, the mourners turned to go, but Herbert the Strong called out, "There's one last thing! An announcement, if you please."

Tobias's heart sank. There was *more*? He wanted to go home now. Read a book. Stare at the wall. Anything that wasn't being here.

Slowly, the assembled pirates quieted, tense and waiting.

"Most of you know that, before his untimely departure from this world, Captain Blackbeard called a meeting of the pirate captains, to decide the Future of Piracy. What you probably don't know," Herbert continued, "is that at that meeting, Blackbeard intended to announce his retirement."

Another rumble made its way through the crowd. Blackbeard, the world's most famous pirate, retire? Unthinkable!

Tobias was equally confused. He'd never imagined his pa retiring. Ever.

"Pirates don't retire!" someone—who sounded suspiciously like Captain Vane—called out.

"Oh, shut your gob!" yelled a woman—obviously Bess—from the crowd. "They do, too!"

"Not if they're real men, they don't!"

"What does that even mean, *real men*?" Bess fired back. "You see? This is why I broke it off with you! Well, that and you're an arse!"

"Everybody calm down," Herbert said. "Now is not the time to get into personal grievances. It is true, I assure you, that Blackbeard intended to step down as the Pirate King. He meant for there to be a new Pirate King, Blackbeard's heir and successor, one extraordinary man to represent the Golden Age of Piracy to the entire world."

That's when Herbert looked directly at Tobias.

Then everyone else looked at Tobias.

Tobias contemplated whether or not he should leap off the dock and into the water.

But then Herbert the Strong turned to regard a line of men who'd come forward.

"In the wake of Blackbeard's death," he said, "these three captains have come together to form a new organization. They call themselves the Admirable Association of Retired Pirates, or the AARP for short."

"But pirates don't retire!" Vane yelled again.

"Oh, be quiet!" screamed Bess.

"Don't tell me what to do, woman!"

"SHUT UP!" This was from Herbert, who'd clearly reached the end of his patience with Captain Vane's relationship drama.

"THIS IS A FUNERAL, FOR PETE'S SAKE! SHOW SOME BLOOMING RESPECT!"

"Er, sorry," rasped Vane.

Herbert sighed. "Now where were we? Oh yes. The AARP. I give you Benjamin Hornigold! James Hook! And Henry Morgan!" As Herbert called out each name, the pirate captain in question lifted his hat and waved it, which incited more shouted comments from the crowd.

"Captain Morgan died a long time ago, didn't he?" said one.

"No, I think he makes rum now."

"And I thought Captain Hook was fictional?" said another.

Herbert the Strong stepped back and gestured for one of the retired captains to take over as MC. Captain Hornigold shuffled to the front and cleared his throat. "The AARP would like to honor Blackbeard and his wishes to crown a new Pirate King."

Everyone swiveled again to look at Tobias.

Tobias looked into the water. He could do it. He could swim for it and hope there weren't any sharks this close to the shore. He'd prefer being eaten by sharks than being the king. How could he continue to rage against the machine of arbitrary titles if he inherited an arbitrary title?

"But, of course, a Pirate King must be chosen in the most democratic way possible," Hornigold added sagely, and then everyone was back to looking at him.

"Of course, of course," the pirates agreed. "Democracies are important."

"Will there be a vote?" one pirate asked. "Will it be a proper election?"

"There's a lot of pirates. Maybe captains should vote on behalf of their crews. That way every ship is represented equally."

"Well, that's not fair to the bigger crews!" declared another pirate, probably from a bigger crew. "Everyone's vote should be equal. One man, one vote!"

"And why do only pirates get to vote!" someone in the audience cried indignantly. "The whole town should get to vote!"

A bunch of pirates cried "Aye!" or "Nay!" or "Arrr!"

They were about two seconds from a brawl.

"Calm down!" Hornigold yelled over the noise. "I'm trying to tell you how it will work!"

The pirates calmed down. As much as they were able, anyway.

"We all know there's only one way to handle this," Hornigold said, "only one way that's fair to everyone, that gives every man a chance to become the next Pirate King. We're going to hold a contest!"

Well, that sounded ridiculous.

But, Tobias realized suddenly, a contest meant that no one expected *he* would inherit the title of Pirate King.

It was a great idea. He started to clap.

"The competition will officially begin in three days." Hornigold grinned toothily. "May the best man win!"

SIX

Jack

"May the best man win," Bonn grumbled, pacing back and forth around their room later that night. She raked a hand through her hair, sending red curls flying. "Why do they always have to say it in such a way? May the best *man* win. Ugh."

"Yes, I know," Jack sympathized. "So damned unfair."

"A woman could be the Pirate King!" she ranted. "It doesn't say anywhere in the rules that women can't enter the contest."

"The rules?" Jack inquired politely.

She fished a wrinkled piece of parchment out of her pocket and handed it to him.

Jack scanned down the curly pirate writing with its random capitalized words. It did, indeed, appear to be a set of rules for the Pirate King contest. "Interesting. The AARP is really taking this seriously, it seems. Rule number one: *No accidental Murdering of another Contestant.* That's a wonderful rule. I'd hate for anyone to be accidentally murdered."

"Go on, read the rest," Bonn urged quietly.

"Rule number two," Jack read. "*No Deliberate murdering of another contestant.*"

"So, no murder, period," said Bonn. "To keep the contestants from simply eliminating one another as the competition."

"Sounds reasonable." Jack continued to read. "Rule number three: *Sabotage, be it of Ship or Person, is allowed, so long as it does not result in the breaking of rules one or two.*"

"Get to the part about the violence!" Bonn ordered.

Jack glanced down. "Oh. Yes. Here it is. Rule four: *Violence is Encouraged, but please continue to refer to rules One and Two.*"

Bonn rubbed her hands together. "I love me some good mayhem. Really gets the blood pumping. Nothing more exciting than getting into a proper tiff with a bloke."

"You're amazing," Jack said softly. He cleared his throat. "Rule number five. *All contestants must be Captains with a Crew of at Least twenty.*" He frowned. "Is that all?" Jack turned the paper over, but there was nothing written on the back side. "No murder, but it's okay to sabotage and fight one another, and you have to be a captain?"

"That's all," Bonn said. "Nothing about being a woman. So we could have a Pirate Queen! Like Grace O'Malley, the great Irish pirate queen from a hundred years ago!"

Jack set the paper down in his lap and settled back in the bed, watching her stomp from one end of the room to the other. Great Waters, but she was beautiful when she was plotting something nefarious. He wished fleetingly that it would be possible to introduce Bonn to his mother. The two of them would get on nicely, he thought.

Bonn was still going on about Grace O'Malley. "Why, she used to sail right past my hometown of Kinsale! She was a clan chieftain! That's like a queen, you know!"

Jack did know. He'd heard Bonn talk about Grace O'Malley so many times that he almost felt like he knew the woman personally. He always imagined her with red hair and an attitude. Which was just his type.

"And there's Sayyida al-Hurra," Bonn continued hotly. "She basically ruled the entire Mediterranean Sea, some two hundred years ago. And she was an *actual* queen. The name Sayyida al-Hurra is her title, not her name. Al-Hurra means 'a woman sovereign who bows to no superior authority.' So she was *literally* a pirate queen."

Bonn sure knew a lot about pirates. She had even crafted her own personal set of hand-painted cards upon which she'd recorded the information of all the famous pirates throughout history. How she came by this information was a mystery, as he'd never seen Bonn read much or have any conversation with scholars. But somehow she knew. As evidenced by what she said next:

"And what about Artemisia of Halicarnassus? Elyssa of Tyre? Queen Teuta? The Vikings: Sela, Rossa, and Lagertha? Alfhild the Beautiful? Joanna of Flanders? Jeanne de Clisson? Gunpowder

Gertie? Sister Ping? Sadie the Goat?"

"Those were *all* women pirates?" Jack was amazed.

"Aye," said Bonn. "And I mean to be like them, Jack. If they could do it, so can I."

"Indeed you can, darling," he said. "So are you planning on entering the contest?"

She scowled prettily. "I was when I first heard of it. I thought to meself, *Self, you could go straight to the top!* But then the rules say you must be a captain. So no, I can't enter the contest. But I still mean to become a pirate, just you watch me. I'll get there."

"There's not a doubt in my mind that you will, my love," Jack said. "I can't wait to see how you're going to make that happen. You'll be an ideal pirate. And I'll be your best mate."

He was trying for a joke there, but her expression faltered. "Gawl!" she cried. "Why did Blackbeard have to die?"

"His death does put a damper on your initial plan," he agreed, but then, because he was Jack and therefore inclined to see the bright side, he said, "But perhaps that's for the best?"

She stopped pacing and looked at him, outraged. "What. Did you not like my plan?"

"It was a solid plan," he said quickly, "but perhaps there's a less dangerous path to becoming a pirate than you fighting your way to the top."

"Oh yes?" She crossed her arms. "What would you suggest?"

"My cousin is the quartermaster of the *Ranger*," he pointed out. "So perhaps—"

"You think she can talk our way onto that ship?" Bonn gave him a skeptical look.

"I think she can be very persuasive when she sets her mind to a course of action. She—" He paused. "Wait. You know Mary's a woman?"

Bonn rolled her eyes. "It's plain enough to anyone who really cares to look. Why do you think I was so steamed when you went off alone with her the other night?"

"But she's my cousin!" he protested.

"So you say." Bonn gazed at him assessingly. "There's something you're not telling me. I smell something fishy there. You're not *kissing* cousins, are ye?"

He shuddered. "Ew, no! Never!" Then he guiltily remembered, well, not never. Once when they were kids he and Mary had seen a picture in a book of two humans kissing (which was not really a thing among the Mer except in the most dire of emergencies), and of course they'd had to try it out on each other. But it hadn't been a good kind of kiss. It had been like kissing his . . . cousin.

"Uh-huh," Bonn sniffed. "Then what was all the hugging and standing there gazing rapturously into her eyes?"

She must have been watching the entire time.

He smiled, delighted at her obvious jealousy. "Darling, you seriously can't believe that I would have eyes for any other woman but you."

"No, perhaps not," she admitted. "And I suppose Mary—that's her name, is it?—doesn't fancy you, either. Seeing as she's so clearly flying a flag for Blackbeard's son."

"Right?" Jack said. "They are so obviously more than just friends."

"But anyway, it doesn't matter," Bonn said, shaking her head. "We can't get aboard the *Ranger*. It makes no difference that your cousin's the quartermaster, because the captain—Captain Vane— is a notorious woman hater. Ask anyone in Nassau. Ask Bess, the madam of the Saucy Siren. She'll tell you, well enough."

"Hmm." Jack stroked his chin. "That does present a problem. If only my cousin was the captain of the *Ranger*, instead of this Vane fellow."

Bonn stared at him for a moment. Then she started putting on her boots. "Get dressed!" she ordered.

He reached for his shirt, which was dangling on the bedpost. "Where are we going?"

"To find your cousin," she said. "I've got me an idea."

Finding Mary turned out to be a difficult task, on account of the fact that neither Jack nor Bonn, even with her encyclopedic pirate know-how, knew where Mary lived when she wasn't aboard the *Ranger*. So Jack suggested they go to the Scurvy Dog, the last place they'd encountered Mary outside the funeral, and ask around.

So that's just what they did.

Most of the pirates in the Scurvy Dog knew of Mark Read, sure enough, but nobody knew exactly where the illustrious Mr. Read resided. They did say that many crew members on the *Ranger* lived on a street in the northern part of town called Okra Hill.

"We should start there," Bonn said. "But I want a drink before we go. I never did manage to get a rum last night, and it's supposed to be the best in all Nassau. Let's sit at the bar for a bit."

There wasn't a line this time, and they were able to find two spots at the bar together.

"Good evening. What can I get ya?" the barmaid asked cheerily.

"Two rums, if you please," Bonn answered, and the woman smiled and set two mugs of rum before them.

"You're Anne Bonny, aren't you?" she asked Bonn.

"Who's asking?" Bonn said, but Jack could tell she was pleased that she was becoming so well known in town.

"I'm Maggie O'Brien, from Cork," said the barmaid.

"I'm from Kinsale meself," said Bonn.

"Pleased to meet a fellow Irishwoman. And what about you?" Maggie's gaze slid over Jack curiously. "No, wait, don't tell me. You're Calico Jack."

He tipped his hat at her, because women seemed to like that. "At your service, miss."

She smiled, revealing dimples. "And where are you from, good sir?"

His heart immediately began to beat faster. "Not from anywhere you've ever heard of."

"Oh, so Liverpool, I'm guessing," she said.

He laughed a bit nervously. "No. Not Liverpool." Although

he didn't exactly know where Liverpool was. He hadn't had time yet to learn much about the geography of the human world.

Thankfully just then the bell over the door rang, and a large man entered and lumbered up to the bar.

"Ahoy there, lass!" the man said loudly.

"Good evening to ya," Maggie said. "What will it be?"

"Two," said the man.

She nodded and poured two cups of rum.

He grinned at her with blackened teeth. "Not rum."

"That's all we've got," she replied matter-of-factly. "Oh, did you want rum with lime in a coconut shell? You put the lime in the coconut and drink them both up."

The man burped. He'd obviously already had some rum. "No. I want dairy."

She put a hand to her hip. "We don't serve milk here. Just rum."

The man smirked at her. "I think you do." His gaze fastened on a part of the barmaid's body that was absolutely off-limits. Two parts of her body, in fact.

Maggie sighed. "I think you need to mind your manners, sir, or I'm going to have to ask you to leave."

"I want dairy," the man slurred again, and then he leaned across the bar and tried to grab her.

That's when Bonn leapt to her feet and punched him.

Hard. In the nose.

The man howled. Bonn stepped lightly around her barstool,

took the offending man by the ear, and tossed him out into the street before he could get his wits about him.

"Have a nice day," she said sweetly as she slammed the door.

Jack pressed a hand to his chest. What a human!

"Thanks," said Maggie. "Your drink's on the house."

Bonn slid back onto her stool. Jack was afraid she'd pick up the conversation about where they were all from, but happily a new topic was now being loudly discussed all over the bar, and Bonn's attention was diverted once more.

The topic was, of course, the Pirate King contest. Who could enter said contest. Who should enter. And who was the most likely to win.

"It's a dangerous business, that," one man said gleefully. "Did you hear? The *Squirrel* was scuttled tonight. And Captain Pipp went down with her."

"But that's murder and therefore against the rules!" said another incredulously.

"And the contest hasn't even officially started yet," cried still a third man. "Who did it?"

"Captain Stocking," the first man said. "The AARP disqualified him immediately, and then they put him in a gibbet, to show how serious they are about the no-murder rule."

A gibbet, dear reader, was a big iron cage like a birdcage, only you could put a live man (or sometimes a dead man) inside and then hoist the cage up somewhere as a warning for everyone to see, as the man inside slowly wasted/rotted away. In other words, the

AARP was murdering Captain Stocking to make a statement about not murdering people.

It was a confusing time.

"I think the new Pirate King should be Tobias Teach," said another pirate stoutly. "To carry on the legacy of his pa."

"But he's not even a captain. He's a navigator. So, according to the rules, he can't enter the contest."

"But mayhap he could be a captain."

"Babybeard? No way. He can't even grow a beard now, can he?"

"He might, once he's older. I bet he'll be just as hairy, in the end. He could shape up into a fine captain, given time."

"ARRR!" said another pirate, scowling, and Jack took this to mean that he didn't approve of Tobias as a choice, either.

"But he hasn't got time, has he? The contest is happening now. So it can't be Teach."

"But if not Teach, then who should we root for?" the first pirate asked.

That seemed to be the question of the hour.

"Me," came a raspy voice. "You root for me."

Everyone in the pub swiveled to look at the man sitting farther down the bar. He was a rough-looking fellow, true enough, and he certainly did have a beard, albeit a short one.

Jack shivered. "Who is *that*?" he whispered to Bonn. "His voice sounds familiar."

Bonn scoffed. "Probably because you just heard him in a

shouting match with Bess, at Blackbeard's funeral. That's Vane."

"Yes, I'm Charles Vane," said the man, again with the smoky voice. (*Maybe he has a cold*, Jack thought.) "And I said it today, and I'll say it until the day I die and go down to Davy Jones's locker, pirates do not retire!"

Who was Davy Jones? Jack wondered. And what was in his locker? And how was that relevant?

"But what about the AARP?" someone asked.

Vane suddenly grabbed his pistol and fired it, obscuring the room with a puff of smoke. Then the smoke cleared, and the framed portrait of the shaggy white dog that was mounted over the bar fell heavily to the floor.

The pirates in the room gave a collective gasp. "He shot the dog!"

Vane kicked the portrait aside. (Thereby kicking the dog—we know, he's a monster. Thankfully no real dogs were hurt in the making of this book.) "I'm the captain of the *Ranger*!" he yelled.

"Okay, okay, we've got it," a pirate said. "We all already knew that you were 'very scary Captain Vane, captain of the *Ranger*.' You're badass. We're aware. What do you want?"

"I'm the captain of the *Ranger* for now," Vane said, "but soon—mark my words—I'm going to be the Pirate King." He took a long drink from his mug of rum, then wiped his mouth on the back of his hand and scowled. "And I'm going to be a better Pirate King than Blackbeard ever was. He was too soft, Blackbeard. Too willing to negotiate and ingratiate himself with the various authorities who would see our way of life come to an end. He was mad, too—everyone knows it. But I'm sharp enough, and strong enough, and bold enough to lead us into a new era of piracy. And so I will. I swear it. I'll be the king."

A murmur rose among the collected pirates in the bar.

"And the first order of business," Vane continued, "will be to take care of this damn woman problem we're having." He sneered. "Women, thinking they can rise above their natural place in the world. Talking back. Embarrassing you in front of your coworkers. Disguising themselves and hiding among us." He took another drink. "When I'm the Pirate King, I'll root them out, one by one, and they'll get what's coming to them."

Jack met Bonn's eyes, which were blazing with fury. He half expected her to leap up the way she had with that bloke only moments ago, punch Vane in the nose, and throw him out. She wanted to; he could see that by the stiff set of her shoulders, the tightness of her jaw. But she did not move from her place at the bar this time.

"Do you see?" she said quietly. "A woman hater."

Jack did see. If this man had his way, if he "rooted out" all the women, he'd surely discover that Mary was a woman. (Vane already knew quite well that Mary was a woman, dear reader, but Jack didn't know that he knew, or he would have been even more worried about her.) "What can we do?" he whispered.

Bonn finished off her rum in one long gulp and tossed a coin to Maggie. "We go to Okra Hill to find your cousin." She jumped to her feet. "Let's go."

She didn't spare a second look at Vane as she strode from the bar. Jack had to run to catch up.

They walked north toward the harbor, ARRRing at the various pirates they encountered along the way, stepping over drunks and around puddles of dubious liquid that was pooled here and there in the street. On any other evening, Jack would have stopped to admire the sights—like the red petticoat hanging on a clothesline between two brothels, the color so bright and perfect—but tonight he just silently followed along behind Bonn as she strode toward Okra Hill, lost in his own thoughts.

He'd felt a bit hurt, he could admit to himself, when he and Mary had been reunited. He'd thought he was her best friend and closest confidant, and yet she'd been content to let him think her dead for all this time. (He couldn't wait to tell his mother, who would also be shocked at this revelation.) And now Mary had a new best friend, so she didn't need Jack anymore. She'd seemed happy enough to see him again, but then she hadn't sought him out since learning of Blackbeard's death. They hadn't truly had a chance to talk or catch up about things. She was so focused on Tobias now.

Jack didn't consider himself to be the jealous type, but the situation niggled at him. He didn't like it. And he didn't like that he didn't like it.

But he liked the thought of Mary outed and humiliated, maybe even hurt or killed, even less. Vane clearly had to be stopped.

They came around a corner, and the street started to incline up a steep hill, topped by the overlooking fort. Okra Hill.

"What do you think," Bonn said, "should we start knocking on doors?"

But Jack had a better plan.

"Mary!" he called out in Merish, turning in a wide circle. *"Oh, Mary!"*

"Mary, oh Mary," he used to call out to her when they were both minnows and he'd wanted to play. And then she would inevitably appear out of a side door of her father's palace, a slip of a Mer with her long blondish hair and bright eyes, and they would take hands and swim off together. To explore a sunken ship, perhaps. Or to work in her garden, chatting all the while about humans and questions they had about their world. Or to curl around a book together, devouring and deciphering it, before the sea disintegrated the fragile pages.

But this time there was no answer to his call.

Perhaps he wasn't being loud enough. He took a deep breath. Concentrated his Mer voice.

"MARY! COME OUT, COME OUT, WHEREVER YOU ARE!"

"Gah, Jack! What the fish?" A door farther up the street banged open, and Mary rushed out, holding her hands over her ears, even though her ears had nothing to do with the noise Jack had made in her head. She spotted him. *"WHAT?!"*

"We need to talk to you. It's important."

He became aware that Bonn was gazing at him strangely.

"Oh look, there's Mary right over there!" he cried, pointing at his irate cousin standing in the doorway of a charming little sea shack. "Hooray! We've come to the right place. Mary! Hello, cousin! How lucky that we were able to find you. May we have a word?"

She stared at him, too, for a moment, deciding. Then she sighed. "It's been a long day, but . . . of course. Come in."

She led them both inside the shack, where Jack's eyes cut straight to Tobias Teach, who was lying on a bed in one corner of the room, reading a book.

"So you live together," Jack surmised.

Tobias swung his legs around and got up. "Hello again." He looked better than he had at the funeral, but still a bit peaked.

"What are you reading?" Jack inquired.

"*Robinson Crusoe*," Tobias answered.

"And what's that about?"

"A man stranded on an island," Tobias said.

"Ah!" Jack said approvingly. "Is he saved by a mermaid?"

Tobias's brow crinkled. "A mermaid? No."

"*He doesn't know about the Mer,*" Mary informed him tensely.

"*So you can't be that close,*" Jack replied. "*If he doesn't know who you truly are.*"

"*He knows who I am, just not who I was.*" Mary glanced briefly at Bonn. "*Does she know?*"

Jack's face heated. "*She does not. Yes. I see that I am being a tad hypocritical. What the humans call a pot and kettle situation. My bad.*"

During this silent conversation, Tobias had been explaining the plot of *Robinson Crusoe*. "So I'm not going to finish it. It turns out I hate the title character. I'm not into the whole 'white man's burden' thing."

"Same," said Mary.

"Amen," said Bonn.

"I agree, one hundred percent," said Jack. (He had no idea what they were talking about.)

An awkward silence fell.

"I didn't get a chance to say this earlier," Jack said after a moment, "but I'm terribly sorry about the untimely death of your father. We both are. Aren't we, Bonn?"

"Sorrier than you know," she muttered.

"Uh, thank you," Tobias said.

Mary gestured to the rickety table in the center of the room, and Jack and Bonn sat. Tobias joined them.

There was another awkward silence.

"So," said Mary, "why are you here?"

"Couldn't I just be here to visit you?" Jack said.

Bonn gave him a sharp look. "We're here because something has to be done about Captain Vane."

He loved that about Bonn. She just came out with it.

Mary and Tobias exchanged a look Jack couldn't interpret. "I'm not sure what you mean," Mary said. "Vane hasn't been performing his duties lately, but—"

"He means to become the Pirate King." Bonn leaned forward urgently. "And once he gains that title, he will seek out and remove all the women pirates, even the ones hiding themselves. So you're in danger, lass."

Mary looked at Jack, betrayal in her blue eyes. "You told her," she said softly.

Bonn scoffed. "I figured it out meself. It weren't hard to do, really."

"And you know this about Vane, how?" Mary asked.

"We heard him say so."

"He talks big," Mary said, almost like she wanted to argue.

"He seemed to mean it," Jack said.

"Vane cannot become the Pirate King," Bonn said. "I think we can agree that such a thing would be disastrous for us all."

"But how could we stop him?" Tobias asked. "He's stubborn. If he takes it into his head to—"

"He must be removed," Bonn said. "Someone else must become the captain of the *Ranger*."

This sounded like an excellent idea to Jack. Why hadn't he thought of it? Oh, wait. "How does one become the captain of a pirate ship? Some kind of duel to the death, I assume?" Gulp.

Tobias shook his head. "The captaincy is decided by an election, and every member of the crew, from the quartermaster to the lowliest cabin boy, no matter their color or creed or social standing, gets to vote. At least in that regard there's equality among us. Which is why this notion of a Pirate King is so backward," he added.

Mary was gazing hard at Bonn. "And who, pray tell, do you have in mind?"

Bonn stole a glance at Tobias. Then they were all looking at him.

"No," he said fiercely. "I won't do it, and you can't make me. Find yourself another bloke."

"A bloke?" Jack's eyes widened as he realized he was the only other bloke present. "What, *me*? I just got here."

The corner of Bonn's mouth turned up into a smile. "You'd do fine. You're bonny as blazes and everyone likes you. But no, you're not qualified to be a captain, given that you've never even been a pirate before."

"It should be Mary," Tobias said suddenly.

"It should be me," Mary repeated, sitting up straight. "I'll become captain."

There was a glint in Bonn's eyes now that suggested to Jack that this was what she'd been intending all along. And he had a feeling that this was only the beginning of her nefarious plan.

"Now that's an idea I could get behind," she said.

Mary
SEVEN

"The crew of the *Ranger* is fifty-seven men," Tobias reminded them the next morning, as he, Mary, and Jack strode up the gang-plank and onto the ship. (Jack was along because he'd said he wanted to see where Mary worked, but Anne couldn't come, even though she'd clearly wanted to, since there was no way her "saucy lad" disguise would hold.) "By my tally," Tobias continued, "I figure about thirty of them will already vote for you outright. That's a majority, which is all you technically require to take the captaincy, but we need more like fifty, I reckon. We want to win by a wide margin."

"I know," Mary said tightly.

She was a bundle of jangled nerves this morning. Still, part of her had known that it would eventually come to this. All the time she'd been rising up in the ranks on the *Ranger*, Vane had been, well, falling. She'd been considering ousting him ever since this Bess business had begun to affect his work. Taking the captaincy from one of the most infamous pirates in the Caribbean was a huge risk, especially for someone like Mary, but now, the risk of *not* taking the captaincy felt greater. If what Jack and Anne said was true, and Vane entered the Pirate King contest, he would likely win. And if Vane won the contest and scoured all the pirate crews in search of hidden women, he'd find her out. Then she knew what would happen. Vane would trot her out in front of everybody, unmask her, and make an example of her. Whether that was by plank, gibbet, or being burned at the stake—she was a woman, after all, and she'd been fooling men all this time, so why not accuse her of being a witch?—Vane would certainly humiliate her before he executed her.

Vane could not become Pirate King.

Which meant Vane could not be allowed to enter the contest.

So he must be removed as captain.

And Mary should be the one to do it.

"We'll win them over," Tobias insisted. "You just have to make your case."

"I know." She tried to smile to reassure him—or maybe to reassure herself. She wasn't looking forward to this part, the campaigning bit, but it had been the same when she'd been elected quartermaster—except that Vane had been public in his support of her, therefore putting his thumb on the scale, so to speak.

And this time she'd be betraying him.

It's him or me, she thought.

"And then, when we've got the numbers," Tobias went on, "we'll call for a vote."

"All right," she said. "Let's get this over with."

The first pirate on their list was Nine Toes McGee. He looked up from his mop as the group approached him. "What's this about? I've got work to do."

Mary took a deep breath. She could do this.

"It's not an easy job, is it?" she said. "Swabbing, I mean." Actually, it *was* an easy job. You just mopped the deck over and over again.

Nine Toes shook his head. "The deck is always full of salt. And just when I've got it clean, the men step all over the wet boards. They leave boot prints on my nice clean deck."

"You work hard." Mary clapped the man on the shoulder and leaned in. "How's Tallulah? Are you still seeing her? Are you treating her right?"

He met her eyes, startled. "I'm trying."

"I'm sure your portion of the booty's not stretching far enough, what with flowers to buy your sweetheart and romantic dinners to pay for."

Carefully, Nine Toes said, "My portion would be fine if it weren't paid to me in fruit."

Mary gave a sympathetic nod. "Tallulah's not a fan of bananas, huh?"

Nine Toes blinked a few times. "She's more of an apple lass."

"Well, what if you had one *and a half* portions of our next prize? And every prize thereafter?"

Nine Toes narrowed his eyes. "I need more than a half. I can't take a pay cut."

"No, no," Mary hurried to explain. "You'll get your one portion—and then a half portion more. It's a raise. Because you're such a vital part of our crew."

Silence. Nine Toes started counting on his fingers. Then his toes. "So I can pay my bills and then have some left over?"

"Yes," Tobias said. "For Tallulah."

"And how would I go about getting this raise?" Nine Toes now had a greedy gleam in his eyes.

Mary and Tobias exchanged glances. Then Tobias said cheerily, "Just vote for Mark."

There was a pause. Finally Nine Toes nodded. "I see. Well, Mr. Read, I always liked you. You've got my vote."

"See?" said Tobias as they walked away. "This is going to work."

"It's such an interesting way to choose a leader," Jack said. "But it's not very fast, is it?"

"It's as fast as we make it," Mary said. "So help me convince these men to vote for me."

"Good point." He turned to Tobias. "Who's next?"

Mr. Child and Mr. Swift were sitting together in the galley eating their bowls of mystery-meat stew (it smelled terrible) when Jack, Mary, and Tobias came marching in.

"If you vote for Mark as captain, we'll get a better cook," Jack said right off.

Mr. Child scowled. "Hey, I'm the cook!"

"He means better tools for the cook," Mary said quickly. "Better ingredients, fresher, more identifiable meat, maybe even some vegetables."

Mr. Child scratched his cheek. "I would like to serve some beets now and then. I like beets."

"And so you shall have them," Mary promised, and continued the list. "So, better cook . . . ing. And Fridays, you can wear your comfortable clothes instead of your fancy ones."

"We're calling it 'casual Fridays,'" Tobias added.

Mr. Swift, the ship's musician, frowned. "But what if you've only got the one cardigan?"

"Then you can do casual hair," Jack suggested.

"And what else?" asked Swift.

"Monthly prosthetic maintenance," Mary said. She was starting to get the hang of this.

"Prost a what now?"

"Like your hook." Mary gestured to the bent-up curl of rusty metal on the end of Swift's arm. "You bring that in, and we'll get it shined up like new. Once a month. And the same would go for anyone with a peg leg, or an eye patch that needs darning."

"That sounds like my wildest dreams," said Swift.

"And"—Mary lifted her chin, because this was the winning promise, she just knew—"free parrot training."

Both men's faces lit up. "Free training?" said Child. "Croaky's always trying to peck me eyes out. And whistles when I'm trying to sleep."

"All things that could be remedied with training. So can I count on your vote?"

"Aye!" said Mr. Child. "You've been doing the job anyway, while Captain Vane's been moping about his lady love."

"Aye, aye!" said Swift. "In my opinion, Bess and Captain Vane are never ever getting back together."

Mary dug around in her pockets. "Say, would you two mind wearing these?"

Both men nodded eagerly, and Mary handed them each a little button that bore the words VOTE FOR MARK.

The group continued down Tobias's list for the next hour, striking up conversations, handing out buttons, and making promises Mary hoped she would remember later. All in all she found the men receptive to the idea of her replacing Captain Vane. There were only a few holdouts.

Like the beady-eyed twitchy-type fellow by the name of Coop Cooper, who, yes, was the ship's cooper. When they spoke about parrot training and better cooking and casual Fridays, he didn't blink an eye. He didn't even seem convinced when they offered to raise his pay.

"I like Vane," he said roughly. "I know him. I don't know about you. I'll vote for whichever man won't get us killed." His beady eyes cut to Tobias. "There's that Jonathan Barnet fellow roving about, sinking ships and killing pirates. Not even Blackbeard was safe."

Tobias's posture went stiff, his expression guarded, but if he had anything to say about Coop's lack of decorum, he didn't say it out loud.

"Aye," Mary said carefully. "Barnet is bad news. And he knows about Vane, too, as Vane's one of the more notorious pirates in these waters. He'll be gunning for him. Which is," she added quickly, "no fault of Vane's. But if Barnet has it out for our current captain, then we've always got a target on our backs."

Coop nodded slowly. "So if I vote for you as captain, you won't go getting us caught?"

"Definitely not," Mary promised.

"Mark is smart and careful," Jack said.

"A real pirate's pirate," Tobias added.

"Then I suppose you've got my vote." Coop accepted a button and went off.

"He seems like a good fellow," Jack said.

Tobias made some kind of noncommittal noise and checked the list. "Coop Cooper was the last one. We've got forty-nine yeas, by my count, which should do it. Now we just need to call for a vote." He looked at Mary. "Are you ready?"

She swallowed. "I—"

Just then, the door to the captain's quarters burst open, and Captain Vane burst out.

Mary went motionless. "Finrot," she muttered. She'd assumed that Vane was still on land, either drinking himself into a stupor somewhere or fighting things out with poor Bess.

"Look alive, boys!" Vane yelled, and everyone aboard the ship swiveled toward the sound of his voice. "I have an announcement to make!"

"Double finrot." There was only one kind of announcement Vane would be making at a time like this.

Vane cleared his throat, which didn't help his raspy voice in the slightest. "As you may have already heard, I've decided to enter us in the Pirate King contest! As soon as the AARP puts out the sign-up sheet, the *Ranger* is going to be at the top! And we're going to win this, lads!"

"So . . ." Nine Toes scratched his head. "We'll all be the Pirate King?"

"I don't see how that works," muttered Swift. "Can we all be kings?"

On the quarterdeck, Vane sighed. "No, you dolts. *I'm* going to be the Pirate King. And you'll be my subjects."

"Oh." A few of the crew exchanged nervous glances.

"Or most of you will." Vane swept his gaze across the deck, looking at all the men in turn. "My first order of business will be to do some housekeeping. Because there are some here who don't belong on a pirate ship."

Was it Mary's imagination or did his gaze linger on her a little longer than the others?

A shiver marched up her spine, but there was no way he could know about her. No way at all.

Mary took a long breath, trying to calm her fear. And excitement. And nerves. And the tiny sliver of guilt over what she intended to do to Captain Vane, who'd generally been good to her. But in this moment she steeled herself against him. If he'd known she was a woman, he wouldn't have been so kind. Plus, his first name was *Charles*.

She felt the familiar surge of anger then. There was always some Charles telling her what he thought she could or couldn't do. Some Charles to make some rule restricting her.

She was going to stop Vane from making rules for *all* pirates even if it killed her.

And the crew would be better off with her, she told herself.

They'd all be better off.

Time was running short.

It was now or never.

It's him or me, she thought again. *I have to do it. I must.*

And this time she could do it.

"And the second order of business," Captain Vane was saying, "is to get rid of the AARP. Because pirates don't retire. They die, me hearties. They die in violent, bloody deaths. It's the only dignified way for pirates to go out."

"Or," Mary said, because she knew her moment had arrived, "we could not die. Not for a while, anyway. We could live. That's what I would offer you, if I were captain."

The crew looked back and forth between Mary and Vane.

"Wait," Vane said. "What did you say?"

"I'm calling for a vote," Mary said, her voice ringing loud and clear on the quarterdeck.

Vane's eyes narrowed. "You. You want to be captain. You cannot be serious."

"I am quite serious." Mary nodded at Tobias, Jack, Nine Toes, Mr. Swift, Mr. Child, and her other supporters. Someone rang the bell, calling for all hands on deck, and within minutes, everyone had gathered. A good many were wearing VOTE FOR MARK buttons. "It is my assertion that you, Charles Vane, are not fit to serve as captain. For weeks, you've hidden away in your cabin, moping about your broken heart. Well, I've had my heart broken before. It didn't kill me. What's more, it didn't make me neglect my duties. But you've been absent during raids and fights, leaving others to do your work for you. Therefore, I assert that I should take command of the *Ranger*."

"Preposterous!" Vane sputtered. "The men will never—"

Tobias stepped forward. "Time to vote, mates! Let every man who wishes for Mark Read to be captain of the *Ranger*, instead of Charles Vane, raise his hand or hook."

Mary closed her eyes and took a long, fortifying breath. *Please be me. Please be me.*

"That settles it!" she heard Tobias say. "The decision is clear."

Mary opened her eyes. All around her were raised hands (and hooks). One guy had even lifted a live chicken into the air. It had a VOTE FOR MARK button stuck into its breast feathers.

"Begawk!" it shrieked.

She'd done it. She'd really done it.

"Congratulations, Captain," Tobias said, clapping her on the back. "I knew you could."

"I swear to be the best captain possible," Mary called out. "I know I made you promises. I will keep them. Things are going to be better on this ship. We're going to fight smart, harm few, and score big!"

A cheer went up.

"No!" The shout came from Vane, who'd been staring at all the raised hands (and hooks, and chicken) in disbelief. He reached into his vest for his fancy pistol, pulled it out, and took aim right at Mary.

Everyone froze.

"You'll find it difficult to captain a ship with an iron ball lodged in your head," Vane rasped.

Mary lifted her hands, but she also started talking, quickly, in case Vane's trigger finger got itchy. "That's undoubtedly true," she said. "But do you have an iron ball for everyone's head?"

The men who'd all been raising their hands (and hooks and chicken) a few minutes ago were now raising their cutlasses (and pistols and angry chicken). Mary felt relief and gratitude dissolve her momentary flash of fear. They meant it. These men wanted her to be the captain, and they were willing to defend her.

Just to be safe, though, Mary grabbed Vane's gun-toting arm and looped a rope around his hand. She nodded at Tobias, and suddenly Vane was upside down, hanging by one arm twenty feet above them, his pistol lying uselessly on the deck.

"See Mr. Vane off the ship, if you please, Mr. Quint," Mary directed.

"Aye, Captain," Mr. Quint said.

"You'll pay for this, Read!" Vane yelled after they brought him down. Then, when he was on his feet again, he leaned toward Mary and lowered his voice, so the painful rasp was extra menacing. Gold glinted in his teeth as he snarled at her. "I know your secret, Read. You're one of those playing dress-up in a *comely pirate costume.*"

He knew.

How?

Mary's blood felt like ice in her veins, but she kept her expression neutral, her voice equally low. "It doesn't matter what you think you know. You're not the captain anymore. No matter what claims you make about me, the crew won't have you back. Not after you repeatedly proved yourself unfit."

His expression faltered. "I'll get them back," he said.

"Like you're getting Bess back?"

His face paled. "I'll get my revenge upon you, *Mary* Read. I swear it. At the right moment, I'll expose you for the fraud you are."

"Yeah, good luck with that." She forced herself to sound casual about this, like she wasn't worried, like her heart didn't feel like it was about to beat itself out of her chest. She jerked her head at Quint. "Get him off my ship."

Quint grabbed Vane and escorted him from the *Ranger.* Mary could hear his raspy ranting all the way down to the dock.

"I'll get you, my pretty," he called, "and your little navigator, too!"

"What was that about?" Tobias asked. "What did he say to you?"

"It's nothing," she said. "Nothing I can't handle," she amended, because that felt true, at least.

But she couldn't shake the feelings that she'd just made things worse.

Mary went first to the captain's quarters, where she threw open the windows to let in some fresh air. After Vane, the cabin reeked of spilled rum and regret. Oh, and body odor. Then she spent the better part of the morning directing her crew (her! crew!) here and there, getting Vane's belongings cleared out to make room for her own things: some books (her TBR was a mile long), a whetstone (for keeping her cutlass sharp), and a blank book to serve as a captain's log. And then, when the men were finished carrying a box of her clothes in, she realized the fanciest, most luxurious part about being the captain: private chamber pot.

It was good to be captain.

A knock sounded on the door. "Come in!" she called, and Jack entered.

He assessed the space with a low whistle. "Very nice, cousin. The captaincy looks good on you."

Mary lifted her chin. "Thanks. I don't feel ready to celebrate just yet, but—"

"Are you kidding? We have to celebrate! Cabin boy to captain in a year. That has to be some kind of record."

It was, Mary thought. But she couldn't shake the unease that had filled her when Captain Vane had said he knew her secret.

"And while we're celebrating," Jack went on, "we should get you some curtains for that window. Some yellow ones, maybe, to brighten up the place. And perhaps a bouquet of flowers to keep everything smelling fresh."

Mary rubbed her temples. "Jack, why do I feel like you're trying to butter me up for something?"

"Butter you—" He frowned. "What an interesting expression. I don't think I've ever tried butter before. Perhaps, now that Bonn and I are pirates, we could consider taking a ship carrying butter?"

"Now that . . ." Mary shook her head. "Anne isn't a pirate. You can be, if you want, but Anne is not currently allowed to be a pirate."

"But you could change the rules," he said. "Isn't that so? You could decide that women are allowed to be part of the crew."

"I can't change the rules *immediately*," Mary clarified. "Jack, I just got elected. It's too fast."

"Yes, you can." Jack crossed his arms. "Bonn said all that must happen is for the new rules to be voted upon. And if you just quietly remove the parts we don't like—and never mention that everyone agreed to rules that *don't* prevent women from being pirates—you'll have done the job without ruffling any feathers. That's another interesting expression, isn't it? Ruffling feathers.

What kind of bird are they referring to, I wonder."

"Jack."

"Mary." He took a step toward her. "This is all Bonn wants in life!"

"Being captain isn't enough!" Mary shouted. At Jack's hurt expression, she closed her eyes and attempted to school the frustration from her face. "My position is still precarious," she tried to explain. "They could hold another vote at any time, and then I'd be out. They're giving me a chance to be their captain, but I haven't proven myself yet."

"Then do it," he said. "Prove yourself."

"I *will*."

"Do it now," Jack pressed.

"Oh right now, right this minute?" she asked sarcastically. "How?"

He bit his lip thoughtfully, then nodded. "Enter the Pirate King contest and change the rules for everyone, including Bonn. If you become the Pirate King, they'll have to—"

"I agreed to be captain," Mary said sharply. "I didn't agree to enter the contest."

But at the thought of the contest—and her newfound eligibility for the title—something deep inside her began to stir.

"You *should* be the Pirate King," Jack argued. "You'd be a strong, fair king. Plus, you actually are royalty, so you're more qualified for the role than any of these simple humans. Think about all the good you could do."

"It's too public. I'd be found out." She lowered her voice. "Vane *knows* about me, Jack. I don't know how he figured it out, but Vane knows I'm a woman. And he's already threatened me. If I enter the contest—he'll ruin me. I will never be allowed on another ship. And where will *that* leave your precious Anne Bonny, or any other woman who wants to be a pirate? Let me prove myself to the crew the normal way: we'll capture ships, find some treasure, and stay out of trouble with the law."

Jack shook his head. "If Vane already knows, then you have no choice but to win the contest." Before she could argue again, Jack turned and marched toward the door. "I'm going to see Bonn. We need to decide what to do."

"About?"

He threw a look over his shoulder. "You."

The door clicked shut behind him.

Mary allowed herself, finally, to breathe. Her hands were shaking a little. Her heart was still thrumming in her ears. So she did what she always did when she was stressed out. She lit a candle, curled up on her new fancy bed with the feather pillows, and read a book.

Or she tried to, anyway.

Jack doesn't understand, she thought to herself as she turned a page and then forgot the first part of the sentence and had to look back at the previous page again. It wasn't like she got any joy from denying Anne a place on her crew. She wasn't trying to keep all the pirating for herself. It might be nice, in fact, to have a few more women on board the ship. But Jack was demanding she make *instant* change when she was the one who'd face the biggest consequences.

Jack just couldn't understand what it meant to be a woman and a human at the same time.

"Littlest!"

Mary jerked, dropping the book onto her face.

She pushed it aside and listened. Perhaps she'd imagined someone calling to her.

"Littlest! I know you can hear me, young lady! Get out here right now if you know what's good for you!"

Mary groaned. That definitely wasn't her imagination.

It was her father.

She heaved herself up and stepped out onto the main deck, where her men were swabbing, carting bananas back and forth, and taking inventory of their supplies. Nothing seemed out of the ordinary.

"There's a cove on the north side of town. Meet me there so I don't have to yell."

Oh, that definitely wasn't happening.

She would, she decided, ignore him. It was the only way.

"I see you ignoring me, young lady. Don't make me turn that ship upside down."

Just then, waves splashed higher on the *Ranger*'s hull, even though the sky was perfectly clear and there hadn't been any wind. The ship rocked up and down, and water trickled along the deck, exactly where Nine Toes had just finished swabbing.

"Argh!" Nine Toes yelled, hurrying to clean the water before it dried and left a crust of salt.

"Odd," Tobias said, coming to stand beside her. "Perhaps there's a storm coming? No clouds, though." He peered into the distance, frowning.

"I'm sure it's fine," Mary said. "We just need to focus on making ready to sail. Those merchant ships won't capture themselves."

"Littlest!"

Mary groaned. He was going to keep yelling at her—and maybe sinking her ship a little—until she agreed.

"Is everything all right?" Tobias asked. "I saw Jack leaving the cabin earlier. He looked upset."

"He wants me to enter the Pirate King contest now that I'm eligible."

Tobias's brown eyes widened. "That's the worst idea I've ever heard. Second only to the idea of *me* being the Pirate King."

Mary snapped her gaze to him.

"Not," he said quickly, "that you aren't capable of such a thing. But pirates don't—"

"Need a king," Mary finished. "Yes, I know. Trust me, I have no intention of trying to become the Pirate King. Managing this lot is going to be enough to keep me on my toes."

"Right," Tobias said. "Well, I'm glad that's settled."

But it wasn't the Pirate King that was consuming Mary's thoughts right now. It was a different kind of king entirely.

"Get to the cove right now or I will sink every ship in the harbor!" Another

wave—a bigger wave—punctuated his threat. The pirates were all drenched from the knees down.

"Fine!" Mary shouted in Merish. *"Stop hurling water at my ship!"*

She hated giving in to him, but what choice did she have?

What the Sea King wanted, the Sea King got.

Dread in the pit of her stomach, she marched toward the gangplank. Tobias trailed after her, and she stopped. "I need to go speak with my—myself," she said. "I need to think about something. Alone, I mean. Mind the crew, won't you?"

"That's Quint's job. But all right." He gave her a tight smile, but she didn't see it, because she was already stomping down the docks and practicing what she would say to her father—something so biting it would send him swimming back to Underwhere in abject shame.

Perhaps something like, "You're not the boss of me!"

No, that wasn't good enough.

Unfortunately, by the time she reached the cove, she hadn't thought of anything better.

The cove was quite nice, it turned out, sheltered from the city by a large hill and scattered palm trees, with a gentle slope of the land into the water. Seagulls called above, while crabs burrowed through the sand. And out in the water, not ten feet away, was Mary's father. The Sea King himself.

For a moment, she felt like a minnow again.

"Hello, Littlest," he called.

Mary stared out over the water. It was hard to believe that, after two whole years, her father was *right there*. He hadn't changed much. He still had a head of abyss-black hair, jellyfish-pale skin, and crab-legs around his eyes (like crow's-feet but in Mer). And he still had that commanding presence, an aura of power that radiated from him in all directions, like the wind itself was waiting for his orders. And it kind of was. He was, after all, the ruler of the ocean.

Mary swallowed.

I hate you, she'd said the last time they'd seen each other. *You don't understand me.*

Yeah. He was probably still angry at her. Mer lived for three hundred years, and the Sea King was nearly two hundred. That was a lot of time to perfect the art of holding a grudge.

"Come here," he demanded. *"I want to see you up close."*

Mary considered saying no, making him drag himself up the shore and flop around on land like a beached whale. Just because he was king didn't mean she should acquiesce to his every command.

Then she recalled a moment when she'd been just a minnow. She'd escaped from Karen's not-so-watchful eye and gone off exploring by herself, immediately getting trapped inside a closet. For what seemed like ages (but probably hadn't been more than a quarter hour), she'd struggled with the door and called for help, until finally she'd exhausted herself. Sea foam seemed imminent.

But then she'd heard her father's panicked calling—*"Littlest! Littlest!"*—and her heart had soared with hope and relief. At her answering cry, he'd burst in and scooped her up. Safe. She'd been safe.

With a sigh, Mary removed her boots and stockings, then rolled up her trousers. Wet sand squished between her toes as she strode into the waves.

He watched her approach, his expression hard with judgment. *"You're looking well,"* he said as she got closer.

Quickly, she loosened her ponytail so the short strands of her hair covered up her earring. *"Life as a human has worked out for me,"* she replied. *"I'm happy here."*

He lifted an eyebrow. *"No hello? No 'nice to see you, Father'?"*

Well, she'd *run away from home.* To a completely different world. She hadn't planned to ever see him again. *"How did you know where to find me?"*

He shrugged. *"I have my ways."*

Silence stretched between them. (And it was a really big silence, as talking in Mer didn't make any sound.) He twisted his coral ring on his finger. Mary scratched the back of her neck.

"What do you want, Father?" she finally gathered courage enough to ask.

"I want you to come home. In fact, I demand it."

Ah. There was the father she knew.

Mary was shaking her head before he even finished telling her. *"I am not going home."*

He crossed his arms. *"Littlest—"*

"My name is Mary! Call me Mary."

A pained expression flashed over his face. *"Fine. Mary. Come home, Mary, to your family."*

To the family that had named her *Littlest*? To a world that made her feel small and silly for having different interests from everyone else? The only other Mer who'd ever understood Mary was Jack—and now he was here. So what was left for her back in Underwhere? Nothing.

"Also," her father added, *"Big Deal wants the crown. You should make things right with your sister and bring it back to her."*

"The crown?" Mary's face twisted while she tried to think of why Karen (aka Big Deal) thought she had their mother's crown.

Then she remembered the wedding.

She shook her head. *"I already looked for it when she asked. It wasn't there."*

The Sea King closed his eyes and blew out a long breath, as though mentally preparing himself for Karen's reaction to this news. Then he straightened. *"Littlest—"*

"Mary!" Ugh. Why couldn't he get it right?

"Mary, I mean. I was hoping that you'd want to return to us on your own. But I will force you if I must."

Mary scoffed. *"And then what? I drown? I'm a human now! Unless you got Aunt Witch to make a potion to change me back."* Mary really hoped Aunt Witch hadn't made a potion to change her back.

"You won't drown. Someone will kiss you."

Mary's mouth dropped open. What he was talking about was the magic of "the mermaid's kiss," the gift of underwater breath that a Mer could bestow upon a human. Mary had used it once, on Charles, when he'd been drowning in the storm. It lasted, according to the latest Mer research, for twenty-seven minutes before you had to kiss the human again.

So what her father was proposing was that somebody—who? the royal daughter kisser?—would kiss Mary every twenty-seven minutes for the rest of her life. Which could possibly be for the next *283 years*.

She'd rather die.

"I won't go back, and you can't make me. This is my home now. I'm making a difference here."

He rolled his eyes. *"By being a pirate? Oh yes, I know what you are now. A thief on a boat?"*

"I'm the captain of a ship!" she countered. *"I matter to people here."*

"You matter to people at home, too."

"Not like I do Above. People rely on me. And no one tells me what to do. Not anymore."

"At home, you're a princess."

"And here I'll be the Pirate King!"

The words were out before she realized.

"Is that so?" asked the Sea King, sounding amused. *"You think you can be a king?"*

"I will be," Mary said. *"By this time next month, I'll be the ruler of all the pirates on the seas."*

Her father studied her for a moment, as though assessing whether he believed she could do it. He probably didn't. She was still *Littlest* to him. The baby of the family. No one expected her to do anything great.

Then he reached into his kelp pouch at his hip and removed a small hourglass, made with driftwood and mother-of-pearl, filled with sparkling sand. One chamber had a puffy cloud painted on it, while the other had a series of waves. He spoke a few words to it—murmuring in Merish—then handed it to her. It was warm.

"What is this?" she asked warily.

"You have until the full moon," he said.

"What happens at the full moon?" The moon wasn't visible currently. She would have to ask Tobias what phase it was now. He would know.

"I'll come back and take you home." He sighed. *"Little— Mary, my sweet minnow. I want you with me. I want to protect you from the big world."*

"I don't need your protection!"

"Prove it, then. Prove that you truly can do this all on your own. Become the Pirate King. Or say goodbye to the human world forever."

Then, before Mary could form any kind of response, the Sea King turned and swam away, creating a massive wave that completely doused Mary from head to toe.

"You don't understand anything!" she shouted in Merish. *"You're not the boss of me!"* But it was too late. He was already gone.

Dripping, Mary looked down at the little hourglass. It was small enough to fit in her palm, and no matter the way she held it, the sand ran from the cloud side to the wave side, defying gravity. It was magic, of course. Probably Aunt Witch's.

Mary hurled the hourglass far out into the water, where it disappeared beneath the waves. She didn't need his deadline. Or his permission. And once she was back on her ship, he wouldn't be able to find her. She'd keep her freedom.

Jaw and fists clenched, Mary marched awkwardly out of the water and pulled her stockings and boots back onto her wet feet. Then she unrolled her trousers and straightened all her clothes.

That was when she felt it. A small object in her pocket.

Grimacing, Mary pulled out the hourglass.

Experimentally, she hurled the hourglass into the ocean again.

And found it in her pocket.

Then she buried it in the sand.

And found it back in her pocket.

She even tried stomping on it and mixing the broken shards with someone's pile of trash.

But, of course, before she could take two steps away, it was in her pocket once more.

Which meant her father would (probably) always be able to find her. And when the sand had moved from one chamber to the other . . . he'd come to take her away from everything that mattered to her. Her ship. Her crew. Her friends.

And all the things she could accomplish here.

Being captain isn't enough.

Mary screamed silently for a few minutes, quietly shaking her fists and stomping her feet on the sand. Then, super-secret screaming fit complete, she combed back her hair into its neat ponytail.

"Fine," she grumbled, shoving the hourglass deep into her pocket again.

She would enter the Pirate King contest.

And she would win.

But first, she had to tell Tobias.

EIGHT

Tobias

"You want to WHAT?" Tobias wasn't sure he was hearing her right. "Why? Why would you do that?"

"It actually makes a lot of sense when you think about it," Mary argued from behind the privacy curtain.

No. Nothing about this made sense to Tobias. After winning the election, Mary had specifically told him that she was *not* going to enter the Pirate King contest. In fact, he believed her exact words had been, *Trust me, I have no intention of trying to become the Pirate King*. But then she had run off to *talk to herself* and had shown up at the shack close to dinnertime, salt crusting her clothes and hair, a fiery look in her eye.

Then she'd told him about her decision.

Tobias was still reeling.

Now Mary was behind the curtain, changing her clothes. (A fact that Tobias was trying not to think about.) "If I'm the Pirate King," she was saying, "then I can decree that all crews must accept women. They must compensate us as full members of the crew, too. Equal pay for equal work. Oh, and of course, women should have the right to vote in captaincy and quartermaster elections, same as any man."

Tobias wasn't sure it would be as simple as a decree, but Mary wasn't stopping even to breathe.

"Furthermore, if a woman has a child, she should be permitted to take some time off the ship—and then be welcomed back whenever she's ready. Men, too, you know? Just because they're pirates doesn't mean they don't want to spend time with their children."

"Mary," Tobias said, "where is all this coming from?"

"I didn't like everything about where I grew up," Mary said, "but they did have the right idea about a few things. And considering how pirates love to talk about how democratic and equal things are aboard a pirate ship—well, I have some notes."

Tobias rubbed his temples. *Where* was Mary from? He'd never heard of any place that was like this bastion of equality she was describing.

"Also"—Mary, fully dressed now, threw aside the curtain—"if I become Pirate King, that will get Jack off my back about Anne Bonny joining the crew, and everyone will be happy."

"Is that why you're doing this?" Tobias asked. "For your cousin and his sweetheart?"

She scoffed. "No, of course not. I'm doing it because it's the right thing to do."

Tobias scoffed right back at her. "It's a preposterous thing to do! It's risky and reckless and downright foolish!"

"I know that!" she snapped. "But that doesn't mean it's wrong. If I can do this—if I can really become the Pirate King—I can do more than just make things better for women. We can be smarter about piracy, more unified and organized in our efforts. We can temper the excessive violence, and champion real equality among men *and* women. We can do it together, Toby."

Tobias narrowed his eyes. "Who are you trying to convince? Me or you?"

"I'm not trying to convince anyone!"

"You practically just pitched me free parrot training," he countered.

"And it's still a good idea!" she cried.

Tobias crossed his arms. Then uncrossed them. "But it's dangerous, Mary. There will be so much scrutiny on you—on all the contestants, but you especially, since you *just* won the captaincy. What if they find out that you're a woman?"

A brief look of panic crossed her face, but she smoothed it away quickly. "No one's going to know," she said, which was so clearly a lie. (Mary was good at many things, but lying to him was not one of them.)

"Mary." He made his voice lower. "What is it?"

"It's nothing."

Tobias waited.

"All right, it's that Vane knows."

Tobias sat down on his bed. Hard. A few feet away, their table collapsed again. He ignored it. "How?" he asked hoarsely.

"I'm not sure," she admitted. "But that's what he told me after the election. He said he was going to wait for the right moment to expose me."

"Then we need to go." Tobias reached under his bed and pulled out his bag. They would have to pack light. It would mean leaving their books. A tragedy. But they could get more books where they were going.

They would need supplies—food, water, and a few changes of clothes.

"What are you doing?" Mary caught Tobias's arm just as he was shoving a rolled map into his bag. They would need maps, of course.

"We're getting out of here. I've been preparing for this. I have a plan. First, we'll make our way around all the islands—lead everyone on a wild-goose chase and get them lost. Then, when we've shaken any tails, we'll sail down to Aruba. There's no gold there— at least according to the Spanish—so no one will expect us there. I'll set up a small cartography business, and you can decide what you want to do when you're ready." He wrested his arm from her and pushed the map in with his change of clothes. "We'll have to change our names, naturally. I've been thinking about that, too. I might go by Leonardo—"

"No." Mary pulled the map out of his bag. "We're not going anywhere. We're not switching careers. And I am definitely not calling you Leonardo."

He grabbed the map back. "If Vane tells everyone what you are, that's it. You're done here."

They had to go. They had to get somewhere safe.

He'd already lost his family. He couldn't lose Mary, too.

Mary took the map again. "I'm not running away, Toby."

His jaw muscles flexed.

"I'm entering the Pirate King contest. And I'm going to win. It will all work out. You'll see."

She was being *awfully* naive, Tobias thought, which wasn't like her. "And do you think Vane is just going to sit on his hands in the meantime? You said he was going to wait for the right moment. When do you think that will be?"

She shook her head. "I don't know. After I win, when he thinks he'll be best able to ruin me. But by then I'll have won the hearts and minds of Nassau."

"Mary. You can't effect change—for anybody—if Vane tells them who you are."

Another look of panic crossed her face. Which meant that she was *aware* that what she was proposing was a bad idea. She was just ignoring the fact. But why?

"I have to do this, Tobias," she said urgently. "I have to. If I don't—I lose everything."

He frowned. "What does that mean?"

She put her hand into her pocket, worrying something there. "Nothing."

Another lie. An obvious one. But just because he knew when she was lying didn't mean he could read her thoughts to find the truth.

"Is there anything I can do to make you change your mind?" he asked tightly. "Anything at all?"

"I have to do this," she repeated. "Trust me."

Tobias closed his eyes and exhaled. "Fine. But if things start getting hairy with Vane, promise me you'll consider running. This is your freedom, Mary. Even if you don't value it, believe me when I say that I *do*."

Her gaze lifted, and their eyes met. "This is about my freedom," she said softly. "My freedom to be here. With you." She blinked a few times. "And everyone else, obviously. The ship, of course. Ah—" All at once, she seemed to realize that she was still holding on to his arm, and she had been the entire time they'd been going back and forth with the map.

She let go of his arm. The map fell to the floor.

They were still looking into each other's eyes.

Mary pulled away first. She always did. And just as she did, someone pounded on the door.

Tobias's cheeks were hot, like they'd been caught somehow. His breath felt thin and his heart beat too hard. And he couldn't stop thinking about what she'd just said. Her freedom to be here. With him.

The pounding on the door came again.

Mary looked just as disoriented as he felt, but she straightened her hat and said, "I'll answer it." Then she pulled away and called out, "I'm coming! Gah! Don't break my door down!"

She yanked open the door to reveal Jack and Anne.

"Oh good," Jack said. "You're here. And were you going somewhere?" His eyes cut to the half-packed bag on Tobias's bed, then the table still collapsed on the floor. "I hope everything's all right."

Tobias sighed. Everything had been right in his world—or fine, anyway—until this strange cousin of hers had shown up in their lives.

"Everything's fine," Mary said tightly. "What do you want?"

"We were just coming to tell you," Anne said quickly, "that sign-ups for the Pirate King contest are happening at the Scurvy Dog tonight, and if you were interested . . ."

"That is," Jack said, "if you've changed your mind."

Tobias rubbed his temples. So Jack didn't know. Which meant Mary hadn't gone to see him in the time she'd been talking to "herself." Something else must have happened. Something that made her go from laughing off the idea of becoming Pirate King to most desperately wanting it.

Mary and Jack exchanged one of those odd, silent looks they did sometimes. It was just as awkward now as it was every other time.

Then, without so much as tossing a look over her shoulder at Tobias, Mary said, "Yes. I have changed my mind."

"Three cheers for that!" Anne cried, and Jack smiled brightly, but Tobias's heart sank, even though he'd already known she wouldn't be talked out of it. When Mary decided she wanted something, truly wanted it, she was—how did Quint put it?—as tenacious as a dog with a tooth in a towel. She didn't give up. So there was nothing left for Tobias to do now but follow her to the Scurvy Dog.

They reached the Scurvy Dog and took a spot at the end of the line.

And what an impressive line it was, stretching nearly out the door. Everyone who was anyone (and a captain) was waiting to sign up. Ahead of them were Captains Obvious, Ahab, Penzance, Crunch, and half a dozen others Tobias knew. Anne pointed them out for Jack. And Mary simply stood with her hand in her pocket again.

What the heck was she holding on to? A coin, perhaps?

They shuffled forward as captain after captain wrote his name on the list of candidates.

"The formal announcements will be held at GIRLS GIRLS GIRLS tomorrow afternoon," Hornigold informed them from behind the table. Hook and Morgan were with him. They wore their fanciest waistcoats and hats, as though to demonstrate how seriously they were taking this competition. "Everyone who enters will be officially presented to the pirate community as a contestant and will be allowed an opportunity to speak and answer some basic questions about their qualifications. Oh, hello, *Captain* Read," he said as Mary reached the front. "Congratulations on your promotion."

If they were congratulating her, that meant Vane hadn't outed her. But Tobias didn't feel relieved at all. Vane would do it. That was a certainty. The only question was *when*.

"Thank you," Mary said to Hornigold. "I'm fortunate to have a crew who believes in me."

"And you'll be entering the contest?"

She nodded.

"Bold of you to enter when you got your position as captain only yesterday. I like it!" He jabbed a finger at the page. "Sign your name there."

Mary glanced back at Tobias just once. He tried to hold her eyes, tried to communicate one last time what a terrible, dangerous idea he thought this was. But if she understood his look, she ignored it.

Mary dipped a quill into the ink and signed her name on the paper.

Captain Mark Read, the Ranger.

There was no turning back now.

NINE

Jack

"Away to the cheating world go you," the man on the stage sang out. *"Where pirates all are well-to-do. But I'll be true to the song I sing, and live and die a Pirate King."*

This guy, Jack had to admit, was pretty good. He had a great voice, big and boomy, and a very snazzy outfit: tight black pants with a little red-and-black sash cinched around the waist, thigh-high shiny black boots, and a white billowy shirt open nearly to his belly button. (Centuries later, Halloween stores would sell this exact pirate costume.) It wasn't even really a captain's getup so much as it was a sexier version of the typical pirate garb, but it was getting the job done. The general noisy hubbub that was always happening inside GIRLS GIRLS GIRLS had quieted down. And now the audience was gazing raptly at Chest-Hair Guy as he sang his catchy little tune.

"I am the Pirate King!" he belted out. *"And it is, it is a glorious thing to be a Pirate King!"*

"Great, now I'm going to have this song stuck in me head all day," grumbled Bonn, dropping into the seat beside Jack. She made a face. "What's singing got to do with pirating? Nothing! This is a waste of time."

"Well, darling, it's entertaining," Jack said, glancing around at the pirates seated near them in the audience, who clapped their hands (and hooks) and tried to sing along. "And that makes this fellow—what's his name? Captain Penzance?—memorable. And you have to admit, he has style." He wondered fleetingly if Penzance was the man's first name or last name, and, if it was his last name, what his first name could be. Ted, perhaps? He had dark hair and eyes. Sure, this man was a pirate, and Jack's mysterious missing father was a sailor, but there wasn't such a big difference between the two professions. A man could easily start out as a sailor and end up as a pirate in the space of seventeen-odd years.

Jack leaned forward to scrutinize.

No, he decided. Even accounting for the difference in how humans aged compared to Mer, this man didn't seem old enough to be his father.

Jack didn't know whether to feel disappointed or relieved.

"For I am the Pirate KING!" Penzance sang out again, and suddenly the man's crew ran out from behind the curtains and sang, *"You are! Hurrah for our Pirate King!"* The room filled with their voices.

"Bah!" Bonn rolled her eyes. "How is he with a cutlass, is what I want to know. So he can sing a little. But how presumptuous is it to be already singing that he's the Pirate King?" She scoffed. "Cocky lout, isn't he? He's all flash and no bang. Your cousin, on the other hand, is the whole pirate package."

Jack smiled. That was one of the things he most loved about Bonn. She was loyal. And it warmed his heart that she'd now so clearly given her steadfast allegiance to Mary.

"Indeed," Jack said.

Bonn grinned slyly and reached into her inner coat pocket as if she had some great surprise to show him.

"What's that?" he asked. He adored surprises.

She opened her fist to reveal a handful of coins, plus a watch and a very nice set of nail clippers. "Pocket money."

"Pocket . . . money?" Jack was unaware that this was a category of money.

"It's twenty pieces of eight," Bonn clarified. "Plus some odds and ends I was able to scrape up."

"Where did you get it all?"

She glanced around and then returned the "pocket money" to her pocket. "Oh, you know. This pocket and that pocket."

Oh.

"Darling, I assure you, there's no need for that kind of petty thievery," Jack said. "I told you, I can get the thousand pieces of eight for us. I will handle this."

She arched an eyebrow at him skeptically. "Oh yes? How

much have you gathered so far?"

He swallowed. "Uh . . . oh, look, he's about to get to the big finale."

They watched as Captain Penzance worked himself up to a fever pitch. All his men formed a line with their arms linked together, kicking their legs out in sync.

"I AM THE PIRATE KING!" he sang/yelled.

Then he fell to his knees at the end of the stage, his hairy chest heaving.

That was it. End of song.

"Go on with your silly self, now!" yelled Bonn. "Boo! Boo, I say!"

But the rest of the audience had surged to their feet, clapping and cheering wildly. Several painted ladies threw certain articles of clothing at Captain Penzance, which he graciously accepted. He stood and bowed deeply, motioned to the men around him, then bowed again. More wild applause. More things (like roses and undergarments) thrown at him by the ladies.

The three captains of the AARP, who were seated behind a long table at the front of the crowd, also stood, and the audience sat down again and quieted to hear what they would say.

"What a spectacle that was!" Captain Hornigold cried.

"What pizzazz!" exclaimed Captain Hook, clapping so hard he almost stabbed himself in the hand. "Wow!"

But everyone knew the tough one to win over was Captain Morgan. He was more difficult to impress, partially because he was always drunk, and therefore not paying the best of attention, and also because he was just meaner than the other two.

Captain Morgan wiped his mouth on his sleeve. Belched. And then he said:

"Yes, that was quite the *performance*, even though the contestants are not required to give a performance here, Penzance. All you had to do was state your name and answer a few basic questions. It was overkill, don't you think?"

Penzance, his arms full of petticoats and petunias, wilted at his words, and the energy in the audience was greatly dampened.

"Boo!" Bonn yelled again.

But then Morgan smiled. "Even so, I would hate to be the poor bloke who has to follow *that*!"

Penzance grinned, tipped his hat at the audience one more time, and sashayed from the stage.

"Who's next?" Bonn asked.

Jack looked down at the paper in his lap, a rudimentary program. "Oh dear," he said. "I'm afraid it's us who's next."

Mary stepped out from behind the curtain.

Jack felt a burst of pride. She had allowed him to advise her about her outfit for today, and she was therefore wearing a simple but elegant white shirt he'd been able to scrounge up, plus a gold satin waistcoat, a deep blue damask overcoat with gold buttons and gold embroidered thread on the chest and arms, brushed black breeches, white silk stockings, and gleaming buckled boots. She had pulled her tawny hair into a short tail tied with a blue silk ribbon and topped her head with a brand-new captain's hat, a red feather stuck into the brim.

She looked *good*.

She strode across the stage with her head held high and a kind of challenge in her eyes, which looked amazing, by the way, set off by that blue coat. She stepped lithely around the various flowers and undergarments, and then, at center stage, she stopped and turned to face the audience.

"I am Mark Read, captain of the *Ranger*," she said in a loud, clear voice.

Jack's breath caught. This was a big moment. He'd been so pleased that she'd listened to him and changed her mind about becoming the Pirate King. She'd be a wonderful piratical monarch, he just knew it, and her ruling the pirates would neatly solve the problem of Bonn wanting to become one and also set them both up nicely to start earning up their thousand pieces of eight. And now that Mary was a captain, she could even be the one to officially marry him and Bonn. All good things.

But he was also, in this big moment, a little bit afraid for her.

He'd seen the tight fear in Tobias Teach's eyes when Mary had signed up for the contest, and this morning, as they'd walked to GIRLS GIRLS GIRLS together.

It was possible that this Pirate King business would be a dangerous undertaking. Jack knew the rules. No murder. That was a relief. But he hadn't forgotten that cheating, sabotaging, and general mayhem, as Bonn called it, were all still on the table. *Violence is encouraged*, the rules had stated.

Mary could get hurt.

He pushed the thought away. Everything would turn out all right, he told himself. It always did.

And then Hornigold was talking again.

"Thank you, Captain Read. I don't suppose you, too, have some musical number prepared to present to us? A secret talent? A magic show?"

Now, that would have been a good idea, Jack thought. He loved magic shows.

"No, sir." Mary shook her head. "I can present only myself, for your consideration."

"All right," said Captain Hook. "Tell us, then. Why do you wish to become the Pirate King?"

"I wish for world domination," she said, which was what most of the previous contestants had answered when asked this question. (Kind of the pirate-y opposite of world peace, dear reader.) "But let me tell you why. It's because we live in a world of *real* kings, a world in which we are told to accept the life we've been born into and not seek anything greater. But as pirates we know that our fortunes can change as the tide changes. We can make a difference. We can rise up in the world. I want to be the Pirate King—yes—but I don't mean to be a ruler who puts on an air of superiority and tells everyone what to do. We pirates don't need some fancy, highfalutin king. We need a leader who will work for the true equality of all pirates."

"So you believe in a *brother*hood of pirates?" Captain Hornigold asked her, and she frowned at the word.

"More like a community," she clarified.

"So like a *fellow*ship?" he pressed.

"An alliance," she amended.

"A *fraternity* of like-minded *men*?"

Mary smiled tightly. "A union of hardworking individuals striving for the common good of all piratekind."

Jack beamed. She was nailing this. "Three cheers for Captain Read!" he called out impulsively.

Bonn whooped from beside him. "Equality for all pirates! Preach!"

Their enthusiasm seemed to infect the pirates around them. "That's right! A union," Jack heard one fellow say from just behind him. "Working for our common good!"

"ARRR!" said another, and Jack took this to mean that this pirate very much agreed.

Hornigold held up a hand for everyone to be silent.

"That's very interesting, Captain Read," he said. "Is there anything else you'd like to say?"

Mary nodded. "I have ideas," she began. "Little ways to make things better, right from the start. Like free parrot training, which is proving to be very useful on my own ship. And casual Fr—"

"Liar!" someone yelled out from the crowd.

Mary's words trailed off. She had caught sight of the person who'd spoken, someone standing in the audience. The color drained from her face.

"Who said that? Who's she looking at?" Bonn asked, craning her neck around to see.

Jack didn't know, but he had a pretty good idea who it might be.

Mary cleared her throat. "Casual Fridays," she repeated. "And monthly prosthetic—"

"Traitor!" came the voice again. A familiar voice. A raspy one.

"Uh-oh," said Bonn.

There was a flurry of motion in the crowd as a man—Tobias, Jack realized—started to push his way to the front. "Get out of my way!" Tobias said urgently. "Let me through."

Jack followed Mary's gaze, which was still fixed on the person in the audience. A man dressed all in black. Leathery face. Badly groomed beard. Gold tooth.

Vane.

He was smiling in such a menacing way that a shiver rippled down Jack's spine.

"I know what you are, *Mister* Read," Vane said loudly.

"What he is?" someone in the crowd asked. "He's a captain, isn't he? I'm confused."

But Jack was not confused in the least. Vane was about to out Mary in front of everyone.

His moment had arrived.

Beside him, Bonn let out a low curse. "Get your frying pan ready, Jack," she hissed. "I've a feeling all hell's about to break loose."

Mary glanced down at her feet for a moment, collecting herself, and then looked up again.

"There's something else I need to say," she announced. "Something you all must know."

The room grew quiet. There was a loud sudden tinking noise. Everyone swiveled to look.

"Sorry, sorry, everyone," said a pirate. "I dropped me pin."

Everyone turned their attention back to Mary. Jack saw her take a deep breath. Whatever she said next, it would change everything.

"Oh gawl, don't do it," Bonn breathed from beside him. "Not like this."

But Jack knew the expression on his cousin's face. It was one he recognized from a time when he and Mary had been chased by a couple of really nasty eels when they'd been exploring once. At first they'd swum away, but then, when it had become clear that they wouldn't be able to escape, Mary had turned to face them.

And then she'd kicked the eels' butts (if eels had butts, that is) with nothing but a half-rotted wooden oar.

"My true name is not Mark Read," she said then. "I'm not who you think I am."

Mary

TEN

So much for winning the hearts and minds of Nassau, Mary thought as she stared at Vane. He had a hungry look in his eyes she was familiar with, the cunning glint he had when he was about to take a ship. Only now it wasn't a ship he was after. It was her.

She was the target. Her humiliation was the prize.

She could almost hear his rasping voice saying her name—her true name—in front of everyone. She could halfway see the looks of shock and horror on the faces below. And she could nearly feel the noose around her neck.

But Mary had never respected the captains who'd just surrendered. She'd liked the ones who decided to fight back—even when resistance was futile. They'd gone out on their own terms.

And she would do the same.

She would fight.

"My name is Mary Read," she said. "I'm a woman."

And just like that, it was out.

"What?" Hook lurched up from his seat. "No, you can't be!"

Morgan jumped up next. "I knew it! You're a fake!"

Then all hell seemed to break loose. The other contestants began to shout and complain, the audience pushed forward, and Vane was lost in the crowd.

"She's been tricking us!"

"Has she been a girl this whole time?"

Then someone asked: "Hey, if she's a girl, is she even allowed to compete to be the Pirate King?"

A resounding "NAY!" filled the auditorium. "NO GIRLS ALLOWED!" And then, right there in the middle of GIRLS GIRLS GIRLS, a bunch of pirates drew cutlasses, rapiers, and machetes. They glared at her.

So it was to be a fight. She could handle a fight.

Mary drew her own cutlass.

At which point a few pirates drew pistols.

Oh. Well. She didn't have one of those on her.

Before she could come up with a plan, Penzance, Obvious, Ahab, and the other contestants had rushed up behind her and grabbed her arms, twisting them behind her back hard enough that she dropped her sword. Grunting, Mary stomped directly onto someone's foot. Bones crunched under her heel, Penzance screamed in a high F♯, and then there were two fewer hands gripping her shoulders.

Then, while she had them on their toes, Mary jerked her head backward into someone's nose. Ahab shouted and moved away. Then Mary ducked and grabbed her sword off the stage.

She spun to face the contestants, lifting the blade to guard.

She would start by removing the competition. Literally. No murdering, but violence was acceptable.

"ARGGGGH!" There was a fierce cry, and Anne Bonny came barreling out onto the stage to Mary's aid, a dagger in each hand.

The two of them turned so their backs were nearly touching, surrounded by the angry crowd of men. "Why don't you try it," Anne growled. "It's been far too long since I've had to clean blood off me blade."

"Wait!" Tobias—with Jack close behind—ran forward. "Wait!" he called. "Calm down, all of you!"

No one calmed down. A dozen men started climbing up the stage, yelling about how it wasn't fair that Mary had tricked them, so why should they do what anyone said?

Then, Tobias drew a pistol (to Mary's great surprise, since he rarely carried one) and fired at the stage floor. The musket ball shot through the wood, creating a huge, splintering hole.

"I said calm down!" Tobias shouted, and this time they did.

On the stage, Ahab held his hand over his bleeding nose. Penzance was sitting, cradling his broken foot to his chest. (Wow, that guy was flexible!)

Mary scanned the audience for Vane, but he had melted back into the crowd. Which seemed unfair, that he could just force her hand this way and disappear again. She would have liked to fight it out with him.

"Thank you!" Tobias said, shoving the pistol back into his belt. "Now pay attention."

"Is that Teach?" someone asked. "As in *Tobias* Teach?"

"Babybeard," someone else confirmed, a note of awe in his voice.

Tobias heaved a long sigh. "That's right. You know me. I'm Blackbeard's son—the pirate *prince*, many of you have said. And I'm here to make the case that *Mary* Read should be allowed to compete for the title of Pirate King, just as much as anyone else."

"No girls allowed!" someone cried again. "Why is that so hard to understand?"

"I read the rules, same as everyone else." Mary lowered her sword but didn't lighten her grip as she moved to stand beside Tobias. "They don't say anything about needing to be a *man* to compete."

"Yeah!" Anne shouted from the back. "We all read the rules!"

"It was implied," said Hornigold. "Being that all pirates are men."

Mary cleared her throat.

"Except Read," Hornigold amended, clearly irritated. "But the rules of the *Ranger*, if I remember correctly, specifically state that no women are allowed to be pirates. So how is it that you are allowed to be here, as a captain?"

"My crew didn't know," Mary said quickly. "Not a one of

them. But now that I'm captain, that particular rule will *not* be on our books."

"Right," Tobias said. "Mary Read is a skilled and outstanding pirate. Why, she went from cabin boy to captain in only a year!"

"Aye," Hook said, "that's true. A bit of an overachiever, that one."

"Perhaps the rest of you are *under*achievers," Mary muttered.

"Not helping," Tobias said. Then, louder: "Look, the Teach family stands behind Miss Read participating in the competition."

Mary's chest squeezed. Tobias hated using his family name in this way, but here he was, using it to help her. Publicly. Loudly. And he hated the competition—hated that she was determined to win it—but he was supporting her now, all the same.

"Well, you still cheated your way aboard the *Ranger*," said Hornigold.

"I didn't. The maleness was assumed." Mary shrugged. "I just didn't correct anyone. And when I'm Pirate Queen, I'll make a royal decree that any woman who wants to be a pirate should be allowed to be one. Equality for everyone!"

Only a few people cheered, and as Mary looked around, she saw they were all women. Everyone else looked like they wanted to keelhaul her.

"I move that Mary should remain a contestant for Pirate Queen," Tobias said.

"Aye!" Anne agreed. "Me too!"

"Me three!" Jack called.

"Well, the lass's aye doesn't count," Hornigold said, "but the pretty boy's does. Gentlemen? Shall we allow *Mary* Read to compete in our competition, or should we take her out to the deepest part of the ocean and force her to walk the plank, where she'll likely be eaten up by sharks before she drowns?"

"What's the point of it being the *deepest* part of the ocean if she's to be eaten by sharks before that?" Hook wanted to know.

"So that her bones are lost to the depths of Davy Jones's locker, of course, and can never be retrieved."

At that, the other two AARP members nodded in complete understanding.

"Let us discuss." Hornigold motioned Hook and Morgan to huddle close to him.

The audience went quiet as the three old pirates spoke, but their conversation was too low to carry.

Nervously, Mary looked at Tobias, but his gaze was fixed on the council. This was exactly what he'd been worried about yesterday, when he'd tried to get her to run away with him. Now it wasn't only Vane who knew her identity, but everyone.

"All right!" Hornigold and the other AARP members broke apart. "We've come to a decision."

Mary tore her eyes away from Tobias. "Well?"

"*If* your crew allows it, and you remain captain—keeping in mind that you deceived them, too—you may remain in the contest."

The resulting BOOOO from the audience was immediate and overwhelming. Someone threw a tomato. Another person threw a shoe. Someone (hopefully not anyone from the *Ranger*) threw a banana.

That was when Vane climbed onto the stage. When he held up a hand, the audience quieted. "I would like to announce my candidacy for Pirate King," he rasped.

"You have to be a captain," Mary told him. "And in case you've forgotten, you no longer hold that title."

Vane sneered at her. "Oh, don't worry about me, lass. I've been doing a little campaigning."

"Just now?" Mary asked. Surely her crew wouldn't turn on her so quickly. But Hornigold was right: she had been deceiving them.

"Aye, just now." Vane grinned, showing his teeth. "I spoke with many fine men a few moments ago, men who miss the way things used to be. No women. More rum. No blathering on about the *Future* of Piracy. Bah!"

Mary risked a glance out at the audience, but she couldn't see any of her crew now.

"After I made my pitch to the crew of the *Conspicuous*," Vane said, "their choice was obvious."

"Hey!" Captain Obvious cried out. "The *Conspicuous* is my ship!"

"Not anymore." Vane turned toward the audience, where the crew of the *Conspicuous* had bunched together. "All who want me to replace Captain Obvious, raise your hands or hooks!"

Dozens of hands and hooks lifted into the air, including some who weren't part of that crew.

Hornigold counted, then nodded. "Well then, Captain Vane, I

suppose all that's needed is for you to sign your name here."

Vane hopped down from the stage, signed his name to the sheet, and then returned to stand in front of everyone.

"You all know what I advocate." He looked across the crowd, eyes narrowing. "And, most importantly, you know *who I am*. I should be the Pirate King."

"Very well," Hornigold said. "If you'll all put away your weapons and return to your seats, it's time to announce how the contest will be decided."

Nobody put away their weapons *or* returned to their seats. Tobias remained on the stage beside Mary. Jack and Anne stood nearby, their eyes on the other contestants like they were expecting another attack. And Vane stayed put, his glare firmly on Mary.

"A Pirate King must be well endowed," Hornigold declared. "And by that, obviously I mean he must be rich."

Ahab dabbed his nose with a grimy handkerchief. "So it's to be a contest of who has the most money?"

"Aye," Hornigold said. "Our captains will go out in search of treasure! That is what makes a king, after all: the ability to take ships, take treasure, and take power. Whoever returns with the most gold and jewels—by the noon bell at first of next month— will be crowned the Pirate King!"

So that was it. Treasure. Bring it back to showcase their incredible pirating abilities.

In three weeks.

Mary reached into her pocket and touched the magical

hourglass. "Tobias," she said softly, "when is the next full moon?"

He tilted his head, thinking. "In about three weeks. Why?"

"No reason." She let go of the hourglass.

"Worried, Read?" Vane sneered. "You can always give up."

"Not a chance," she said. "I beat you once. I'll do it again."

But if winning had seemed like a long shot before, it looked impossible now.

Back on the *Ranger*, Mary called the entire crew to the main deck. She stood on the quarterdeck where they could all see her. Wind tugged at her jacket as she gazed down at them: Nine Toes, DuPaul, Child, Swift, and all the rest.

"If you were at the presentation earlier," she said over the sound of water hitting the hull, "then you already know what's happened. But for those of you who weren't—I wanted you to hear it from me first."

They *definitely* wouldn't be hearing it from her first; pirates were the worst sort of gossips. But still, she had to pretend. For their pride.

"I'm a woman," she said quickly, before she could lose her nerve. "I know that's probably shocking to many of you, but I'm the same person you voted for. We're still going to do all the things I promised. We make a good crew, all of us together. And I want you to know that nothing is going to change—except I might let my hair grow out. And I'd like this woman, Anne Bonny, to join us." She motioned to where Anne stood before her, red curls flying in the wind. "And the fact that if we don't win, we'll probably all be killed. But that's it!"

"Honestly, Captain," Quint said, "we already knew you was a girl."

"What?" Mary stared at the boatswain. "Since when?"

He shrugged. "Since you first came aboard."

"That's right," Howser (the ship's doctor) said. "We all thought you'd cry and want to go home after the first day, but you didn't. Then we thought you'd only last a week, but you kept going." He shrugged, too. "Some of us lost good money on those bets, but I guess it's working out for us now. Look at you, Captain Read!"

"Hear, hear!" the others shouted.

"So you all knew?" Mary frowned.

"Show of hands from everyone who knew!" Gaines, the ship's carpenter, called.

Everyone except the parrot, the chicken, and three other guys raised their hands.

"Oh." Mary wasn't sure how she should feel about that. Proud that she'd defied their expectations? Annoyed that they'd known about her this whole time and just . . . never said anything?

She eyed Tobias, who wore that crooked smile of his.

"Shake it off, Captain!" Swift called. "We're with you."

"Aye," agreed Gaines. "And now we're *against* Vane. I don't like that he took command of the *Conspicuous* just to get back at you. That's mean-spirited."

"The *Conspicuous* crew will pay for their mistake," Quint said. "Mark my words, they'll regret voting him in. Meanwhile, we've got the best captain in the Caribbean!"

There was a round of ARRRs and AYEs and a single (but enthusiastic) BEGAWK!

Their faith set a fire under her.

"Very well!" Mary shouted. "Then it's time to vote on a new rule. Everyone who wants to allow women aboard the *Ranger*, say aye!"

"AYE." It was unanimous. Every pirate (and chicken and parrot) was in agreement. Mary tossed her copy of Vane's rules into the ocean and immediately started thinking about what she would call hers. *Captain Mary's Definitive Guide to Piracy*, perhaps. Or *Piracy for a New Generation*. Hmm, not quite. *How to Embrace Your Inner Pirate*.

Well, it was a work in progress.

Mary turned back to the crew. "Well, what are all of you still doing here? Get to your stations! We need to move! The other competitors will be gunning for us first. They think we're weak. But we'll show them."

Once the *Ranger* was sailing out of the harbor at top speed (so about six miles per hour), Mary found Tobias, who was leaning against a rail and scribbling a note in his logbook. She watched him, waiting until he finished and put the book and pencil back in his pocket.

"So," she said.

"So," he agreed.

This was hard to admit. She leaned next to him. Their shoulders were nearly touching. "I think you might have saved my life today."

"You think I *might* have?" That smile was back. "Read, they were going to peel your banana this afternoon. I *definitely* saved your life. I think that puts me one ahead of you."

Mary's mouth dropped open. "You're not ahead. Or are you forgetting about the lobster incident again?"

"That one doesn't count, and you know it."

She scoffed, but that was a fight for a different day. Instead, she turned to face him directly. "What I really came to say," she said, "is thank you. I know what it must have cost you to stand up there in front of everyone, to use your pa's name like that."

Tobias closed his eyes and let out a breath. "Pa would be proud I finally did it. He always wanted me to throw my weight around a bit more, lean into his legacy, be a better pirate."

"Of course he'd be proud of you."

"I didn't do it for him." Tobias lifted his eyes to hers. There was an urgency in his gaze, like he was working himself up for something. He kept his voice soft. "What did it feel like today? Standing up there and telling everyone the truth?"

Mary drew in a sharp breath. That wasn't what she'd expected him to ask about. "Freeing, I suppose. Once it was out, that is. I didn't like getting forced into it and I didn't think I was ready for everyone to know, but now that it's done—well, it's one less thing I have to worry about, one less secret I have to keep. Why?" She let out a nervous laugh. "Is there a huge secret you're keeping? I thought I knew everything there is to know about you."

He shook his head. "I was just thinking about how you told everyone else the truth today. *A* truth. But when are you going to tell me your other secret?"

Mary's shoulders tensed. "What . . . do you mean? You knew about me from the beginning?"

He sighed. "There's something else. Your past. Where you're from. The reason you suddenly changed your mind about entering the contest. You're holding on to something big, I know it. And, well, after everything, I was hoping you might decide to trust me with it."

Oh. The Mer thing. She couldn't tell him that. What if he hated her after learning the truth? What if he was disgusted? Humans could be unpredictable when it came to unfamiliar things. "Does it really matter?" she asked hoarsely. "You know who I am now. Who I was—that's all in the past."

"Of course it matters," he said. "You're my—"

"Ship!" cried the lookout. "Ship off the port bow!"

Mary stepped back from Tobias in alarm and looked into the . . . harbor? They hadn't even left the harbor yet.

But sure enough, there was a small sloop just floating there, anchored. With the contest on, parking was obviously a real problem, but who in their right mind would leave a sloop out where *anyone* could just take it?

Then Mary spotted the single figure on the poop deck, waving their arms over their head, as though *trying* to get her attention.

Mary strode toward the helm, where DuPaul was waiting for her orders.

"Take us to her," Mary said. "But it could be a trap, so be

ready to maneuver away at a moment's notice."

"Aye, Captain."

A few minutes later, the *Ranger* came alongside the *William* (that's what the other ship was called) and a plank was set between them. "Keep your eyes peeled," Mary cautioned as the boarding party crossed. "We don't know who left this here. If you even get a *whiff* of a dance number starting . . ."

But it wasn't a trap set by Penzance or any of the other competitors. Instead, Effie Ham strode down to meet them, a folded slip of parchment in hand.

"Good afternoon, Captain Read. This is for you." She handed Mary the note.

> *Captain Read,*
>
> *I hope this missive finds you well. Thank you for saving my little sister during the Chango incident. Given your announcement today, I hope you'll be willing to take Effie on. She comes with the ship, four cannons, and supplies for a whole crew.*
>
> *In any case, the Ham Fam wishes you all the best in the Pirate King contest.*
>
> *Warmest regards,*
> *John Ham*

Mary lowered the note. "You're willing to serve under my command?"

"Eager to, Captain Read. I asked for this specifically." Effie lifted her chin. "I've been sailing all my life. I was born on the ocean, in fact. And I know everything about the *William*."

Mary smiled. Nodded. "You'll be an asset, Ham. Glad to have you with us." Then she called out to the rest of her men, "Heave the anchor!"

All the pirates with her cheered.

Then she headed back to the *Ranger*, ordered DuPaul and a few other men to help crew the *William*, and settled herself at the helm.

They had a contest to win.

ELEVEN

Tobias

Tobias had been thinking about treasure—THE treasure—since his father's funeral. When Hornigold had announced that the winner of the Pirate King contest would be the person who could come up with the most treasure, Tobias had thought, *Well, that's easy enough*. They needed treasure. He knew where to find it. Bam. Contest won.

But Tobias also knew Mary (or thought he did, anyway) and he knew what wouldn't be as easy would be convincing her to take the particular treasure he had in mind. She wouldn't like to simply have a treasure handed to her. She would want to earn her place as Pirate King. She would want to win fair and square.

"Our goal is to come up with the most treasure we can in the next three weeks," she was saying to the crew now. "And how do we do that?" It was a rhetorical question, but the guy with the chicken raised his chicken. "Uh, yeah, you?"

"We rob a bank."

Mary blinked a few times. "I like the creativity, but considering we're on a ship, we should think about focusing on other, more water-based methods of acquiring treasure. Such as . . ."

"Flipping ships!" Gaines shouted.

"Say what now?"

"We can capture a ship, fix it up, make it pretty—maybe add some shiplap—and then sell it for an insane amount of profit."

"No. We take the ships, and we keep the treasure." Mary rubbed her temples. "Or, if we had enough ships, crew, and firepower, we could siege a port town. But I don't think this is a viable option, given our limited amount of time."

"We could take treasure off other pirate ships," Anne Bonny suggested, leaning back against the rail and flipping a dagger over in her hand. The woman had impressive knife skills. "We could simply wait for the other captains to collect their treasure, and then we could take it." Flip, went the dagger. Flip. "That might be fun."

Tobias smiled faintly. Mary was going to hate that idea.

"Fun, yes, but I don't wish to become the Pirate King by doing harm to other pirates," she said. "So ships it will have to be. Merchant ships, preferably."

"What if they just have bananas on them again?" Mr. Child asked. "There's only so much I can do with bananas."

Ah. Tobias could help with this. He pulled the banana recipe book from his pocket. "We have several options," he said, holding out the book, "if you'd like to borrow this."

Mr. Child climbed onto the quarterdeck, took the book, and eagerly flipped through the pages. "Banana soufflé. Interesting . . ." He wandered back down to the rest of the crew.

"You kept that on you?" Mary asked Tobias.

He shrugged. "I liked to imagine that I was eating anything but raw bananas." He cleared his throat, addressing the crew. "I have another idea, regarding our acquisition of treasure."

Mary turned to him, blue eyes curious. "Yes, Mr. Teach?"

"We take Blackbeard's treasure," he said.

A sizzle of excitement went through the crew, and the men all began murmuring at once.

"Blackbeard's treasure! Is that real?" Quint asked.

"Blackbeard prolly didn't even have a treasure," DuPaul added doubtfully. "You know how pirate captains love to claim they have this huge stash of booty, but few actually have more than a chest or two saved up."

"Blackbeard's treasure is real. I've seen it," Tobias assured them. His heart was beating fast now, but he kept talking. "He used to joke it was enough loot to satisfy a dragon. A treasure fit for a king. Or, in this case"—he nodded at Mary—"a Pirate Queen."

"Three cheers for our Pirate Queen!" Anne Bonny whooped, and many of the others joined her.

"So what are we talking here?" the guy with the chicken asked. "Gold? Jewels?"

"Chest upon chest of gold coins," Tobias reported. "Gold bars. Golden jewelry and crowns. Solid gold statues. Sacks of gold dust. Silver ingots. Trunks full of jewels. Ivory. Indigo. Bolts of silk and other expensive fabrics. And I know exactly where it is. All we have to do is go get it."

Now the crew was becoming really darned excited.

Jack raised his hand. "What about pieces of eight? Are there any of those in this treasure? Say, a thousand of them?"

"Uh, yes," Tobias said. "Thousands and thousands of pieces of eight."

"Excellent," Jack said. "I say we procure this treasure at once!"

But Mary was biting her lip, brow rumpled. She pulled him aside slightly, lowering her voice to whisper, "That treasure should be yours, Toby. We can't take your inheritance."

"I'm happy to share it," he said.

Her eyes lifted to his, and he wondered if she heard what he wasn't saying. *With you.*

It had seemed impossible before, to think they might have any kind of relationship other than being best mates. But her secret was out now. She'd stood on that stage and declared herself a woman. He still couldn't believe she'd done that.

The gall of her.

The guts.

The indomitable pluck she had.

His gaze dropped to her mouth for just an instant.

Mary pulled back and shook her head. "No. I have to do this

myself. I have to earn it."

Which, again, was exactly what he'd expected her to say.

But the crew was already worked up. The idea of so much treasure had put a glint into the eyes of every member of the *Ranger*.

"Everything has changed!" exclaimed Mr. Swift. "When do we leave?"

"Yeah," said Effie Ham. "What are we waiting for?"

"This won't be an easy task. We'll have to work for it," Tobias said to Mary quietly. "It's not like we can just show up and take this treasure."

"It's not?"

Tobias raised his voice again. "First, we'll have to take some more ships, because the amount of treasure we're after would be heavy enough to sink the *Ranger* straight to the bottom!"

"All right, then!" yelled Quint. "Let's get to taking more ships!"

"Then we'll have to sail like the devil is chasing us and hope the wind is in our favor enough that we'll reach the treasure in time," Tobias added.

"Is it very far?" Mary asked.

"We'll make it if we push ourselves," he promised. It was about a week to sail there, depending on the wind, and a week back. Which should give them plenty of time.

"Trea-sure! Trea-sure!" chanted the crew.

"And then, once we arrive, there are booby traps," he said.

"Booby traps? Those don't sound so bad," Jack said, and

Anne smacked him in the chest.

"Booby traps?" Mary repeated.

"A few," Tobias lied. There was one booby trap. And he wouldn't really call it a trap so much as poor engineering on his pa's part. But the more arduous he could make this task sound for her, the better.

"Let's go! Let's go!" shouted the crew, and Tobias turned to Mary and arched an eyebrow.

"Come on," he said. "This is more treasure than a single man could spend in a lifetime. I want it to go to a good cause. Equality for all pirates, men and women alike."

The corner of her mouth tilted up, and he knew he had her.

"Oh, all right, if you insist," she said, then turned to the crew with her usual grin. "What do you say, lads—and, er, Anne? And Effie? Shall we get after Blackbeard's treasure?"

"Aye!" they answered in one voice.

"Very well," she said. "You heard the man. If we're going to transport all this booty, we're going to need a bigger ship. So let's get one. And you . . ." She stepped close to Tobias again, her mouth near his ear. "Chart us a course, Mr. Teach."

"Aye, aye, Captain," Tobias said.

It didn't take them long, cruising the nearest shipping route, before they came upon a ship. A large one, just like they needed.

As they drew closer, this ship was identified as the *Jester*, a rather odd name for a merchant vessel. *Please*, Tobias prayed, *don't let this one be full of something ridiculous.* He didn't think the crew could stand to eat any more bananas.

The crew—half of them leaning over the rail to peer across the water—looked as though they were thinking the same thing.

"Shall we do this, then?" Mary asked, and the men cried, "Yea!"

"Raise the black, lads!" she shouted. "Ready your guns!"

But the *Jester* ran up the white flag of surrender just as soon as the *Ranger* flew the black one. An easy take, then. They were alongside her within minutes, and the captain of the *Jester* waved at them almost merrily from the rail.

"I'll come aboard as your hostage," he called over. "So our men can avoid any fighting and we can come to friendly terms."

Mary assented. A plank was laid down between the two ships, and the captain stepped carefully across onto the *Ranger*. Then Mary cordially invited him into the captain's cabin with her for the negotiation of his surrender. Tobias found an excuse to be the one to escort the man there. He needed to update a chart, he said, so he lingered by his worktable as Mary and Captain Gregory—that's what the man said his name was—discussed what would be done now that the *Jester* was captured by pirates.

"So you're an honest-to-goodness pirate ship," Mr. Gregory said jovially. He was a portly man with a sharp, almost orange colored goatee, dressed in what looked to be the long black robes of a priest, which was confusing. "And captained by a woman, to boot!" he added. "How progressive is that?"

Tobias glanced at Mary. Was this man trying to flatter her? And how had he discerned she was a woman so quickly? To Tobias she didn't appear much different from the way she always had. She wore a captain's hat now, the one with the red feather in it, and the same damask waistcoat she'd worn at GIRLS GIRLS GIRLS. Her hair did inexplicably seem slightly longer than it had yesterday, but perhaps that was because she was wearing it loose today, in tawny tousled waves about her face, instead of drawn back in its usual tail or hidden under a cap. Her voice was a bit changed, higher, maybe, but still hers.

But then he realized: she'd clearly forgone whatever she'd been doing previously to flatten her chest.

She had bosoms now. Well, she'd always had. But now Tobias could see them. Well, not *see them*, see them, as they were well covered by both her shirt and waistcoat, but he could discern them. The shape anyway.

Good Lord, what was he doing?

Tobias averted his eyes. His face was very hot. He must get ahold of himself. He bit the inside of his cheek and forced himself to concentrate on what this Captain Gregory was saying.

"We're but a company of traveling players," said the man, "on a mission to entertain the masses. We're based out of Charles Town, but we like to sail a circuit around the Caribbean this time of year—Barbados, Jamaica, the Bahamas."

Mary's posture straightened, as Tobias knew it would, at the mention of Charles Town. Whatever had happened to Mary at

Charles Town had been significant.

He wished, for the thousandth time, that she would tell him what it was.

If only she would.

"It's miraculous, when you think about it," Captain Gregory was saying, "that we've never encountered any pirates before now."

Mary did not look impressed. She looked annoyed, in fact, her brows pinching together in almost a glower. Tobias understood why. A merchant vessel, loaded with valuable goods, would have been so much better than a boatful of professional actors. The men would probably think this worse than the bananas. At least the bananas had come with a helpful manual about what useful things might be made from them.

"And what provisions are you carrying, sir?" she asked lightly.

Captain Gregory wiped his brow—the only sign he showed of being frightened at the prospect of a watery grave, or worse. He was clearly an actor himself, Tobias decided. "Not much to speak of, booty-wise. We have a few casks of a good wine. Some decent food stores. Several canisters of pancake stage makeup—I won't expect you to know what that is if you're not in the entertainment business. We also possess many fine articles of clothing, which we wear when we do a show involving nobility or royalty. Some costume jewelry. And an amusing dog."

Mary frowned. "You're right. That isn't enough. Not nearly."

Tobias cleared his throat. "We don't really need their cargo, remember?"

"Oh dear." Captain Gregory held out his hand. "Please. If

you will consider not outright murdering us, we will perform a show for you tonight," he promised. "And our chef will whip you up a five-course meal of the likes that your men have never experienced." He suddenly grasped at Mary's arm, his voice turned pleading. "We'll give you dinner and a show, and then you can . . . you can let us go."

It was a weak offer. Captain Vane might have keelhauled the lot of this company of players, to suggest such scant booty as "dinner and a show."

But Mary was not Captain Vane.

"Don't worry yourself, sir," she said, clearing her throat. "We will accept what you are proposing. The men will find your show most diverting, I'm sure, and they never say no to a well-cooked meal. But I cannot let the *Jester* go."

Captain Gregory's face paled. "You cannot?"

She shook her head gravely. "I need your ship, I'm afraid. You see, my crew and I are engaged in a pirate competition of sorts. I—"

"Of course! The Pirate King contest!" interrupted Captain Gregory. "The entire Caribbean is talking about it! So you're going to make a go of it? A woman! How marvelous is that?"

Her chin lifted, and Tobias's chest swelled with pride for all that she'd done and all that she was. "Indeed. And now I'm competing for the benefit of all women who want to become pirates. Our task is to return to Nassau with the most treasure."

"I see." Gregory stroked his pointed goatee. "Well, since we do not have much in the way of treasure to offer you, what will become of my men? They're good chaps, all of them, but not many of them are decent sailors, and none that I'm aware of have any ambition to become pirates."

"Ah," Mary said. She looked like she was trying to decide how to let them go without compromising her reputation as a fierce pirate, someone everyone should respect and fear. "In that case . . ."

"However," Captain Gregory said, "I have been thinking of writing a play of my own. An original. Something the world has never seen before. And now that I see you and your quest to bring women into piracy, perhaps *that* is the story I am meant to tell. Your story. If you would permit me to observe you for the duration of the contest, I would be most honored to tell the tale of the great Captain Read and her crew."

Mary's eyebrows lifted. "Indeed? How would you portray me? As a woman playing pirate?"

Captain Gregory shook his head urgently. "Oh, your character would be formidable—terrifying to this simple play actor, who found himself captured. I will tell people that I was allowed to return to my regularly scheduled programming only as a warning to others."

Mary tapped her chin. "I would need to read this play first, of course. And if there's anything I find objectionable . . ."

"I will make the requested revisions or walk the plank. Whichever you prefer."

"And royalties," Mary said. "The story is about me, after all. I'm a pirate. I require gold."

"A flat fee, perhaps," Gregory said. "Let's say one hundred pieces of eight, to be paid at a time when I have any money at all. It's easier to keep track of, and if for some reason the play doesn't take off, you still get compensated."

"Very well," Mary said. "I accept those terms. Now, when it comes to the crew, no harm will come to your men, as long as you do as I tell you. You may remain captain of your ship, in spirit, if not in an official capacity. Hopefully you and your ship will not be worse for wear when we part ways, although I cannot make you any promises in that regard, seeing as how we're pirates and that does involve some element of risk."

Then, in spite of all his confident negotiating, Captain Gregory began to literally cry with gratitude. It was a quite dramatic weeping session.

Perhaps, Tobias thought, the previous exchange had all been an act. Or perhaps he was acting here, with the weeping. Tobias couldn't tell.

Man, this guy was good.

"That's very kind of you, ma'am," Gregory sniffled at last. "Thank you." He bowed. "Thank you. Thank you very much." He kissed her hand. "Thank you, gentle lady."

"You overstep, sir." Mary whipped her hand away. "I am no gentle lady. I am a captain, like any other."

"I beg your pardon, Captain," sputtered Gregory. "I didn't mean you any offense."

"Mr. Teach will see you back to your ship, Captain," she said, effectively dismissing them both. "Oh, and what shall I tell my men about your show tonight?" she added when they reached the door to the cabin. "When will it take place, and what kind of performance should they expect?"

Captain Gregory's eyes brightened. "Ah! We'll serve dinner at six, and the show shall begin at eight. It's Shakespeare, which your men should find most engaging."

Tobias rather doubted that, but okay.

"This season," continued Gregory in a voice like he was formally announcing the lineup to a large crowd, "the production is all about star-crossed lovers. It's called *Romeo and Juliet*."

"*Romeo and Juliet*, you say?" Jack clapped his hands together. "That's our favorite story, isn't it, Mary? Oh, what good luck!"

It was evening now, the sky a deep blue with stars just beginning to poke out, and dinner was about to be served. Tobias was feeling oddly nervous about dinner, like this was somehow more than just a dinner. It was the first dinner that he and Mary would share in which they got to be themselves, a man and a woman, going out in public together.

In other words, it felt like a date.

Tobias had ironed his shirt and shined his boots. He'd washed. He'd tried to do something different with his hair that hadn't worked out, so he'd washed again and rubbed some old spices into his armpits until he smelled less, well, pirate-y. (Old Spice was a thing even back then, dear reader, but Axe was considered too dangerous.)

Mary seemed to have gussied herself up a bit, too. She was wearing a clean white blouse and a dark blue skirt, which she must have borrowed from somebody because Tobias knew she didn't have her own. Her hair gleamed in the lantern light, and it seemed even longer now than it had this morning. She looked good. *Beautiful* is the word Tobias would have used, if he was allowed to use such a word.

"Look at us, so clean and sweet smelling," Jack said. "We're adorable."

It was actually like a double date, Tobias realized.

Jack turned to Anne with a smile. "Do you enjoy Shakespeare, my love?"

"Can't say I've ever seen him before," Anne said. "Is he good?"

"He's very good," said Jack dreamily. He closed his eyes for a moment, as if remembering, then said, "*But, soft! what light through yonder window breaks? It is the east, and Juliet is the sun! Arise, fair sun, and kill the envious moon, who is already sick and pale with grief, that thou her maid art far more fair than she.*" He frowned. "Hmm, and I'm forgetting a few lines, but then he says, *It is my lady; O! it is my love: O! that she knew she were.* I love that bit."

"That is good," admitted Anne, looking Jack up and down, and even Tobias felt a bit flustered by Jack's passionate delivery of the lines.

"But the two of them don't even know each other at that point, to say such things about love," Mary said softly. "And what are they, like fifteen years old? Anyway, enough, Jack. You're spoiling it. Let them hear it themselves and make up their own minds about the play."

Jack's mouth opened in shock. "But Mary! You used to love this story. You said—"

"I didn't understand it then," she said, and there was the look in her eyes—the one she got when she was remembering the guy from Charles Town.

Tobias hated that guy.

But maybe this was his chance to make her forget that guy. Maybe this was his chance, period.

Above them, the bell rang for six o'clock. "It's dinnertime!" Mary said, and went to locate Mr. Child, who had been busy all afternoon working with the *Jester*'s cook, Mr. Ramsay.

Dinner was a thing of beauty. The starter was a spicy banana-zucchini ball in a red pepper curry sauce, followed by the main dish: casserole de jambon au fromage et de bananes. (Reader, this was a ham and cheese casserole with bananas in it.) For dessert, banana cream pie and a ginger banana cake. The men were markedly less cranky about the banana situation after that. They ate and ate and ate so much they forgot to drink as much rum as they usually did.

So they were remarkably sober when it came time to view the play.

The actors from the *Jester* were all men, even those playing the female roles. Captain Gregory played the priest, which explained his outfit earlier. Romeo was a talented actor named Oscar. The boy playing Juliet was pretty, Tobias could admit, but obviously a boy. He found that his gaze kept drifting from Juliet to Mary, who was seated next to Tobias in the front row. On her other side sat Jack, gazing rapturously up at the quarterdeck, which they'd established as a kind of stage. And at his other side was Anne.

"Come, gentle night; come, loving, black-brow'd night, give me my Romeo: and, when he shall die, take him and cut him out in little stars, and he will make the face of heaven so fine that all the world will be in love with night," the boy Juliet was saying sweetly, and he was good, too, better than Jack, even, and as he/she spoke about love, Tobias could see something wavering in Mary's steadfast expression, an aching vulnerability in her face. Then she caught Tobias looking at her, met his eyes for a long moment, and gave him a sad smile that made something twist in his heart.

She was beautiful. And strong. And brave. And he loved her, he realized. Not just like. Love.

Like Romeo loved Juliet.

And she was right that Romeo and Juliet hardly knew each other, and they were so young, but he and Mary knew each other well. They were best mates. They'd been roommates for a year. They were partners in so many ways. And while nineteen wasn't that much older than Romeo, it was enough for Tobias to know his mind, and what he knew was this: he loved Mary.

He had to tell her.

But instead he settled back to watch the play, and as the moments passed between the lovers, Tobias came to slowly understand why Captain Gregory had dubbed them "star-crossed" earlier. Because nothing was going right for them suddenly.

"Wait," Jack piped up after Juliet took a potion that made her appear dead, so that she might be stolen away by Romeo for their happy ending later. "This is going to turn out all right, isn't it? True love will conquer all?" (Jack clearly didn't understand that you were not supposed to ask your questions out loud at a play.)

"Shh!" said a pirate next to them.

Tobias swallowed. He had a bad feeling about where the play was going.

"Wait, wait, WAIT," Jack exclaimed near the end, as the two lovers lay dead in each other's arms. "This isn't right. This story is supposed to have a happy ending. You're telling it wrong! The messenger does get to Juliet in time, and then Romeo wakes her with a kiss, sweeps her off her feet, and carries her away to their happily ever after. That's what's supposed to happen."

"I'd hoped there was going to be more fighting," grumbled Anne.

Jack huffed. "Well, it has a happy ending where I come from!"

Tobias couldn't stand it any longer. "Where in the hell do you come from?" he asked.

"Shh!" said the pirate's parrot from the shoulder of the pirate next to him. "Be quiet, you two."

"The ending was washed away in our copy of the book," Jack whispered urgently. "But they loved each other. They deserved to be together. We thought it must end well for them."

Mary had said nothing this entire time, but now, as she looked up, there were tears sparkling in her eyes. She dashed them away with the back of her hand. "Sometimes love ends in tragedy," she murmured. "That's why Vane had a heart on his flag. Love is dangerous."

Then she got up abruptly and walked off just as Captain Gregory stepped forward to perform the last little bit of the play.

"I still think their story is beautiful," whispered Jack. "I don't know what her problem is. She never used to be so jaded."

"Some bloke did her a bad turn, is all," mused Anne. "She probably doesn't mean it."

But Tobias thought she did mean it.

"Love is dangerous," he repeated dully. Was that what Mary really thought?

Captain Gregory cleared his throat loudly to deliver his final line. *"For never was a story of more woe,"* he said mournfully, *"than this of Juliet and her Romeo."*

"Well, crap," said Tobias.

Their date—which Mary didn't seem to even realize they were on—had not gone well.

"I liked our version better," Jack said, "even if we made it up."

To which we, your narrators, have this to say:

Same, Jack. Same.

TWELVE
Jack

BOOM!

Jack opened his eyes. For a moment he forgot where he was—why was he swaying? where was Bonn? what was that most unpleasant smell?—but then it came to him. He was a pirate now. On the *Ranger.* Which meant that he was lying in a hammock in the crew's berth, a large room below the main deck where most of the ship's crew slept.

In the hammock above his, he caught Bonn's dainty snore.

She'd insisted that she be treated no differently from any other crew member, no special allowances made on account of her being a woman. Which meant they were stuck in the berth with about fifty other men. Every night for the foreseeable future. Ugh. It really did smell foul in here. But such was life as a pirate, or so he'd been told. Jack supposed he'd get used to it.

Boom!

What *was* that? Jack slid out of his hammock and glanced around. It was very dark in the room, the only light a sliver of moon cast down from the stairwell that led to the deck. He took a moment to listen, and through the creaking of the ship and the hushing of the waves, he thought he could hear voices. Faint shouting, even.

He turned and gently shook Bonn by the shoulder.

"Oh, leave off it, Jim," she murmured, pulling away. "I'm beat."

Jack frowned. Jim. Aka James. Her soon-to-be-ex-husband's name. She'd told Jack there'd never been love there, between her and Jim, but did she still think about him? Dream about him? She was probably having a nightmare.

Boom!

He shook her again. "Darling, I think there's something happening up on deck."

She pulled the woolen blanket over her head and grumbled something. Her voice was muffled and Irish, but he thought he understood what she was asking: "What is it?"

"I don't know. I—" He paused to listen again, this time picking up the sound of boots on the deck above them. Running boots. More muffled shouting. "I think we might be under—"

"Attack!" Mr. Diesel came stomping down the stairwell, banging a pot with a wooden spoon. "Wake up, lads! We be under attack!"

Jack was confused. He was under the impression that, as pirates, they should be the ones doing the attacking, not the other way around.

Bonn rolled out of the hammock. She gathered her mass of curls in one hand and tied it back with the other. Then she yanked on her boots and began to arrange her various daggers and pistols into position within her clothes.

"Oh no, do you think there's going to be actual violence?" Jack asked, dread pooling in his gut as, all around them, men swarmed like a colony of angry ants up and out onto the deck.

She grinned. "Aye. Find yourself something to fight with, won't you?"

He looked around helplessly. Now, we've already established that Jack was just plain bad when it came to fighting with a cutlass— that one time he'd tried, he'd almost taken his own foot off, and he was really precious about his feet, as they were brand-new to him— and he loathed the use of muskets. (They were so loud, they took ages to load, and they misfired about half the time.) "Oh, bother," he muttered. "I didn't think to bring a frying pan."

Bonn darted in between the rows of hammocks, searching someone out, and then she made a triumphant aha noise and held up a frying pan like she'd conjured it from thin air.

Jack gaped at her. "Where did you—"

She held a finger to her lips and then stepped aside, smiling slyly, to reveal Mr. Child, who remained fast asleep somehow. Apparently he'd been sleeping with his frying pan, and Bonn had just yoinked it off him.

"Come on," she said, tossing the pan to Jack. "Let's get up there! I don't want to miss the fighting! I sharpened my knives last night, just in case!"

She was cute when she was bloodthirsty.

Jack took a second to admire the prime condition of the frying pan. It was cast iron, sturdy, and obviously well cared for. Then, saying a silent apology to Mr. Child, he dashed after Bonn and up the stairs.

The main deck was in utter chaos. The air was filled with gunpowder smoke, and pirates were scrambling about in various states of undress, shouting at one another as the *boom*s kept coming and the ship rocked violently, sending sprays of water onto the deck. Jack jumped back to narrowly avoid being soaked.

Whew. This would not be a good time to make his public debut as a Mer.

Maybe being a pirate wasn't the *best* career path for him, he realized.

But Bonn was clearly having the time of her life. She jumped into the rigging like she'd been born to it, rising to get above the fray enough to see what was going on, and then she climbed quickly down again while Jack moved here and there to avoid getting splashed.

"It's the *Pequod*!" She took Jack's hand and dragged him toward the quarterdeck.

"The what now?"

"Captain Ahab's ship."

Ah. Jack thought he understood. They were being attacked by

another contestant for the Pirate King contest. Which made sense. Violence was encouraged, after all.

"Let's find the captain!" Bonn cried.

It wasn't difficult to locate Mary. She was standing at the helm, steering the ship herself, barking orders to everyone around her. Tobias was in his regular spot right beside her, casually consulting a map like there wasn't madness and mayhem going on all around them.

"The problem is the *Pequod* and the *Ranger* are fairly evenly matched in size and cannons," Tobias was saying calmly, stepping aside as a parrot flew past him shrieking, "WE'RE ALL GOING TO DIE!" "So we need to find some way to get the advantage. Otherwise we're only going to sink each other."

"No one is sinking my ship," Mary growled. Her mouth pressed into a line when she saw Jack. "Go below! It's not safe up here!"

"I know!" he agreed.

A cannonball whizzed past their heads.

Jack held up his frying pan. "But I want to help."

She shook her head. "You can best help by staying out of the way, so I don't have to worry about you getting hurt."

Or getting wet.

This was reasonable, but Jack was still mildly offended.

It was almost like she didn't see him as a pirate.

"Hey now, see here, Mary—" he began.

She ignored him and turned to Bonn. "Bonny! So go find Diesel. He'll be on the gun deck by now. Tell him we're going to need him to get creative here. Jack, you go below."

"I'm going to stay with Bonn." He was not going to let her out of his sight, he decided. Getting wet wasn't the true danger here. If the ship was sunk, at least he'd be able to save his love from a watery grave. Would it be an awkward conversation later? Certainly. But her life was what mattered now.

"You're going to do what I tell you," Mary said sharply. "Because I'm the captain, and you're part of my crew, and that's how it works. Go below, cousin. That's an order."

"No." Jack folded his arms across his chest, trying not to flinch as another cannonball tore through one of the sails over their heads. "I'm with her." Then, silently, he added, *Unless you want to make me walk the plank.*

"Don't push me," she shot back. *"You're not going to get special treatment just because you're my—"*

"Jack, it's all right. I'm fine. Just do what she—" Bonn started to say, but suddenly there came a tremendous *BOOM!* and the ship rocked so hard to one side Jack feared they would capsize.

Bonn cocked her head. "That boom sounded different."

"It wasn't a cannon." Mary ran to the side and lifted her spyglass to her eye. "That was something else."

Jack, Tobias, and Bonn joined her at the rail just in time to see an enormous white whale glide up beside the *Pequod* and smash the entire front of the ship with its massive tail.

Bonn's mouth fell open. "Now there's something you don't see every day."

Tobias looked, in a word, relieved. "It destroyed the bowsprit. Their ship is now effectively disabled. We're . . . saved."

This was, of course, excellent, excellent news. But Mary's expression remained tense. And Jack thought perhaps he knew why (and he hoped it wasn't because she was now going to make him walk the plank).

Jack and Mary both knew their fair share of whales—big ones, small ones, in-between ones—and not one of them, to Jack's knowledge, ever tried to harm humans or Mer. Whales were fairly chill, as a species (those orcas could be feisty, no doubt, but they tended to keep their aggression limited to fish and seals). Why would a whale attack a human ship? Was it trying to help Mary somehow? Which brought up a bigger question: had this whale been *instructed* to help Mary? And if so, by whom?

Jack could think of only one person with the power and will to do such a thing.

The Sea King.

And if Mary's father (aka Jack's uncle) knew that Mary was alive, and knew her predicament and current whereabouts, there was no telling what was about to happen next.

While he was pondering all of this, the *Pequod* was slowly sinking beneath the waves. Her remaining crew was doggy-paddling toward the *Ranger*, calling out for help.

"Send out the dinghies," Mary instructed Quint, who came running up breathlessly. "We need to save as many of their men as we can."

Quint turned and ran back the way he'd come.

"Isn't that Ahab in the rowboat?" Bonn squinted. "I think he's coming over here, too. The nerve of that guy!"

Indeed, that's what appeared to be happening. Captain Ahab had abandoned his ship, and, flying a white flag of surrender, was making his way as fast as he could row toward the *Ranger*.

"New plan." Mary touched Jack's shoulder. *"I have a mission for you, cousin. Go talk to him,"* she ordered him silently.

"Who, Captain Ahab?" he asked.

"The whale. I don't know what its problem is, but I don't want it attacking us next."

Jack nodded. Talk to the whale. He could do that. His whale dialect was rusty, but he would do his best.

He really, really hoped this was not about the Sea King.

"Wait, where are you going?" Bonn called after him as he turned to walk away.

He turned back and handed her his frying pan. "Below. Like she said."

She looked like she would argue, but then Mary gave her an order—something Jack didn't hear—and reluctantly Bonn turned and headed in the other direction. Jack let her go. She was out of danger. For now. And he could be useful.

He found a spot near the rudder and glanced around to make sure that no one was watching him. No one was. Everyone was on the other side of the ship, pointing and staring at the *Pequod* and the frantically rowing Captain Ahab.

Jack stepped out of his pants and folded them neatly over the rail. Then he gasped at the feel of the cold night air against his bare legs and jumped off the side of the ship.

Into the deep, dark water.

Which welcomed him home like an old friend.

"Where in blazes have you been?" Bonn asked him later, stomping up to him. It was morning now, the sun peeking up against the blue horizon, and Jack was sitting on a crate on the main deck, sleepily picking through an armload of fabric in his lap. It had taken him hours to converse with the whale, climb up the side of the ship again—he would have to work on his upper-body strength if this was going to become a regular thing—wait for the opportune moment when no one was looking to heave himself over the rail, thoroughly dry himself, locate and re-don his pants, and report to Mary what he'd learned. He was exhausted. But here's what he'd discovered:

The Sea King had nothing to do with the vengeful whale.

It turned out that Captain Ahab was a vicious whale killer, and he and the great white leviathan had one heck of a history.

Mary had therefore put Ahab back in his rowboat and left him for the whale to deal with as he (the whale) saw fit. Then she'd recruited the rest of Ahab's men to her cause (there was a charming fellow on board called Ishmael who told the most amusing stories), and they all went on their merry way. (Ahab, by the way, was never seen again. But that's a retelling for another time.)

But Jack couldn't explain any of this to Bonn.

"Where have *you* been?" he countered. "I was looking for you earlier."

"I was with Gaines making repairs to the hull," she said, and for a moment he thought he'd managed to divert her question, but then she asked again. "So where were you, exactly?"

"Yes," came a voice from behind them, and they both turned to see Tobias standing there. "You were going a bit—how do I put this?—mutinous for a minute there earlier, and then you just walked away."

"Mary told me to," Jack said.

Tobias shook his head. "She didn't say anything."

"Yes, she did. She told me to go below. And so I went Below." (This was technically true.)

To change the subject, he held up a square of red cotton to show them. "Mary has asked me to design her a new flag for the ship. What do you think of red?"

"It has to be black, so she can say, 'Raise the black,'" Bonn said.

"Oh, right! Of course. Black it is."

Tobias frowned. "Mary wants you to do some sewing for her?"

"We don't want to be using Captain Vane's old flag anymore, do we?"

"I suppose not."

"She's made me the ship's official sailmaker," Jack said, his chest puffing out. He might not be a good fighter, but he was an absolute menace with needle and thread. He'd picked up the skill in the first week he'd been Above, when he'd stumbled upon a tailor's shop in Port Royal looking for some decent human clothes.

He unfolded a long strip of black fabric on the crate and picked up a sketchbook he'd grabbed from the captain's cabin earlier.

"Hey, that's mine," Tobias said.

"Oh. Can I borrow it? I need something in which to sketch the design."

"All right. Above all, I think, the flag should inspire fear," Tobias said, and then he grabbed the notebook himself and made a quick drawing of a flag, then turned it around for Jack to see. "I always thought, if I made a pirate flag, it'd look like this. Scary, right?"

He'd drawn a mermaid with long hair waving down her chest. But this mermaid had jagged eyebrows and fangs. With one hand she was holding her own tail. With the other she held a trident, upon which was speared a heart.

Scary mermaid. That was a little on the nose.

"This is . . . uh, terrifying," Jack said. "Well done."

Tobias shrugged. "Thanks."

"But the captain said no hearts on her flag. That was her only stipulation, in fact. No hearts."

"Right," muttered Tobias. "No hearts."

"I think the flag should be simple." Bonn snatched the sketchbook from Tobias and drew her own flag upon it. "It should plainly convey what we want people to do when they see us." She showed them. Her flag was just one word—SURRENDER—in all caps.

"That's very nice, darling," Jack said.

"But not everyone here can read," Tobias pointed out.

"Oh, that's right," Jack said. "Where I come from, everyone is well educated. I keep forgetting it's not like that here."

He was tired, and this kind of slipped out, and it took him a moment to realize that both Bonn and Tobias were now staring at him.

"I've been meaning to ask you," Tobias said slowly. "But where do you come from, exactly?"

Uh-oh.

"Why, Nassau, of course," Jack answered.

"No, before that."

"Before that, I was in Port Royal."

Tobias wiped his hand down the front of his face. "No, I mean before that. Where were you born? Where did you grow up?"

"Hasn't . . . hasn't Mary told you?" Jack stammered.

"She doesn't talk about her past."

"Well. Nor do I," Jack decided.

Bonn turned to Tobias. "Don't be offended, Teach. He won't even tell me where he's from."

"A fellow has to maintain some mystery," Jack said, trying to sound, well, mysterious.

"Does he, though?" Tobias questioned.

"Surely there are some things you haven't told Mary about

your own past," Jack said, "even though you're apparently such good mates."

Tobias shook his head. "No. I've told her everything."

Well, that was annoying. "You should try holding something back," Jack advised. "It could do wonders for your relationship."

"I don't see the point of mystery," said Bonn. "You wouldn't want to withhold such key information about yourself from the woman you intend to marry, would you, Jack?"

Oh, bother. She was finally going to push this issue.

"Well, uh, darling," he began. "You wouldn't have heard of where I'm from." And this much was true.

"I've heard of most places," Bonn countered. "I've had a fine education, don't you know. So try me."

"Uh . . . It's far away from here." This was not true. Under-where was actually quite close, as the swordfish swims.

"Like how far?" Tobias pressed. "I've always thought Mary's accent strange, like she's Dutch, perhaps?"

"That's exactly right," Jack said. "She's Dutch. I mean, we both are."

"Interesting," said Bonn, her bright green eyes watching his face closely. "So you grew up where, then? Paris?"

Jack's cheeks felt hot. This was terrible. He hated lying nearly as much as he hated fighting. "Yes," he coughed. "Paris. That's where we grew up."

Now both Bonn and Tobias were staring at him so intently that Jack knew he'd been trapped somehow. He squirmed. "Anyway, we lived in Paris for only a small time. We moved around a lot. Here and there, in Dutch-uh-land. With the wild . . . animals, of some kind. And the mountains."

Tobias gave a snort. Then he jumped up because Mary had come out of the captain's cabin.

"What are you all doing sitting about?" she asked, frowning at the way they were congregated around Jack.

"I'm working on the new flag, as you told me to, Captain," Jack said, holding up the sketchbook. "Because I'm a good and faithful member of your crew."

"Help, help, they're asking questions I can't answer," he pleaded silently.

"Toby, I need you," Mary said simply. Then to Bonn she ordered: "Up above with you, Bonny. You may relieve Mr. Keyes as lookout for today. I want your sharp eyes looking for another ship for us. We need more ships if we're going to bring back so much treasure."

"Aye, Captain," Bonn said, and in moments she was in the rigging, climbing to the crow's nest, and Mary and Tobias went back to the captain's cabin, and Jack was alone again.

Whew.

He spent the rest of the day working in an inspired fervor on the flag. He thought hard about all the pirate flags he'd seen thus far. Most of them had a skeleton stabbing something. But normally you were too far away to see what the flag depicted. Jack's design would need to be bolder, bigger, with more contrast. Something that inspired fear and communicated "SURRENDER" without the use of words.

It was almost dusk when he went to present his work to Mary.

"Look, I can't talk right now," she barked when he entered the captain's cabin. "Oh, it's you."

"Here's the new flag." He held it up.

It was a plain black flag with a large, grinning skull in the center and two crossed bones underneath that made a letter X.

That was it. Skull and crossbones.

"I call it the Jolly Roger," Jack said. "Jolly, because the skull is kind of smiling, see? Which I think is more frightening than if it were scowling, like what is it up to? And Roger, because the men tell me that's another name for the devil—some mystical figure that they're scared of. Hence the skull. Plus I just like how it sounds."

She was silent for a long moment, staring at it.

"I can do it again, if you don't like it," Jack said stiffly.

"I like it," she replied. "It's perfect. Now you need to make a few more exactly the same. For the *William* and the *Jester*, and any other ships we acquire."

He stifled a grin. "I'll get right on that." He turned to leave, then paused. "I may or may not have told Tobias and Bonn today that we were Dutch. Sorry."

She stared at him. "You what?"

"I didn't know what else I could tell them. They were insisting that I give them some point of origin."

She looked miffed for a moment, but then broke into a smile. "I guess we're Dutch, then. I hear Holland is nice this time of year."

Jack didn't know what Holland had to do with it. But he didn't ask, because right then he caught sight of the tiny hourglass on Mary's desk.

"Jumping jellyfish!" he gasped, rushing over to look at it more closely. "Where did you get this? My mother used to have one just like it. She'd give it to me whenever she wanted to make sure I returned home on time. I kept losing it, so she put a spell on it that made it so—"

"You couldn't get rid of it," Mary finished for him flatly.

He glanced up at her stoic expression. "Wait, how did you get this?"

She sighed. "My father gave it to me last week."

His stomach dropped. "Last *week*? What is it counting down to?"

"The end of the Pirate King contest." She rubbed at her eyes. "If I don't win, if I don't prove that I have what it takes to be a success as a human, then my father is coming to get me and take me home."

Jack stared at her, aghast. "But how would you breathe down there?"

"He'd get someone to kiss me," she answered.

"Ugh," he said with a shudder. "That's awful. So that's why you changed your mind about the contest! Why didn't you tell me before? I could have, well, not helped any more than I have, I suppose, but I could have at least understood what's at stake for you. Did he . . ." He gulped. Long ago, when they'd been assigning human names to Mer they knew, they'd named Mary's father Kevin, kind of as a joke. As in King Kevin. But try as Jack might, he'd never been able to think of the Sea King as Uncle Kevin. The guy was too imposing, and Jack had always been intimidated by him. Especially since he knew well enough that King Kevin considered Jack to be a bad influence on Mary. Which was fair. "Did he say anything about me?" he asked.

"No, but here's something I've been wondering," Mary said, picking up the hourglass and stuffing it into her pocket. "How did he know?"

"Pardon?"

"How did my father know I'm alive? How did he know where to find me? You said—" She took a few steps toward Jack, her fists clenching at her sides. "You told me that everyone thought I was sea foam. That there was a funeral. That they all mourned. So how did he know?"

"Oh." Jack's shoulders hunched. "That's probably my fault."

Mary closed her eyes. She nodded grimly. "And how is it your fault, Jack?" she asked lightly.

He winced. "I told my mother all about finding you again."

Her eyes opened. "You spoke to your mother? The Sea Witch?"

"I only have the one mother, Mary. And I talk to her every week."

"You swim back to Underwhere every week and talk to her?"

"No, silly." He pulled on the leather cord around his neck

until the clamshell pendent he always wore came free of his shirt. "I talk to her on my shell phone."

She stared at him, then stared at the clamshell. "Your shell phone?"

"It's one of my mother's more ingenuous recent magical inventions," he explained gleefully. "It allows us to speak in Mer over great distances. This is just the prototype, you understand, but I think it's going to become all the rage in Underwhere once we figure out distribution. It truly is an amazing little thing. You can talk and send messages to one another, and it has a map function to help you find your way—although this one only works underwater, unfortunately. It can tell you what the weather is going to be like tomorrow, it recites some of the more popular whale songs, and you can even play a few games on it. All in a device that fits in the palm of your hand."

"That is amazing," Mary said, stepping even closer to eye the shell phone with a half-envious, half-reverent expression. "May I see it?"

"Of course." He pulled the cord from around his neck and handed the phone to her.

She opened and closed the clamshell a few times. "You used this to talk to your mother about me?"

"I couldn't help myself. It was too good not to tell her all about you, *not sea foam after all*, living as a *pirate*! But I made her promise not to tell anyone."

"Oh, like you promised me you wouldn't tell anyone."

She had him there.

"So you told your mother about me being here, and she told my father."

"That does seem like the most likely explanation," Jack said. "I'm sorry."

"You're sorry," she repeated. "Jack. This is all your fault."

"Yes, which is why I apologized just now."

"And what else did you tell her?" Mary demanded, closing the clamshell firmly.

"Hey, be careful with that; the hinge is delicate. I, uh, may have told her about how you were dressing as a man because of the unfair rules about gender that exist Above, and about how you have a dear friend, Tobias Teach, the son of the most famous pirate in history, but unfortunately he died, because pirates don't live very long comparatively with other humans, and about how you were such a mild, unassuming little minnow before, but now you've become this fierce, scary, pirate-y woman."

"In other words, you told her everything."

He sighed. "I always tell her everything. She always wants to know every detail of my life. I'm supposed to call her tonight, in fact."

"Oh no, you don't." Mary closed her fist around the shell phone, walked briskly to the window in the back of the captain's cabin, opened it, and hurled the clamshell into the churning ocean.

"It's bad enough that he found me," she said crossly, "and that he interfered, because he *always* wants to interfere, and of course he had to give me some kind of ultimatum, didn't he? But he's not going to know about my every move up here. I am my own person. This is my life, and I refuse to live it with him bubbling down my neck. I'm going to win this contest and become the Pirate King, all on my own, without his meddling!"

Jack was still staring in agony out the window, his hand outstretched as if he could reach back in time and snatch up his precious shell phone. "Why, why would you do that?" he whispered. "I was almost at level one hundred on Crabby Crush!"

Her jaw set. "I won't have my father spying on me!"

"He's the Sea King! If he wants to spy on you, he can do it without my shell phone!" Oh, Great Waters, what would his mother think when he didn't call her? What would she do when she found out that Mary had destroyed his phone? His mother wasn't evil, but Jack didn't know what she'd do if she got truly angry on his behalf—one time in third grade she'd gone all Mama Shark and turned a boy who was bullying him into a cuttlefish. He didn't think his mother would turn Mary into a cuttlefish, seeing as she was family. But he couldn't be sure.

"When I saw the whale today, I thought maybe . . . ," she began.

He sighed. "Me too. I thought we both might be in some kind of trouble. But it turned out just to be an angry whale."

"What else did your mother give you?" Mary asked.

He shrugged. "Not much. She packed a bag for me with a few provisions: that organic kelp I like, a bag of seaweed chips, the face tonic she makes for me because I occasionally get those red spots on my chin, and a couple magical potions she thought might be useful, although I'm not actually sure what they all do." He shook his head, seeing the clamshell tumble through the air again in the back of his mind. "I can't believe you just threw away my shell phone!"

She scratched at the back of her neck. "I thought it might magically return to you. Like the hourglass. I was attempting to make a dramatic statement."

"I said it was a prototype!" he huffed.

Suddenly there was a shout from directly over their heads. An Irish shout. Bonn. "Sails! A ship! A ship!"

"I hope it's a big one," Mary said as she fetched her cutlass from behind her desk. She sighed. "I hope this whole treasure of Blackbeard's is more than just wishful thinking."

It was the first time Jack had seen her anything but confidant in their plan to get the treasure.

"Me too," he said. "I need that thousand pieces of eight."

"To get married?" she said doubtfully. "That is one expensive wedding."

"To get divorced," Jack said.

"What?"

"Bonn. Not me."

"Did anyone hear me yelling, SHIP, SHIP!" came Bonn's voice again.

"Anyway, there's no time to explain," Jack said, and then he and Mary both ran for the door.

Out on the deck, the ship was in an uproar (again), everyone running about preparing. Bonn was still up in the crow's nest. Jack followed Mary to the helm. As always, Tobias appeared beside her.

"What's the prize?" Tobias asked.

Mary put her spyglass to her eye. "Merchant ship." She squinted. "The *Kingston*?" She frowned and lowered the glass. "They are already flying a white flag, and I don't see the crew on deck."

"Like with the *William*? Someone offering up a ship?" Jack asked. "How about money? Do you think they'll be carrying, say, a thousand pieces of eight for each member of the crew?"

Mary snapped her spyglass shut. "Let's go get it. Full sails, men!" she called out. "Heave to! Take us straight to her, Mr. DuPaul. And Tobias, signal the other ships to stay back. It could be a trap from one of the other Pirate King contestants."

They set off at top speed for the *Kingston*.

"Wait, it could be a trap, and we're going to sail right into it?" Jack had questions.

"We're tough. We can handle anything," Mary said. "Besides, what do we have to lose?"

Jack could think of a few things. "Uh, our lives? Our ship? A lot of bananas?"

"The *Kingston* isn't any pirate ship that I've heard of," said Tobias. He unrolled and consulted a map. "But we're nearly within sight of Port Royal. We'll need to move fast."

Mary clapped him on the shoulder. "It's exactly what we've

been looking for. Do you reckon that's a big enough ship to hold your pa's treasure?"

He nodded. "A good portion of it, anyway."

"But it seems too easy, doesn't it?" Jack said. "A ship just there for the taking?"

"You don't know, Jack," Mary said. "That's how we got the *William*. Sometimes the ocean just gives you what you need, right at the moment you need it."

Jack hoped that was true.

Within the hour they were alongside the *Kingston* and could confirm that it was abandoned, save for a small crew of ten men, who were meant to keep the ship anchored and afloat.

"What are you doing out here?" Mary asked them when she'd crossed over to parley. They did not look like pirates. They were dressed in nondescript sailor's clothing, but something about their bearing was more rigid, more straight-shouldered, than the typical buccaneers. "What say you?" Mary demanded.

"We're messengers," one of the men said.

"And what is your message?" Mary asked.

Jack had a bad feeling about this. His squid sense was tingling.

The man gave Mary a tight smile. "Death to all pirates," he said with a sneer. "Courtesy of Jonathan Barnet."

"Sails!" came Bonn's distant voice from the *Ranger*. "Sails! SAILS!"

"Where?" Tobias yelled up.

"Three to starboard. Four to port!" Bonn screamed. "Seven

big ships, led by a frigate flying the British flag. All of them closing fast. Get back here! It's a blooming trap!"

A trap. Not one set by another captain in the contest.

One set by the notorious pirate hunter. Meant for any wannabe Pirate King.

"Oh ship," muttered Mary. "Retreat!"

Once the boarding party was back on the *Ranger*, Mr. DuPaul attempted to turn about, but the wind was against them. The British ships were closing in like pincers. They were vastly outmanned and outgunned, and everyone on the *Ranger* well knew it. The crew was already starting to panic.

"At least we sent the other ships away." Mary paced the deck. "It will only be us they capture."

"What will they do, if they capture us?" Jack asked tremulously.

Mary shrugged. "Take us back to Port Royal, I imagine, and then we'll hang."

Jack swallowed. "And how can we prevent that from happening?"

Mary stared at him, helpless. "You can go," she said.

"Go?"

"Swim away. Go home, Jack. Save yourself."

He let out a breath. "I can't do that. I won't. What else is there to be done?"

"Nothing," she said. "It would take a miracle."

"Right," Jack said. "And what's a miracle?"

"Something wondrous and unexpected," Tobias explained weakly. "Like magic."

Mary's eyes widened. "Magic," she gasped. She turned to Tobias. "Toby, go tell Diesel to lighten our load. We're going to run."

Tobias hurried away. The moment he was out of earshot, Mary grabbed Jack. "Go get your mother's potions. Maybe one of them can help us."

Jack thought he knew just the one that would do it. He dashed down to the berth, fetched his bag from under his hammock, and ran as fast as he could back to Mary.

"We can use this one to escape!" Jack held up the dark blue vial with the lightning bolt on it. "I accidentally mixed it up with my face tonic one time, and then it started to rain and thunder all around my head, and it was a mess. Thankfully Bonn wasn't there."

Mary took the vial from him. "So what does it do?"

"It conjures a storm."

She nodded eagerly. "That could work. Good! There's no time to lose!" She uncorked the vial. "We'll need a lot of it."

"Mary, wait! We should—" Jack called, but it was too late. Mary had already run over to the side and dumped the entire contents of the vial into the water.

The result was instantaneous. A thick fog billowed up all around them, obscuring any sight of the oncoming ships. Black clouds rolled in over their heads. Lightning cracked in the sky as an enormous wind filled the sails.

Jack grabbed Mary by the shoulder. "I SAID WAIT!" he yelled, but it would have been hard to hear him over the rolling sound of thunder.

"AND I SAID THERE WAS NO TIME TO LOSE."

The ship lurched violently to one side.

"YOU PUT IN TOO MUCH!" Jack groaned.

"I'M SORRY!"

Many things happened quickly then:

The ships that had been chasing them, lost them. Yay!

They almost got driven aground on the island of Jamaica. Boo!

The storm pushed them toward the rest of their fleet—the *William* and the *Jester*. Yay!

And then the storm was directly on top of them. Boo.

Bonn came down from the crow's nest just before it got struck by lightning. Jack ran toward her, relief filling his chest. She was safe. Yay!

But just before he reached her, a huge wave crashed over the ship, and Jack slipped. He fell. He was caught up in the wave as it raged across the deck, and he was swept away.

Boo.

Mary →

THIRTEEN

Mary watched in horror as Jack slid overboard.

"Jack!" Anne screamed, running to the rail after him. Then, with the heavy wind bearing down on her, she nearly went over herself.

Mary hauled Anne back onto the deck just in time. "Don't be a fool, Bonny! Get back!"

Frantically, the girl shook her head, wet curls plastered to her face. "I have to get Jack!"

They both looked into the choppy water just as Jack's head surfaced above the waves. *"I'm all right. Get Bonn to safety! Please!"* Jack shouted in Merish.

"I will!" Mary called back. *"Be safe! Storms are dangerous underwater, too."* As Mary very well knew.

Anne hadn't heard any of that, of course. She glanced around wildly, grabbed a piece of a broken barrel, and threw it down into the water. "Use this to stay afloat!"

But it was no use. The wind caught the wood and carried it away. The storm was turning into an actual hurricane, lightning cracking across the slate-gray sky. Wind keened across the deck, forcing the rest of the crew to grab handholds as they moved across the planks.

"Storm sails!" Mary shouted as another gust of wind roared up, sending wave after wave across the deck. "Drop the sea anchor! Secure—"

Lightning flashed. Thunder boomed. Rain sheeted, obscuring everything. A wave rushed over Jack's head. He didn't surface again.

"I'll never let go, Jack! I'll never let go!" Anne sobbed as Mary hauled her away from the rail.

"Stop. Making. This. Harder," Mary said, pulling her along the deck.

"Please!" Anne begged. "There's got to be something we can do! Some way to at least give him a *chance*. He'll drown!"

"I'm sorry," Mary growled, fighting both the wind and Anne to move up the deck. "There's nothing we can do for him now."

"You're heartless," Anne cried. "There should be *something* on this ship to help save him, some sort of flotation device."

(Your narrators here. Anne has a point. There *should* be something. Like a life preserver. Or a life jacket. It turns out that

233

humans have always had some sort of floatation device, basically since ancient times. In the ongoing effort to avoid drowning at sea, humans have used things like inflated animal skins, bits of driftwood, and other floating debris. This worked just fine when ships were mostly made of wood. Though, of course, if you got thrown overboard like Jack here and the ship was still intact, then there probably wasn't as much floating debris to grab hold of. It wasn't until much later, when ships were constructed from less-floatable iron, that life jackets as we might recognize them were invented— think 1850s—with cork vests. And it wasn't until quite a while after *that*, with the sinking of a very famous ship—yeah, you know the one—that life jackets (and lifeboats) were required for every passenger on board. But none of that could help Jack right now, could it? Fortunately, Jack couldn't drown, being that his legs just fused into a tail and he was back to breathing water. *Un*fortunately, Anne didn't know any of that. Now, back to the hurricane.)

Still holding fast to Anne, Mary scanned the slick decks for the rest of her crew. "Get to cover!" Mary shouted, hooking her other arm around a nearby pole to brace against the wind. They were all in action, everyone moving to secure barrels and spars and anything that might come loose. This storm was serious. It was a ship killer if she'd ever seen one.

Maybe she shouldn't have dumped the *entire* bottle of storm potion into the sea.

"Captain!" Quint was hauling himself toward her. "Should I send the crew belowdecks?"

"Do it. And take Bonny here. Tie her up if you must." Mary shoved Anne at Quint. Anne fought, of course, but they wrestled her down the stairs and into the crew quarters.

Mary went back up to see to the rest of the crew. She gripped the rail as wind shoved at her. With the sea anchor down and the storm sails up, the *Ranger* had turned, and now the bow was pointing directly into the wind. They rode up a huge wave, crested, and slammed into the trough on the other side.

Every movement was an effort as the ship rolled and yawed violently along the waves, but slowly, Mary made her way to the main deck and counted her men as they went below—into the safety of the crew quarters.

But someone was missing.

Tobias.

Mary squinted against the sheeting rain, scanning the yards and decks. But with the storm, her visibility was shot. And when she called out for him—"Tobias!"—the wind sucked her words away.

The ship rose and fell over another immense wave. Water crested and surged, dragging at Mary's legs as she braced herself until the deck was horizontal again. Several minutes passed as she searched the weather decks, calling Tobias's name, until an enormous gust of wind knocked her down hard enough to bruise. Mary skidded across the deck, grasping for something to hold on to, and then, before the wind threw her overboard, she caught hold of a line. Quickly, she looped the rope around her wrist, ignoring the chafing pain as she pulled herself upright again.

She couldn't stay out here. If anything, the storm was getting worse.

And Tobias? She hoped he was safe below.

One painful step at a time, Mary hauled herself to the captain's quarters—but her fingers were so wet she couldn't grasp the knob. She wiped her palms on her sodden clothes, then tried again. But the door wouldn't budge with the wind and pressure.

"ARRR!" she screamed.

Then the door burst open, and Tobias reached out, grabbed her, and dragged her into the cabin. It took both of them together to pull the door closed again.

Mary dropped to the floor, her legs too weak to hold her up any longer. Every muscle was aching, slowly stiffening thanks to the cold and overexertion. But . . . she'd found Tobias? So yay?

"Have you been in here the whole time?" Her voice was thinner than she'd intended. Everything hurt.

"I came to secure the maps and logbook. The astrolabe and sextant." He motioned to the cupboards where they kept the navigational instruments. All of them were delicate, irreplaceable, and totally necessary if they were going to figure out where they were once this storm was finished. Without them, they'd be lost.

Mary blew out a long breath. "Right. That makes sense. I should have thought of that."

The *Ranger* rode up another wave, then crashed down.

Tobias pulled the blanket off Mary's bed and draped it over

her shoulders. "Hang on," he said. "I'll get you some dry clothes."

Mary shivered, holding herself against the bulkhead as the ship pitched and rolled. She hoped Jack was all right. And the other crews, whose lives were her responsibility.

While Tobias rifled through the wardrobe and chest of drawers, Mary closed her eyes, remembering, as the ship pitched beneath her, another storm. Her first.

The one that had changed her life.

She recalled with perfect clarity darting between broken beams and planks, searching the raging waters for Charles's sinking body. And then—once she had him—pressing her mouth to his. Later, after the storm died down and she'd dragged him up onto dry land, she'd dropped, trembling, by his side, relieved to see his chest rising and falling, breath puffing from between his parted lips. She'd traced along his cheekbone with the tips of her fingers, finding his skin, so clammy before, now warm under the sun.

He was so, so beautiful, she'd thought.

He was alive. It had taken all her strength to save him but save him she had. Her kiss had worked.

"Here." Tobias passed her a bundle of clothes. "I'll turn around while you change."

Mary shook herself, returning to the present—*this* storm, which she knew how to weather, and *this* man, who saved her life (almost) as often as she saved his.

"Thank you." The moment Tobias was facing away, Mary

peeled off her boots, stockings, trousers, and shirt. They were all sopping wet. Using the blanket, she dried her damp skin as best she could, then pulled on the fresh clothes.

"I'm decent," she said, drawing the blanket over her again. "Still freezing. The rain is like musket balls."

"Here." Tobias slipped into the blanket den with her. "Is this all right?"

He was warm. *Really* warm. Mary found herself leaning toward him, pressing her arm against his. She cleared her throat. "Listen, I've been meaning to thank you for offering your pa's treasure. You don't have to do that. You know that, right?"

Tobias twisted to look at her. "I want you to win," he said softly under the rumbling thunder and keening wind. "Even if I don't know why it's suddenly so important to you."

She swallowed a knot in her throat. The ship rolled over another wave, causing her to press even more into Tobias. When it settled again, she reached into her pocket and removed the magic hourglass. (She hadn't transferred it from her wet clothes to her dry clothes. But then, she hadn't needed to. The wretched thing always jumped into whatever pocket she happened to be wearing.)

"What is that?" Tobias asked.

Mary turned it over in her hands, watching as the sand continued to move from the cloud chamber to the water chamber, even when it was upside down.

Tobias gasped. "Is . . . it supposed to be doing that? How? Just—*how*?"

"Magic," she said with a sigh. "It's magic."

"But there's no such thing?"

Mary tossed the hourglass across the cabin, where it rolled under the door and out onto the deck. Unfortunately, it wasn't lost to the storm, because seconds later, she fished it out of her pocket again.

"Oh my God." Tobias was very still, staring at the hourglass in her hand. "That's— That's not possible. But I just saw it with my own eyes. Unless you have several in your pockets?" He shook his head. "No, that's ridiculous. Why would anyone have a pocket full of gravity-defying hourglasses?"

The corner of Mary's mouth turned up with a smile. "A good question."

"Okay," Tobias said. "I'll bite. What does this, uh, magic hourglass have to do with you winning the contest?"

Mary bit her lip. "My father found me," she said finally. "Jack told his mother we ran into each other, and she told my father and, well, he's demanding that I go back."

"Your father found you," Tobias repeated softly. "Mary, did you— Did you run away from home?"

"It's complicated, but yes. That's what happened. And unless I can prove myself to him, he'll force me to return home when the sand runs down. That'll be the full moon."

"And to prove yourself to him, you have to win the contest." Tobias was quiet for a long moment, like he was absorbing it all. Outside, the storm raged on. "That's why you said this is about your freedom," he said at last. "Not just your freedom as a woman on a pirate ship, but your freedom to be who you are, go where you want, and do as you please."

Her freedom to be with him. "Yes," she said softly.

"Mary, *where* are you from? Because I'm certain it's not Holland. Or Paris."

She closed her eyes and exhaled. It was now or never. "I'm from Underwhere."

His brow rumpled. "Under . . . where?"

"Yes."

"I'm not following," he said.

She pointed down. "Under there. Far, far below the ocean's surface. And when I lived there, I was a princess."

"In Underwhere."

She smiled. He understood. "Yes."

Tobias opened his mouth. Then he closed it. Then he said, "I have follow-up questions."

Mary laughed a little. "Fine. I'll start from the beginning."

There, under the blanket, while the storm raged outside, Mary told Tobias about her life before this, when she'd been the littlest of princesses, overlooked and babied, laughed at for being fascinated by the human world—and all the scraps of Above that floated down around Underwhere.

"Jack and I had a secret hideout where we kept all our human stuff," she admitted. "That's where we learned to read—at least until the books disintegrated—and learned about human culture. Obviously there were some gaps in our knowledge. There were no pirates in the books we read. And the stories all had happy endings."

Or so she'd thought.

When she finished telling him about her fight with her father, visiting the Sea Witch for help, and then everything that happened in Charles Town, Tobias was quiet. He was quiet for a long time.

Perhaps she had revealed too much. "Toby, say something."

He cleared his throat. "I apologize. I was merely thinking about how everything I thought I understood about science, nature, and humanity in general is wrong. This is a lot."

"I know. Why do you think I didn't want to talk about it before? It's not only my secret, but the secret of a whole world. I can't trust just anyone with it."

"And you trust me?" he asked.

"I always have." Mary tilted her head. The ship's rocking had stopped, and the sound of wind had died. Finally, the storm was done, the potion's power spent. She pushed aside the blanket and got to her feet. "I'm sure the storm blew us way off course, so find your fancy instruments, Mr. Teach, and figure out where we are. I'll see to the crew."

"Aye, aye, Princess."

Mary shot a look at him. "That's *Captain* Princess to you."

Tobias smirked. Then he got to work.

* * *

The ship was a mess. One of the masts had cracked, though according to Mr. Gaines, a quick repair would get it back into working condition—as long as they didn't come across more unusually bad weather. The storm sails were in tatters, though those could be mended. And, obviously, the deck was in dire need of swabbing, a fact that Nine Toes was ranting about.

"Stop stepping where I just mopped!" he cried as the rest of the crew scurried about, hauling up the sea anchor and trimming the mainsail. "You're getting boot prints everywhere!"

As Mary strode across the deck (keeping clear of Nine Toes's mop lines, if only to spare the rest of the crew more of his wailing), she paused to assess the damage, give orders, and ask after anyone she hadn't already seen. That was when she spotted Anne at the bow, leaning over the rail and looking forlornly out at the water.

"Need a job to do?" Mary asked, approaching her. "Or is there something wrong down there?"

Anne glanced up, unshed tears shining in her eyes. Her voice was rough. "I don't see him."

Oh. She was looking for Jack. Mary wasn't sure what to tell her, though.

"He's probably fine, though, right?" Anne asked. "He's a good swimmer. He told me that before. So he might have made it."

"Nope," said the guy with the chicken. "After a storm like that, he's surely down in Davy Jones's locker. No one can outswim a hurricane. Poor fellow."

"Begawk!" agreed the chicken.

Anne gave a noisy gulp and a sniffle, and tears slipped down her freckled cheeks.

Mary shooed away the guy with the chicken. "Off with you! Find something useful to do." Then she put a hand on Anne's shoulder and they both faced the waves while Anne fought to keep her tears under control and Mary wondered where her cousin was. Or if she should say anything to comfort Anne. And if perhaps the hurricane had gotten Jack. Those winds had been strong, and if there'd been any debris in the swirling water—well, Mary knew from experience how difficult it could be to swim through it. Still, she wasn't ready to count Jack out just yet.

"There, there," Mary said after a few minutes. Because she had to say something. "Sorrows, sorrows. Prayers."

Fortunately, Anne was too busy with her own feelings to notice that Mary was oddly unemotional about her cousin's (unlikely) untimely demise.

"I can't believe he's gone," Anne said hoarsely. "He only wanted to be a pirate because of me. I got him into this."

"You can't blame yourself," Mary said.

"I thought—" Anne wiped her face with her sleeve. "When he went over, I thought I saw . . . something. So I was hoping . . ."

"Uh, what did you think you saw?" Mary asked.

"It sounds mad," Anne said quietly, "but I thought I saw—"

"What are we looking at?" asked a voice right behind them.

Mary and Anne spun to find Jack there, fully dressed (thank goodness) and craning his neck to see around them.

"Jack?!" Anne shouted incredulously. "Gawl! I thought you were—" She threw her arms around him.

Jack lifted Anne and spun her around, then kissed her right in front of everyone. A few pirates whooped.

Mary watched the reunion, hardly aware of her own small smile. It was good to see them both happy. "Glad you made it, Jack," she said. "Not that I was worried. I knew you would."

"How *did* you make it?" Anne asked, stepping back from him. She looked him up and down. "And not a scratch on you!"

"I, uh—" Jack shot Mary a frantic look. "*Help?*" he asked in Merish.

"Like you said earlier," Mary said out loud, "he's a good swimmer. One of the best I know."

"That's right!" Jack let out a nervous laugh. "A little squall can't keep me from you, darling." He kissed Anne again.

"But the storm went on for hours," Anne protested. "I don't see—"

"Don't you both have jobs?" Mary clapped her hands together twice. "Go find something useful to do, or I'll put a mop in your hands and you can swab the deck with Nine Toes."

"I wouldn't mind the help!" Nine Toes called.

"I'll get to mending the sails," Jack said cheerily. "And Bonn, I'm sure there are sharp objects that could be made sharper."

"Aye," Anne agreed. "I'll take care of that right away."

Mary smiled as they headed away. *"I'm glad you're not sea foam, cousin,"* she called to Jack in Merish. *"But you'll want to keep an eye out on*

Anne. She suspects something."

"I'm sure everything will be fine," he replied.

And for the first time, Mary thought he might be right. Tobias had taken the Mer thing remarkably well.

Perhaps not *every* relationship was doomed, after all.

FOURTEEN

Tobias

Things Tobias had learned during that talk with Mary: mermaids were real, she was a princess, and Jack could swap between the two forms as needed. Oh, and *mermaids were real*.

It was blowing his mind a little bit.

Partly because Blackbeard had been *right*.

There'd been a moment when Tobias had been a lad of just eight or nine, and Blackbeard had decided to "teach him the stars."

"The best captains are their own navigators," he'd said. "You must learn how to find the ship's latitude. You must know how to read a map." Blackbeard shuffled through several papers on his desk—a fascinating pile of various maps and charts. Then Tobias spotted the drawing of a mermaid.

"Why do you have this?" he asked with a fearful shiver.

"Mermaids are bad luck, Pa. If you look into the ocean and say the word *mermaid* three times, one will appear out of the water and eat your face off!"

Blackbeard drew back. "Who told you such a thing?"

"Johnny Silver in my class."

Blackbeard gave a hearty laugh. "Well, that's not true." He pulled the drawing out from under the other papers to show Tobias. This mermaid was beautiful, with long flowing hair and a piercing yet somehow kindly gaze. No fangs. "Mermaids are magical, my son. They're *good* luck, they are. Count yourself most fortunate if you ever encounter one."

Well, now Tobias had.

He couldn't help but wonder what Blackbeard would think of his current circumstance.

The existence of mermaids kept popping up in Tobias's thoughts at the strangest of times, such as when he wandered down to the galley to see what was for dinner, and Mr. Child had a dozen fish spread out on cutting boards. *Mary used to have a tail like that*, he found himself thinking, and later he couldn't eat anything but the beets Mr. Child had served up as a side.

And, of course, whenever he looked out into the water, he found himself straining to see some kind of kingdom under the surface. Maybe a mermaid looking back up at him. Should he wave if he saw one? Or pretend like nothing was going on? What if he said *mermaid* into the water three times? Would one actually appear?

Finally, there was that time he was on the main deck taking

noonday sights and caught Mary with the hourglass in her hand, a brief, worried expression passing over her face.

If they didn't win the contest, her father—the actual king of the sea—would come find her and take her away, and Tobias would never see her again.

He could not let that happen.

And so, he focused fully (or, rather, as much as he was able, given this new reality he was getting used to) on the task at hand: getting his pa's treasure, returning to Nassau, and seeing Mary crowned Pirate Queen.

Unfortunately, they hadn't been able to take the *Kingston*. Nor did they have time to go looking for another ship. The three they had would have to be enough.

The first part of their journey was simple enough. They sailed to North Carolina, which took nearly a week. Once they reached North Carolina, they had to leave the fleet of ships in a place called Pamlico Sound and take a rowboat up the river to Plum Point, a large expanse of property the governor of North Carolina had bestowed upon Blackbeard when the old pirate had made a deal with him that he wouldn't attack any of the governor's ships.

"I'm coming, too," Anne insisted when Mary assigned herself, Jack, and Tobias to the initial scouting party. "You'll need another person who can scrap, if there's a fight."

"There won't be a fight," Tobias said.

"There will be if I don't get to go with you," she pointed out.

So they all piled into a single rowboat, and off they rowed.

It was the dead of night and pitch-black out when they finally made it up the river to Plum Point. All around were trees with Spanish moss hanging in dark clumps, fireflies swinging in and out and out of them, a pale blue mist rolling over the ground. Tobias and Anne kept stumbling as they came up the path from the shore. They were having a much worse time of it than Jack and Mary, he noticed, who could see better in the dark than he could. (It must be a Mer thing.)

They passed a creepy little shack where an old man was playing an out-of-tune banjo on the front porch. Then Plum Point Manor loomed out of the dark ahead of them. Tobias's breath caught. Even though his feelings about Blackbeard were complicated, he still couldn't help the thrill that shivered through him. His father's house.

Was it Tobias's house now? He didn't know.

They reached the front steps of the house, which was dark—no lights in the windows, no smoke curling from the chimney, no creepy banjo music. It was clear that no one was home. Tobias stared at the house for a long moment, looking into the space where his pa should be.

"He never felt at home here," Tobias said. "He couldn't find his land legs."

He turned and started walking briskly away.

"Wait!" Mary called, running to catch up with him. "Aren't we going in?"

"Nope."

"But isn't the house where we'll find the treasure?"

He didn't answer. He just led them behind the house to a rocky field where, at the far edge, he knew they'd find an oven-like structure made of bricks.

"What's this?" Jack asked, baffled.

"It's called the Kettle," Tobias said. "It's where Pa made tar for sealing the hulls of his ships."

Anne eyed the thing doubtfully. "It doesn't look like any kettle I ever saw."

"It isn't like any kettle you ever saw." Tobias kicked around in the dirt at the base of the structure for a while. Then, presently, he bent and picked something up. A large, rusty key.

The group swiveled again to look at the oven.

Tobias brushed aside a bit of greenery from the top of the Kettle, revealing a hole in the brick just big enough for a person to fit an arm into. There was a message etched into the brick right above it in surprisingly fancy script: *Give me a Hand*.

His father had made a joke of that, every time they'd come here. Which had been often.

Tobias glanced around, keeping his expression sober. "Anyone know how to stop excessive bleeding? Because if I don't do this right . . . well, there's a reason so many of my father's men had hooks."

Anne, Jack, and Mary gave a collective gulp.

"No? Oh well, here goes." Tobias thrust his hand (which was holding the key) into the hole.

"Be careful," said Mary.

There was a bit of scratching and the sound of metal on metal. Then came a loud metallic click.

And Tobias screamed.

They all rushed to him, Anne yanking off her belt to serve as a tourniquet, Mary tearing a piece of her shirt off as a bandage. Jack found a stick that he could bite.

But then, as they pulled him back from the hole, Tobias gave a halfhearted laugh.

"I'm just kidding," he said. "I'm fine."

He held up his hand and wiggled his fingers for them to see.

Jack gave a grudging smile. "Oh, I see," he said. "You wanted to scare us in order to be humorous and entertaining."

"Yes, that was the plan," Tobias said ruefully.

Anne grinned. "Classic!"

Mary said nothing. Her hand was at her chest, clutching the shirt/bandage. Then she scowled and hit him hard on the arm.

"Don't ever do that!" She blinked several times and dashed the strip of torn shirt against her eyes. "That's an order!"

"Aye, Captain," he said. "Sorry, Captain."

"Now, about that key?" Jack said.

They all turned their attention to the hole again. Under the hole a metal plate had popped out from the wall. Tobias swung it open, revealing a crank.

"Anyone want to volunteer to turn the crank?" Tobias laughed again weakly.

No one did.

Tobias put his shoulder against the wall and turned the crank smoothly. They all heard another metallic grinding noise, and then a trapdoor began to slide open in the floor of the Kettle, leading down into a dark passageway.

"Gawl," said Anne.

Tobias lit the lantern and led them through the narrow passageway until it opened into a small cave, and at the other end of the cave was a set of long wooden stairs leading farther down into the dark. There was another little message posted: *Walk on the Left side.*

"Now we're getting somewhere!" Mary grabbed the lantern away from Tobias and started enthusiastically down the stairs.

"Wait!" Tobias called after her.

Mary hated waiting, as he knew well. But she only got about halfway down the stairs (treading carefully on the left, as the sign had instructed) when the wooden steps gave way beneath her and she plunged down, down, down. She only just managed to catch herself by one hand on what was left of the stairs, swinging and then dangling from the edge. Her lantern smashed on the rocks (and a nasty assortment of sharpened spears) below her.

"Mary!" Tobias ran down the steps (smartly keeping to the right) and grabbed her hand and sleeve and whatever else he could reach. "Here—"

"I'm all right," Mary gasped, still dangling. "I can manage myself."

The corner of his mouth quirked up. "Oh, can you now?"

She reached for him with her other hand, and he caught it. He hauled her to her feet, drawing her close to his chest for the briefest of comforting moments, but she pulled back from him as Jack and Anne descended to meet them. "Why in blazes did he instruct us to walk on the left side?"

"Pa had an odd sense of humor," Tobias admitted.

"Like father, like son," Mary scoffed, and then stepped back against the wall and gestured for Tobias to go first as they proceeded. He took the scrap of shirt from Mary and the stick from Jack and made a handy torch out of it, which was good, because the lantern was long gone. Much more slowly and carefully, the group went down the stairs. At the bottom there was a locked metal door, which Tobias opened using the same key he'd retrieved from the hole earlier.

They had to push hard to get the door to open, as it was partially rusted.

"This is it," Tobias said. "Treasure enough to win the contest."

"This wasn't nearly as hard as you made it sound like it would be," Mary said. "I thought you said there'd be more booby traps."

"Well . . ." Tobias shrugged. "The stairs counted as one."

"I'm not complaining," Jack said. "All I want is a thousand pieces of eight."

"I want more than that," Anne said. "I want to dive into a vault of gold coins and swim around—"

"Let's not count our coins before they clink," Mary said as they stepped inside.

On the other side of the door was still another cave. Tobias had always felt cozy in there, with some of the walls covered with sails to give the impression of a real interior. It was also crowded with an assortment of odd furniture: a tiny table bearing a chessboard and ivory and ebony pieces, an old pianoforte with several missing keys, the top of a ship's crow's nest braced against the ceiling of the cave with various trinkets and bottles and brightly colored fabric hanging down from it. A chandelier fashioned from the wheel of another ship. A bar (of course) and an assortment of barstools, flanked by a few barrels of what could have once held gunpowder or rum.

But now, Tobias's heart was sinking.

"Look!" Anne exclaimed behind him. "Blackbeard's flag."

Anne, Jack, and Mary stood a long time looking at the flag. (Tobias barely gave it a second glance, as he'd seen it many times before.) It was a horned skeleton who with one hand held up a goblet (apparently to toast the devil) while the other hand grasped a sword and stabbed it into a perfect red heart with three drops of blood spilling out.

"What does it mean?" Anne asked, awe filling her tone.

"Who can say?" Jack shook his head. "The messaging is all over the place."

Anne patted Jack's arm. "Your flag is much better. I'm sure soon enough all pirates will come to stand behind the skull and crossbones. Now that's a message. But can I have this?"

"Sure, whatever," said Tobias. "But the treasure . . ."

Mary glanced around furtively. "There is no treasure here."

Anne turned a small circle, her sharp eyes scanning every corner. "It's just . . . stuff."

The hard truth settled over them all. There wasn't a gemstone in this room, nor a single coin. The only promising items were a few old trunks scattered about, but upon inspection they were stuffed with damp, moth-eaten old clothes. Even the candlesticks on the large table in the center of the room weren't real silver, but pewter, and the table itself was strewn with ruined books and inscrutable maps.

"What the fish?" Mary spat. "Tobias? You said it would be here."

"I thought it would! He must have moved it somewhere else before he . . ." He glanced around, but there was nothing but maps and books.

His heart grew heavy. If Blackbeard had moved the treasure, then it meant that he hadn't wanted Tobias to have it. All that talk about being the heir . . . and in the end, their final argument had won out. Tobias had said he didn't want to be the Pirate King—and clearly Blackbeard had, in the end, agreed with him.

"What are you looking at?" Mary stepped into Tobias's line of sight and he realized he'd been staring into space. "This?" She pointed at a map.

Wait . . . a map!

He surged toward the table and began rummaging around, pulling out maps and discarding them. "Maybe there's a map here, to where he's stashed the real treasure," he said. But even as he rifled through his pa's old papers, he knew it didn't make sense. Blackbeard had often said that the only people who knew how to find his treasure were himself and the devil. And Tobias, allegedly.

He swallowed a knot in his throat. Now was not the time to feel sorry for himself.

Mary picked up one of the largest books and started to shake it, as though a secret map would fall out. None did. But then Tobias noticed the writing in the book. The same neat, curly handwriting as the messages on the wall of the Kettle and the space above the booby-trapped stairs.

"Wait." Tobias took the book from her. "This might be something. Anne, Jack, light those candles."

They did. The group circled around behind Tobias and all tried to make out what was written.

"May 12, 1719," Jack read over his shoulder. "Why, I think this is a diary!"

"His journal," Tobias agreed softly. He wanted to close it, to keep everyone from seeing whatever Blackbeard had written about him. But Mary was already touching the page, reading aloud.

"'*The mermaid is laughing at me*,'" she read. "What does he mean mermaid?"

"My father was obsessed with mermaids," Tobias admitted. "He had a tattoo of a mermaid over his heart, in fact. Recently, he"—Tobias paused, something working in his throat—"went on some wild-goose chase looking for them. He thought he saw mermaids everywhere, in every wave, on every big rock in a bay. He kept saying only a mermaid could cure him of his malady, that he had definitive proof that they existed."

"His malady?" Anne asked.

"It was, uh, the French disease." Tobias felt heat moving up his neck. "He was quite mad, by the end."

You're mad! The shame of those cruel words welled up in him again.

Mary touched his arm, the smallest form of comfort she could offer him, but it made him feel better in so many ways. Then she read a bit further. "*'She has begun to sing to me, songs of my own death, songs of love, songs of all the secrets of the deep. I think she means to give me away to my enemies. . . . I think she wants me to leave. To return to her. But I won't part with my gold. It's mine—more than I could ever spend in a lifetime, but mine. My own. My pr—'*" Mary rubbed at her eyes. "I can't read any more. It's smudged."

"So he does have gold," Jack said. "At least now we know for sure."

"He did have it," Anne corrected him. "He doesn't have it now. He doesn't have anything now." She glanced at Tobias. "Sorry."

He nodded sadly. "It's all right. It's the truth."

"But he did have a treasure recently," Jack persisted.

"And he was definitely paranoid about losing it," Mary said.

Paranoid about losing it . . . and intentionally moving it away from the one place Tobias knew to look.

They were all quiet for a moment, considering.

"Perhaps he was in the *process* of moving it. Which means his treasure would have gone down when Pa went down," Tobias said. And they all knew what he meant.

The treasure could be with the *Queen Anne's Revenge*. And the *Queen Anne's Revenge* was somewhere off the coast of North Carolina.

At the bottom of the sea.

"Well, the good news is that we can find out, can't we?" Tobias said cheerily. "Jack can go down there and check."

"He can?" Anne looked at Jack.

"Uh, on account of what a good swimmer I am," Jack said quickly.

"Yes. Swims like a fish, Jack does," Mary added.

"Ha! A fish!" Jack tried to laugh.

Anne looked from Jack to Mary and back again. "What's going on?"

"Sorry," Tobias said. "This is my fault."

"It's nothing," Mary insisted. She blew out the candles. "All right, then. Let's get back to the ship. We're wasting time."

It took them until morning to row back to the *Ranger*. Once there, the group compared notes with the crew. What stories had the men heard about where, exactly, the *Queen Anne's Revenge* had gone down? Then everyone started yelling names they knew of towns in North Carolina or rumors they'd picked up: about how Blackbeard had grounded the ship on a sandbar on purpose when he couldn't outrun Jonathan Barnet, or how he'd sent Caesar, his loyal quartermaster, down below with orders to set the powder room alight when defeat had seemed inevitable. Tobias felt a great, sorrowful tension rising up in him at every story, but he didn't have time right now for grieving what he'd lost. The point of the stories was this: his father's ship could be in a thousand pieces on the sandy bottom right now.

Eventually the guy with the chicken said he knew a guy who knew a man who'd spoken with a fella back at Nassau who claimed he'd been the cabin boy on the *Revenge* and escaped in a dinghy before it went down and had given them an approximate location of where the shipwreck could be: near an island. Ocracoke Island.

(The game of telephone hadn't been invented yet, dear reader, but only because telephones hadn't been invented yet.)

Still, it was the best they had to go on.

Tobias consulted the map, then scoffed in disbelief. "We're practically there already." He oriented himself and then strode to the starboard rail and pointed. "Ocracoke Island should be that way, about seven or eight miles due east. We can almost see it from here."

"Let's go, then," Mary told DuPaul, and the men sprang into action to heave the anchors and pass down Mary's orders.

"We'll be there within the hour," DuPaul said.

Tobias hoped the treasure would be there this time. Otherwise, he was out of ideas.

He was about to go find his pa's journal again when Anne

bounded onto the deck. "Jack, my dearest darling, I must show you something. In the captain's cabin."

"In *my* cabin?" Mary asked.

Jack, however, looked thrilled. He immediately followed Anne into the cabin. Mary was close behind them, scowling. And Tobias went after them because he just had to know.

The moment the door shut behind them: *SPLASH!*

A bucketful of wash-water flew straight onto Jack, dousing him, and in the space it took Tobias to blink, Jack was on the floor, his trousers in tatters thanks to the enormous tail he was now sporting.

A tail.

To be told that the Mer existed was one thing.

To see it, though. That was something else.

Jack's tail was a shimmering, iridescent green, which darkened into a bronze color at the large, fluted end. There were two smaller fins on either side, a little higher than Jack's knees would have been. Tobias couldn't take his eyes off the place where skin met scales and how *seamless* it was.

It did seem to be magic, after all.

He glanced quickly at Mary, wondering what *her* tail had looked like. Then he glanced back at Jack, wondering if he should offer a towel. But before he had time to do anything more, Anne spoke.

"I knew it," she said hoarsely. "I just knew it!"

FIFTEEN

Jack wiped water off his face. He tried to get up, to go to Bonn and take her in his arms and explain everything, but all he could manage to do was slide toward her on the slick and soapy floor.

"Darling," he said helplessly. "I was going to tell you, I swear."

She let the bucket drop from her hand and thunk noisily to the floor. "When were you going to tell me, Jack? It's not like you haven't had the opportunity." She scowled. "You asked me to marry you, for Pete's sake!"

"Who's Pete, and what does he have to do with this?" Jack asked. This was all so humiliating. He looked to Mary for help, but she, too, seemed to be stunned by what had just transpired.

"I suppose it's safe to assume that you're not Dutch." Anne's green eyes were near dancing with fury. "So you lied to me, Jack, bold as brass, straight to my face."

This was what she had a problem with? Him lying? Not him, you know, being half fish?

"I never lied about what's important," he said. "You're my person. I love you."

"I dunno," she said. "If you love someone, don't you tell them the truth?"

"That's not entirely fair," he protested. "You didn't tell me the truth, either." He knew this was a mistake, arguing, walking down this road with her (metaphorically speaking, because he still wasn't walking anywhere, obviously), but he couldn't seem to help himself. "You weren't going to tell me you were already married."

"Wait, she's already married?" Tobias's eyebrows lifted. "Perhaps we should leave you alone to talk this out."

But Mary clearly had no intention of leaving. She rounded on Bonn. "Look here, Bonny," she said, that scary captain tone creeping in her voice again. "I let you come aboard this ship as one of the crew, but I can just as easily toss you overboard. If you say a word about Jack's . . . condition . . . to anyone, I will have no problem with having you keelhauled."

This was a terrible time for Mary to go all protective on him.

"No, she won't, my love," Jack protested. He looked at Mary pleadingly. "No, you won't. I love her, and she's angry at me right now, as she has every right to be, for my deception, but she loves me, too. Don't you, darling?"

Bonn didn't answer.

Jack's heart gave a great squeeze. "Wait," he gasped. "This is just a misunderstanding."

"She needs to understand that she can't tell," Mary said.

Bonn lifted her chin. "I won't tell anyone! I would never! Gawl!" she cried, and barreled out of the room, banging the door open to reveal a very startled Mr. Quint, who'd been about to knock.

Tobias rushed to Mary's bed, grabbed the blanket, and threw it over Jack's lower half, for which Jack was quite grateful.

"What's all this?" Mr. Quint asked as Mary hurried to meet him in the doorway. "Captain? We've, uh, reached Ocracoke Island."

"Very good, Mr. Quint," Mary said quickly. "We're just going to need a moment here."

He nodded and stepped out again. Mary shut the door.

"I'm sorry," Jack said tremulously. "I thought—"

"No, I'm sorry, cousin," Mary said. "I should have seen this coming. She kept saying that she saw something when you went overboard during the storm."

"I'm sorry, too," piped up Tobias. "I kind of outed you before, at the Kettle. It's my . . . bad."

"It's fine," Jack said, struggling to not go flopping after Bonn. "I will talk to her. Later. In the meantime, we should see to the business at hand, should we not? I can swim down and look for the wreck." That would give him time to think of something to say that would make this right.

If there was anything that he *could* say to make this right. He knew that Bonn could hold a grudge with the best of them.

"Thank you, Jack," Mary said, and took Tobias by the arm and left the cabin, to give Jack a chance to dry off and collect himself, but he didn't know why she bothered, because he was only going to get wet again.

Ocracoke Island was lovely, really, with white-sand beaches and a herd of wild ponies running about free. He would like to vacation there someday, Jack thought. Only an hour ago he'd been able to picture him and Anne together, seeing sights such as these. Traveling the world. Living that human life.

But now—he didn't know what to think.

He'd work up the courage to talk to her later. To beg her to forgive him. To tell her everything he'd ever held back about himself, down to the most minute detail. He wanted her to know. Why hadn't he told her before this?

Oh, right. Because he'd been a coward.

But he couldn't think about that now because he had a job to do.

He removed his hat and handed it to Tobias. This felt like a lot of pressure, swimming down there alone, either discovering Blackbeard's treasure or coming back empty-handed. He peered over the side of the ship. "It looks dark down there. Maybe we should wait until tomorrow." (Reader, it was not especially dark down there. It was only midmorning, and the sun was shining bright overhead.)

"It will be fine, Jack," Mary said. "And anyway, I'm going with you."

He glanced up at her, surprised. "You're going? Below?"

"This is my quest," she said. "Tobias will watch the ship while we're gone."

"No, I won't," said Tobias quickly. "I'm coming as well. Mr. Quint will watch the ship."

"But neither of you can—I don't know—*breathe* down there?" Jack pointed out.

They were both staring at him like they knew something he didn't.

"What?" he asked.

Tobias scratched the back of his neck. "Mary told me about the mermaid's kiss thing, when a mermaid—or, excuse me, merman, is that what I should call you?—kisses a human and that temporarily gives them the ability to not drown underwater."

Oh. The mermaid's kiss. That.

"So you want me to kiss you? Both of you?" He glanced at Mary and Tobias, who were studying the deck now.

"*Want* is a strong word," Tobias said.

"If you must," Mary sighed. "It's preferable to drowning."

"Very well," Jack agreed. He didn't mind kissing them. And it didn't seem nearly as daunting if they were all going to go find the shipwreck together. He stepped up to the rail again.

"You should probably take off your pants," Mary said.

Right. He took off his boots, untucked his shirt, and shimmied out of his second-best striped trousers—his first-best striped trousers having been horribly ripped when Anne had doused him a moment ago. (He would have taken his shirt off, too, but then he would have been naked, and he was fairly certain *that* would be inappropriate.) Mary and Tobias set to removing their shoes and stripping down to their undershirts and breeches.

"Well, this is going to be awkward," Jack said, trying to sound cheerful. "Who's first?"

"Make it quick," grumbled Mary, coming to stand before him. Jack gave her a perfunctory peck on the lips that felt a bit like kissing his mother. Then Mary voluntarily walked the plank and jackknifed into the water.

Tobias stepped forward. Jack kissed him even more quickly, both pulling away from each other the moment after their mouths touched. It was a bit like kissing his brother, if he'd had a brother, that is. Tobias mumbled something about never mentioning this again and followed Mary into the water.

Jack sensed movement behind him, and he turned to see Bonn, her hands on her hips, staring at him, her mouth open a little. She'd obviously just seen him kiss Tobias.

"Bonn," he said quickly. "That wasn't what it looked like. I can explain."

"Oh, like you've explained everything so well, up to now," she said.

He couldn't think of what to say to her then. He was struck with the urge to kiss her, too, and bring her along with them. He wasn't even sure she'd have need of his kiss, at this point. Since the night they'd met he'd kissed Anne as often as he'd been able to find the time. It was his favorite human thing, in fact, kissing Anne Bonny. It was just so very human, pressing his lips to hers, sharing his breath, a little bit of his soul. She always kissed him with her whole self, making his heart thunder, such heat and salt and fury all in one. Like a beautiful storm.

"I'm sorry," he said. "I have to . . ."

"Well, go on, then," she said.

He nodded and stepped back on the edge of the rail and into the water, leaving her behind while he followed Mary and Tobias.

At least she was still speaking to him. That was something.

In the water his legs instantly fused back into his tail, and he could move so swiftly and easily down there, in the wavering coolness of the deep, that he felt a surge of euphoria. Sometimes he missed being Mer. (And sometimes—like ten minutes ago—it was a literal pain in the ass.) But things seemed so much simpler Below.

Mary and Tobias were waiting beneath the ship, making treading-water motions with their arms and legs. Mary was waiting patiently, breathing under the water with no trouble. The kiss seemed to have worked. Tobias, however, was thrashing, his body panicking at being under the water without taking any breaths. Jack took his hand, looked into his wide, frightened eyes, and made an in-and-out gesture with his chest. Tobias quieted and did the same.

"The Queen Anne's Revenge should be somewhere nearby," he told Mary in Mer.

"I feel like it's that way." She pointed to the south, and he didn't ask her how she knew such a thing. She was human now, but she

was also, somewhere still deep inside her, Mer royalty, and sometimes that came with inexplicable powers over the things in the ocean. He'd always been a bit jealous that she had some remnants of magic in her, when that was so absent in him, the son of a witch. *"There are sharks,"* she added. *"They've been following the Ranger. But I told them to stay away."*

He turned south. Mary swam over clumsily and grabbed Tobias's hand, and Jack grabbed Mary's, and all in a line he towed them, using the superior strength and control of his powerful tail and fins to propel them through the water.

Mary was right. Not even a league from where they'd parked the *Ranger*, resting against the sandy bottom, was a newly sunken ship. It was largely intact—Jack saw that at once—with a large hole blown out of one side. Jack pulled the humans down the hatch and into the cargo hold. It was murky and dark inside, too dark to see much, even with Jack's and Mary's superior Mer vision. But then, a moment later, a school of lantern fish swam into the hold, illuminating the scene.

"Did you do that?" Jack asked Mary.

She didn't answer. Instead, she was turning a slow circle around the space, her expression gloomy. And Tobias also seemed downtrodden.

Then Jack realized why.

He could practically see the bubble of their hopes all popping at roughly the same time.

There was nothing here. Not one jewel. Not one gold bar. Not one single piece of eight.

Only a few useless weapons scattered about the floor.

Cutlasses, cannonballs, and crabs.

No treasure.

And no real idea where to look next.

"What now?" he asked Mary in Merish.

"We're not far from home," she said.

And by home, she meant Underwhere.

"Not very far at all," he agreed. He was tempted to swim back to the little cottage he'd grown up in and see his mom. He really missed his mom. And she would be worried that he hadn't called her. He would have loved to ask her for relationship advice about now.

"Do you remember the necklace we found that one time?" Mary asked out of the blue.

"Necklace?" Jack thought back. *"Oh, the pretty, sparkly one with the big blue heart-shaped jewel? The one some idiot just tossed overboard from a ship?"*

She nodded. *"That's got to be valuable."*

"Right! A little treasure all by itself."

"We could get that. It's not Blackbeard's hoard, but it's something. And there might be other items there we could take back with us, now that we know what humans find precious."

"That sounds like a plan," he said.

They turned to Tobias, who was hovering in the water beside them, looking confused. Jack swam up to him and motioned that he was going to return them to the surface. He offered his hand,

and, after a moment of hesitation, Tobias took it. Then Jack grabbed Mary and headed back Above.

"Well, that was a whole lot of nothing," sputtered Mary the moment her head breached the surface. "Except for this." She held up her fist and then opened it to reveal a rusted belt buckle. "This could have been silver," she reasoned. But it wasn't. It was iron. And it was rusted.

"What now?" Tobias asked. "I'm sorry, but I don't know where else he could have stashed it."

"We have somewhere we can search," Mary said.

"For my pa's treasure?" he asked.

"No," Jack said. "For *my* treasure." He met Mary's eyes, and for the first time since he'd come Above, he felt that old camaraderie between them, the excitement that had lit them both up every time they'd ever ventured out to find human artifacts. "*Our* treasure," he amended, because yes, it had been his idea, way back when, but Mary had been right there with him. "To the grotto?"

She returned his smile. "To the grotto."

"Wait, and where is this grotto, exactly?" Tobias wanted to know.

"It's where we come from," Mary said.

"Oh," said Tobias, wiping water out of his eyes. "Under-where?"

"Under the water," Jack explained.

"Yes," said Tobias. "I know. Underwhere."

Underwhere! Jack didn't know whether to be excited or

terrified. He went with excited. He swam quickly to Tobias and kissed the lad on his startled mouth (just to be extra safe about the time limit), and then Mary.

"Are you ready?" Mary asked him.

Jack's heart was pounding, and it was from more than just the inappropriate kissing.

He was going home.

Mary

SIXTEEN

Underwhere looked different, somehow. Bigger than she remembered. More beautiful and magical than she'd thought when she'd lived here, with its brilliant coral buildings, shining mother-of-pearl streets, and intricate rock gardens. The city was so full of life, with hundreds of Mer swimming about their daily lives, schools of fish flashing in the watery light, and plants wafting in the gentle current.

How had she never seen it before, the absolute wonder of her home? How had she missed it all those years?

The group kept to the outskirts of town, swimming in the shadows. The last thing they needed was to get caught. Mary couldn't imagine how her father would react finding her here—and with a human, no less.

What was the single biggest rule in all of Underwhere?

Don't interact with humans.

Whoopsie.

But she wasn't her father's subject anymore.

Still, as they swam toward the far edge of the city—the place where the seafloor dropped straight into the abyss—Mary couldn't help but stare at the palace. It stood in the center of the city, tall and proud, with its windows thrown wide open. She imagined she could see her father on his throne, making important decisions, and—occasionally—checking how much longer before the full moon. And Karen, of course, flitting about her business. And everyone else's business. Her hair would have grown back by now, Mary thought, after she'd cut it to pay Aunt Witch for the knife.

She *had* missed them, she realized. A little, anyway.

Jack touched her arm. *"Come on. There's no time for that now."*

Mary set her jaw and gave a mighty kick—though swimming with legs wasn't nearly as good as swimming with a tail. As far as Mary was concerned, swimming as a human was absolute whale rocks. Tobias, too, was clearly struggling.

Meanwhile Jack was swimming circles around them, grinning.

"I always was the superior swimmer out of the two of us," he teased. *"But now there's no question."*

"Oh, be quiet, you, and help us."

"Aye, aye, Captain." Jack took their hands and helped tow them through the water. At last they made it to the grotto where Mary and Jack had spent half their childhoods loitering about.

She sent another school of lantern fish in ahead of them. She felt stronger in the ocean, more connected to the currents. The sea creatures listened to her, obeyed her, because she was the daughter of the Sea King.

She'd forgotten that, too.

The cavern was just as Mary remembered. She couldn't help but smile as she spotted the cannonball they'd discovered one afternoon. And there was the old, rotting box of pots and pans they'd collected. *"Jack, look!"* She pulled a busted spyglass out of a different box. *"Remember when we didn't know what this was for?"*

He grinned. *"Your best guess was that they used it in gardens!"*

She laughed and shoved the spyglass back into the box before moving on. *"And our collection of silverware!"* They'd been *really* confused about what spoons were for. The knives had made sense—they were sharp, clearly for cutting—and the forks were obviously for stabbing, but spoons? They'd seemed so unexplainable at the time, more like digging tools than cutlery.

"Mary." Jack's voice went soft, even though Mary was literally the only other one who could hear him. *"Something's wrong with Tobias."*

Following Jack's gaze to the cavern entrance, Mary saw Tobias treading there, not quite in, not quite out, wearing a pensive expression.

He didn't want to come in. (And can we blame him, dear reader, for not wanting to enter a dark cave at the bottom of the sea? No, no we can't.)

Mary frowned, realizing suddenly that Tobias had been distant since he'd seen Jack transform earlier. His face had gone ashen, and he hadn't spoken much. It was one thing to hear that some of your friends were magical sea creatures—and another thing to see it with your own eyes. Perhaps it was too much for him.

Mary swam to him and held out her hand. She wished she could speak to him, wished she could make him understand that she was the same person she'd always been. Nothing had changed. Not really.

She was startled when Tobias reached out suddenly and took her hand. He squeezed it. And then he managed a faint flicker of his usual, crooked smile.

Show me, he seemed to be saying with his eyes.

Mary felt a flutter of nervousness, the way a girl might be flustered to show the boy she liked the inside of her bedroom, with her stuffed animals on the bed and her old posters on the walls. It felt . . . intimate. But she drew him into the cave anyway, to the shelf full of the old bottles she'd found on the seafloor. There was an array of styles, colors, and shapes; some even had scraps of labels still on them. She pulled out her favorite one—a round pinkish bottle with tiny handles you could barely stick a finger through on either side—and handed it to Tobias.

Clearly confused, he took it. Gave it a little pat. And then replaced it on the shelf. But he was smiling, amused.

They swam from shelf to shelf, perusing the things she and Jack had collected over the years. With a grin, Mary pointed out various trinkets and treasures—rather, things she'd thought were treasures, back when she'd been little. Now it was clear the large metal hooks were incredibly common pieces of ships, while her waterlogged compass was a relatively normal item.

So most of it was junk. But it had been *her* junk. (And Jack's.)

That's when she found the necklace.

She took it from its velvet-encased box and brought it over to a lantern fish so she could inspect it. It was as striking as she remembered, a necklace like she'd never seen, before or since. The huge blue jewel, cut into a heart shape, was bordered by smaller, clear diamonds that glinted in the dim light. Even underwater, the piece had heft; on land, it would be downright heavy.

It probably wasn't enough to win the Pirate King contest, but it was something.

She held it up for Tobias to see. His eyes grew round as he mouthed what might have been, *Holy crabs!*

Mary nodded.

Gently, Tobias took the necklace from her, fussed with the clasp, and then swam around behind her. His fingers grazed the back of her neck as he brushed aside her hair, then—quickly, before her hair could float back—he placed the necklace around her neck and clasped it.

Mary took a small hand mirror and gazed at her reflection. The necklace looked nice on her, she thought. It made her eyes stand out, and all the tiny facets made her sparkle as the lantern fish swam around.

She glanced up. In the foggy glass next to her, Tobias was

watching her in that thoughtful and admiring way that always made her heart pound. It felt good and warm and a little overwhelming, to be looked at like *she* was the treasure.

Mary placed the mirror back on the shelf, blushing. Tobias picked up the next item: a small, leather-bound volume with gilding on the front cover. It was a stunning example of human craftsmanship, though many of the pages had disintegrated. Too many pages.

The Complete Works of William Shakespeare, read the cover.

Mary bit her lip. This had been one of the most precious pieces of the whole collection.

She took the book from him and carefully opened it to the story of *Romeo and Juliet*, the drawing of the star-crossed lovers as they gazed into each other's eyes.

This had been her whole understanding of love for so long. She'd looked at Charles, and she'd seen Romeo, and later resented him because she hadn't turned out to be his Juliet. And when she'd seen the play after they'd captured the *Jester*, she'd thought the story simply a warning about the dangers of falling in love. But now, looking at the book in her hands, she wondered if she might have been wrong about it again. The love Romeo and Juliet had for each other had been true. Yes, they'd died in the end (an absolutely *rotten* ending, if you asked her), but didn't that say something about the strength of their feelings? Their devotion?

They only died, she thought sadly, *because their families wouldn't get along.*

It wasn't *love* that had killed them, but the lack of it.

Mary didn't realize her hands were trembling until Tobias pulled the book away, closed it, and placed it back on the shelf.

She touched his arm. His fingers brushed her cheek as he smiled, a little sadly, a little hopefully.

Things could be different between them now that everything was out in the open.

Her gaze dropped to his lips. They were perfect, she noted.

"AHEM!" Jack said from the other side of the cavern. *"I found some coins and a pair of candelabras."* He showed off a palmful of gold in one hand, and a pair of (very tarnished) silver candelabras in the other. *"We should go before that last kiss wears off. Unless you want me to do it all over again."*

"Right. Yes. I mean, no, no more kissing." Mary's cheeks felt red hot, like she'd been caught doing something illicit. Tobias, too, looked a little bashful.

Jack pulled a face. *"You're not the only one who's uncomfortable with this situation. But maybe you'd rather be kissing someone else—"*

"Shut up, Jack!" Mary kicked her way toward the exit, but then stopped short.

Because outside was one very angry Karen.

"Well, well, well—if it isn't the littlest princess," Karen said. *"And Son of a Witch."* Her eyes flickered from Jack to Tobias. *"And who is this? A human? Littlest! You know the rules!"*

"Hello, Big Deal." Mary moved in front of Tobias, like she could somehow shield him. *"My name is Mary now. Don't call me Littlest anymore."*

"Oh, right, your human name." Karen rolled her eyes. *"And I suppose*

Son of a Witch has one, too? He was always such a landlubber. Is that still true?"
Karen looked at Jack. *"Do you still wish you were human?"*

"Go swim with the fishes, Karen," said Jack.

"Leave him out of this," Mary said. *"I don't see why you care so much if he's interested in humans. It doesn't affect you at all."*

"It's unseemly." Karen sniffed. *"But anyway, I suppose I'm glad you're not sea foam. I was so surprised when Dad informed me that you were still alive. And I see you kept those."* She pointed at Mary's legs. *"How can you swim like that? And why aren't you drowning?"*

"It's the mermaid's kiss." Mary tried to tuck her floaty hair behind her ear and failed.

Karen's eyebrows lifted in surprise. *"Ew!"*

"We just came by to get a few things," Jack said, swimming up beside Mary. *"We'll be on our way."*

"You have no right to be here anymore," Karen said. *"You gave up all your toys when you left Underwhere. And if you don't want to be here, you shouldn't have returned. Father was so upset for days after he visited you. Not to mention how upset he was when he thought you were dead. You're so—I don't know—selfish."*

She was correct, Mary thought, but the words stung. She gripped the blue diamond necklace (which she was still wearing around her neck) in her fist. *"You can't kick me out of my own secret hideout. You're not the boss of me."*

Gah, she really had to come up with something better than that.

"Actually," Karen said, planting one hand on her hip, *"I am. Or I will be very soon."*

Mary went still. *"What do you mean? Is Father—"*

"Oh, he's fine. He wants to retire. Then I'll be the Sea Queen." Karen's eyes flickered to the top of Mary's head. "But before I can take over, I need the crown. I believe Dad ordered you to give it back to me."

Mary sighed—which underwater was basically a burst of bubbles. Not this business with the crown again. "And I told him that I looked for it, and I didn't find it. It's gone."

Karen scoffed. "That crown wasn't even yours to begin with—it was both of ours—so you taking it was technically stealing."

"I didn't steal it," Mary said. "I brought it Above with me as a way to remember my family."

"I'm still going to need it back. For the coronation, you see."

Impossible. At this point, the crown could be literally anywhere. "I can't give it to you. I don't know what more you want from me."

"I want you to look harder!" Karen glanced at Jack and Tobias. "How about you go Above and look for it, and in the meantime, I'll keep those two here. To ensure you come right back with my crown."

"I can't leave them here. Tobias will drown!"

The corner of Karen's mouth turned up in the hint of a smile. "Oh, don't worry. I'll kiss him. Even though I'm sure it will be gross, I have to admit I'm curious."

Over Mary's dead and drowned body was that ever going to happen. But how could she resist Karen down here? All her sister would have to do is scream, and she'd alert hundreds of nearby Mer, and her father would probably take this opportunity to just keep Mary home for good, Pirate King contest or not. "Just let us go," Mary pleaded. "I'll get your crown back."

After the contest. Maybe. If she ever saw Charles again. (And she really hoped she never would see him. What a *codfish*. She was so over him.)

"Why should I trust you to keep your word?" Karen asked. *"You were always so needy, Littlest. But now I need something. You can collect your human once you've brought me the crown. I'll take him back to the palace and that Son of a Witch can kiss him every now and then, too. I think that's very reasonable of me,"* Karen added. *"Considering."*

It might have been reasonable if Mary had any earthly idea where the crown was. But she didn't. She would have to find another way out of this.

"Get ready, Jack," Mary whispered only to him. *"Grab Tobias. We're going to have to swim for it."*

Then Mary sent the school of lantern fish swarming around Karen's head.

"ARGH!" Karen waved her hands around her hair (which had, indeed, grown out), trying (unsuccessfully) to shoo the lantern fish away.

While Karen was distracted, Jack linked arms with Tobias, who linked arms with Mary, and they pushed out of the grotto and started up toward the surface.

It didn't matter. Because Karen—who was also the daughter of the Sea King and therefore also had some influence over the ocean—suddenly called out, *"Yoo-hoo, sharks!"*

In response, seven large hammerhead sharks wove through the water toward them, teeth red with whatever they'd eaten last.

Now, it was Mary's experience that sharks were generally more afraid of you than you were of them, but that didn't mean they weren't still really freaking scary.

"What the fish?" Jack shouted. *"Why would she— Is your sister really trying to kill us? That seems a bit extreme!"*

"Uh, maybe? Swim faster!"

Jack swam faster, shooting up and up toward the brighter water above them. Mary glanced behind. Karen was metaphorically right on Jack's literal tail.

"Faster, Jack, faster!" Mary yelled.

"I thought I was going faster."

"You're supposed to be this superior swimmer, this great legendary thing! And yet she gains!"

"Well, I am carrying two people, and she's got only herself."

"I do not accept excuses, Jack! I'm just going to have to find myself a new cousin, that's all."

"Don't say that!"

Mary glanced down again. The lantern fish had spotted the sharks and were swimming away in a different direction. But the sharks had gotten distracted by the fish—so they were swimming away now, too.

And then there was Karen, now *literally* on Jack's tail. Her hand closed around Mary's foot, yanking her down.

Mary was still hooked to Tobias, though, and Tobias was still hooked to Jack. Their ascent came to an abrupt halt while Karen tugged on Mary.

"Stop! Being! So! Selfish!" Karen shouted. *"I need that crown!"*

Mary did the only thing she could think to do: she wiggled her toes in Karen's face. The tips of her toes brushed Karen's nose.

"Ew, it's so gross!" Karen shrieked, and let go.

"Sorry, Big Deal!" Mary said as she kicked upward. She heard a scream of outrage and glanced over her shoulder to see Karen frantically wiping at her face.

"I'll get you for this, Littlest!" Karen yelled. *"And your little human, too!"*

"Don't call me Littlest!" Mary yelled back.

Mary spared a glance at Tobias to make sure he was all right. She wanted to tell him that they were safe now—the sharks had moved off, and Karen was too busy gagging to come after them—but just then, his eyes widened in panic and he began to clutch at his chest.

"Jack!" Mary cried. *"The kiss is wearing off!"*

Jack was already swimming as fast as he could, but towing two people was clearly taking its toll. Two people who were in the process of drowning? Worse.

Wait.

Only *one* person was drowning. If Jack had kissed her immediately after kissing Tobias, shouldn't Mary be drowning a little bit now, too? But she wasn't.

Mary let go of Tobias.

He thrashed, reaching for her, clearly thinking he'd lost hold of her, but Mary shook her head.

"Go, Jack!" she called, kicking after him.

Jack went—and went faster now that his load was lightened.

Mary only hoped it was fast enough.

Slowly, so slowly with these bad-for-swimming human legs, Mary rose up to the surface, finally reaching the bright blue of the world above.

Jack and Tobias were already up, coughing and sputtering.

Tobias lurched toward Mary as she wiped water out of her eyes. "I thought I'd lost you!" He threw his arms around her. "I thought—"

"I'm fine," she said out loud. "I can—I guess I can still breathe underwater."

That would have been helpful to know when she'd jumped off the *Fancy*.

"So I kissed you for nothing?" Jack made a gagging noise.

Mary leaned her forehead against Tobias's shoulder, letting the heat of his embrace spread through her. But only for a moment. "We should go," she said.

"Come on," Jack said. "I'll pull us in."

They chained up again, kicking while Jack took everyone toward the nearest spit of land: a beach with a thin forest behind it. At the northern end, a ribbon of smoke trickled upward.

Legs burning with exhaustion, they struggled up the sandy slope and onto the beach, and—when Jack could go up no farther—the two with legs hauled him up as far as they could.

"I can't believe," Tobias panted, flopping onto the beach,

"that we were just attacked by a killer mermaid. Jimmy Silver was right."

"Fortunately, she wasn't actually going to kill anyone." Jack threw dry sand over his tail.

"Then what was all of that about?" Tobias burst out.

Right. He hadn't been able to hear any of her conversation with Karen. To him, it had once again looked like an extremely intense staring contest.

Jack explained: "Karen wanted a crown that Mary took two years ago. She wanted to keep us down there until Mary gave it back."

Tobias's brow rumpled. "A crown?"

Mary shrugged. "I lost it a long time ago, so you would have been down there indefinitely. And Jack would have had to kiss you to keep you alive," she added. "Every twenty-seven minutes."

"A fate worse than death," said Tobias gravely.

"Hey now," said Jack. "I've been assured that I'm a very good kisser." Then he looked sad.

"That mermaid's name is Karen?" Tobias asked.

Jack shuddered. "She's the *worst*."

"She's my sister," Mary admitted.

"Oh," said Tobias awkwardly. "Well, I'm glad I got to meet some of your family. I'm sure she's a delightful person under different circumstances."

"You don't have to be nice about it," Mary said with a laugh. "I hate that beach."

SEVENTEEN

Tobias

At this point Tobias would have been happy to never set foot in the ocean again. He was cold and wet and, frankly, disappointed. They hadn't found his pa's treasure. They had risked their lives for a diamond necklace and a handful of gold coins. (Jack had dropped the candelabras in their mad rush to get away from Mary's sister.) Tobias had no idea how they were going to win the Pirate King contest now.

But they'd survived. He supposed that was the important bit. And Mary was currently holding his hand.

Jack stood up triumphantly. "I'm dry!" he exclaimed. "Check out these legs!"

Tobias was the first to turn around, and then quickly finished the circle to face away. "Sit down, Jack. You're not wearing any pants. Again."

Jack sat down. "Sorry. I can't seem to help it."

"Go back into the water," Mary directed him. "Swim to the *Ranger* and tell them where to pick us up—"

"And explain myself how, exactly?" Jack asked. "Plus, I still won't be wearing pants."

"Hmm. Well, there's a fire over there." Mary gazed down the beach to where they'd seen smoke rising earlier. It was still there, a curl of black against the azure sky. "Which means there's a person. Perhaps they can assist us."

"Or rob us," Tobias said, eyeing the huge diamond necklace still around Mary's neck. He shivered, remembering how his fingers had brushed the tender skin at the back of her neck when he'd put it on her. (Or maybe he was just shivering because he was really cold.)

Mary tilted her head to one side to smirk at him. "We're pirates, remember? We're the ones who rob."

"It could be a traveling towel salesman," Jack said hopefully, even though traveling towel salesmen didn't exist. "You never know."

"All right, Mary and I will go," Tobias said. "Jack, you stay here. If there's a decent person over there, they don't need to be exposed to your un-pantsed state. Mary, you should hide that rock."

Mary took off the necklace and stuffed it into her pocket. The two of them headed toward the smoke. Sand squished under their feet. Palm trees whispered. Waves crashed against the shore.

"I'm sorry," Mary said after a moment.

"What for?" Tobias said.

"Well, there's getting to be quite a list of things I should apologize for," she admitted. "But just now I was talking about bringing you to the grotto. I didn't think my sister would be there."

"Family is complicated," he said. "Mine isn't exactly normal, either."

She chuckled. "Yes, I know."

Then Tobias stopped walking because the campfire had come into view. Sitting at the fire was a large brown man staring into the flames with a pensive expression. "I don't believe it," Tobias breathed. "I don't believe it!"

"Tobias?" Mary asked.

But Tobias was already running toward the fire, shouting, "Caesar!"

Caesar looked up, a smile growing on his face. "Toby!"

Tobias threw his arms around the man. He was nearly in tears, he was so relieved to see Caesar, the one person who'd always been there, looking out for him, for nearly as far back as Tobias could remember. "You're alive!" Tobias gasped. "I thought you'd gone down with the *Revenge*!"

Caesar shook his head. "Barnet didn't get me. I doubt he knows, but if he does, I hope it keeps him up at night." He laughed and pulled away from Tobias, clasping him behind the neck for a moment, before patting his shoulder and turning to Mary, who was walking up behind them. "And who is this?"

"Oh. Allow me to introduce Mary Read," Tobias said a bit

haltingly. "She's the captain of the *Ranger.* My . . . captain."

Caesar glanced at Mary in obvious surprise, then back at Tobias. "I see. What happened to Vane?"

"He got beat by a girl," Mary said.

That earned a short laugh from Caesar. "I think I like this one," he said.

Wonderful. Tobias cleared his throat. "Mary, I'd like you to meet Caesar, my father's second-in-command." There was so much more that he wanted to tell her about Caesar. About how the man had once been a tribal war chieftain who'd been taken from his home in western Africa and fought his way to freedom. How he'd spent years captaining his own ship, targeting and freeing slave ships. About how, in some ways, he'd been more of a father figure to Tobias than Blackbeard had been; the one who'd taken an interest in Tobias as a person, not just an heir. It had been Caesar who'd taught Tobias how to be a man.

"A pleasure to meet you, sir," Mary said, and Tobias felt a wave of emotion rise in his chest, that these two people who were so important in his life were now able to meet.

"How'd you get away from Barnet?" he asked. "What happened?"

"No stories until you've dried off and warmed up," said Caesar. "You're both soaked through."

Mary moved to sit on the large piece of beach wood near the fire that Caesar had been using as a makeshift bench. She closed her eyes, took a deep breath, and then abruptly opened them again.

"Wait—I almost forgot Jack. We have another companion down the beach."

Caesar motioned toward a large chest near the fire. "Take whatever you need."

Tobias threw back the lid. The chest was full of clothing and supplies. Blackbeard's clothing and supplies, he realized immediately. He removed a velvet bathrobe that he'd often seen his pa wear, deep burgundy and trimmed with silver threads. "Think Jack will like this?" he asked.

Mary laughed. "He'll love it."

Tobias tossed it to her, along with a large black coat. "One for you, too. Now, if you don't mind, I'd like a private word with Caesar."

"Of course." Mary slipped the jacket over her damp clothes, then carried the other away.

"I'm glad to see you." Tobias pulled a deep blue dinner jacket from the trunk and took his own place by the fire.

Caesar smiled. "I'm glad as well, my boy. But I will say I'm surprised to find you so far out this way. How came you to be here?"

"It's a long story," he admitted. "After word came that Captain Blackbeard had died, the AARP—"

"Ah," said Caesar. "The Admirable Association of Retired Pirates. I thought that a silly name, but I can appreciate the notion."

Tobias frowned. "You know about the AARP?"

"Aye. It was technically Blackbeard's idea."

Tobias thought for a minute. "So the meeting, the one he set up with all the pirate captains at the Scurvy Dog, that was—"

"To announce his retirement and the formation of the AARP," Caesar said. "And set up the promotion of his successor."

"His successor . . ."

Caesar nodded. "He had some cockamamie notion of a contest to determine the next Pirate King."

Oh. So his father hadn't planned to announce Tobias as his successor. Tobias didn't know whether to be relieved or ashamed. "The contest being whoever could come up with the most treasure?" he assumed.

Caesar nodded. "Which would be you, naturally, seeing as you're the one he gave his treasure to."

Ohhh. And we were back to his father wanting him to follow in his footsteps. Trust Blackbeard to rig the game. The rules had said that cheating was allowed.

"Yeah, about that," Tobias said, and very quickly gave Caesar a rundown of the past couple weeks. By the time he finished his story—leaving out the mermaid bits, as that wasn't Tobias's secret to tell—Caesar was frowning.

"Wait. You're not competing to become the Pirate King yourself?" Caesar asked.

"No. I'm with Mary." Tobias jerked his head back in the direction Mary had gone. "She wants to be the king."

"And you're helping her out of the sheer goodness of your heart?" Caesar said, an edge to his voice.

Tobias didn't know how to answer that. "I . . . She's my . . ."

Caesar sighed. "So it's like that between you, is it? She's the one for you? And you for her?"

"I don't know if she'll let me be the one for her," Tobias admitted, ignoring the barb behind Caesar's words. "Things are changing between us. Right now we're focused on the hunt for Pa's treasure. But I went to Plum Point, and it was all gone. Every bit of it. So maybe he didn't intend for me to be king. Maybe he'd decided I wasn't his favorite son, after all. We didn't part on good terms, last I saw him."

Caesar looked troubled. "He wasn't well, last you saw him. That was just before he laid siege to Charles Town. He was behaving very strangely."

Tobias swallowed hard. "Why on earth would he besiege Charles Town?"

"He was trying to get medicine for the malady that plagued him," Caesar replied. "But all he got for his trouble was a pirate hunter on his tail, and a swift and bloody death."

"It was . . . violent?" Tobias asked softly.

Caesar nodded. "Aye. But he wouldn't have gone out any other way. And when it came to his legacy, he never wavered. He wanted everything to be yours. He meant you to become the Pirate King. But if you want to, you can take the treasure and never have to be a pirate again. You can build whatever kind of life for yourself you want." Caesar's jaw tightened, and he gazed off, clearly frustrated. "But instead you want to give it away to a woman you fancy."

"More than fancy," Tobias protested. "A woman I—"

He still could not quite produce the word out loud.

Love.

He was about to attempt to explain the depth of his feelings to Caesar, but now the others were coming back, both wrapped in their borrowed clothes. Tobias threw a pair of pants at Jack, who faced away and slipped them on.

"Will you tell us the story of what really happened to Blackbeard?" Mary asked as they sat at the fire, warming themselves. Caesar could never resist telling a story, so he told them of how Barnet had caught Blackbeard by surprise here in the shallow water off Ocracoke, sailing in with two sloops and his men disguised as pirates themselves.

"Blackbeard was suspicious from the first, though," Caesar said. "He called out, 'If you shall let us alone, we shall not meddle with you.' But then Barnet called back, 'It is you we want, and we will have you dead or alive!' and the fight was on. Brutal, it was, as tough a fight as I've ever been in. And when it was clear that we would lose, Blackbeard saved my life. He sacrificed himself so I could escape. I still hardly made it out of there. I jumped in the water just as I saw him fall. I washed up here sometime later, along with that." He gestured to the trunk.

"He saved you," Mary asked, and it made sense why she was confused, because that didn't exactly sound like the Blackbeard everyone knew and feared. "Why?"

Caesar met Tobias's eyes. "Because he wanted me to find you."

Jack frowned. "So were you just going to stay here, hoping we showed up?"

"It didn't have to be you," Caesar said, "but I knew eventually I'd see familiar sails on the horizon." He was quiet a moment. "Anyway, it gave me time to think." He cleared his throat and stood. "So that's my gruesome tale, and I am glad to be alive to tell it. But enough of Blackbeard's death. I hear it's his treasure you seek."

"Did he have it with him?" Mary asked Caesar urgently. "We searched Plum Point and the *Queen Anne's Revenge*, and it wasn't there."

Caesar cocked his head, troubled. "You searched the *Revenge*? How did you manage that?"

"That's another long story that we probably shouldn't go into," Tobias said.

"The captain didn't have the treasure with him," Caesar said after a pause, like he'd just decided something. "He relocated it to Booty Island months ago. Everything is there. Every last coin."

"Booty Island? That sounds made up," Mary said doubtfully.

"He never took me there," Tobias said. "I didn't even think it was a real place. I thought he was just . . . mad."

"It's real enough," Caesar murmured.

"Where is this island?" Mary asked.

"He left a map for you." Caesar reached into an inner pocket of his coat and drew out an oilskin envelope, which he handed to Tobias. Inside was a folded sheet of parchment. Tobias smoothed it out on top of the trunk and gazed down at it.

Mary peered over his shoulder. "It looks like a regular map to me. Except these bits around the edge." She pointed at the border. "I can't make heads or tails of what that's supposed to be."

"It's in a code," Caesar said.

"Oh." Mary sat back. "Can either of you read it?"

Tobias scanned the markings, the lines, and the numbers. "I can."

The next morning, the four of them walked up the beach until they could see the *Ranger* and Mary's other two ships in the distance. They set a signal fire, and a short while later, a rowboat came rowing in to take them back to the *Ranger*.

Tobias was half expecting Anne Bonny to confront Jack again the moment they set foot on board. But she remained aloft in the rigging, discernible only by the flash of her red hair under the sun. Tobias couldn't tell if this was a good or a bad thing. He felt for Jack, who kept looking up again and again. Relationships were hard.

"Impressive fleet you have here," Caesar told Mary as they traversed the *Ranger*'s deck.

"Thank you," she said. "I'd be honored if you'd take charge of one of the ships. The *Jester* doesn't have a proper captain yet, just an actor pretending to be a captain. The men could benefit from having someone with your experience."

"I'll think about it. For now, let's get after that treasure."

Soon the whole fleet was heading south again—toward the Caribbean—and Tobias, Mary, Caesar, and Jack all squeezed into the captain's cabin and spread Blackbeard's map onto the table.

Tobias traced his finger along the row of symbols that

bordered the map. "It reads, *'Get kicked by the boot at midnight and call my name.'*"

"How do you know that?" Jack asked, peering down at the map, befuddled. "I don't see anything about footwear."

Tobias grinned. "Navigator magic. They don't call me the Artist for nothing, you know."

Mary rolled her eyes, but with a smile. "All right, so we're looking for a boot."

"Is it an actual boot we need to find?" Jack asked. "Finding *the* boot we need in a world full of people wearing boots is going to be a challenge."

"It's got to be a landmass," Mary reasoned. "Somewhere we must go to call Blackbeard's name. And the part about getting kicked must tell us where, exactly, on that landmass to be at midnight."

"There's Nassau. And here's Port Royal. And here"—Tobias's finger touched a tiny island that was hardly visible between them—"is the little boot."

They all crowded around the map to squint at the spot he'd showed them.

"I don't think that looks like a boot at all," Jack said.

"Yes, more like a slipper," Mary said.

"Just go with it," Tobias said. "Let's call it a boot."

"So that's Booty Island?" Jack asked hopefully.

"No, that's the island that you have to stand on, at midnight, to say Blackbeard's name and be shown the location of the real Booty Island."

"That doesn't make sense," Mary said. "So we go to the island and say the thing at midnight and then something magical will happen? That seems unrealistic. Was Blackbeard magic, then?"

"I don't think so," Tobias said. "It's more likely that it's just another puzzle to figure out, like the keyhole at the Kettle. Pa was clever, but not, as far as I know, magic."

"Not as far as I know," Caesar agreed. "But he did have a way about him. He could be spooky."

That was true. It had helped his reputation that people weren't sure what he could do, exactly. And that he did unusual (and unwise) things, like putting fireworks in his beard. And he'd been awfully obsessed with mermaids. It seemed possible that Blackbeard had known magic *existed*, even if he wasn't magic himself.

"That island is awfully close to Port Royal," Mary noted. "It'll be risky to sail anywhere near Barnet again. He'll be watching out for us."

"You could always change your mind about the contest," Caesar said. "You could wait. The treasure will be there whenever you feel that it's safe to fetch it. I hear Aruba's nice this time of year."

Tobias had a feeling Caesar was speaking more to him now than to Mary.

"Definitely not. There's too much at stake." Mary jabbed her finger at the island. "We're going there now. We're getting the treasure. And we're winning this contest. No matter what it takes."

"She won't even speak to me," Jack said wistfully a few days later as the three of them—Mary, Jack, and Tobias—settled into the rowboat (which was starting to feel familiar). The *Jester* and the *William* were stashed away in a cove off another island, well out of sight from Port Royal, so it was only the *Ranger* now, just off the tip of the boot island, where you'd have to be in order to be properly kicked. "What do you think that means? Is she angry? Hurt? Simply too occupied in her new position as lookout to have time for me? Yearning for me, as I am her? Plotting my demise?"

Mary heaved a weary sigh, and Tobias knew the feeling. Jack had been like this for days, asking a string of questions that none of them could answer about the possible state of mind of Anne Bonny. Still, he felt for the guy.

"Give her some space," Tobias suggested. "She'll find you when she's ready to talk."

"To break things off with me," Jack said grimly.

"At least then you won't have to worry about coming up with a thousand pieces of eight," Mary said. "Now row!"

Jack rowed the boat for a few moments in silence. Then:

"If only she'd talk to me, I feel certain that I could mend things between us. I could try to make her understand the depth of my feelings. How I love her. How I'm devoted to her, and her alone. How me being half Mer won't be an impediment to our relationship . . . unless we happen to get caught in the rain, I suppose . . . but it could be an advantage, too."

"You're a good man, Jack," said Tobias to bolster him. "Mer or otherwise. Anne would be a fool not to see that. She'll come around."

Jack beamed. "You think so?"

"I do," Tobias said, then mumbled, "Of course, I'm no expert on the ways of the heart, myself."

"You're doing all right," Mary said quietly.

Tobias looked up, startled. The corner of her mouth was turned in a tiny smile. He found himself smiling back. "Really?"

"I think we're here," said Jack.

They'd come upon a rickety old dock, where they secured the dinghy.

"This way," Tobias said. He'd figured that the very tippiest tip of this island was the edge of a craggy cliff, which jutted out above the water about fifty yards down the shoreline. And sure enough, when they approached the cliff, he spotted a series of steps carved into the side, which allowed them to quickly climb to the top.

For a minute they all just stood there, looking out.

"I think I can see Port Royal from here," Jack said, squinting. "Ah, good times. It feels like a lifetime ago, when I first crawled out of the ocean there and became a man."

(Reader, it was roughly six months ago.)

"We should do this and get out of here," Mary said.

"BLACKBEARD!" Jack yelled.

Nothing happened.

"It's not midnight," Tobias pointed out. "We'll have to wait."

They passed the time by playing some cards and drinking some rum and singing YO HO, YO HO, A PIRATE'S LIFE FOR ME a bunch of times. Then they fell asleep, because it turns out that rum makes you sleepy. The next thing Tobias knew, Jack was yelling, "Get up! It's almost midnight!" Tobias checked his pocket watch and gasped. "One minute to midnight!"

"Mine says two minutes!" Mary said, peering at her own watch.

"The moon would suggest more like five minutes," Jack said.

"Darn but we need a standard unit of time," Tobias cried.

They all stood on the very edge of the boot (on the cliff) and yelled, "BLACKBEAAARD!" into the moon-glimmered waves.

But nothing happened that Tobias could see. The moon kept glimmering the waves. No magical island appeared.

They tried some variations: "Captain Blackbeard!"

"The Pirate King!"

"Pa!" Tobias exclaimed for good measure.

Still nothing.

But then they did notice something. But it wasn't a magical island full of treasure.

It was the *Ranger*, anchored just where they'd left it.

But it was not alone. There was another ship alongside it.

Mary put the spyglass to her eye. "Oh no. It's the *Conspicuous*!"

Tobias's heart skipped.

This was not a good time for Vane to show up.

(Actually, dear reader, there was never a good time for Vane to show up. That guy was an ass.)

"We've got to get back to the *Ranger*!" Mary cried, and started running down the cliff stairs and then straight for the dinghy. Tobias and Jack followed, and a moment later, they were pushing off.

"Bonn's on that ship," Jack said. "Row faster! I thought you were this legendary pirate!"

Somehow, even though the boat was small and slow, it reached the ship quickly.

"Haul us up!" Jack cried as he secured the dinghy to the *Ranger*.

Some of the men began to run for the pulley that would hoist the anchor. In moments, Jack, Mary, and Tobias all tumbled out onto the deck.

"What a strange catch we have today," came a raspy voice. They looked up to find Charles Vane smiling down at them. "Oh good," he drawled. "You're just in time for the vote."

EIGHTEEN

Jack

"What is Vane trying to accomplish here?" Jack whispered to Tobias out of the corner of his mouth as they all got to their feet.

"I don't know, but I would guess he's trying to get his ship back," Tobias murmured.

Vane beamed at them. "Indeed," he said. "I'm taking back what's mine and putting things right at long last."

Jack's eyes darted around frantically, looking for Bonn, and he found her—yay!—but she was gagged and tied to a chair just behind Vane.

Boo. She must be one of the things Vane had decided to "put right."

But, to look on the bright side, she was still on board, and not at the bottom of the ocean. At least Vane hadn't already made her walk the plank because she was a woman who dared to be a pirate. She was alive.

She looked, well, pissed off. But Jack hoped that this time she was angry at Vane, and not Jack.

Mary drew herself up to her full height, her hand resting lightly on her cutlass. "So you want to vote again, Vane? Is that it? Well, then, go ahead. Make your case." She looked around at her crew.

It was hard to know, thought Jack, looking around at them himself, what they were thinking.

"I was just reminding the men of all the good times we had together, when I was captain," Vane said. "The adventures we enjoyed. The ships we took. The treasure we plundered. Those were the days, weren't they, lads? You were paid with more than bananas then."

"Hey, I quite liked that spicy banana-zucchini ball we had a few nights ago," Quint said. "Bananas ain't all bad, really."

"In any case, the banana thing happened on your watch," Tobias pointed out. "Technically speaking."

"Perhaps," Vane said coolly, "but what have you gained since then? I don't see a lot of treasure to be had around here. Having a rough time of it, are you?"

"We'll get treasure," Mary said stiffly.

Would they, though? Jack wondered. Everywhere they'd looked so far held no significant treasure (outside of one pretty necklace). And the "get kicked by the boot" thing hadn't worked.

"Some hypothetical treasure you're chasing, no doubt," Vane

sniffed. "Let me guess. You're searching for Blackbeard's treasure." He scoffed. "I knew Blackbeard, and he loved nothing more than to spend whatever capital he had on women and wine. He probably died without a penny to his name. If you vote for me to be your captain again, I'll give each of you two hundred pieces of eight, right now."

Behind the gag, Bonn uttered something indecipherable (but obviously rude) and one of Vane's men elbowed her sharply in the ribs.

Jack's fists clenched at his sides. He might finally be willing to do some violence. The intensity of the feeling surprised him. He just really, really wanted to make that man suffer right now.

Mary scoffed. "My men won't be bribed. Not by you."

"Won't they?" Vane nodded to another of his men, who dragged forward a heavy chest. "Better to have a bit of cash now than imaginary money later. And this is merely a taste of my booty."

Jack stifled a laugh. His booty. But then Vane's man opened the chest. It was full of gold coins.

There were definitely a thousand pieces of eight in there, Jack surmised. It was very shiny.

"So that's my argument," Vane concluded. "Reinstate me as your captain, and you'll be rich men. Who's with me?"

No one spoke. (The speech sounded good, dear reader, but let's remember that two hundred pieces of eight was the equivalent of about $2,500 in today's cash. Which was nice, sure. But didn't exactly make a man rich. But think of how many bananas one could buy with that much money.)

"So I am officially calling a vote now," Vane said a little more loudly. "Every man who wishes for me, Charles Vane, to captain the *Ranger* again, raise your hand or hook."

No one did. Not one of Mary's men abandoned her.

"See?" Mary's eyes were alight with triumph. "No one wants you back."

"Let me put this a different way," Vane said, ignoring her. "If you don't choose to join my crew again, here's what will happen."

He nodded to one of his men, who lit a flare that shot up into the sky and popped loudly overhead.

Then, from around the entrance to the bay, came, not one, not two, but *six* other ships—big ships, ships with cannons, ships flying the British flag.

"Whose are those?" Jack asked. "Also, why are they familiar?" Then he blanched, because he realized why. "Oh no! Barnet?"

"Yes, it's true," Vane said, a dangerous glint in his eye. "Those ships you see out there are under the command of Jonathan Barnet. You're familiar with him, are you? Anyway, they will arrive shortly, and Barnet and his soldiers will kill some of you and imprison the rest. Then they will take you back to Port Royal, where you will be tried and hanged as a pirate. So in that scenario it's quite simple. You will die."

Even Mary looked unsettled by the idea.

"Or, alternatively, you could elect me as captain again," Vane continued. "Barnet and I have a very special understanding, and he will let you all go free as long as you pledge your allegiance to me and sign a silly little pardon thing later. So if that's what you choose to do, you will live."

Bonn said something again that was muffled by the gag.

"You're in league with Barnet?" Mary spat out—which is probably what Bonn had just said. "You're a traitor, Vane."

"I'm an opportunist," Vane said. "As all pirates must be." He turned to address the men again. "You can choose which of these paths you wish to walk. But you must choose. And you must do it quickly."

"He's right," Tobias said tensely. "Barnet's nearly on us."

Jack glanced past the stern, where, indeed, the six large ships were closing in fast (wow, at maybe even seven miles an hour). He gulped. He didn't doubt that they would hang if Barnet caught them. Or they'd die fighting, like Blackbeard. Dread bloomed in his stomach. He didn't want to die. He also didn't want to fight. (Except that one bloke who'd just manhandled Bonn.) He wondered vaguely where he'd put his frying pan.

"Now let's try this again," Vane said. "What do you say? Who votes for me and gets to live?"

Slowly, keeping their eyes downcast, about a third of the crew started to raise their hands. It wasn't enough for Vane to be captain again, not by the rules of piracy, which said he needed more than half the crew to vote for him, but maybe with the Barnet factor, Jack thought, it didn't matter.

Suddenly Bonn jumped to her feet, the ropes she'd sawed

through dropping to the deck behind her. She wrenched the gag from her mouth.

"Don't let him bully you, lads!" she yelled. "He's full of empty promises, that one. Do you really think that Jonathan Barnet—the infamous pirate hater—will just let you all go, easy as that? I say we fight!" She tossed her hair back and drew her cutlass, which gleamed in the moonlight. "Are we men or are we pirates?"

Jack's breath caught. She was glorious.

"*You* are neither, lass," Vane said coolly. He turned his attention back to Mary. "And, *Mary* Read, wanting to be a man and a pirate doesn't make it so." His lips curled into a sneer. "I should have known you were nothing but a conniving woman, set on rising above your proper station."

"I've no desire to be a man," Mary retorted. "But I *am* a pirate. And I am still the captain of this ship!" She turned to the other men. "We can fight. We can win!"

The crew looked . . . doubtful. Afraid. They'd been hearing scary stories about Jonathan Barnet for months now. He'd killed Blackbeard, after all. He'd nearly killed them, just last week.

"But we can try to run first, right?" Jack asked tremulously. "Avoid violence if we can?"

He really wished he had another storm potion. Something very bad was about to happen, he could feel it in his swim bladder. Everyone on the ship seemed poised for action. Mary went ahead and drew her own cutlass, her eyes fixed on Vane. Jack knew she'd fight him now if she had to, and then she'd fight Barnet.

But she didn't get the chance, because right then, without missing a beat, Vane lifted the pistol in his hand and fired it. Not at Mary—the musket ball whizzed by her, barely missing.

But at Tobias.

He fell to the deck and didn't move.

Then, when they were all standing there, frozen, Vane reached into his belt and drew out a second pistol. And fired at Jack.

He didn't realize what had happened at first. He heard the shot and felt something hit him, like he'd been whacked by a big stick, but he couldn't have said where. There was no pain, but after a moment he felt an intense prickling, and then he looked down at himself and saw blood pouring out of a hole in his thigh.

"Oh . . . ship," he said softly, before he dropped to the deck like a rag doll. "I'm shot."

"I know, I know. Where?" Bonn slid to her knees beside him. So maybe she wasn't still mad at him. Which was the silver lining in this terrible situation.

"My pants! And my beautiful leg!" He gestured down at the hole. There was so much blood that he wondered if he would change into a Mer. But blood was thicker than water, apparently, because he remained a gravely injured human being.

Bonn's face was suddenly close to his, her worried green eyes framed by charming golden lashes.

"I love you, Bonn," he whispered, reaching to touch her hair with a bloodstained hand. "Even if I'm sea foam, I will love you. It was all worth it."

"Stop talking nonsense," she barked. "If you die on me, I'll kill you myself."

He made a noise that was meant to be a laugh, but it came out like a whimper.

"That doesn't make sense," he said. "Nothing humans do makes sense."

"We must stop the bleeding!" She fussed with his leg, tightening something around it, and then tore at her shirt to serve as a bandage, pressing it down hard on his thigh. He cried out as a great wave of pain crashed over him at last. His leg was on fire!

"Water!" he begged. "Put me out."

Mary appeared beside Bonn suddenly, her face very pale under her tan. "Water! We need to get him into the water! If his tail forms, it will heal the wound, I think. It's worth a try, anyway."

Each girl grabbed him under the arms and began to drag him painfully toward the rail of the ship. "Is Tobias all right?" he asked Mary, but she didn't answer. Then they were blocked by Vane and a couple of other men with cutlasses.

"You're not going anywhere," Vane rasped.

Great Waters, the man's voice was annoying.

"You need a lozenge," Jack said weakly. He was losing so much blood. He was most likely dying, he realized, right this minute. He glanced around wildly, looking again for Tobias, but the spot on the deck where his friend had fallen was now empty.

Mary struggled to her feet, picked up her cutlass, and faced the crew.

"We can't run from this," she said. In the time she'd been seeing to Jack, Barnet's ships must surely be nearly on them now, although Jack couldn't see them. "So we must fight."

"Surrender!" came the disembodied voice of Captain Barnet from the other ship as it slid up alongside the *Ranger.* "If you lay down your arms now, I promise you will be shown mercy."

"Ha!" said Bonn. "What a crock! Don't listen to him, lads!"

"Hanging—that's another way to die," Jack rambled deliriously. "That's what they'll do if they catch us, right? They won't truly show mercy, because Jonathan Barnet has sworn to bring death to all pirates? And we're all still pirates, aren't we?"

"That's right, Jack," Mary affirmed. "And I, for one, would rather die like a pirate, with a sword in my hand and a curse on my lips, then see myself imprisoned and hanged!" She raised her cutlass in the air. "Who's with me?"

She was awfully brave, Jack thought.

"You have salt, Mary," he said. "I've always thought so."

"Shut up, Jack," his cousin said tenderly. "I've got to fight now." She gave a fierce battle cry as a group of Barnet's soldiers swung aboard the *Ranger* from the rigging.

Most of the *Ranger*'s men turned to fight as well. But a few of the men (those who had voted for Vane earlier, it must be noted) retreated, slinking below, away from the action.

"Where do you think yer going?" Bonn bellowed after them. "Get back here, ye sniveling dogs!" She pulled out one of her pistols and leveled it at another of the crew. "Vane! Stay and fight, or I'll kill ye meself."

Vane—for all his big, raspy talk before—shrugged and bolted away toward the *Conspicuous*.

Bonn fired the pistol at his retreating back, or at least she tried to. The pistol misfired. She screamed in rage, clobbered one of the attacking soldiers with the butt of the faulty pistol, and hurled it overboard. "Come at me, then!" she yelled, and cut and slashed and spun and parried and whirled.

"Be careful, my love," Jack panted, but there was no denying that she was brilliant. It was like she'd been born to pirate. Oh, she must be so pleased with herself.

But though she held her own for several minutes, they were quickly overwhelmed by the sheer number of Barnet's soldiers. It was one woman against twenty men, and even Bonn could not prevail against such odds.

"Behind you, Bonn!" Jack cried as the circle of soldiers closed around her. "Watch out!"

Bonn took a swing with her cutlass that brought down two of the soldiers, but two more of them grabbed her arms from behind. They took her sword and pistols. She tried to bite them, scratch them, even kick them in the tender bits, but then they promptly tied her up and gagged her again. Which was really going to piss her off.

"Unhand her!" Jack protested, but he never found out what happened after that, because that's when he passed out.

Mary

NINETEEN

Everything was going so wrong. Anne was already down, disarmed, but struggling against the soldier clapping irons around her wrists. Then there was Jack on the deck, bleeding badly from that hole in his leg. And finally, Tobias, who was up on his feet, fighting.

If there was anything Mary was grateful for today, it was that: Tobias was alive.

When he'd fallen to the deck, everything in Mary had felt like it was spinning. She'd seen gray for a moment, lost her breath. But then Vane had shot Jack, too, startling her into action.

Quickly, she'd discovered the musket ball had hit the trusty compass Tobias always kept in his breast pocket. The force of the impact had knocked the wind out of him, dropping him to the deck, but he was unhurt, save a few shallow cuts from broken glass, and what would become an impressive bruise just over his heart.

When he'd opened his eyes and his mouth had made the shape of her name—well, Mary had never felt such relief. If Jack hadn't been hurt—bleeding profusely, in fact—and a fight hadn't been heating up, Mary might have bent and kissed Tobias. He was *alive*.

But then she'd heard Jack call for water, gone to help him, and the battle was on. Tobias, having recovered somewhat, was on his feet and swinging his cutlass at a soldier closing in on him.

"Good," Mary said as Tobias moved toward her. "I thought you might have decided to get a nap in."

"And miss this? Never!"

But when Mary caught his eye, there was a glimmer of fear there. They were so far outnumbered.

Mary cut and slashed at her enemies, ducking and dodging as they closed in on her. She needed to get to Tobias, to fall into her usual pattern with him. But as she scanned the noisy deck, she realized that he'd moved. Somehow, he'd been forced back against a wall.

"Ha!" cried the soldier she'd been fighting, taking advantage of her distraction. He thrust his blade at her, but Mary blocked and disarmed him. Before he could react, she scooped up his sword and hurled it at him, blade first.

He hit the deck. The sword whirled past him and struck one of the soldiers advancing on Tobias. Right in the arm. While those two were busy, Mary grabbed the nearest line and swung toward

Tobias, feetfirst. She kicked another man, sending him straight into the water.

Pistols went off as Mary landed, moved a soldier around her to use as a shield, then threw him—and the musket balls now embedded in him—into the ocean after his friend.

Then there was only one left, who Tobias took down with a swift kick to the groin. Together, they sent him over the edge, too.

Musket balls were still flying and soldiers were still coming after them, but Mary needed to take care of one more thing.

Mary called out in Merish: *"I've got something for you!"*

"Mine?" came a voice from atop the mainmast, a voice between Merish and out-loud animal calls.

Another "Mine?" echoed from a different ship.

Suddenly, a flock of seagulls appeared out of nowhere, divebombing Barnet and his men. White feathers flew as the soldiers tried to fight them off. But there were hundreds of seagulls.

Mary turned to Tobias and sheathed her sword.

"I don't know how we survive this," he said urgently. "The men—"

"I know." At this point, she didn't care why some of them had turned on her, only that they had. "The only thing I'm worried about now," she said softly, "is you. If they catch you—"

Tobias glanced down. Port Royal wasn't Nassau. In Port Royal, Tobias wasn't likely to lose his life. He would lose his freedom. Which he'd said many times before would be a fate worse to him than death.

Around them, the seagulls were still going after the soldiers, but they wouldn't last much longer. They'd soon run out of shiny buttons and snacks to claim. Then they'd be gone, and Mary would be an easy target.

"I want to—" No, there was no time to explain. Instead, she grabbed Tobias's jacket, dragged him close, and kissed him.

He seemed startled at first. Surprised. But an instant later, he kissed her back, sweet and careful—just like he was. And the whole world melted away. The pistols. The swords. The screeching seagulls. Even Jack groaning on the deck.

The kiss felt exactly like she'd imagined, with those perfect, warm lips lingering over hers. His fingers touched her jaw. His other hand fell to her waist.

Mary wanted to stay like this forever.

But then the shrieking of seagulls stopped, and the fight came rushing back—and what she had to do.

She drew back from Tobias, her fists still clutching his jacket. He gazed at her, something between shock and elation on his face. And then he went all the way to shock as Mary pushed him over the rail of the ship.

He hit the water with a splash just as the last seagull flew away.

Mary lunged for Jack, ready to send her unconscious cousin overboard next, but she was too late. Hands clamped around her arms. Someone pried her sword off her belt. And then she felt the cold bite of iron around her wrists.

Jonathan Barnet came to stand in front of her, gazing down impassively. After the seagulls, he was a little more ragged than before, but it was clear to see he was a man who was usually well put together, with a red coat, shiny shoes, and a white wig.

"So this is the woman pirate, the fierce Mary Read I've heard so much about. I'm not impressed."

Mary spat at him, but before she could say anything, one of the men shoved a filthy rag into her mouth, gagging her.

"And was that Tobias Teach you just threw overboard? The son of Blackbeard?" Barnet sighed and shook his wig-topped head. "Ah, well, I'd have liked to murder him, too, but you win some, you lose some."

Mary bit into the gag as she scanned the deck for Anne Bonny. The girl's hands were bound with two pairs of handcuffs, and there were four pistols trained on her at all times. She, too, was gagged. Mary wondered what Anne had done while the birds had been attacking, because while she looked just the same as before—hair windblown and cheeks red with heat—she wore a feral little smile, made even wilder with the rag in her mouth.

At least until her eyes fell on Jack again. Then, pain.

She met Mary's eyes, seeming to ask, *Why didn't you save him?*

Mary shook her head, wishing to all the great waters that she'd been faster.

"Now," said Barnet, "you filthy pirates will be taken back to Port Royal, where you will be tried and assuredly found guilty of piracy, and then you'll be hanged." Then Barnet stepped directly in front of Mary and reached down for her neck. "What's this?"

Mary grunted and struggled, but there were too many men holding her back.

With a cruel smile, Barnet pulled the diamond necklace out from the collar of her shirt, his face so close to Mary's as he examined the blue diamond that she could smell the wine on his breath. "How pretty," he said. "Do you always wear diamonds on a pirate ship?" (Actually, Mary was wearing the necklace because it was priceless and she didn't want to lose it, and she'd figured the best place not to lose it was around her neck. Which she understood now was a mistake.) "Do you fancy yourself some sort of—I don't know—*queen*? Ah yes, I've heard about your little contest. Ha ha. I thought you pirates called yourselves a democracy. A brotherhood, of sorts. Pathetic. But there is one element of this silly game of yours that interests me." He loomed over her, his fingers closing around the diamond. "Treasure. And the acquisition of said treasure." He lifted the necklace from around her neck and began to pace back and forth in front of her, still holding the necklace aloft, letting the moonlight play along the facets of the stone. "Fun story: When I killed Blackbeard and his crew aboard the *Queen Anne's Revenge*, I kept one or two of his men alive because I'd heard a rumor that Blackbeard had a treasure."

Mary fought to keep her expression neutral as the pirate hunter looked at her assessingly.

"After a bit of light torture," he continued, "one of these men told me there was indeed a treasure. At a cute little farm in North

Carolina. Plum Point. Have you been? It's charming. Of course, I had to go see for myself. But alas, I could find no treasure. Not even one single piece of eight. It was gone." He pouted. "I thought the treasure was lost to me forever, but now—happy day!—here you are, a known associate of Blackbeard's son. Do you, perchance, happen to know where Blackbeard's treasure is?"

He waited. Then he realized she had the gag in her mouth.

"Oh, excuse me," he said, and pulled the gag free.

Mary glared daggers at him. "Even if I did know," she said, "I'd die before I'd tell you."

He gazed at her for a long moment and then sighed. "Unfortunately, I believe you." He pushed the gag back into her mouth. "Oh well." He shoved the necklace into his pocket and signaled someone from another ship. "All right, men, let's take these criminals back to Port Royal for due process!"

They didn't have to go far. Port Royal was, like we said, very close. They'd been sailing into dangerous waters when they'd gone to the boot.

Why, Mary wondered for the tenth or twentieth time, *would Blackbeard hide the key to his treasure so close to Port Royal?*

Perhaps because he'd understood very few pirates would ever think to look there. Only Tobias, with his knowledge of the maps and codes. Regardless of the reason, Blackbeard had gotten them caught. And Vane. That bilge rat.

By morning, Mary, Anne, Jack, and the rest of the crew of the

Ranger were crowded into the courtroom for the trial. Vane was in the audience, looking smug.

It was obvious from the judge's face that this wasn't going to be a long event. He'd already made up his mind.

Mary sat stiffly in the chair they'd provided, Anne next to her. And Jack, poor Jack, was awake, but obviously in incredible pain.

"Is Tobias all right?" Jack asked in Merish.

"I don't know." Mary hoped Tobias had made it to the safety of the other ships, but she couldn't begin to guess. And even if the mermaid's kiss worked—which she didn't know if she could still do, now that she was human—it would be a long swim. A *very* long swim. Much longer than twenty-seven minutes.

Her heart sank the more she thought about it, so she tried not to think about it. Instead, she nudged Anne. "I'm glad you came aboard," Mary said quietly. "You've been an asset. A real pirate's pirate."

"I only wish I'd been able to make a name for meself," Anne said. "Like Grace O'Malley."

"I'd like to hear about her sometime," Mary said.

Just then, the judge banged his gavel and everyone went quiet.

"State your names," the judge ordered.

Mary lifted her chin. "Mary Read."

Anne seemed to think for a moment, then said, "Anne Brennan Cormac."

And finally, Jack said, "Jack Rackham, but please call me Calico Jack. I'm hoping it catches on."

The judge did not look like he was about to call Jack *Calico* Jack.

"Your Honor," Barnet said, standing from his seat with a flourish, "these people are pirates. They were caught on the pirate ship *Ranger* engaging in suspicious pirate activity. Inspection revealed that the cargo hold was full of bananas—and as you know, the *Chango* was raided recently. Indeed, that ship was on its way here—to deliver much-needed bananas to Port Royal. It never arrived."

The judge gave a slow, thoughtful nod. "Those bananas would have fed a lot of people on this island. And you're certain the bananas found on the *Ranger* were stolen from the *Chango*?"

"Yes, Your Honor. On that fellow"—Barnet pointed to Mr. Child, the ship's chef—"we found this recipe book. If I may approach the bench to present the evidence."

"You may." The judge took the book and flipped through it. "Well, this is terribly suspicious. What other evidence can you present?"

Barnet unfurled a black flag—the skull and crossbones. "They were flying this."

The judge put on his spectacles. "That's not a flag I've ever seen before. Is it new? It's quite good, as far as pirate flags go."

"You think so, Your Honor?" Jack leaned forward. "I don't want to brag, but I designed it. I call it the Jolly Roger, because—"

"Shut up, Jack," Mary hissed in Merish. *"The trial is about whether or not we're pirates. And you're confessing."*

"I mean," Jack said out loud, "I designed it as a joke. Not as anything serious. Obviously if I'd designed it in a serious manner, I'd be a pirate. Which I'm not. None of us are." Then, in Merish, he said to Mary, *"Lying is so easy when you just say it out loud!"*

"Nobody believes you," she replied, also in Merish.

"Interesting." The judge motioned for Barnet to put away the flag. "And is there anything else?"

"Tobias Teach was aboard the *Ranger,* Your Honor," Barnet said. "Sadly, he jumped overboard before he could be apprehended. But as you know, he's Edward Teach's son—Blackbeard, that is. And, finally," Barnet said, "perhaps the worst crime of all is that these two were aboard the *Ranger.*" He pointed at Mary and Anne. "And that one"—now he pointed only at Mary—"is said to be the *captain* of the ship."

The judge's face twisted. "But she's a girl."

Barnet pinched the bridge of his nose. "I know. It's— Well, it's disgusting, frankly. I knew pirates were low, but I didn't think they allowed *women* to command."

"Absolutely indefensible behavior," the judge agreed. "Now, have you any witnesses?"

"I do." Barnet motioned for Vane. "This is Charles Vane, former captain of the *Ranger.* He and I have reached an agreement. In exchange for testifying today, he'll retire from his life as a pirate and live the rest of his days as an upstanding and useful member of society."

Mary snorted.

The judge raised an eyebrow. Then he turned to Vane. "Is that so? You're willing to retire?"

"Aye," rasped Vane. "All I want now is to settle down with my lady love, Bess."

"He's lying!" Anne burst out. "They broke up ages ago. Bess will never take him back."

"Order!" The judge banged the gavel. "Order!" He turned back to Vane. "Well, let's hear what you have to say about your former crew."

Vane narrowed his eyes as he looked at the assembled crew of the *Ranger*. His glare lingered a moment on Mary. Then he grinned, showing the gold glint in his teeth. "I can attest that all these men and, uh, women, are indeed pirates. They've engaged in all manner of pirating activities, from stealing to mutiny to forcing innocent folks to walk the plank. That Read is one of the hardest, most heartless pirates I ever met. Why, she started calling for all men to be thrown off ships—"

Mary slammed her hands against the table and surged up. "That's a lie! I never said—"

Bang, bang! The gavel hit the bench again. "Order!" ordered the judge. "I'll not be having any *he said, she said* nonsense in my courtroom. Now, Vane, is there anything else you wanted to say?"

Vane clasped his hands in front of him, the picture of a remorseful and reformed pirate. "I'll conclude by saying only that Mary Read made me afraid for my life. If she and her crew are permitted to go free, no man will be safe."

"All right," said the judge. "I suppose I've heard enough to make my decision."

Mary cleared her throat. "Wait, aren't I allowed to defend myself? And my crew?"

The judge practically rolled his eyes. "All right. What do you wish to say?"

"We were not engaging in any illegal activity when Barnet found us. We hadn't done anything wrong. And I don't know how those bananas got on my ship. Clearly that so-called evidence was planted."

Jack gasped and, in Merish, said, *"You are so good at lying!"*

"What about the *Kingston*?" Barnet said. "You tried to take that."

"Did I?" Mary tilted her head. "Did you find the *Kingston* while rifling through my pockets or something? Or was it also in the *Ranger*'s hold?"

A few people from the audience laughed.

"That's enough," the judge said. "You walk like a pirate. You talk like a pirate. You're clearly a pirate."

Mary couldn't help her proud smile.

"Therefore, I sentence you—and your entire crew—to hang until dead." The judge checked his pocket watch. "We'll do it in the square at sundown, to give everyone something to discuss over dinner. Until then, you will be held in Fort Charles."

Mary's smile fell. Why was there always a mention of Charles?

Beside her, Jack looked utterly miserable.

But then Anne stood. Fierce Anne Bonny. She turned to Vane and the men who'd joined with him, standing behind them, all shame-faced and guilty. "If you had fought like men," she accused, "then you wouldn't hang like dogs."

TWENTY

Tobias

She had *kissed* him. Tobias still couldn't fully believe it. He raised his hand to his lips, as if he could find some evidence lingering there, but all he tasted was salt. Still, he didn't think he'd hallucinated the moment between them: Mary grabbing his jacket, jerking his body to hers, her lips finding his. It had been the most wonderful surprise of his life.

Of course then she'd pushed him overboard.

By some miracle, Tobias hadn't died upon hitting the water. Nor had he died when he couldn't immediately surface. Instead, he'd found he could breathe underwater—just like before, when Jack had kissed him.

Because *Mary had kissed him.* She had the magic, too.

Not that it mattered, because the moment he resurfaced,

Tobias immediately started climbing back onto the ship. So he'd been clinging to the hull just a few feet below them when Jonathan Barnet had been interrogating Mary about Blackbeard's treasure. Tobias had briefly considered jumping up onto the deck and declaring that he knew where to find the treasure, making some sort of devil's bargain to deliver the treasure to Barnet, in exchange for letting Mary and the crew go free. But Tobias was a realist, and he knew he had no leverage here. There was nothing to stop Barnet from then taking the treasure and hauling them all back to Port Royal for due process. Tobias knew he couldn't save them, not single-handedly. Not now. He needed help.

So, with a heavy heart, he let himself drop back into the water. Mary, Anne, and Jack were transferred to one of the British ships—the *Kingston*, ironically—in chains. Barnet's ships, with the *Ranger* and the *Conspicuous* in tow, set off in the direction of Port Royal. So he turned and swam in the opposite direction, toward where they'd sent the *Jester* and the *William*.

He'd wondered, during this long swim, if Mary had known she could still give him the ability to breathe underwater. Either she *had* known, and she'd been letting Jack kiss him this whole time, or she hadn't known, and she'd sent him overboard with nothing but hope to go on. But clearly she'd been trying to save his life.

It gave him something to think about as he swam. The kiss's magical properties didn't last long, but then (in the second most wonderful surprise of Tobias's life), a pod of dolphins found him and made him understand that they were there to help him on his way. Like Mary had sent him the dolphins, too. Like even now she was looking out for him.

In any case, Mary was probably winning their who-saved-who competition right now. But not for long!

At last he made it, with the dolphins towing him in turns to the cove where the *Jester* and *William* were anchored. He called out to them, and in moments someone hauled him up onto the *Jester*. And then, from flat on his back on the main deck, trying to catch his breath, he'd explained the situation to Caesar.

"We have to get to Port Royal," he panted. "We have to save them."

"If we aren't already too late," Caesar said grimly. "They're quick to hang pirates, these days."

Tobias refused to believe it was too late. He thought for a second. "Get me the *William*. Fly the *Jester*'s flag—the original one, not the Jolly Roger. And I need men—anyone brave enough to risk Port Royal to rescue our captain."

Half a dozen men sprang into action, and minutes later the *William* was sailing as fast as she could manage toward Port Royal. And the *William* was fast—she was a tiny sloop, even speedier and more agile than the *Ranger*.

But was she fast enough?

Tobias gritted his teeth the whole way to Port Royal, and as they came up on the harbor about midday, he scanned the gibbets hanging over the water, searching for familiar faces.

They weren't there. Not yet.

Tobias's relief was short-lived; he couldn't afford to relax at all. Because while Mary wasn't hanging inside a gibbet, she might be hanging from a noose.

He wouldn't let that happen. Not ever, but especially not now. Not when they'd just . . . Not when she might begin to understand how much he loved her, every part of her.

As the *William* berthed and Gregory—the most respectable-looking white fellow among them—acted as the captain, Tobias took his father's treasure map out of the oilskin envelope he'd stowed in his jacket pocket and tore the long piece of parchment in half. He handed one half to Caesar and returned the other half to the envelope, which he placed back into his jacket pocket. Then he shoved a cap over his head, nodded to the crew, and hurried down the gangplank—into the town of Port Royal.

"Good luck, lad," Caesar called after him. "Be careful."

A vague, distant part of Tobias knew he should be afraid here. He'd steered clear of Port Royal all his life, a place where people like him were considered property and not human beings. But he had to be here.

I'm coming for you, Mary, he thought. *Just be alive when I get there. Please.*

The city was loud and chaotic, with people pushing from every side. No one gave Tobias a chance to get his bearings, but he could see one promising location from here: a fort on a hill.

He hurried in that direction.

And as he did, he kept his eye on the people around him, noting who was brown and who was white and adjusting his course accordingly. He couldn't afford to be stopped. He scanned the streets and squares, looking—always looking—for signs that Mary, Jack, Anne, or any of the others had been here. But soon, he realized the town was abuzz with news.

The first significant item was about the Pirate King contest itself. It seemed the townspeople had all heard about it and were taking bets on which pirate captain would win the crown. Among the snippets of updates, Tobias learned that Captain Penzance had quite a lot of treasure (although no one could agree how much), Captain Ahab was out (Tobias knew that already), and Captain Crunch was dead. Oh, and Captain Vane—the clear frontrunner, according to everyone in town—had *three* ships full of treasure. Where he'd procured this treasure, no one knew.

The second bit of news was more urgent to Tobias, who could hardly think of the Pirate King contest at a time like this. The talk was of *lady* pirates and a hanging scheduled for this evening. The people were planning what they would wear and taking bets on whether or not they thought the pirates might scream during the short drop.

Tobias pushed himself faster toward Fort Charles. And now that he knew Mary was alive—for the next few hours—a new plan started to form in his head. Half a plan, anyway. More like a quarter of a plan.

But it was better than nothing.

"I need to speak to Jonathan Barnet," he told the soldier at the door. A white man.

The soldier looked him up and down. "You?"

Tobias forced his voice to be steady. Confident. "I was sent to bring him a message."

"Not possible. He's busy today. He's got a big execution coming up this evening."

"I need to speak with him before then," Tobias said. "It's about Blackbeard, you see. A most urgent message."

"A message from whom?" the guard demanded.

Oh crap, from whom?

"Leonardo," he blurted out.

"Leonardo who?"

"Leonardo Di—"

"Oh, yes. I've heard of that guy," said the guard. "Come with me."

As Tobias followed the soldier inside, he had the strangest sensation of being here and not here. Like it was someone else walking through the narrow halls of the fort. He passed closed doors and crowded rooms and a long stairway down, and finally, the soldier deposited him in an empty office at the end of a hall.

"Wait here," the soldier said. "He'll be along soon."

Awkwardly, Tobias stood by the desk and waited for the soldier's footsteps to recede.

He stared at the chair but wouldn't allow himself to sit. He went over the details of his haphazard plan in his mind. He would tell Barnet about the treasure. He would produce his half of the map. He would take Barnet outside onto the ramparts, give him a spyglass, and point out the *William* anchored there. On the ship, Caesar, who would be waiting for his signal, would hold up the second half of the map. And then Tobias would offer Jonathan Barnet a trade.

Was it a foolproof plan? No. Was it all he had? Yes.

Tobias reckoned that there was about a 50 percent chance that with this plan, he'd get captured, too. Maybe tortured. Possibly killed.

But a 50 percent chance was good enough for him.

Unfortunately the key part of this plan relied on Tobias being able to locate Jonathan Barnet.

Who wasn't here.

And the sun was dropping lower in the sky.

He started rifling through the papers on Barnet's desk, looking for a schedule or some clue of where the man might be. Then the desk drawer caught his eye. It was slightly open. Inside, something sparkled.

Tobias slid the drawer the rest of the way open to find the heart-shaped diamond. It was just . . . sitting there. In Barnet's desk. Mary's necklace.

Faint gray gathered at the corners of Tobias's vision as all the urgent, terrified energy that had gotten him here began to abandon him now, leaving him with bone-deep exhaustion and numb dread. He was running out of time. He couldn't wait any longer.

Tobias started for the door. But now he heard someone coming down the hall.

Barnet?

No. When Tobias peered out, a pair of soldiers were coming up the stairs, a prisoner, still shackled, between them.

Anne.

Tobias's heart jumped at the sight of her.

"Your father paid quite handsomely for your release," said one of the solders. "We're to deliver you straight to his ship."

"Already here on business, he was," agreed the other soldier. "So that's lucky for you."

Anne grunted but didn't say anything.

And before he could think better of it, Tobias let out a short whistle to the tune of "A Pirate's Life for Me."

Anne's shoulders stiffened. She glanced back. And her eyes narrowed slightly.

It wasn't like Anne Bonny to go down without a fight.

Tobias smiled. Because now his brain was finally catching up to his body and a new plan was forming in the back of his head. A better plan.

First things first, though: he had to get out of here before Barnet arrived. And then he needed to join forces with Anne.

Tobias followed Anne and the soldiers back to the docks, where a man was waiting for her in front of a large merchant ship. He was an older man with bright red hair—clearly her father.

The soldiers removed Anne's shackles, pushed her at her father so hard she nearly fell, and turned back to the fort.

"Ah, come here, my darling!" her father said loudly, and Anne stiffened at the term. He opened his arms wide, but Anne didn't step into his embrace. "Aw, don't be that way. Give your father a kiss now, lass, because I've rescued you from certain death. And for once I'd see you grateful for it. I'll take you home now, where you belong."

Anne didn't reply.

Tobias whistled, drawing her eye to the shadowy overhang where he was hiding. Her gaze lighted on him. He gave a little wave.

Anne turned back and took a long look up at the ship, at the man waiting for her, the safety he offered.

"Go to hell, Da," she said, then stomped on her father's foot and turned and ran in the opposite direction.

Her father ran after her, of course. Even the soldiers and more than a dozen men from her father's ship chased her, but Anne was too fast. Tobias watched as she darted and ducked around people and buildings alike, then as the soldiers and her father's men gave up chase, she looped back to Tobias's hiding place.

"So how are we going to do it?" she asked him breathlessly.

"Do it?"

"Rescue our sweethearts. We have to move fast. It's nearly sundown."

Tobias nodded. For the first time since midnight, he felt like there was a real chance this was all going to work out. "I have a plan."

TWENTY-ONE

Jack [5]

As you're no doubt aware, dear reader, Jack considered himself to be an optimistic person, able—even in the most seemingly dire of circumstances—to see the good in any given situation. (When life gave him bananas, he could definitely make banana cream pie.) But at this moment, Jack was curled up in a miserable ball on the cold, dank floor of Fort Charles's coldest, dankest prison cell, and all he could think was some variation of *poor me, poor me, poor me.*

He was going to (gulp) die.

The humans were going to kill him, which felt like such a betrayal. He'd defended them when some of those in Underwhere said humans were a terrible, bloodthirsty species that would hopefully destroy themselves before they ended up wrecking the planet. Oh no, he'd said, humans were brilliant. Look at their inventions, he'd said. Look at their art, their writing, their appreciation of beauty. He'd never imagined that one day he'd be locked up, waiting for men to come and lead him to one of humanity's less fun inventions: the gallows.

Jack curled up even more tightly, shivering, the shackles around his wrists and ankles biting into his flesh. He didn't know what time it was, but the judge had said they'd hang at sunset, and Jack sensed that the sun was getting awfully low. Any time now, and they'd come for him. And then he'd (gulp) die.

It felt so impossible, at his mere seventeen years of age, to be faced with his own untimely demise. Mers, if you'll recall, live to be approximately three hundred years old. What did it mean for his life expectancy, he had often wondered in the time since he'd come Above, to be half human? Would he still get three hundred years or only one hundred? But now he was never going to find out.

He was never going to find Ted and solve the mystery of his parentage.

He was never going to see Tobias again.

Or Mary.

Or his mom. What must she be thinking now that he hadn't checked in on his shell phone?

Sniff. His shell phone.

And (gulp) he was never going to get to hold Bonn's freckled face in his hands and kiss her salty, chapped lips one last time. She'd been taken somewhere—he'd heard the guards move her, they'd said something about her father—and he thought maybe she'd get out of this somehow. He hoped she'd get away from here, disappear and live out her life in some safe obscurity. Never look back. He wanted that for her. But he was also devastated by the idea that he'd never hear her sweet brogue again.

He reached up to swipe the wetness from his face. Such a bizarre thing, crying. Perhaps if he cried enough tears, he could make a puddle large enough to wet himself. (He'd tried the number one way to wet yourself earlier, but he was just so darned dehydrated from the copious blood loss that even that didn't work.) He wanted to revert to his Mer form, not to escape, since Mer Jack would have been even less capable of getting out of this cell than human Jack was, but on the off chance that if he changed, the transformation might fix the *hole in his leg*.

Yep, he still had a musket ball in there, and it still really hurt. His thigh had become swollen and hot to the touch. Infected, probably.

It might be better to quickly die now, he reasoned, than to die slowly and painfully of blood poisoning later.

See now? Hanging would be better. Perhaps Jack had found a silver lining here, after all.

Heavy boots sounded in the hallway. They were coming.

Jack scrambled back against the wall farthest from the door. Nope, no silver lining here. Dying still sucked, hanging or otherwise.

The door opened and three burly guards shuffled in. The one in front grinned at him, which was rude, considering the circumstances. It wasn't polite to enjoy the misery of others.

"Time's up, Calico Jack," the guard said.

Oh, good. The name had finally caught on.

"Careful now, I'm injured!" Jack protested as they hauled him painfully to his feet. But they only laughed and goaded him.

"That leg won't be troubling you for long, lad," said the rude guard, and they dragged him from his cell and toward the bright door at the end of the hall.

Jack really, really, didn't want to go into the light.

"No! No!" he cried, dragging his feet, reaching out with both hands, trying in vain to grab hold of something—anything—that he could use to stop himself from exiting this world. "I don't want to die yet! I'm not ready! No! NOOOOOOO!"

His fingers caught in the bars of another cell, and he clung to them for dear life. The guards shouted their displeasure and began to hit him: first a fist to the stomach that brought him wheezing to his knees, then a hard, fast blow to his leg, which hurt so much he saw starfishes. But he did not let go.

"Get up, you dog!" yelled the rude guard next to his ear, and Jack closed his eyes against the brutal noise of it, but he did not let go.

Then a hand closed around his on the bars.

"Get up, Jack," said Mary softly.

His eyes opened and he gazed through the bars at his cousin. There was despair in her expression, an undercurrent of fear, but there was also determination. Fury. Salt. Mary had salt. And she was trying to impart some of hers to him.

"Littlest," he whispered. "I am sorry."

She shook her head. "I'm the one who should apologize. You wouldn't be here if it weren't for me."

"You're right," he agreed. "Thank you for owning up to that."

"GET UP!" bellowed the guard, and hit Jack again, but Jack held Mary's gaze.

"Have courage, cousin," she said, a shimmer of tears in her eyes. "I'll be right behind you."

Courage. Yes. If she could be so brave, he could, too.

He struggled to his feet, bracing against the terrible pain in his leg, and stepped back slowly, releasing the bars.

"Goodbye, Mary." He struggled to keep his voice even. "You're the best pirate I ever saw."

"Goodbye, Jack," she replied, squeezing his hand. "You're the worst pirate I ever saw, but that's to your credit, I think. You give them one hell of a splash."

Ha! A splash! He could almost laugh at that, imagining it as he walked between the guards toward the light. Perhaps he should ask them to put up a sign. *Warning: Splash Zone!* it would read. *Any onlookers standing in the first three rows will get wet.*

But he stopped laughing when the guards marched him out of the jail and into the square, where a small crowd was gathered, and at the sight of him, they immediately began to jeer.

"You're about to feed the fish now, boy!" one man shouted.

"You bilge-sucking, scurvy dog!" a woman cried.

"That's not fair. I like dogs," he gasped. Dogs had been one of his favorite things about being human. Gawl, there were so many things about being human he'd loved.

Someone hurled a head of rotten cabbage at him, which struck Jack full on the chest with such force that he stumbled and the guards had to drag him to his feet again. Then they were pushing him up the steps and onto a tall platform fitted with a noose, a trapdoor, and a lever.

The gallows.

The hangman—a large fellow wearing a hood over his face—put the noose around Jack's neck. Jonathan Barnet came forward and read some things off a piece of paper, but Jack couldn't make sense of the words. His heart was a riotous clamor in his chest, his breath sharp and shuddery, and his hands and legs began to tremble so that he was afraid he'd fall again. He scanned the crowd, unable to keep himself from looking for the flash of Bonn's beautiful red hair. He didn't see her. She hadn't come. Perhaps she was still angry with him. Or perhaps she was far away from here by now.

He swallowed.

It was for the best, that.

Barnet asked him if he had any last words. The crowd fell silent. He felt his terror subside. The sun had just set, and the sky bloomed into a rosy lavender color he'd never seen before. He turned his face up to feel the soft Caribbean breeze against his skin. Breezes were good. Sunsets were good. Somewhere he heard a bird singing, and he looked around until he located it, perched in a gnarled tree just beyond the edge of the fort wall. A little gray bird with a bright yellow head. Its song was beautiful, a run of several sweet notes on one pitch, followed by some at a lower pitch, ending with a single note on the original pitch.

Birdsong. Another one of his favorite things.

"Thank you," he said softly, and then cleared his throat to address the crowd.

"Does anyone know a man named Ted?" This was, he supposed, his last chance to ask.

The crowd murmured among themselves. These were pretty strange last words.

But one man—miraculously—stepped forward. "My name is Ted."

"Oh! Really?" Jack stared down at the fellow in disbelief. The man was tall, with dark hair and eyes! He was a most friendly-looking man, with a large bushy mustache and a big smile. He was holding up a sign that read, *BELIEVE*.

"You're Ted?" Jack said breathlessly.

"Yep, that's my name," said the man, in the funniest accent Jack had ever heard. He must be from Holland. "Ted Lariat, at your service."

"Pleased to meet you, Mr. Lariat," said Jack. "And are you now, or have you ever been, a sailor?"

"Nope. I'm a coach."

Jack had no idea what that was.

"And have you ever met a mermaid, sir?" Jack asked.

"Well, that would be real neat," said Mr. Lariat, "but I can't say I've ever had the pleasure."

Jack deflated. This was not his father. "Well, thanks for coming to my Ted talk."

"No problem. Good luck with the hanging, son," Ted replied kindly.

Oh. Right.

"Any *other* last words?" asked Jonathan Barnet with a sniff.

"Hmm," said Jack. "Let me think."

We'd like to pause for a moment here, dear reader, to address a legend about Calico Jack Rackham. History would report that he was indeed hanged at Port Royal for piracy and then put in a gibbet (the birdcage thing, remember?) at the entrance to the harbor, as a warning to anyone who sailed into the town. His last words, or so the legend goes, were: "Woe to him who finds my many treasures, for no ship can carry them all." To which we, your faithful narrators, say, HUH? That makes no sense at all. Jack never had much in the way of treasure, unless you counted his friends as treasure, and, well, we do.

But why would Jack say this?

Had he decided to mess with the people who had come to see him hanged? Was he going for mystery here? Was he trying to stall, like maybe if people thought he had a great treasure, they'd wait to hang him until after he could tell them where to find it?

Did he say it at all?

We don't know. What we do know is that, whatever it was that he said at that moment, they weren't his *last* last words.

Because right then, with the hangman's hand on the lever and the rope chafing against Jack's neck, a trumpet sounded on the far side of the square.

Everyone spun around to see what was going on. Then the crowd was confused, because there, having just entered the square, was a man in a bright-red-and-gold jacket, a broad-brimmed hat with a large purple plume, and a sheathed rapier at his hip. He raised his voice to be heard over the crowd.

"TO BE, OR NOT TO BE," he intoned dramatically.

Jack felt an incredulous grin spreading over his face. Because it was Mr. Gregory, the captain of the *Jester*, come to give Jack one final performance. And because Jack had also noticed that, while everyone else was looking at Captain Gregory, another figure had emerged, riding a horse at full speed toward the gallows.

Bonn.

Her copper curls bounced in the air with each stride of the horse. She'd smeared her face with some kind of blue paint. And, strangely enough, she was carrying a stick of dynamite and a squawking chicken.

"THAT IS THE QUESTION," said Gregory.

"GAWLLLLLLL!" yelled Bonn, and Jack's chest swelled with love and terror at the sight of her. Love because he loved her. Duh. And terror because she was taking such a big risk, all for him.

Everything happened very quickly after that:

Bonn hurled the chicken up into the air, where it fluttered for a moment before launching itself at a nearby spectator, pecking violently at anyone who came too close. "BEGAWK!"

"Wait. I think this is a distraction. They're attempting to free the prisoner!" a man from the crowd said loudly.

"You're right! Release the trapdoor!" shouted Jonathan Barnet. "Kill the pirate!"

The hangman dutifully pulled the lever. Metal clanked. The floor dropped out beneath Jack's feet.

Oh ship.

The rope burned at his throat, but before the noose had a chance to tighten, a blade whistled through the air, and the rope split apart. Jack landed on the packed dirt beneath the gallows with a *thunk* and a strangled cry—his poor musket-ball-filled leg was jarred by the impact, enough to have him seeing starfish again. Did it hurt? Oh, yes. It was agony. Was it better than being hanged by the neck until dead? Absolutely.

"Get that pirate!" screamed Jonathan Barnet. "Five pieces of eight for the first man to bring him to me!"

Ted Lariat, who was still at the front of the crowd, dropped his sign and blew a whistle. "Be a goldfish, son!" he coached. "Go! Go!"

What a time, Jack thought, to be unable to properly run.

"Get him!" The crowd roared and converged on Jack, and, as he turned to flee, he realized that he still had three significant problems: his hands, which remained shackled; his blasted leg; and the noose still around his neck—now with a convenient tail for anyone to grab.

He reached around, grasping for the end of the rope, at the same time as he ducked and pushed between half a dozen men running toward him.

"Get out of my way, you!" Bonn's voice rose above the frenzy. Hoofbeats thundered toward the gallows, forcing people to flee or be trampled. "Run away! Get out of here! Git!"

The crowd began to run away. Then the horse was right beside Jack. "Come on!" Bonn cried, and Jack limped out from under the gallows. But before he could climb onto the horse, someone grabbed the rope, which sent him sprawling to the dirt again, gagging.

It was Barnet. Who was, strangely, smiling. He jerked on the rope again, tightening it on Jack's neck.

"Rude!" Jack sputtered. He spun and kicked Barnet in the knee (with his good leg), forcing the man to let go of the rope.

"Here. I brought you a present." Bonn reached back into the horse's saddlebag and retrieved a large black item. She tossed it down to Jack, and he caught it between his chained hands.

A frying pan.

He grinned. "How well you know me, my love!" he said jovially, and then clocked Barnet on the back of the head right as the man was getting to his feet, and Barnet went down again, this time for the count. "Perfect!"

"I'll be taking this back." Bonn pried her knife out of the wood where it had stuck after cutting Jack's rope. Then she looked down at Jack. "Well, don't take your time about it," she rasped in her adorable brogue. "Climb up!"

That was going to be difficult, considering the leg, the shackles, his general inexperience with horses, and the frying pan. Jack heaved himself back up onto the platform, ducked the hangman's punch, bopped the rude guard on the head with the frying pan, and then tried to figure out if there was a good way to get on the horse from up here. And the answer was, no, not really.

"Let's go!" Bonn called to him, then brandished her dagger at one of the men trying to get to Jack. "Get back! He's mine!"

"Hold this, will you, darling?" He tossed the frying pan to her, and she jammed it hastily back in the saddlebag. Then, before he lost his nerve, Jack threw himself bodily onto the horse, landing half across Bonn's lap (which, all right, wasn't so bad) and halfway across the pommel of the saddle (which was quite painful where it jabbed at his ribs).

"Gawl, Jack," Bonn said. "Don't you know how to get on a horse?"

"I'm a little tied up now, darling." From Jack's vantage point—which was, unfortunately, right by the horse's front shoulder—he could just see the angry mob closing in on them again. "Um, I don't mean to alarm you, but we seem to be surrounded," he called up.

"I see that! We have to wait for—"

"BEGAWK!" A weight thumped onto Jack's left butt cheek. Talons dug into his skin.

"Is that the chicken?" he inquired.

"Stay down." Bonn's hand pressed on Jack's back as she kicked the horse again, twisted them around—and the mob pressed in more tightly. Above Jack, Bonn heaved a great sigh. "Well, I didn't want to have to do this, but here we go."

"Wait, what?" Jack couldn't see what was happening.

But then he heard a hiss, and very, very quickly, the angry mob started to move back. "Run away!" they shouted. "She's gonna blow!"

There was the sound of screaming, the violent jerk of Bonn throwing something, and then the rush of the wind (and horse's mane) in his face as they took off at full speed. The chicken held on to Jack's trousers (and butt) even more tightly.

All this running was really making his leg throb.

"What's happening?" Jack shouted. But because he was lying half on Bonn's lap and half on the pommel as the horse galloped out of the square, it came out as "Wh-ah-h-ah-t-ts-ts ha-ha-ha-owww-pen-in-ing" followed by a pained groan because the bruise developing on his ribs was really starting to bloom.

"They're getting away!" cried members of the angry mob.

Which was the wrong thing to pay attention to, because at that very moment, a loud *BOOM* shook the square, the gallows exploded, and screaming crescendoed.

"Gawl, that was more fun than a frog in a cup of milk!" Bonn shouted. Then she urged the horse faster with a "Yah!" and they were careening through the streets of Port Royal at top speed.

They fled for their lives for several more minutes. The horse's mane continued flying into Jack's nose and mouth. And the pommel continued jabbing him in the ribs. The chicken clutched tighter. And not to mention the musket ball in his leg. If this was riding a horse, Jack wanted nothing to do with it ever again.

It was fully dark by the time Bonn allowed them to slow and stop. Jack slid, groaning, off the side of the horse. His legs crumpled underneath him. The chicken flew off to safety.

Whale rocks. Everything hurt.

"What about Captain Gregory?" he asked. "We left him."

Bonn dismounted gracefully and knelt in front of him. Quickly, she loosened the rope still around his neck and slid it over his head. "He'll be all right." She hurled what was left of the noose to the other side of the road. "He has something else to do right now. You were the only one I was after."

Jack's heart gave a great lurch as he gazed up at her. "I really thought I was going to die. It was most upsetting."

"Not on my watch." Bonn removed a lockpick and tension wrench from her boot, then got to work on his shackles. "Of course I came to rescue you, you daft bucko. You're my man. And I'm your woman."

"I am? You are? But what about how angry you are because I didn't tell you I was a Mer?"

"There were a few things I didn't tell you, either," she said. "We'll get to that later."

"But what you said at the trial—about me hanging like a dog—"

She snorted. "Oh, I didn't mean that about *you*. I was addressing the other men from the *Ranger*. The ones who went to cower below when the real fighting started. You were shot, Jack. You couldn't very well fight, now could you?"

"Oh. Well, that's a relief." The shackles fell off, and Jack rubbed at his wrists. Then he rubbed his ribs. Then leaned to rub his left butt cheek. And before he could go for his leg, Bonn was standing over him with a bucket of water and—

Splash.

Again? "Why do you keep doing that?" he cried.

But then he understood. Water poured across him, soaking him instantly. His pants ripped the rest of the way as his legs fused into a tail, pushing the musket ball out onto the street. Everywhere the water touched, the pain subsided.

Jack exhaled slowly. "Not being in total agony feels amazing," he said.

Bonn bent to pick up the musket ball. "Do you want to keep this? For good luck?"

"Of course. What a souvenir that will be." Jack closed his hand around the tiny ball of pain. "How about a towel? Do you have one of those stashed somewhere?"

Bonn pulled a blanket out of a pack on the horse.

A few minutes later, Jack's legs were dry and he was wearing the pair of too-short pants that Bonn had stolen for him. They weren't calico, but they covered up all the things that needed to be covered up.

"You had this all planned out to the last detail, didn't you?" Jack said.

She shook her head, sending a tumble of curls into her eyes. "Nah. It was Toby, mostly, who did the planning."

Jack gasped. "Tobias survived Barnet's attack? He's alive?"

"He was last I saw him," Bonn said. "He's a clever one, sure enough. I'm sure he's fine."

"Then will you—will you go back to your father's house now?" Jack asked tremulously. "He can take care of you, right, shield you from the law?"

She snorted. "Not after what I just did."

"But perhaps you should try to go ba—"

"Gawl, Jack." She stared at him, brows drawing low over her green eyes. "Did you not hear the part about you being my man and I your woman?"

"Yes, but I desire you to be safe."

"When are you going to understand?" she asked, leaning to catch his face in her hands. "I don't care about being safe. I never have. I'm a pirate, Jack, in my blood. And I realized somewhere along the way, even though you're green as a wee little pup sometimes, even though you're prettier than me, even though you're part fish, that I'm actually quite fond of you. I want to be with you. I love you."

Jack's chest felt like it would explode from happiness. She loved him. "I'm so honored, Bonn," he murmured. "I am so—" He couldn't even put into words what he felt. Alive. Full of wonder and hope and joy, because he was loved by Anne Bonny, and that was a miracle indeed. "I—"

She rolled her eyes. "Just say it back, fish boy."

He laughed. "I love you. But you already knew that."

She kissed him, but then quickly pulled back. "We have to go now. We've a boat to catch."

"The *Ranger*?"

She shook her head. "Barnet had the *Ranger* taken to the impound dock, locked up tight. Impossible to steal, even for us. We're going to have to leave her. Toby has the *William* and a small crew of men."

"Where is Tobias?" Jack asked, but then he realized he already knew the answer to that question. "He's gone to get Mary, hasn't he?"

"Aye, and we're to meet them both presently." She tied the horse to a post, slung the saddlebag over her own shoulder, and picked up the chicken, which squawked approvingly. "Shall we take a stroll, my love?"

Jack's chest swelled with warmth. My love, she said. And she loved him. She'd said that, too. Out loud. With words.

In spite of the near-death thing, in spite of the pain he'd been put through, today was, quite possibly, the best day of his life.

Mary →
TWENTY-TWO

This was, by far, the worst day of Mary's life.

She'd tried to put on a brave face for Jack earlier, when his voice had cracked with fear, and when he'd gathered those last scraps of his courage because she'd told him to, but the moment he was up the stairs, she'd sunk to the floor and buried her face in her arms.

He was gone. *Gone* gone now, if the cheering crowd was anything to go by. The explosion. The screaming. She'd never heard of such a lively execution (though to be fair, her experience was limited), but all this chaos suggested it had been especially horrible. Perhaps Jack had indeed erupted into sea foam. And perhaps it had made a sound—an explosion. She'd never seen anyone go foam before, and who knew what kind of sound it made on land.

Mary's face was hot and slick. Her eyes felt swollen with too many tears.

This was her fault. All her fault.

Jack was a good man. Kind. Thoughtful. Her best friend since they were minnows.

And now he was gone.

It had been a mistake to put so much of her sense of worth into the contest. Who cared about being the Pirate Queen anyway? Why should such a thing even exist? She'd only done it because she'd let her father get to her—because she'd thought winning the contest would be enough to prove she didn't need him anymore.

She pulled the hourglass from her pocket. Of course the wretched thing had come back to her after the soldiers took it. And as she gazed at it, she estimated the land chamber still held several more days. Her time would run out before the hourglass did.

When the Sea King came looking, he would be too late.

She could see his face now, the grief returning after learning of her death. *Again*. What Karen had said about him being upset after he'd visited her—it had stuck with Mary. At the time, she'd assumed he was upset because she hadn't given in and gone home. But now, it seemed obvious that he'd been upset because he'd wanted her to return, and she would have chosen *death* over that humiliation.

"I wish you could come get me now," she whispered. But the hourglass wasn't like the shell phone. It wouldn't relay her words to anyone.

The sound of a seagull outside drew her gaze toward the tiny, barred window. It squawked at her.

"Oh, bird!" Mary scrambled to her feet. *Bird, listen to me!*

"Squawk." It rustled its feathers.

"Go find my father," she said. *"Tell him I need him to come get me now."*

"Squawk." It tilted its head.

"My father," she tried again. *"The Sea King."*

The bird settled down onto the windowsill. "Squawk."

"Gah!" Mary scooped up the hourglass and threw it at the seagull, causing it to fly off. *"Go get my father!"* she shouted out the window.

"Squawk!" called the bird, and then it flew to a roof in the town and—as far as she could tell—went to sleep.

Mary let out a wordless shriek, then fell against the wall and slid back down to the floor. Tears burned her eyes.

She should never have entered the contest. Tobias had been right about the danger.

She should have gone to Aruba with him.

And *where was* Tobias now? She had no idea. For all she knew, he'd drowned when she'd pushed him overboard.

Mary sobbed harder. Soon, her nose was running, her eyes were aching, and her head was throbbing. And the only things she could think about were every mistake she'd ever made.

There were so many of them.

She was so caught up in her grief that she didn't notice as the noise around her died down. Her crew—previously discussing which one of them was going to be called out next—had stopped talking. She didn't hear the screech of metal on metal. Or the heavy footfalls.

The only thing she noticed was someone approaching her cell.

She scrambled to her feet, moving to the back of the cell as quickly as possible. She wiped her eyes and nose on her sleeve, but it wasn't a guard, come to take her to the gallows. It was Tobias, holding an iron ring bristling with keys.

She hadn't killed him after all.

"Ready to get out of here?" he asked, flashing a grin.

"How'd you get here? And what about the others? And I think Jack—" Her voice broke on her cousin's name.

"Jack is fine." Tobias tried a key in the lock on her cell. "As for the others, I set them all free and told them to meet us at the *William.*"

"Jack's alive?" She could hardly believe it. "Are you sure?"

Tobias finally found the right key and opened the door. "Quite sure."

Mary rushed out of the cell and threw her arms around him, squeezing him as hard as she could. "I'm sorry," she whispered by his ear. "I'm sorry for everything. I should have—"

"Don't worry about that right now." Tobias's fingertips dug into her sides for a moment, then he stepped back. "Just add another point to my tally. I'm saving you."

A faint, disbelieving laugh bubbled out of Mary. "How? I pushed you off the ship! Did you swim?"

"Let me explain," he said. "No, there is too much. Let me sum up. After you pushed me overboard, all I had to do was swim for the *William*, sail here, steal Anne, and plan everyone's escape. After I found a stick of dynamite."

"And the keys?" Mary asked, wiping her face on the last clean spot on her sleeve.

"We had a significant liability. By sundown, the fort gate was guarded by sixty men. We didn't have very many assets. My brains, Anne's steel, and a troupe of actors. But then we got a wheelbarrow, so Captain Gregory impersonated Barnet, sneaked us into the fort, and then I—"

Into the fort! Barnet!

Right. They weren't out of danger yet.

Mary seized him by the arm. "Even the sum-up is too much. Let's get out of here."

Their escape was swift, with only a handful of guards chasing them down the crowded streets (which smelled eerily of explosives), one detour around a cart accident (no one was hurt, but it did bring traffic to a standstill), and then a series of hiding spots while they approached the *William* sitting in the harbor like it was any other ship. It was flying the *Jester*'s flag.

Clever, Mary thought as they climbed up the gangplank and the rowers started to row the ship away from the docks. The flag switcharoo must have been Tobias's idea.

But what of the *Ranger*?

Her heart sank as she turned and scanned the docks. There, in the impound section, her gaze caught on the *Ranger*. As the *William* moved out, Mary watched her ship fade into the darkness. It had been her home for an entire year. It had been the place she'd finally understood herself—who she was and what she could do in this world.

She'd thought she was all cried out, but another tear found its way down her cheek. *Not everyone made it out of Port Royal*, she thought, blinking a few times before she turned to face the crew.

"Mary!" Jack ran toward her, Anne just behind him. "You're alive!"

"*You're* alive," she countered, throwing her arms around him.

He hugged her back. "Bonn got me out just in time. It was very exciting." He grinned widely. "She loves me."

"Well, yes, obviously," Mary said. "We all knew that."

Jack gave her a fierce squeeze, then let her go. His smile had faded, and he was staring at something beyond her. "Well, finrot."

Mary spun to see what had caught his attention. The rest of the crew, too, was pointing. There were audible gulps of fear.

Which was fair enough. Because there, blocking the entrance to the harbor, were half a dozen ships flying the British flag and three ships flying Vane's flag, most notably the *Conspicuous*.

"Well, finrot," Mary agreed. The *William* was small and fast, but it would be impossible to get through without taking some damage. "Tobias, the liabilities are obvious. What kind of assets do we have, besides your brains, Anne's steel, and a troupe of actors?"

"Your strength," he said.

She couldn't exactly hop from one ship to another and fight all those men individually, though. But she supposed . . .

"Full speed ahead!" Mary climbed up to the helm. Her fists closed around the wheel. "Hoist the sails! The wind is with us."

"Uhh," said a bunch of pirates all at once.

"You want us to sail directly into nine heavily armed ships, all of them carrying our various enemies?" Jack asked.

"Do it now!" Mary ordered. "And get the Jolly Roger flying. I want them to know who's coming for them."

"Aye, Captain!" Anne said cheerily. Then she was up in the rigging.

Slowly, the *William* began to gain speed. The skull and crossbones flapped in the wind. And when Mary peered through her spyglass, she could see the crews of the other ships—all staring at the *William* and scratching their heads.

At first, it seemed like nothing was going to happen—nothing except the very small *William* about to ram several much larger ships. But that was when everyone noticed the rushing sound around the hull of the ship. The seagulls flying in formation around them. The dolphins and sharks swimming alongside the ship.

And the wave growing ahead of them.

"What the heck?" Mr. Gaines shouted.

"Oh, look what you made her do!" called Mr. Swift gleefully. "Look what you made her do!"

Mary grinned as the wave surged before them, rising up and

up until the water frothed and broke upon the nine ships blocking the exit.

Like toys, they spun out of the way. Water raced along their decks, sweeping soldiers and pirates overboard. And now there was a narrow path for the *William*, which was picking up speed with all the sails trimmed and the sea creatures swimming ahead to let the ship sail in their wake.

Mary laughed as they slipped through the gap. Then she waved at the soldiers and pirates who hadn't been pushed overboard but were wringing water out of their clothes.

From the *Conspicuous*, Vane glared at her, murder in his eyes.

"Enjoy your retirement party," Mary called.

And then they were through, into open waters. The sharks and dolphins left. The seagulls went back to Port Royal. And Mary let out a long, exhausted breath.

The crew whooped and hollered. Jack cheered, while Anne dropped down from the rigging, a huge grin on her face. Tobias clapped Mary on the shoulder. "Wow," he said. "I didn't know you could do *that*."

Mary gave a tiny shrug. "The ocean is a friend of mine."

"Well, Captain," DuPaul said, when Mary let him have the helm again, "where to now?"

Mary bit her lip. She'd been thinking about this. "That depends." Slowly, she looked down at the men gathered on the deck. There were a few faces missing—the men who'd sided with Vane—but most were still with her. They gazed up at her, waiting, Effie Ham among them, and the actors from the *Jester*. "Now that we're free, we have a decision to make."

"What's that?" Anne asked.

"The contest. I know I've been pushing the crew. We've been all over, braving storms, other contestants, and just now, Barnet. And we don't have a bit of gold to show for it."

"You didn't find the gold on the boot island?" DuPaul asked.

"No," Mary said simply. "It wasn't there."

They were all quiet, the only sound the *William* cutting through the waves.

"You all voted for me. You trusted me. And under my watch, we've gotten into more trouble than we've ever been in before. Jack almost died."

"I'm fine, though," Jack piped up. "I didn't end up hanging by the neck until dead, and the musket ball is finally out of my leg. Look!" He held up the small piece of iron.

"You kept that?" Mary wrinkled her nose. "Whatever floats your boat, I guess."

"It does float my boat." Jack shoved the musket ball back into his pocket.

Mary shook her head. Only Jack would keep something like that.

"So what's this decision you're talking about, Captain?" Quint called.

Mary took a steadying breath before she said, "We need to decide whether we should keep going in the contest. Or if we should drop out."

"Why would we drop out?" DuPaul asked.

"Because a title isn't worth your safety. Your freedom. Besides, we're pirates. What do we need a king for, anyway?"

"That's what I've been saying," Tobias said faintly. He looked ready to drop. Had he slept at all since the encounter with Barnet? Caesar, who was standing behind him, looked worried, too.

All this time, Mary had been focused on *her* freedom. She hadn't spent any time thinking about what that would mean for everyone else.

But as captain, it was her duty to protect her crew, even if it meant she had to go home to Underwhere.

"Well," DuPaul said, "I think we should go back to the boot island and try again."

Quint stepped forward. "Aye. I want to finish the contest."

"Really?" Mary said. "We could go somewhere else. Settle down. Stay out of sight. I hear Aruba is nice this time of year. . . ."

"None of us want that," Swift said. "We want to win this."

"But why?" Mary asked.

Swift took off his hat to let a mess of blond hair fall around his face. Then he adjusted something beneath his shirt. And he . . . *changed.* "You see," Swift said, "I've been a woman this whole time."

"Aye, me too!" Gaines wiped a film of dirt off his—uh, *her*—face. "You have no idea how happy I was to see you on the stage that day saying you're *Mary* Read."

Child lifted Croaky into the air. "Us too, Captain. Croaky and I have both been hiding for years. But no more!"

Mary's head spun as she gazed out across the crew, men *and* women. More were coming up from the lower decks, now that they were out of the harbor and the wind would take them in the right direction. "This is— I never expected—" She could hardly believe it. Her heart felt so *full* with love for them.

All this time, she'd thought she would win the contest for herself. But it mattered to her crew, too. Anne, Effie, and all the rest.

So Mary had to win. Nothing would stop her.

"All right," she called out, "let's go get that gold."

TWENTY-THREE

Tobias

Back they went to the island shaped like a boot. This time, at exactly midnight, under the light of a nearly full moon, they took out the map. Or the pieces of it, anyway.

"What the fish did you do to the map?" asked Mary.

Tobias shrugged. "I was trying to rescue you. It's fine." He pushed the torn pieces of the map together and held it up. "Blackbeard!" he called.

Still, nothing happened.

"Maybe you broke it," Anne said. (She'd come along this time.)

"If only there was a way to put it back together," Jack said. "Like some sticky paste on a clear substance that you could use to join the pieces again."

But alas, dear reader, tape had not been invented yet.

362

"What does the map message say exactly?" Mary asked, and Tobias read the exact words: "'*Get kicked by the boot at midnight, and call my name.*'"

"It doesn't say *stand* on the boot at midnight," Mary pointed out. "It says get *kicked*."

"And how do we do that?"

Mary peered over the edge of the cliff. "Perhaps he means us to jump. That would be like getting kicked."

"It also might be like getting killed," said Tobias.

"We have about thirty more seconds before it's no longer midnight," Anne pointed out. "Let's do something."

"Making people jump sounds like a thing Pa would do," Tobias said, and so, before any of them could think too much about it, they joined hands and leapt from the cliff, down, down, down, into the sea, screaming "CAPTAIN BLACK-BEAAAAAAAAAARD!" as they fell.

None of them died.

What happened was this: the map (the pieces, we mean) got wet.

And when it was wet, to their great surprise, the ink did not run. Instead, another set of words and numbers formed—a second message, below the first.

Coordinates.

Mary sputtered and blew a strand of wet hair out of her eyes. "So the map just needed to get wet. No magic. Just water."

"Apparently," said Jack.

"Classic!" chortled Anne.

"It didn't have to be midnight," Mary thundered, "and we didn't have to jump, and we weren't even required to say Blackbeard's name, were we?!"

Jack shrugged.

"GAWL!" Anne cried, splashing around furiously. Then they all made their way back to the rowboat.

"Have we found the treasure yet?" the crew wanted to know when the four of them, dripping, returned to the *William*.

"Not yet. But soon," Mary promised. "We'll get there."

They better.

Getting there turned out to be the easy part. They located Booty Island (an equally small island, but this one shaped like a turtle) right where the coordinates said it would be. The problem then became getting to the treasure alive.

They took the *William* through treacherous reefs that could have clawed open the bottom of the ship. Once they passed that, they had to go through a swarm of man-eating sharks. No one so much as *looked* overboard, just in case the sharks could jump. Beyond them, there was a lagoon filled with shrieking eels, which did indeed shriek so loudly that some of the crew had to go belowdecks.

Finally, they took a rowboat to shore, where Tobias stopped everyone from running forward. "Wait! There will be more traps here."

Anne scoffed. "Booty Island? He should have called it 'Booby Trap Island' instead!"

"Aye, the man loved his tricks," Tobias said. "But watch where you walk." Then, using the pieces of the map, he led them around the spear traps, snares, and pits that scattered the beach. "Now . . . X marks the spot." He pointed to a giant X made of felled palm trees. "There should be a cave somewhere nearby."

"Found it!" Jack tromped down a small slope and motioned directly under the X. "It looks really spooky. Darling, do you have that lantern?"

"Right here!" Anne lifted a lantern high. "Are we all ready?"

Tobias glanced at Mary, who was staring into the cave with a worried little frown. But when she noticed him watching, she sucked in a breath and put on a smile. "Let's go," she said. "I want to finish this."

"We will," he assured her as he followed Jack and Anne to the mouth of the cave. Nailed to a nearby tree was a sign. It read, *Only a true son of Blackbeard may pass.*

"That's ominous," Jack said.

"True son? Did Blackbeard have many false sons?" Anne asked.

Tobias shrugged. "There were always people claiming to be his. And it's fair to say that Blackbeard wasn't so good at keeping track of everyone, so who knows? Perhaps they were his. Perhaps they weren't."

He glanced at the sign again. Caesar had said all this should be his. But what if his father meant this as some kind of test?

"Tobias?" Mary touched his shoulder. "Everything all right?"

"Aye." Tobias shook away his uncomfortable thoughts and said to the group, "Now, there's a list of instructions on this. You all need to do as I say *exactly*. I don't know what will happen if we get this wrong, but remember the traps we had to get through just to get to the island."

"Right," said Jack, "but remember, the sign at the Kettle said to walk on the left. That's what Mary did just before the stairs gave out from under her. What if he's tricking us again?"

"He had a terrible sense of humor," Tobias reminded him, "but I don't think he's tricking us now. Let's assume he wasn't trying to kill me."

He hoped.

After a moment, the other three nodded in agreement. "All right," Mary said, "let's go down the spooky hole."

Tobias consulted the instructions. "Five paces straight ahead. Then stop."

"What if the length of our paces is different from the length of Blackbeard's paces?" Anne hissed.

They took five paces straight ahead, Tobias trying to approximate the length of Blackbeard's stride. Then they stopped.

Immediately, a boulder tumbled past, thundering over the cave's stone floor mere inches from their toes. Apparently thinking the danger was over and done with, Anne moved to step forward, but Tobias whipped his arm out in front of her and stopped her.

They waited . . . and the boulder rolled back the way it had come. Dust and pebbles skittered in its wake, and the surf rushed and crashed behind them, but otherwise, the cave was quiet.

"Gawl," Anne said. "That could have crushed me!"

The group exhaled.

"You all right, Bonn?" Jack asked.

"I might have watered myself a little bit. But I'll get over it."

Tobias recited the next set of instructions. "Turn left, down the boulder path."

This was another tense part. But according to the map, straight ahead would lead to a spike pit, while right would lead to a dead end. A literal dead end, as it would trigger the boulder to start rolling again. And squashing would happen.

"Twenty-four paces. Pause. One pace. Pause."

At each pause, a set of daggers stabbed up from cleverly hidden holes cut into the stone.

They followed the instructions precisely, Tobias continuing to speak them aloud as he went. They kept going, passing by the wall spikes, the spurts of flame, and the second crushing boulder. Blackbeard had always said you couldn't have too many boulders.

Then they came to something a bit more puzzling: a shelf with three goblets. One was gold, one was silver, and one was the deepest black.

"What do you think?" Mary asked.

"There's a sign." Anne pointed. "'*Drink from the cup of*

Blackbeard's blood.' So that would be the onyx one, wouldn't it? Black like the beard?"

"Or gold, because he was the Pirate *King*," Mary said.

"Could be silver," Jack suggested. "Because silver is the least obvious answer and he seemed like the kind of man who loved to trick people like that."

Tobias considered. All those things were true, but they weren't quite right, either. Not for this. In the year before he'd died, Blackbeard had been working on his own special rum, trying to perfect his recipe, but it had never turned out right. They'd all been vile, in fact. No one, not even Blackbeard, had been able to drink the stuff, so they'd poured every batch overboard.

He picked up the gold cup and looked into it. Something dark and murky swirled within.

"Are you going to drink that?" Mary's face twisted with disgust. "I don't think you should."

"We didn't survive getting captured by pirate hunters just so you could poison yourself," Jack pointed out.

Oh, Tobias was absolutely not going to drink it. Instead, he poured the liquid into a small recess at the back of the shelf. It drained through a narrow channel and vanished, but . . . something shifted.

Then he poured out the contents of the silver goblet in the same manner. And then the onyx. With each one, something inside the wall shifted until a mechanism clicked—and a nearby door groaned open.

Jack gasped. "So you weren't supposed to drink any of them!"

"It probably would have killed me," Tobias agreed. "But the weight of the liquid pressed on a lever that opened the door."

"You chose wisely." Mary patted him on the shoulder. "Good job."

They all squeezed through the narrow doorway and into another dark room. This one had man-height models of the *Queen Anne's Revenge* sitting in all four corners, and one in the middle. But something was off about them. Their sails were turned strangely, the acute angles all pointed into the center of the room, even though the ships were all facing the same direction.

Tobias studied the ships. Anne looked around for instructions. Mary and Jack checked the walls, floor, and ceiling for traps.

"There's something back there," Mary announced, pointing at a section of a wall. "There's a seam. Not big enough to be a door, so probably spikes or a flamethrower."

And the only exit Tobias could see was the way they'd come, so if it was a flame spurt, they'd be cooked before they could all squeeze back out.

"So what are we supposed to do?" Anne asked.

"It has to be something with the direction of the sails," Jack said. "Maybe we have to fix them?"

Tobias crouched in front of the nearest miniature *Revenge*. "The mainmasts are levers. Perhaps we need to pull them in a certain order."

"What order, though?" Mary crossed her arms. "There are no hints in here."

"There might be. Douse the lantern," Tobias said.

No one looked happy about it, but they put out the lantern, blanketing the space in darkness. But not *total* darkness.

Faint lights appeared on the walls and ceiling—even the floor. Some kind of glowing algae or mold, Tobias thought. But it wasn't growing there naturally. No, it had been placed in very specific patterns. And all at once, Tobias knew where he was.

"It's the night sky," he murmured.

Against the soft glow, he could see the others gazing about, their mouths open in silent wonder.

Tobias thought back to some of his earliest summers with Blackbeard, searching his memory for clues. And there was . . . something. He remembered standing on the deck of the *Queen Anne's Revenge*, Blackbeard pressing him to name all the constellations and the times of year they appeared. The ones here were summer: there was Draco, the dragon, and Cygnus, the swan. And Libra—the scales. That was it. Blackbeard had said, *Knowing where you are is about balance. You need to trust your instruments—but also your gut. You know where you are. You know where you're going.*

"Tobias?" Mary asked. "Did you figure it out?"

"Aye," Tobias said. "It's not the order the masts need to go in. It's the angle. We should point them at the five stars of Libra. It's there." He pointed out the triangle—three stars—and the two just beneath it.

But just in case he was wrong and set off the trap, he motioned for the others to wait by the exit. Then, one at a time, he pulled on the masts to point them at the correct stars.

A huge *thunk* echoed in the room. The northern wall moved aside. Everyone rushed through in case it closed again, and then Mary relit the lantern.

They had reached . . . another wall.

"What the fish," Mary muttered. "Doesn't he want you to get this treasure?"

Tobias shrugged. "I can't really tell anymore."

Jack had moved ahead of them, poking around some greenery that was growing over the stone. But there was a recess in the wall, just big enough to hold a human skull with gemstones in its eyes. And below the skull was another hole, just big enough to fit an arm into. "There's a sign," Jack announced. "It says, *'Give me a hand.'*"

"Great. Now we have to watch Tobias trick us again, pretending he got hurt. I will not be ripping my shirt for you this time," Mary said, but there was a twist in her smile that suggested she would, of course, if he needed.

"Well, go ahead," Jack said. "Stick your hand in there."

"There's probably a trick to it," Tobias said. "He'd know I know it's like the Kettle. It's too easy to just stick my hand in it this time. Then I'll have to get a hook, assuming I don't bleed out first."

"Use your left hand, then," Anne suggested. "Since you're right-handed."

"Not helping." Tobias inspected the area, but aside from the skull and the sign, there didn't seem to be anything useful. And though he tried, he couldn't remember anything significant about a skull with gemstone eyes. "It has to mean something," he muttered out loud.

"Perhaps he just thought it looked menacing," Jack suggested. "Like, if you're here, then you're not dead, and adding jewels to the eye sockets probably means there's treasure beyond. I think we're done with the booby traps."

Blackbeard was never done with the booby traps, as far as Tobias was concerned.

"I bet he knew you'd get to this point and recognize the joke—even if it's a bad joke—and pop your hand right in there. He's your pa, remember? And you're his true son."

Tobias reached for the hole . . . and then stopped. "I don't know," he said softly. "I don't think I can."

"Because you don't want to get your hand chopped off?" Anne asked. "I was joking about which one to use. Mostly. I can reach in there, if you want. I've always thought hooks looked fetching."

"Because it's possible that he didn't consider me his *true* son," Tobias admitted softly. "The last time we spoke, I told him I didn't want to be."

"But you're the pirate prince," Anne said. "His heir. His favorite."

"And you alone understood that map," Mary said. "You guided us through all those booby traps. And who else could have gotten us past the goblet test and the miniature *Revenge* room? He set it up this way because he knew you'd know how to get here.

He meant for you to have this."

Tobias nodded. That's what Caesar had told him also.

"It feels like a test," said Jack, "but not a trick—not in the same way."

"Just put your hand in there," Anne urged. "What do you have to lose? Besides your hand, I guess. Go on."

So with a deep breath, Tobias stuck his hand into the hole— and yanked it out immediately. "Ow!"

Everyone rushed to help, but when Tobias unclenched his fist, there was only a faint line of blood on his fingertip. "Paper cut," he said. "It really stings."

"Oh, come on," Jack said. "It's not like you got shot with a musket."

Tobias reached into the hole again and pinned the paper between his first two fingers. It scraped the edges of the hole as he drew it out. An envelope. The front simply read *Toby* in Blackbeard's spidery script.

"Open it!" Anne demanded.

Tobias peeled the flap open and removed a folded piece of heavy paper.

My dear Toby,

I knew it would be You to find this. And since you've found This, that means I'm so much Fish Bait by now. I hope I gave em Hell and went Screaming from this world in Spectacular Style, but I suppose, in the end, it don't Matter how one goes.

I wasn't always the Pa you Deserved. I was never much good at the Rearing part. But you always did feel like a True Son to me, in the ways that matter. I've trusted ye and Depend on ye, and maybe that wasn't Quite fair, being that you were a mere Lad, but it's the God's honest Truth.

I know you never liked standing in My Shadow, even though I believe ye to be the best choice for carrying on my legacy. You could captain your own Ship, and to my way of Thinking, should inherit the title of Pirate King that others bestowed on Me. But I can discern now that ye never wished for Such a thing. I'm sorry I never gave you a Proper Choice in the matter. I am giving you leave to make your Choice now, though. Take this Treasure and Build the life you want. Perhaps you still have Caesar—he's not your pa by blood but I know he's like a father to you, too. Perhaps he'll want to Go with you.

I should have told you I'm proud of you. Proud of the man you've Become, the way you've Grown. You're strong and Brave and loyal— everything that a Pa could ever desire in a Son.

I hope One Day you can forgive me for all the Ways I failed ye.

Love,

Your Pa

PS The key is in the Skull, behind the eyes. The gems don't mean anything. I just thought they added to the General Menace.

Tobias finished reading the letter to himself. Then, at everyone's urgent looks—and Anne's "So is there treasure or not?"—he read the letter out loud, hardly caring that his voice cracked when he got to the part about his pa being proud of him, his eyes heavy with tears.

When Tobias lowered the paper, the other three were quiet, blinking rapidly and swallowing like they had something caught in their throats.

"Well," Tobias said after a moment of uncomfortable quiet, "I guess I should check for the key."

It was, indeed, right where Blackbeard had said it would be. And the keyhole, like at the Kettle, was at the very back of the hole the note had been tucked into. Tobias slid the key into the keyhole and turned.

Then they heard a sound. A scraping sound, stone on stone, accompanied by a little squeak of gears. And slowly, so very slowly, the wall began to pivot inward, a door after all, revealing a dark passage beyond, and a long set of wooden stairs.

TWENTY-FOUR

Jack's

"Are you *crying*, cousin?" Mary smirked at him.

"No!" Jack protested. "Definitely not crying. Of course not." He coughed and pressed the end of his sleeve to his face. "It's so dusty in here, is all, and I got something in my eye." But that was a lie, dear reader. Jack had totally been ugly weeping while hearing Tobias read that very touching letter. It had just been so beautiful. What Jack would give for such a letter, for the knowledge of his own family legacy, his place in the world so firmly set. And when Tobias had gotten to the part about Blackbeard being proud of him, Jack's chest had gone tight, and in that moment, he'd come to accept that he would probably never know who his father was. The world was just too big, with too many Teds in it, to find a single one.

But perhaps that, too, was for the best. Not all fathers are good fathers, Jack knew. Some even came with booby traps. Jack had a strong, funny, amazing, magical mother, who loved him. And now he had Bonn, magical in her own way, who also loved him. He had Mary and Tobias, his best mates. He had air in his lungs. (He was never going to take that for granted again.) He had food in his belly. Clothes on his back. It was enough, he thought. It had to be enough. But still he'd gone ahead and shed a few tears right then for Ted.

A small, rough hand touched his arm. Bonn peered up into his face. "You all right?" she asked. "You're not injured, are ye?"

He patted her hand reassuringly. "Only my soul."

"All right then, good," she said. "So. What about—you know—*the treasure*? Shouldn't we get down there and find it? Isn't time a-ticking? Isn't there a contest we still have to win?" She bounced up and down on the balls of her feet impatiently.

"Indeed." He offered Bonn his arm. "Shall we go, darling?"

She snorted at his chivalry but took his arm anyway, and together, very carefully, following closely behind Mary and Tobias, they made their way down the right side of the rickety stairs (there were no more traps, thank goodness) and into a huge, cavernous chamber. Seriously, it was like three times the size of the big cave they'd explored at the Kettle.

Then they all stopped and stared.

"Gawl," Mary whispered from one side of him. "Am I saying that right?"

"Yep. Gawl about covers it," said Bonn.

Mary lifted the lantern higher, taking in the view.

The scale of the treasure could not be overstated.

Imagine, if you will, an area the length and width of about half a football field. Now imagine that whole space filled with gold, silver, and precious gemstones. Everywhere they turned, there were piles and piles of coins. We're talking a Scrooge McDuck, Smaug level of money here. Coins were spilling out of trunks and chests, bulging out of overflowing bags, and amassed in heaps like haystacks. It was an absolute fortune of gold and silver coins, the faces stamped with the kings and queens of every country in the world, even countries no longer in existence. (But mostly, they were Spanish pieces of eight.)

So many more than a thousand pieces of eight.

Jack's heart soared. He laughed, grabbed Bonn by the waist and spun her, and for a few happy moments they danced around in the piles of gold, gleeful as children in a candy store—if candy stores had been invented yet.

"Now *that's* a treasure," Bonn crowed, and pulled Jack's face down to hers to kiss him enthusiastically on the mouth.

Mary and Tobias were also embracing, clutching each other, jumping up and down a bit, gaping in disbelief at the mountains of riches piled all around them.

"I had no idea that he had this much," said Tobias, scratching at the back of his neck.

"It's enough to win ten contests," Mary mused, grinning.

"We're going to need a bigger boat," said Jack, "to get this all back to Nassau." They were going to need more boats in general. The two ships they had would never manage to carry this much. Tobias had been correct in that.

Mary's smile faded. "But are you sure, Toby?" She worried her bottom lip between her teeth. "This isn't mine to take, not really." She turned to Tobias. "It's yours. You're the true son of Blackbeard. He meant this for you. I don't want to take this unless you're certain."

Tobias gazed warmly back at her. "I'm certain. I will gladly give it to you, Mary. For your cause. For equality. For . . . for you."

Aw, thought Jack. That was nice. He also thought they should kiss already, because that's clearly where all of this was headed, but they only looked at each other with moony eyes. Aw.

"Thank you," Mary murmured.

"Don't mention it," Tobias said.

"Hey, Toby, look over here," Bonn called. She'd raced to the far end of the cavern along a narrow trail through the gold and come upon a hodgepodge collection of furniture, fine tables and chairs (all a bit worse for wear on account of the damp sea air), sideboards and wine cabinets, even a throne. The gold chair was narrow, tall-backed, and cushioned in purple velvet.

"A seat fit for a Pirate King," Jack said in awe as the rest of the group moved to join Bonn.

"Not that, silly dear." Bonn motioned to the piles of tomes, scrolls, and parchment spread out on the largest of the dining tables. "Books! You love the books, right, Mary? And maps for Tobias! Perhaps some of these will lead us to even *more* treasure. Can you imagine that? Even more treasure?" She gave a very un-Bonn-like girlish giggle. "And there are all sorts of odds and ends for you, Jack darling. And the gemstones for me. It's like this treasure was made specifically for the lot of us."

"Gemstones?" Jack quirked an eyebrow at her.

She held out her hand and opened her palm to reveal a fistful of bright green emeralds, the exact color of her eyes. "I'm from the Emerald Isle," she explained. "So maybe these could be mine?"

"Jack," Mary said in a strange, almost strangled voice.

"I think it's not unreasonable for Bonn to call dibs on a few emeralds," Jack argued. He was thinking about the ring he'd tried to give her. Which was still back at the boardinghouse, hopefully.

"No, Jack. I don't care about emeralds," Mary said. "Come here. You have to see this."

Jack skirted around the big table to where Mary was standing, staring at something that was leaning against the far wall of the cave.

It was an enormous painting.

Of a mermaid.

Jack took the lantern from Mary to get a better look at the painting. The mermaid was a saucy young lass, sitting jauntily on a rock next to a seagull with her silvery tail stretched out before her, blue hair barely covering her buxom bosoms, a cutlass in her hand, and a knowing smile on her lips.

"Is that your . . . mom?" Mary asked in Merish.

Jack's mouth fell open. *"It is."* It was a bit disconcerting to see a portrait of his mother looking so, well, sexy, but it was undeniably his mother.

"I thought so," Mary said. *"Not that many of us have blue hair."*

"But how?" Jack rasped.

"I told you. My father was obsessed with mermaids." Tobias came up to stand beside them. He of course hadn't heard their conversation in Merish, so he assumed they were just admiring the painting.

"What . . . what was your father's name?" Jack asked slowly.

Tobias tilted his head. "My father was Blackbeard. You knew that."

"But his name wasn't actually Blackbeard," Jack said. "That's not what his mother and father called him, surely?"

"It was Edward," Tobias said softly. "His name was Edward Teach."

"Edward," Jack repeated. "Not—"

"Ted," Tobias added, his eyes widening. "Sometimes that's also a shortened name for Edward. Ted Teach. TED."

So there it was. Jack felt a bit light-headed, like the top of his head had been sheared off and his brains were floating away. His father was Ted. Ted, standing for Edward. Aka Edward Teach. Aka Captain Blackbeard. Captain Blackbeard was Jack's father.

Finally, FINALLY, he knew who his father was.

But also this: his father was dead.

"Are you all right?" Mary asked. "You look like a strong wind could blow you over."

Jack swallowed hard and nodded. "I'm fine. It's just . . ." Now he would never get to meet his father. "It's good to know."

"Wait, what?" Bonn was still catching up. Her eyes widened. "You're saying that *Captain Blackbeard* is this Ted bloke you've been looking for all this time?"

"And *my* pa," Jack murmured. He turned to Tobias. "Which makes us brothers." He shook his head, amused. Wasn't that just the way life Above always went? You could lose a father and gain a brother all in the space of a few minutes.

"So we are." Tobias's lips turned up into his quiet smile. "Although I hate to tell you this, but there are fifty-two more of us."

Jack's eyebrows lifted. "Fifty-two brothers? I shall have to meet them all, then."

He and Tobias awkwardly patted each other on the shoulder, and just like that, their relationship was fixed. They were brothers.

"Wow, that's great, it really is," Bonn said. "But back to the issue of the treasure."

Jack had nearly forgotten about the treasure. Which was something, considering where he was standing.

"She's right," Mary agreed. "We must see to the treasure. We've no time to waste."

* * *

They wasted no time getting word back to their ships about the treasure. After that, the crew was in a very good mood. They didn't know exactly how much of this treasure they'd receive, but they knew they were getting some of it, and even a little bit of it meant that they'd wind up rich pirates.

"This is wonderful," Jack said. "It turned out to be quite easy, in the end."

But then it became apparent that they were only going to be able to carry a fraction of Blackbeard's treasure back to Nassau. There just wasn't room.

"Vane has three ships full of treasure. That's what I heard in Port Royal," Tobias reported worriedly. "Three. And Penzance has amassed a large treasure himself."

"We need more ships." Mary sighed. "I miss the *Ranger*."

"We've got three days, I reckon," Tobias said. "That is not a lot of time."

Mary turned the hourglass over in her hand. "Three days."

"Well, what are we waiting for, then?" Bonn said. "Let's sail!"

So they set out posthaste looking for another ship (or two, even, seeing as Vane was rumored to have three), but they did not find a ship that day, or by noon of the next.

It was awful. Jack wondered if part of this could be his fault, somehow, for remarking about how things had been easy. There was a power in words, he knew, like the spells his mother wove together. But there wasn't much to be done about that now. They had to find a ship. They just had to.

And then, like magic, a ship appeared. It approached them, flying a white flag of surrender.

"But what if it's a trap?" Jack said worriedly.

Mary snapped the spyglass shut. "I don't think it's Barnet."

The ship turned out to be a sweet slender clipper with the words *La Marie* freshly painted along the side, captained by a Frenchman named Captain Caleçons. (In French, Captain Underpants, although this is technically the French word for boxers, not briefs.) He approached their group of ships and offered, as Effie Ham had done, to become part of their fleet.

"But why would you do that?" Mary asked when he came aboard to speak with her.

Captain Underpants dropped into a deep bow before her, and then grabbed her hand and kissed it ardently. "Because I saw you at the presentation all those weeks ago, and I knew it was fate. You are beautiful. I must have you. I am desperately in love with you, in fact. You are the captain of my heart, ma chérie. Please say that you'll be mine."

"I'll rip his heart out for ye," Bonn offered from above, where she'd been working in the rigging. She winked at Jack, which made him feel that he was in on a joke with her.

Captain Underpants waggled his brows at Mary suggestively. "I am a very good lover, you know."

Mary (to no one's surprise) did not accept the captain's generous offer to become his paramour or Bonn's generous offer to rip his heart out. Mary did, however, take Captain Underpants's ship.

(She left the amorous Frenchman on the beach somewhere, still going on about how beautiful she was when she was annoyed.)

So now they had three ships. But the *William* was a small one, so it wasn't a given that they would be able to produce more treasure than Captain Vane.

"I'll gut that scurvy Vane," Bonn said, pacing the poop deck. "If it weren't for him losing us the *Ranger*, we'd be the clear winners. I'd like to slit him across the belly and let his guts all tumble out, and then I'd do a little jig upon them."

"That's nice, darling," Jack said.

"Or"—Bonn pressed her finger to her chin thoughtfully—"I'd tie him to a post in the bay and watch him struggle as the tide comes in. That sneaky snook."

"SAILS!" came the cry from the crow's nest.

"Oh, thank God," said Jack.

He and Bonn raced up to the quarterdeck, where Mary and Tobias were already standing peering through spyglasses.

"Is it really a ship? What kind of ship?" Jack gasped.

"Does it matter?" Bonn cried. "Let's get it!"

"It will matter if it's a warship," Tobias murmured, squinting through his spyglass.

Jack shifted nervously. He really hoped it wasn't Jonathan Barnet.

(Reader, it definitely wasn't Jonathan Barnet. We happen to know that our good old JB was fired after the incident at Port Royal. So he wouldn't be coming after them anytime soon.)

"No, it's—" Mary lowered her spyglass, her face paling slightly. "It's the *Fancy*," she said almost to herself.

Jack, Bonn, and Tobias exchanged a confused glance.

"Uh, what's the *Fancy*?" Jack asked.

Mary
TWENTY-FIVE

It had been a long time since she'd seen the *Fancy*. Over a year, by now. And though it had been the most elegant ship Mary had ever seen then, now it looked . . . tired. The hull needed scraping, the sails mending, and the paint touched up. The polish of Charles Town had worn off, and now it was trying to be something it wasn't anymore.

"Take the *Fancy*," Mary whispered.

No one moved. They were all staring at her, like they were waiting for her to explain.

"Take. The. *Fancy*." This time, she said it with more force, more volume, and everyone launched into motion. Diesel and the other gunners rushed to the gun deck. DuPaul grabbed the wheel and made hard to starboard.

"She's running!" Tobias called. "They're putting out more sails. And I see oars."

So it was to be a chase. Good. It would make the capture that much sweeter.

The crew knew what to do, with every hand in motion. The muskets were made ready. The cannons were manned. The boarding party had their cutlasses.

Here was the thing about the *Fancy*. It wasn't fast. It was a pleasure ship, a vessel meant for spoiled "princes" with too much money and not enough brains. So even though the *Fancy* had started with a lead, it was losing ground (er, ocean) to the *William*, which was one of the swiftest ships in the Caribbean. Plus, they had Mary. She stood on the quarterdeck, her glare locked on the *Fancy* as the waves pushed the *William* faster, wind filling the sails like a hot bellows.

Finally, the distance between them closed. "Raise the black!" Mary called when, even without her spyglass, she could see the well-dressed sailors begin to panic. They were running from bow to stern yelling, "Pirates!" and "We're all going to die!"

She didn't recognize any of their faces, which didn't surprise her. The Worthington family went through staff faster than Jack went through pants.

The crew of the *Fancy* didn't even bother to fight, mostly because they couldn't. There wasn't a gun deck anywhere on the ship. And none of the sailors had weapons beyond (mostly) decorative swords.

"Ready the grapples!" Mary ordered, and as soon as the *William* came alongside the *Fancy*, the grapples went out and her crew began to draw the two ships closer together.

"I'm too young to die!" cried one of the *Fancy*'s crew—right before he threw himself into the ocean.

Mary shook her head and called for her crew to board the *Fancy*. She, Tobias, Jack, and Anne joined them. One or two men resisted, but they were quickly overwhelmed; none of them, apparently, were paid well enough to fight pirates. *Classic Worthington*, Mary thought.

Soon, they were all lined up along the deck, bound at the wrists and ankles.

"So you've been captured by pirates. Now what?" Mary smirked at them. "Well, you have a choice. Either join my crew or walk the plank. But either way, this is my ship now."

How fitting, she thought, that this final ship—the one that would carry her treasure—was the very one where, only a year ago, she'd lost everything.

The sailors looked thoughtful. "What if we're not cut out to be pirates?" one asked. "I've a bad knee. I'm not that good a sailor, honestly."

"You'd be surprised what you can do," Mary said to him, "when your survival is on the line. I suspect you're a better sailor than you think."

"Strangely motivational," the man said. "Thanks. I guess I'll be a pirate."

A few other sailors had questions, but in the end, they all decided to join her crew. And given the other option was drowning, she couldn't blame them.

There was an odd, strangely relieved, strangely disappointed sensation burning in her chest, though. She hadn't seen Charles here, nor any of his family, though obviously that was for the best. Charles was the worst. Still, why was the *Fancy* all the way down here without the Worthingtons?

Just then, the door to the captain's cabin burst open and out came Swift dragging a young man with her. "I found this foolish one hiding in the wardrobe, Captain, and I knew he was trouble."

It was Charles.

He was here after all.

He looked ragged, his hair a wreck and his clothes askew. His face was blotchy and red, with both fear and sunburn. But he still had those dark eyes, that sweep of hair, and an air of refinement about him—a Romeo, though never hers.

A whole mess of feelings rose up in Mary, making her head and heart swim with that old shame and complete humiliation of his rejection. He'd made her feel *so* bad, *so* unlovable.

So unworthy.

But that was the old Mary.

She'd come so far since she'd jumped off the *Fancy* a year ago, learning to take care of herself, finding true friends, and rising all the way to the rank of captain. Indeed, she was just a day away from winning the title of Pirate Queen, once she and her crew returned to Booty Island, loaded up the rest of the treasure, and sailed to Nassau. It wasn't fair that just *seeing* that codfish could throw her back to that miserable place she'd been before, sad and scared and ready to sacrifice anything to be with him.

That's not me anymore, she reminded herself.

But distantly, she registered the scrape of her nails on her shirt, right over her heart.

"Mary?" Tobias asked. "Are you all right?"

At the sound of his voice, the world steadied around her. The swirling emotions settled. The shame faded away.

"Aye." She clapped her hand on Tobias's shoulder. "I'm good. Thanks."

He gave a stiff, uncertain nod as Mary strode toward the captain's cabin, where her men were binding Charles at the wrists.

Mary stopped in front of him. "I'm taking the *Fancy* as my own. You have two choices: get locked in the brig for an undetermined amount of time or walk the plank. You should know that we're in the middle of the ocean, and you're likely to drown before you can reach land."

"I've survived the ocean before," Charles said stiffly. "My other ship went down in a storm two years ago, and I made it to shore just fine. I'll take my chances."

Mary raised an eyebrow. Of course, he didn't know that *she* had rescued him. He never had thought to question his survival, assuming that it was obviously because of something he had done, because of some special quality he possessed.

"But I suppose I should try to negotiate," Charles said. "I don't want to lose this ship. It has sentimental value. I got married on it, in fact. So is there any way I can convince you to just . . . let us go?"

That was when it hit her: he didn't recognize her. He didn't even seem to register that she was a woman, for all that she'd stopped binding her chest and even though her hair was growing out. He just . . . didn't see her. He never had.

"Mr. Worthington," she said, "I will not be negotiating with you. I've given you your options. Now give me your answer."

"Well, I don't want to die. But I don't want to be locked in the brig."

Mary sighed. "The brig it is. Now, where's Lavinia? I'll give her the same options."

"Oh, she was driving me mad, and I had to get away. That's why I'm here, actually, as a little vacation from my wi—" Charles's eyes went round. "Wait, how do you know about Lavinia?"

The idea that she had ever been attracted to this man—ugh, it was embarrassing. "It's me, Charles. Mary."

His face lit up. "Oh my gosh, *Foundling*? Is that you? I thought you looked familiar! Wow, so you're a pirate now?"

Heat rose to Mary's face. "Aye," she said. "Captain. That's my ship. One of them, anyway. And now this one is, too."

Charles took a long (loooong) look at her, his gaze traveling from her hair to the earring to all the way down her body. "This pirate thing is really working out for you, huh? I'm impressed. I didn't think you had it in you. Maybe you want to talk about it sometime? All your experiences, what kind of future you see for yourself . . . and . . . us, now that we've reconnected?"

What. The. Fish.

It was amazing how swiftly those dredged-up emotions sank back down, banished forever to the depths. The way he was looking at her now—it was repulsive. She had to take an actual step back from him.

"You—" Mary shook her head. "You never really knew me. You never bothered. From the very beginning, you were a selfish, egotistical codfish. You use everyone around you and expect them to thank you for it. But here's a free piece of advice: you're not special. You're not a prince. You're not even *memorable*."

Charles's mouth was hanging open. A bug flew in. Then quickly flew out.

"You think I'd want to be with you *now*?" She scoffed. "Look at me. I've got everything I could ever want—every*one* I want. My crew. My friends. People who always believed in me and didn't need me to prove myself worthy." Mary could feel them at her back now—crewmates, Jack and Anne, Tobias. They were with her. They always had been.

"We had such a bond then," said Charles. "And look at you now! You're—well, I don't know that I'd say you're beautiful, but there is a certain something about you, isn't there? A fierceness. A strength. It's actually quite appealing. I didn't think I'd feel this way."

Mary laughed and shook her head. A year ago, she would have killed to hear him give her that kind of backhanded compliment. But now, she saw right through him.

"Can I drown him in a bucket?" Anne asked. "Please."

Charles's eyes snapped to Anne. "All the ladies are becoming pirates, aren't they?"

That was the idea.

"If you let me go," Charles said, "I could offer you a large sum of money. My father would be good for it. Say, one thousand pieces of eight?"

She scoffed. There was nothing he could offer. But wait.

There might be one thing.

Something that belonged to her—and she should probably get it back.

"Where is it, Charles?" Mary asked.

"Where is what? My heart? It's in your palm!"

Mary took a moment to consider Anne's offer to drown him. Then she sighed. "The crown. The one you took to give to Lavinia to wear right over there." She pointed to the bow, where the (apparently *very* happy) couple had been wed.

"Oh," Charles breathed. "That crown. I haven't seen it since the wedding. I'm not sure where it is."

Mary glared at him a moment. He squirmed. Then she said, "Throw him in the brig. I'm going to look for my crown. Jack, make sure Anne doesn't drown anyone in buckets. Yet." She headed belowdecks, to where the *Fancy*'s fancy cabins were located, and went into the room where Charles and Lavinia had enjoyed their wedding night.

Alone, she stared down at the bed, remembering the weight of the knife in her hand, the sweat making her grip slippery. She recalled the bedsprings groaning as Charles had turned onto his back, giving the blade such an easy path to his heart.

She hadn't been able to do it then. Now?

Perhaps.

She hadn't loved him, she realized suddenly. She'd loved the idea of him, the idea of *them*. But those feelings had been one-sided, shallow—a passing fancy. Real love, she understood now, was steady. Kind. Gentle. It was a bond that could not be shaken by titles or rules.

Footfalls sounded behind her, bringing her back to the present.

"Everything all right?" Tobias asked.

Mary smiled over at him. She was done thinking about Charles . . . starting now. "Aye. There's just one thing I need. Help me look?"

"Always." Then, together, they searched through the wardrobe, behind a mostly empty bookcase, and under the bed. That was where Mary found it—along with a single stocking and a whole lot of dust.

Her mother's crown.

"That *is* something," Tobias said. "I've never seen the like."

"You wouldn't have," Mary said. "It was made with Mer

magic. I should have respected it more."

After giving the crown a quick buff against her shirt, she spent a moment admiring the coral and pearls, this priceless piece that had been passed down to her. (And her sister, technically.) She'd taken this to remember who she was—where she'd come from—but now she was different, no longer Littlest, nor Mark, but Mary Read, the best pirate who ever sailed.

And soon, the Pirate Queen.

They returned to Booty Island that evening and spent the night moving treasure from the cave to the ships. Given all the booby traps, it was a slow, tedious process, one that required loading up carts, navigating them through the tunnels, traversing the treacherous beach, and then transferring everything to rowboats to be taken back to one of the ships.

They worked through the night, while Mary checked her hourglass again and again. Time was running short. If they didn't leave by morning, they wouldn't make it.

But at last, all four ships were sitting low in the water from the weight of gold, jewels, and thousands (and thousands) of pieces of eight. They raised the sails and set out for Nassau as fast as they could manage.

Fortunately, the wind was with them. And now, Mary was standing at the helm, her eyes on the smudge of New Providence in the distance, the rest of her ships following along behind. All were flying the Jolly Roger, the black flag with the grinning skull.

"Sails, Captain!" shouted Anne in the crow's nest. "Starboard bow!"

Mary pulled out her spyglass. And there, in the distance, she could just see the points of sails—the royal blue of Captain Penzance's ship, the *Mabel*. Behind it sailed one other.

Worse, as she moved the spyglass toward land, she caught sight of Captain Vane's trio of ships in the harbor, the *Conspicuous* the most conspicuous of them all.

Worse worse, the sun was nearly at its zenith.

"Go!" she shouted. "As fast as we can take her, let's go!"

The ships were so heavy, though, weighed down with all their treasure. It would take a miracle to get there before the noon bell rang.

Mary gripped the rail and imagined wind filling the sails of the *William*, the *Jester*, the *Marie*, and the *Fancy*. She imagined the water swirling around them, gathering, pushing them forward.

And then they were going faster. Six knots, if her guess was right. The ocean pulled them along. And when she looked into the water, there were dolphins and whales swimming just under the surface—ahead of them, too, creating a wake that would make it easier for the ships to gain speed.

She might not be a mermaid anymore, but the ocean hadn't forgotten her.

Just then, a loud *BOOM* sounded from Penzance's ship. A cannonball hurtled across the water and just shy of the *William*.

"Captain!" Quint shouted. "They're shooting at us!"

"I see that," Mary called. "Diesel! Man the cannons! Fire back—but don't kill them, intentionally or unintentionally. Just keep them off us."

"Aye, Captain!" Diesel ran to obey orders.

As Mary's fleet raced into the harbor, several more shots were fired between the two captains.

"Come on," she whispered.

The *William* surged forward, cutting through the water like a blade. The cannons stopped. The whole world seemed to fade away as Mary's fleet half flew into the harbor.

Without a minute to spare.

The AARP met them at the docks, all of them eyeing their pocket watches.

"Mine says twelve-oh-one," Hornigold said.

"Mine says eleven fifty-eight," Hook said.

They both looked at Captain Morgan.

"Eh," he said. "It's five o'clock somewhere."

"So it's fine, then," Tobias said. "We're in time."

"Aye," Hornigold said with a sigh. "Mostly because Penzance came in just a minute after you, and I want him to remain qualified. I'm hoping he has another dance routine prepared."

Well, Mary's crew had an entire acting troupe, but *she* wasn't bragging about it. "Just tally our prize," she said. "I have four ships here, all carrying Blackbeard's own treasure."

The three judges came aboard each of Mary's ships and looked through the holds. It was a ton of treasure, everyone agreed.

"I can't imagine Penzance will be able to produce more booty than this," Hornigold said after the final tally was made. There was a greedy gleam in his eye that made Mary nervous, but the old pirate didn't actually have a chance at stealing anything from them.

"What about Vane?" Mary asked.

"Ah, now Vane." Hornigold shook his head. "Come along. The ceremony is happening at GIRLS GIRLS GIRLS. And you'll see."

They tromped along to the brothel, leaving behind enough pirates to guard the ships—and the treasure. (Mary was really starting to feel itchy about all that treasure lying around Nassau harbor when there were a ton of people who specialized in stealing treasure hanging about.) The auditorium at GIRLS GIRLS GIRLS was packed, just as before, with everyone waiting for the big announcement.

All the contestants took to the stage. Captain Penzance was already mopping sweat from his brow. Mary wondered how much treasure he'd been able to procure.

Captain Ahab was gone, Mary knew, and Crunch had died. Roberts was there, but he looked just as worried as Penzance. None of the others had even bothered coming onto the stage.

Aside from Vane, of course. He stood at the front, just as he had before, looking out at the assembled pirates like he couldn't wait to make his first decree.

Round up all the women. Keep them off pirate ships. Rule

Nassau with an iron first.

Mary's heart pounded as she stood apart from the other contestants. (They'd all shuffled away from her when she'd stepped up.) It was hard to believe that only three weeks ago, she'd been up here, declaring herself a woman to everyone. Forced into it, but relieved to do it herself. And—after learning the truth about her crew— glad of it.

As before, she was dressed well, thanks to Jack; he'd styled her hair, adjusted her hat, and made sure all her clothes fit just right. There was certainly no fault in her appearance.

Then Hornigold turned to address the audience and gave a speech, something about the best *man* winning, something about the Pirate *King*, something about safe spaces for men to do men things . . . Mary wasn't really listening. She was too busy scanning the audience for her crew, who were relying on her to win this thing, and for the women along the margins of the crowd, who were counting on her to win so they could get the chance to be pirates at all. She couldn't stop thinking about the reasons she'd given Tobias after she'd decided to enter—all the good she could do as the Pirate Queen. And this was her chance. If she blew it now, she blew it for all women.

"Our third-place winner," Hornigold said at last, "is Captain Penzance, with three chests of gold, some jewels, and a few other trinkets. Honestly, I'm surprised that's all he brought. I thought he was the obvious choice. I truly expected him to win."

Several members of the audience nodded. Others booed. Someone shouted, "I LOVE YOU, PENZANCE!"

Mary was surprised, too. By all accounts, Mary's main competition was Penzance and Vane. What about that extra ship he'd brought in? Perhaps he'd assumed a ship was treasure enough.

"The contest for first place was much tighter—unexpectedly so, in fact. While *Mary* returned with Blackbeard's treasure, it was Captain Vane who discovered . . . the lost treasure of Cortez!"

The audience erupted with excited screaming. Vane doffed his cap and bowed.

(Reader, in case you're unaware, the lost treasure of Cortez is, well, massive. And legendary. Gold and silver like you've never seen. Treasure hunters from all over have been absolutely *obsessed* with Cortez's treasure for hundreds of years.)

"Our appraiser, Mr. Witherell, has examined both treasures." He gestured to a small, smiley man with pointed ears, almost like an elf, who waved to the crowd a bit shyly. "The values are quite close, but Captain Read has *four* ships, while Vane has only three. So with that in mind—"

BOOM! The sound came from the harbor.

The auditorium went quiet.

"What was that?" Jack asked.

Then everyone looked toward the harbor-facing window just in time to see the *William*—with a fresh hole in its hull—start to sink into the water.

Vane began to laugh, a horrible, raspy sound that made Mary's fists clench.

"You did this," she hissed.

"'*Sabotage, be it of Ship or Person, is encouraged*,'" Vane quoted from the rules. "That's all this is. A little friendly competition. Now, I believe, we are at a tie. I have three ships of treasure. You have three ships of treasure. But I have something you do not have."

Mary had a sinking feeling in her stomach. He probably didn't have *that*.

"I have my reputation—years of being one of the most infamous pirate captains in the Caribbean. Why, I built my name the hard way, picking myself up by my bootstraps. I sought out treasure on my own. I didn't just take gifts from more famous men."

Mary swallowed.

"And you," Vane went on, "have no reputation except that of a liar, someone who deliberately broke the rules to be a pirate on *my ship*." He shook his head. "The fact of the matter is, I'm more qualified for the position. The men know me, the men—"

"Oh, shut up!" Mary took off her hat and hurled it at him.

He ducked, but his gaze flickered up to the top of her head. "What's that?"

Mary reached up, her fingers brushing the coral crown. "This old thing? Just a priceless family heirloom." Carefully, Mary removed the crown from her head and held it up so that everyone could see the perfectly grown coral, the shimmering pearls, and the way the whole thing gleamed like it was caught in a sunbeam just below the water's surface.

At the words *priceless family heirloom*, Mr. Witherell eagerly came forward, pulling on a set of white gloves so he could take the crown in his hands and inspect it.

"This is amazing," he breathed. "I've never seen anything like it. How did you— Where did you—"

"How much is it worth?" Captain Hornigold wanted to know.

Mr. Witherell blinked a few times, like he was holding back tears of delight. "She's right. It's priceless."

Mary placed the crown back on her head. She'd put it on under her captain's hat because she couldn't bear to leave it on any of the ships under anyone else's watch. And, being that she should return it to her sister—at least through the coronation—Mary had wanted a chance to wear it, too. For her *own* coronation as Pirate Queen.

"So you agree that I win?" She lifted her chin. "I have the bigger treasure."

Vane was scrambling, searching through his pockets, snapping at one of his men nearby. "Well, I have— I have *this*!" One of his minions hurried up and handed him an ivory tablet (jeez, could Vane be any more problematic?), inlaid with gold and colorful gemstones. It made what appeared to be a map. "This," he announced, "shows the location of the lost city of Atlantis!"

Mary glanced at Tobias just in time to see his jaw drop at the sight of the map. She resolved to steal it from Vane and give it to Tobias. Later.

"Look, that is a nice little map," she said, "but it's not worth anything close to this crown. Did you see the size of these pearls?"

"It leads to *Atlantis*," Vane reminded them. "*More* treasure, and inventions beyond our wildest dreams! I think we can all agree that is priceless, too."

Everyone looked to Mr. Witherell. He took the tablet from Vane, inspected it carefully, and handed it back. "It does appear to be the genuine article," he admitted. "Which yes, would make it priceless as well."

The judges huddled together to confer.

They were going to choose Vane. Mary knew it. The booty was too close—at least in their opinions. It didn't matter that he'd blasted one of her ships into the water after the contest was technically over. They wanted Vane to win. They needed it, maybe. The idea of a woman winning this contest threatened them too much.

Slowly, the judges turned to face Mary and Vane again. Hornigold was smiling.

Well, she'd given it her best. More than her best. But she would keep her head high, even as they gave the title to their preferred candidate. It was the least she could do now.

"Wait!" Tobias scrambled up onto the stage. "There's one more thing. Mary, you forgot this." He pulled something from his pocket and pressed it into her hand. His gaze locked onto hers as he said softly, "It's your heart."

TWENTY-SIX

Tobias

"Toby . . ." Mary's voice trailed off as she stared down at the big blue heart-shaped diamond in her palm. The surrounding diamonds caught the light and sparkled. The crowd fell silent.

"I thought I lost this to Jonathan Barnet," she murmured. "Where did you get it?"

"I swiped it out of Barnet's desk when I was trying to rescue you," Tobias said lightly. His heart was doing strange acrobatic things in his chest. This was it, wasn't it? Game over? The end? He turned to Hornigold. "This means Captain Read wins the contest, right?"

"Uh, er, well, let's see here . . ." Hornigold pushed his spectacles up on his nose. "What is that? Some kind of big sapphire?"

"A diamond," said Mr. Witherell, pushing Hornigold aside so

405

he could get a closer look. He snapped his fingers, and Mary gently placed the necklace into his gloved hand. He put a mini-spyglass up to his eye and peered through it at the stone. He whistled. "A very rare diamond. I'd estimate it's forty-five carats, the biggest diamond in the world. And cut into a heart shape like that—how very distinctive! What a piece! The diamonds on the chain alone are worth a fortune!" He was growing more and more excited, more even than he'd been by the pearl crown or the map to Atlantis. "Where on earth did you find this, my dear?"

Mary shrugged. "Someone tossed it off the back of a boat right as I happened to be swimming by."

"Why would anyone ever do that?" The appraiser's nose wrinkled. "And you were . . . swimming?"

Tobias stepped in. "Captain Read enjoys diving, sir. A bit of a hobby of hers."

"Ah." Mr. Witherell cleared his throat. "Well, I don't suppose it matters where you got it. The fact is, it's here. It's real. And it is priceless. It's a great treasure all on its own."

"Which means Captain Read wins, right?" Tobias tried again.

"Uh, er, well . . ." Hornigold stepped over to the other two members of the AARP to discuss.

"Oh, come on," Tobias heard Anne complain loudly from nearby. "You said they were tied, and then Mary—er, Captain Read—added a *priceless treasure* to her pile, which put her clearly over the top, and then that filthy scum Captain Vane added what was supposedly another priceless treasure—although it was really just a map, which makes it potential treasure, mayhap, but in my experience, a map doesn't always equal real treasure, but whatever, call it priceless if you like, it's pretty, I guess—which made Captain Read and Captain Vane tied yet again, and now Captain Read has put in *yet another* priceless treasure, which means she's the winner. Unless you're still meaning to try to rob her of her rightful title. Again."

"All right, darling," Tobias heard Jack say cajolingly. "You've said your piece. No need for your dagger just yet."

"And Captain Vane also broke the rules," Anne pointed out.

Hornigold folded his arms over his chest. "It is not against the rules for one contestant to sabotage another's ship."

Anne folded her arms, too. "I wasn't speaking of that—which is a low-down dirty move, too, if you ask me. I was speaking of when Captain Vane betrayed Mary to the pirate hunter, Jonathan Barnet, and testified at her trial, which led to her being sentenced to death. Captain Vane attempted, then, to murder Captain Read. And that's against the rules, is it not?"

"Ah now, don't get hysterical, lass," Vane retorted. "I did not intend for Mary here to be killed."

"You could have fooled me, since you pulled out your gun and shot two of her crew."

"That was an accident," Vane argued.

"Accidental murder is not allowed, either."

"And you did say, sir," one of Vane's crew members piped up, "that you wouldn't rest until Captain Read and every one of her crew were dead."

Vane shifted uncomfortably.

All eyes returned to the judges. After a moment of further discussion, they broke apart. Hornigold looked put out but resolute.

"Let's deal with the treasure part first. It seems that Captain Read indeed has more treasure," he said. "Unless anyone has something more to add?"

No one did.

Hornigold sighed.

"Very well. I pronounce, on behalf of the AARP and pirates everywhere, that Captain Mary Read has won—fair and square—the position of the Pirate King. Er, Queen."

"Three cheers for the Pirate Queen!" Tobias called out, grinning, and Mary's crew (which was quite large by now), burst into raucous whooping and clapping, and their enthusiasm was so heartfelt and genuinely joyful that soon the entire crowd filling the seats at GIRLS GIRLS GIRLS began to cheer for Mary as well.

Equality, you see, is catching.

"Take Captain Vane to the fort," Hornigold added then. "He did indeed seem to be intentionally trying to murder his competition. It's a gibbet for him."

"NOOOOOOOOO," Captain Vane yelled raspily as they dragged him away.

The crowd turned their attention back to Mary.

"SPEECH SPEECH SPEECH!" they began to chant, and Mary's face flushed bright red, but she nodded and held up her hand for them to quiet down.

"Give us a speech," croaked Croaky the parrot from Child's shoulder.

Mary laughed. "All right, you stubborn bird! I do have a few words I'd like to say." She took a deep breath. "My fellow pirates, I am honored and humbled to have such a title as Pirate Queen bestowed upon me. But it is a name only. I don't intend to rule over anyone. If anything, I hope this position gives me a chance to lead us into a new and better Golden Age of Piracy, where there are no kings and queens, no masters, no wealthy, entitled overlords, but in which men and women of every creed and class and color find themselves equals. The Future of Piracy is us!"

Everyone applauded wildly. Tobias felt like he would burst, he was so proud of her.

She put up her hand again, and the crowd quieted.

"I have some people to thank, without whom I wouldn't be here." She glanced around the room, blue eyes shining. "First, I owe my thanks to the best darn crew a captain could ever ask for. We've had our own ups and downs together, but you've made me the woman I am, the captain I am, and you will always have a place by my side, even if our ship is lost."

More than one of her crew broke down into noisy sobs over that.

"Thank you to the other lady pirates—you know who you are—who inspired me to be myself. Especially the fiercest swash-buckler I've ever met, and my friend, Anne Bonny!"

Anne stood up, waved excitedly to the crowd, belched, for

some reason, and blew Mary a series of kisses.

Mary chuckled. "I want to thank my family, who were always willing to sacrifice part of themselves to help me." She fingered the pearl crown. "Particularly my dearest cousin, Jack, who most of you will know as Calico Jack Rackham. Seriously, without you, Jack, I wouldn't be here, in the very best way possible. I'm so glad you invited me into your world. Thank you for believing in me."

"You go, Littlest!" Jack called, and blew her a kiss as well.

Then Tobias's breath caught, because Mary had turned to him now, and her gaze locked with his, so intently that his entire body went warm and fuzzy.

"And last, but not least," she said, "I wish to thank my partner in literal crime, Mr. Tobias Teach. I always thought your name was an apt one, because from the very first day I knew you, you've taught me so much. About how to be a pirate, yes. But also about how to be the truest friend and companion a person could have." She paused for a moment, staring at him as if they were suddenly the only two people in the room. "I should have told you everything from the beginning, and I'm sorry I didn't. You are the cleverest, most trustworthy, funniest, sweetest, kindest, most blatantly attractive man I've ever known, and I've been a fool to wait so long to tell you so. I . . . I—"

"Go on, tell him," yelled someone from the crowd.

Mary smiled a little smile, just for Tobias. He could read her expression, almost like he could hear her soft voice in his head.

Not here. Not now.

Mary finally broke her gaze from his. "What I mean to say is, Toby, thank you. For giving me my heart." She held up the necklace, then closed her fist around it. "For everything." She gave an embarrassed laugh and glanced around. "And that's enough listening to me blabber on, isn't it? Let's celebrate! Drinks on me! Drink up, me hearties, yo ho!"

"YO HO, YO HO, FOR THE PIRATE QUEEN!" the crowd roared, and some of them surged forward and lifted Mary onto their shoulders, carrying her from the stage to the floor.

In the chaos, Tobias took the opportunity to slip out. He walked the nearly abandoned streets of Nassau almost without looking at where he was going. It was fully dark now, and the lanterns had been lit, and he thought this filthy, rickety town had never seemed so beautiful. She had done it. They had done it, together. They had won.

But there was a sadness inside him at this, too, because he knew it meant that things would change between them. He understood now. Their friendship was so precious, more than a crown or a diamond necklace or a lifetime worth of gold. If it changed, he would lose some part of her.

But he supposed that was life.

When he reached their little shack, he unlocked it and spent a few minutes tidying it up. He swept the floors and dusted, pumped fresh water for the pitcher. (He may have also gussied up a bit, washed his face, dabbed some old spices in his armpits, and changed into a clean shirt and trousers.) Then he sat at the beat-up

411

table in the corner and began to draw a new map.

A map of their time together. Charles Town. Nassau. Plum Point. A mark for the *Queen Anne's Revenge* in its resting place off Ocracoke Island. A coral spire in the sea to represent Underwhere. The beach where he'd found Caesar again. The island shaped like a boot. Port Royal. Booty Island. And back to Nassau.

What an adventure they'd had.

He heard the door open and shut, but he didn't look up. "We need to get some oil for that creaky door," he said. "Put that on the list."

"We also need to see about getting that new table." She plunked down in the chair opposite him, took off her hat, tossed it on her bed, and shook out her tawny hair. Then she set one of the heavy bags of gold on the table, along with the coral crown. "We can afford it now, I think."

He nodded. "Aye."

She was wearing the heart necklace again, he noticed. He felt like his own heart was out of his chest, too, dangling there for her to see.

He focused on the map.

"It's been some night," she said with a deep sigh. Then she grinned. "I suppose you should be calling me *Your Majesty* from here on out."

He scoffed. "Yeah, that's not happening. But you did give a pretty good speech."

"Oh, you thought so?"

"Aye. Especially that bit at the end." He glanced up and met her eyes again, as blue as the stone around her neck. He swallowed and glanced away. "But I don't agree."

"You don't agree," she repeated flatly, her smile dropping.

"I don't think you're a fool, Mary."

She sat back, clearly relieved. "Ah, well, that's good, I guess."

"And what was that other part?" He squinted like he was trying to remember what she'd said, like the words weren't already etched on the stone tablet of his heart. "You think I'm clever and funny and"—he made a face—"sweet? How's a pirate to stand being called sweet? How can I show my face on the ship after that?"

"You don't have to be a pirate, Toby," she said earnestly. "Not anymore. Not if you don't wish it."

What I wish is to be with you! he thought, but found he still couldn't voice the words. *Wherever you are, that's where I will be.* Instead, he tried for another joke. "But there was something else you called me. Blatantly attractive, I believe it was. I'm afraid I didn't quite catch your meaning." He'd never had a woman call him attractive before. Heck, he'd never had a woman call him any of those things Mary had up there on the stage. Not because he wasn't those things, dear reader, but because he hadn't spent much time up to now in the company of women. (That he'd known about, anyway.)

"You're beautiful," she said. "Your eyes have this warm depth to them, layers of brown and amber, and they crinkle up around the edges when you're trying not to smile, and your lips are perfect, too, and your ears—"

"My ears?" His ears were burning. Other parts were beginning to feel decidedly heated as well. "You've been . . . looking?"

"Aye," she admitted. "I did try not to notice, truly I did, Toby. But if you'd ever seen yourself from the back." She shook her head. "You're fetching as blazes."

He was really beginning to regret that there was this old crappy table between them. He stood up abruptly and crossed around it. She jumped to her feet, too, but took several steps back, raising her hand between them. He stopped.

"What it is?"

"I have to say this first." She straightened, her eyes on his. "I love you, Tobias Teach."

He closed his eyes, letting the words wash over him. "I know," he murmured, and opened his eyes to drink in the sight of her, flushed and terrified and sweet. "And I love you, Mary Read. Mark. Littlest. My captain. My queen. Whatever name you want me to call you, I love you."

She wet her lips nervously, and it was all he could do not to surge forward and take her in his arms. "So we're agreed?" she said, a bit gruffly. "We love each other, then."

"Aye." He took a step toward her, but she stepped back again.

"But we will still be friends," she insisted. "Promise me. Because I can't lose that."

"I promise, Mary," he said.

She nodded, satisfied by his answer. "All right." Then she closed the space between them in two long strides. At last, at last, she kissed him. And kissed him. And kissed him. (He could have swum to Underwhere and back, is all we're saying.) They explored each other in the cozy, quiet dark of their own little corner of Nassau. Tobias learned so many things about Mary he hadn't known before. What she tasted like—sweetness and salt. The feel of her breath against his ear. Her hand on the back of his neck, reeling him in for yet another kiss. The tangle of her legs with his. The map of her skin. The warmth of her body when later, she slept in his arms.

"Good morning," he said softly, when the sun streamed in the window and she stirred against him. They were squeezed into her narrow bed.

She yawned and smiled at him. "Good morning."

It was a new day. It felt like a new world.

Epilogue

Mary stood on the beach outside Nassau, facing the sea. The warm waves lapped at her feet like a playful dog. The wind ruffled her hair.

She opened her hand to reveal the hourglass her father had given her. Out of habit, she threw it as far as she could into the shimmering water and smiled as she felt it return to her pocket. She took it out again and held it up to the light.

There were only a few grains left of the magical sand running from the land side of the hourglass to the sea side. As she watched, those last grains trickled away, leaving the land side empty. She expected something dramatic to happen then, like a trumpet sounding or a light flashing, but nothing did.

She looked at the water again. Waiting.

Not far away, she could faintly make out the dark shape of the *William* resting along the sandy bottom of the harbor. It wasn't lying far from where she'd initially come upon it that first day, when Effie Ham had so proudly offered it (and herself) up for Mary's service. It felt grossly unfair that Vane had scuttled it—the ship had more sentimental value to Mary now than any other except perhaps the *Ranger*, which she'd also lost. She'd have to remember later to send Jack to retrieve the part of Blackbeard's treasure that the *William* had been carrying when she'd sunk, and then she must find a way to provide Effie with a new vessel, so that the young lady could live out her dreams of piracy for many years to come.

She smiled. Women like Effie Ham could have dreams now. Mary was a realist, and she understood that the world the humans Above lived in was tough and full of injustice. Especially for women. But at least, with Mary serving as the Pirate Queen, she could offer women an alternative to marriage, prostitution, or servitude (which in Mary's mind all felt a bit like the same fate). Now a girl could be a pirate, if she so desired, and it was hard work, and it was often dangerous, but in so many ways there was real freedom to be had in the profession. There was adventure. There was choice. Which made all that Mary had suffered and sacrificed feel worth it.

The water at her feet suddenly surged to her knees, and Mary turned to see her father sitting on a rock not far away.

"*Hello, Father,*" she called.

"*Hello, Mary,*" he said.

Her breath hitched as she reached for something to say. She'd been thinking hard about how she was going to prove to him that she'd accomplished her task—that she had won the contest and become the Pirate Queen—without exposing him to any actual pirates, and without exposing the pirates to the terrifying realization that they lived in a world in which mermaids were really a thing.

She pulled a piece of parchment out of her pocket and smoothed it.

"I know you can't read this," she said, *"but it's the* Nassau News, *an article that discusses how I won the Pirate King contest, and I—"*

"I know you won," he said then, but he still reached out and took the paper from her gently.

"You know?"

"I've been watching."

"The entire time?"

"Well, there was a while there that you were on land, and I couldn't see you," he admitted. *"But I knew you'd be fine. You're my daughter, after all. You've the strength of the ocean in you."*

Right. Right. Mary made a mental note never to tell him how close she'd come to getting her neck stretched on the gallows.

"I am proud of you," he said. *"I've made a mess of showing it. I know that. But I am fiercely proud."*

"Aw, thanks, Dad."

She leaned in to hug him, getting her shirt completely soaked, but she didn't care.

He cleared his throat. *"But I still wish for you to come home."*

She pulled away, her heart sinking. *"No, Father, I—"* How could she explain to him how much the world Above meant to her? How could she make him understand her love for Tobias and for Nassau and for the pirate's life?

"Not permanently," her father clarified. He reached into a Mer's purse at his waist and brought out a slender vial. *"This is from your aunt Witch. If you drink it, your legs will become a tail again, for one day only, and you can use it to come and visit."*

Mary accepted the potion mutely. That would have been a good potion for her to have a year ago, when Aunt Witch's best solution for her had been a knife. *"I will. I'll come and see you."*

"Your sister said you swim very badly with those legs of yours," her father chuckled.

Ugh. Karen. But that reminded Mary.

"I have something for you, too." She took off her hat, then removed the pearl crown and held it out to him. *"For Big Deal."*

"Oh, thank the Great Waters," her dad sighed. *"I was getting so weary of listening to her go on about this."* He gazed at the crown for a long moment, then looked up at Mary again, his eyes shining. *"She would have been proud of you, too, you know. Your mother, I mean."*

Which may or may not have caused Mary to ugly cry. But then she talked to her father for a while, feeling the rift that had been between them finally beginning to heal, and hugged him again, tightly, and promised to visit him soon. He smiled a bit sadly and disappeared beneath the waves, and Mary made her way back to the docks. To the *Jester*, which was still parked in the harbor. Mary walked up the gangplank, past Swift, Nine Toes, Diesel, Quint, and DuPaul. Gregory, who was scribbling his new play furiously into a notebook. Caesar, who'd decided to stay with Tobias. After she'd finished greeting them all, she proceeded to the helm, where Tobias (and Jack and Anne) waited.

"So how'd it go?" Tobias asked.

"It went well," she said. "I'll have to bring you to meet him sometime. He gave me a potion that—well, I'll explain later." She turned to Jack, who was standing with Anne near the rail. "Oh, and your mom wanted you to have this."

She tossed his shell phone to him.

Jack squealed. "My phone! Oh, thank you, thank you!"

"What is that?" Anne wanted to know.

Jack clutched the clamshell to his chest. "Only my most precious possession."

She gave a mock scowl. "Is that so? I thought your most precious possession was me."

Jack shook his head. "I would never dream of trying to possess you, darling."

This was a sticky subject for Anne, Mary knew. Only yesterday had the girl sought out James Bonny, paid him his odious one thousand pieces of eight, and dragged him to the law house to formally dissolve any legal connection she'd ever had with the man.

Then Jack had—right there in the street—dropped to one knee and proposed to her. (Again.)

But Anne had merely laughed and said, "What do I want to be a wife for?"

Mary thought she understood her reasoning. Jack, too—save for a momentary flash of confusion—had understood. He was good, he'd said, so long as they were free to be together.

Now Anne relented, a smile replacing her scowl. "All right, then. But let's get this straight: you are mine, Jack Rackham."

He kissed her. "And happily so."

"Get a room, you two," Tobias said with a groan, but he looked at Mary then like he was thinking along the same lines himself.

"What should we do now?" Anne asked, impatient as always. "Back to pirating, I hope?"

"Of course," Mary said. "But there's something we must do first."

"What's that?" Jack asked.

Mary gazed out toward the horizon. "We need to get the *Ranger* back."

"That will be tricky," Tobias pointed out. "Some might even say foolhardy."

"And dangerous." Anne grinned.

"And fun," Jack added.

"So we're agreed," Mary said. "We're going after the *Ranger*. Jack, can you get in touch with that whale again?"

He considered. "Yes, I think so."

"Anne, what can you do with half a dozen sticks of dynamite?"

Anne grinned. "What *can't* I do is the question."

"What about me?" Tobias asked. "What should I do?"

She drew up onto her tiptoes to kiss him—a peck—on the mouth. "Chart us a course, mate. You're going to get us to Port Royal undetected—they won't know we're there until we're right under their noses." Mary felt the beginnings of a plan forming in the back of her brain. "This should be easy."

"Why did you have to say that?" Jack groaned.

They climbed up to the quarterdeck. Mary glanced around at the crew, both men and women, who were waiting for her order. "Are you ready for an adventure, friends?" she called out.

"Aye!" they shouted.

"Then hoist the black!"

In a moment the Jolly Roger was waving merrily above them as they sailed south, toward Port Royal and the mischief they would surely make there. Mary took off her hat and let the wind play through her hair. The ocean rolled out before her like a deep blue carpet, brimming with opportunity and fun. Beside her, Tobias cast his crooked smile at her. She grinned back at him. This was her life. She could go where she wanted. Take what she pleased.

It was a fine life, indeed.

Acknowledgments

This book was a whale of a tale for us to tell, and as usual, we couldn't have pulled it off without the help of a lot of people:

First off, our swashbuckling crew at HarperTeen, starting with Erica Sussman, our Editor Queen. Our cover designer, Julia Feingold, and our art director, Jenna Stempel-Lobell. Thank you to all the working-under-the-surface people: Alexandra Rakaczki, Clare Vaughn, Sara Schonfeld, Audrey Diestelkamp, and Abby Dommert.

Secondly: Lauren MacLeod, Katherine Fausset, and Jennifer Laughran, our agents, who were always game to go on still one more adventure in the treacherous seas of publishing.

To our families: Jeff, Sarah, and Jill; Dan, Will, Madeleine, Rod, Rob, Allan, Carol, and Jack; and Carter, Beckham, Sam, Joan, and Michael. You're worth your weight in gold.

Special thanks to Kelly McWilliams, who read our book and offered her much-needed insight and expertise on how to deal with issues of race in a funny pirate book. Any mistakes we made with representation are our own.

And finally: thank you to the librarians and booksellers who are fighting the good fight every day to get books to the readers who need them.